After the formal training was over, Harry looked up to see the senior sergeant coming over, wiping the sweat from his face. 'That young dog,' Matthews said, indicating Blade as he pocketed his handkerchief, 'he's off tonight.'

Harry nodded. He opened the back of the wagon and the dogs jumped in.

'What's wrong with him?' Matthews wanted to know.

'He's okay,' said Harry. 'He's just over a virus.'

'Everything all right at home?' Matthews said.

'Fine,' said Harry.

Matthews looked hard at him, reading him. 'Our lives depend on those dogs doing what they're trained to do.'

Harry nodded again.

'See to it,' said Matthews.

GABRIELLE LORD's first novel, *Fortress*, was translated into six languages and made into a successful film. Since then she has published a number of best-selling novels including *Tooth and Claw, Jumbo, Whipping Boy* and *Bones*. She is currently adapting *Bones* for the screen.

The Sharp End

Gabrielle Lord

CORONET BOOKS
Hodder and Stoughton

for Roger

Copyright © Gabrielle Lord 1998

First published in Great Britain in 1998 by Hodder and Stoughton
A division of Hodder Headline PLC
First published in paperback in 1998 by Hodder and Stoughton

The right of Gabrielle Lord to be identified as the Author
of the Work has been asserted by her in accordance with the
Copyright, Designs and Patents Act 1988.

A Coronet Paperback

10 9 8 7 6 5 4 3 2 1

A CIP catalogue record is available from the British Library

ISBN 0 340 71766 1

Typeset by Palimpsest Book Production Limited,
Polmont, Stirlingshire
Printed and bound in Great Britain by
Mackays of Chatham PLC, Chatham, Kent.

Hodder and Stoughton
A division of Hodder Headline PLC
338 Euston Road
London NW1 3BH

I want to acknowledge the tremendous assistance I had from Chris Davies and John Murray. Without the generous sharing of their experiences, this book couldn't have happened.

PROLOGUE

BOOLABIMBIE, 1847

Mara caught the little one in her arms and swung him high out of the water. The baby shrieked with laughter, knowing this game. His laugh rippled through his fat belly and Mara's own laughter came up to meet his. His huge brown eyes shut tight as they both plunged under water, then they opened and looked straight into hers. Bubbles exploded from their mouths as they whooshed to the surface where they bumped into Wanda and Nan who had splashed in to join them. Up on the overhang of rocks from where the waterfall thundered into the swimming hole, she could see the dogs looking down at them, working out how to get down and into the water.

'Give him to me!' Nan called over the roar of the smoking water and Mara swung the baby over. Nan grabbed him and he went for her breast, sucking the whole nipple in. Nan held him and, as she looked down at him, her face became reverent. 'Oh you beautiful, you beautiful,' she murmured, standing in the cooling water while he fed, and he gazed into her eyes, sometimes forgetting to suck, milky with satisfaction.

It was a hot day and the water here was clear, even with the kids' splashing and the strong currents from the waterfall, because the floor of the river was paved with smooth stones. Away from the turbulence of the falls, now only about a third their usual size, the water became almost invisible, so that it looked as if the fish were drifting through air. Despite the drought all around, this hole was still quite deep. The rest of the lower river was only a chain of drying pools, shaded by the huge river gums.

A cloud of gnats swarmed near the shallows. The afternoon was getting on. They should pack up and get home, Mara thought, before the storm. She could smell rain and the sky was becoming darker as huge thunderheads towered in the south. By the time they picked up the rest of the food it would be near dark, the kids would be tired and hungry, and the rains would have finally arrived.

'Okay,' she called out. 'Come on, you lot. Out.'

She knew it was only the first call. It usually took three or four such commands. Sometimes she and Nan had to pretend they were packing up and leaving without them before the kids would finally get out of the water. Soon, she knew, that wouldn't work with the bigger ones anymore. They knew this country like they knew the inside of their mouths and could come or stay as they chose, independent of adults.

'Come on. Out *now*. We need to get going.'

She saw Nan, wading towards the bank with the baby, turn and look back at her with the beginnings of a frown on her pretty face. The dogs started barking. A Willie-wagtail swooped and snapped at insects near the edge of the water. Mara shivered. A huge roll of thunder echoed across the sky and she looked up. Clouds were starting to move; the wind was pushing the tops of the trees.

And there was something else. At the same time, Mara felt something moving, shaking the land and moving up through her feet from the stones on the riverbed; something besides the shuddering crashing of the waterfall. Cattle or horses. Heavy, fast hooves. The dogs were going crazy.

Let it be just cattle, she prayed. Or unbroken horses racing, spooked by the wind. But her senses indicated something else. Let my ears and my feet be wrong this time. Please.

'Come on!' she screamed and the kids knew that tone in her voice. They were swimming and plunging towards the bank. 'Hurry. Now!'

As she scrambled up the bank, Mara looked around. There was nowhere to hide. Why didn't I make one of the kids sit up a tree as lookout? she thought. What are we going to do? Because it *was* horses. Horses with riders. Heavy, fast hoofbeats. She could hear them quite clearly now, crashing down the slope through the last of the thin trees near the upstream waterfall.

'Scatter!' she yelled to the others. 'Go in different directions.' And the kids reached out for the shore and scrambled up the banks, slipping and sliding and finally disappearing over the top. A wild crack of lightning and the thunder crash followed only a second or two later as Nan reached the bank and turned, leaning back, stretching out her free arm to help her sister. The eyes of the baby in Nan's arms were wide with alarm. Now Mara could hear the voices, the yells and curses of the men. She heard the white dog shriek as a bullet tore through his rib cage and lungs. Then the other dog yelped. She couldn't move.

'Take my hand. *Take it!*' Nan screamed.

For a second, the two sisters stood frozen, staring into each other's eyes. The dogs were silent, the sound of gunshots more sporadic. Mara grabbed the outstretched hand, and started to step up the bank. But the sound of a shotgun, very close, deafened them. Nan's hold on her sister's hand loosened. Mara screamed to see that her sister's arm and the left side of her chest had opened in a bloody mess. Nan's huge eyes widened, then she silently fell back into the water. The baby splashed in beside her.

'*Oh no oh no oh no!*' Mara screamed. She grabbed the baby as he sank and pressed him against her waist, trying to support the body of her sister with her other arm. Nan floated with her head underwater, the gaping wounds in her waist and back turning the waterhole red. Mara tightened her hold on the baby, relieved that he wasn't crying, and tried to turn her sister over.

More shots rang through the hot afternoon. Mara heard one of Nan's big boys calling out for the little ones to run as fast as they could, then his voice choked off into silence.

Mara looked at the baby. His legs and arms hung down against her body as if he were asleep. He was not bleeding. There were only a few red-rimmed holes in his neck.

Across the waterhole, she heard a tiny sob and turned to see her niece crouched in the water near the opposite bank, clutching at reeds.

'Dive down!' Mara called to her. 'Stay under the water. Under!'

The child's terrified face disappeared and Mara turned back. She was still clutching the dead baby; tears ran down her face and she tried to control her convulsive sobbing. This was not the time for grief. She crouched near the water's edge, not knowing what to do next. Her legs had no strength to run.

It was quieter now. The shooting had stopped. If she could just get her eyes above the bank level, she thought, and see what was happening. She looked back at the other side of the waterhole. Her niece was still invisible. She crept out of the water, after softly releasing the body of the child to float next to his mother. Red water ran darkly down her arms and chest. She took hold of a twisted root to help her up, because her legs were dragging. Give me strength, she prayed. Please let me get up here safely. She hauled herself up, and just as she could raise her eyes above the level of the bank she screamed in terror, because the boots next to her face belonged to Hunter Wetherill. He was just standing there, waiting for her. He raised his rifle. His hard blue-white eyes sighted the centre of her forehead. He was grinning like a demon. Behind him, the eucalypt leaves whipped in the howling of the storm wind.

'No!' Mara screamed. *'No!'*

Slowly, Wetherill lowered the gun and held out his hand. Again, Mara couldn't move. The man still reached for her but she remained immobile until the huge hand closed around her motionless arm and she was hoisted the rest of the way up the bank. She saw her nine-year-old nephew shuddering in death on the ground nearby. Her heart was bleeding inside. She could feel its red tide filling her body and her mind. A death song came from her lips, bursting out of her like the spurting of blood. Wetherill released his grip on her wrist and she slipped to the ground beside the dying boy. Her strength was ebbing. The first drops of hard rain struck and the dust smoked around them. Although her own body was unharmed, Mara's death song became louder because all around her she could feel the others – their shock, their unreadiness, the terror of their dying. They were calling to her; sister, sister, help us. But there was nothing she could do and her own death was on her as her heart broke.

Minutes later, Hunter Wetherill finished doing what he had wanted to do. He stood up, rebuckled his belt and picked up his gun. But Mara was already dead. In the reeds across the waterhole, her niece raised her head so that just her eyes and the top of her head broke the water. She saw Hunter

Wetherill stand and drag her aunt's slender body to the edge
of the bank, saw the body slither back into the bloody water
to join her own dead mother and baby brother. Before the
sobs burst out of her afresh, she ducked back under the
reedy water.

Now the rain was pounding the ground, cutting little channels in the river banks, turning the surface of the swimming
hole into molten pewter. After the first hour of rain, branches,
small bushes and sticks swirled down new-cut watercourses
into the swimming hole. The water, now densely covered
with foam and debris, was continuing to rise. Little Wanda
still shivered in the reeds. After the second hour, sections of
the banks started to collapse, sliding into the water. Wanda
finally managed to get out of the water, severely hypothermic.
By the third hour, the swimming hole had vanished and was
now just part of a roaring, flooding torrent as the river found
itself again and ran along the bed it had carved eons ago.
At the base of the biggest river gum, its bark gouged by
Hunter Wetherill's shot, Wanda lay, almost dead, as the rain
continued to beat down.

ONE

Harry Doyle had just sat down for dinner in the white- and timber-toned kitchen when the call-out came. Although it was nearly nine p.m., the airconditioning wasn't really coping with the heat of a late November evening and a wall oven. Meg threw the spoon into the baking dish and gravy splattered the white tiles above the stove in the classic blots and exclamation marks of bloodstain patterns, with one long drop reaching the adjacent wall and landing on Hannah's first grade drawing of 'Mum, Dad, my big sister and me' with its caption 'the dogs' mispelled as 'the bogs'.

'Shit!' Meg swore as the mobile rang. Hannah and Alison looked at each other as their father reached for it, and Police Dog Asgard, the young shepherd Harry was minding for an injured mate, stopped licking his balls on the rug. Harry's own partner, Police Dog Razor, sat pressed against his pack leader's boots.

'Yes?' Harry answered, putting his fork down.

It was Ray Gosling, his keen, young ex-army constable. 'Someone from the Drug Squad particularly asked for you to check out a warehouse,' Ray told him. 'Amphetamine factory at Fairfield. It's all cleared and secured. They made five arrests.'

'Why do they want me?'

'They want to make sure there are no other drugs on the premises. The partner of the bloke in charge saw you and Razor in action a few months ago. The sergeant's name's Burgess. Do you remember him?'

Harry grunted. He remembered 'Handbags' Burgess – the sort of police officer that gives the job a bad name, nicknamed because he has to be carried by the rest of his colleagues. 'Give us the address,' he said.

Meg washed up in silence, her back turned to him while the girls wiped up for all they were worth. Harry took three hurried mouthfuls, standing up and swallowing. 'It's beautiful, love – the lamb.'

Meg banged a pot into the drying rack. 'I've had a cow of a day,' she said, looking as if she were about to cry. 'The father of a boy I'm counselling just barges into my office at lunchtime and starts abusing me. I race home to cook something specially for you and then this happens.' She flung the dishcloth back in the sink and left the kitchen.

Hannah was suddenly hugging him, distressed by her mother's anger, and Harry kissed the top of her head, leaned over and took the dog harness off the hook. 'Go and see how your mother is,' he said to Hannah as Asgard rushed over to him, circling with excitement. Harry rested his hand on Razor's head. 'I'm sorry, old fella. I have to take the youngster. You know that, don't you,' he said, fondling the old dog's ears. Razor's dark eyes looked up at him, radiant with intelligence.

'Sit,' Harry commanded Asgard before slipping the harness over his shoulders. Razor's eyes watched every move his master and the young dog made. Am I imagining it, Harry thought, or have Razor's shoulders slumped? 'Wait,' he commanded them both.

Hannah joined him again, squatting in front of Razor, telling him that it was all right, that he was the best dog in the whole world. And she should know, Harry thought, because they had both arrived in his house on the same day – the baby that hadn't been planned, the new puppy that was to live with them.

'She's on the front verandah,' Hannah said, 'just sitting there.' Harry nodded. He knew that lately it was best to leave his wife alone at times like this.

He still had his work clothes on, boots and all, and was ready to go except for his weapon. He went into the small room he used as a home office, where documents and papers covered the desk beneath a Hans Heysen print of dairy cows in the morning mist, unlocked the cupboard above the desk and lifted the gun out, the metal still warm. Usually he strapped it on automatically but tonight he looked hard at it: the neat .38 Smith and Wesson police special, on the way out and due to be replaced by the smart German Glock. He took a couple of Meaty Treats from their packet in a drawer and secured them in one of the pockets of his navy overall. He touched the new message stick he was making and the feathers on each end lifted and resettled, as if remembering flight. It was a piece of eucalypt, about a foot long, with one large fork, like a 'Y' lying on its side. He'd sanded it all over until it was as smooth as skin. The photograph near the door, of Razor tucked up in Hannah's doona, sheepishly dressed in her hooded red raincoat from a time when he had been forced to play various characters from fairy tales, usually made him smile.

By the time he was ready to go, Meg had returned to the kitchen.

'What time will you be home?' she asked.

At least she was talking to him, he thought, even though

the question was a set-up. 'I can't really say. You know that.'

She was shovelling his uneaten dinner into the dogs' dishes. Both dogs looked hard at the roast lamb but neither moved because they only ate on command.

Finally, she turned round and looked at him. The frown lines on her forehead were permanent fixtures now; her fine dark eyes never seemed to smile anymore. Harry felt guilt and anger together.

'I'll be home as soon as I can,' he said, as his wife resumed her position at the sink. Razor was straining after them, although his training made him stay as Harry and Asgard stepped outside. 'Good boy,' Harry called back to him over his shoulder. Something moved heavily in the densely twisted grape and wisteria vines that grew over the shed and pergola and Harry smelled possum.

The dogs' yard, with its concrete, hose-down exercise space and the kennels they never used, took up the far end of the outside area. The remaining space comprised a neglected, overgrown garden which Meg did her best to keep under some sort of control.

Hannah ran out with them and waited while Harry dropped the back of the wagon for Asgard to jump up. 'Oh good boy, good boy, *good boy*,' said Hannah, snuggling her face into the dog's chest and neck, squeezing handfuls of his fur as he stood in the back. 'Can we keep him, Dad?' she asked.

'No, Hanx,' said Harry. 'You know that. His handler wouldn't be able to part with him. You're just missing Blade. He'll be home soon.'

Harry's other dog, the youngster who was gradually replacing eight-year-old Razor, was at the vet's with a mystery virus.

Harry turned, sensing eyes on his back, to see Meg standing

at the kitchen door. 'There's a few of us going for drinks afterwards tonight,' she called after him. 'I could be late.'

Harry tried to read her but her energy was tight and pulled back, with something else hiding behind the anger. 'What about . . .' he started to say, putting his hand on Hannah's shoulder.

'Alison's got study to do. Hannah will be fine with her.'

His wife's face and body were pulling away from him, even though she was facing him; eyes narrowed, mouth set. He wanted to ask her where she was really going, what she was going to do, but somewhere he sensed he already knew and his heart died a little more. He turned away, and Hannah caught his sadness, trotting beside him as he got into the wagon. She wouldn't look at him, but stared at the ground. In the rear-vision mirror he saw Razor nose open the kitchen door and come out to join them. 'You look after old Razor,' he told Hannah. 'He'll be feeling a bit sad.'

She nodded, still without looking up. 'Bye, love,' he said, starting the ignition.

'Dad?'

'Yes?'

'If something happens, can I take Blade? You'd still have Razor.'

'What do you mean "if something happens"?' he asked.

A Willie-wagtail twittered in the moonlight. 'That bird must think it's still day,' she said.

'What can happen?' he persisted.

She shrugged. 'Just things.'

He slammed the door and Hannah stood with her hands behind her back watching him.

'Nothing's going to happen,' he told her through the window as he turned the wagon round towards the road. He drove out of Botanical Avenue, took a right-hand turn, then a left onto Anzac Parade with its Moreton Bay figs and poplars. Dedicated to the soldiers of the First World War, it was the major roadway that joined the eastern and southern suburbs to the city of Sydney. As he drove along, he remembered how years before, when he'd been a division cyclist, he'd had to pick up an old drunk from where he'd been wedged between the buttresses of one of those trees. He'd squashed the old fellow into the sidecar and they'd gone back to the police station with the drunk roaring and singing at the top of his voice, enjoining Harry to sing along with him. Normally, the memory would have made him smile. But not tonight. He glanced at his watch and estimated it would take him about fifty minutes at this time of night to get to Fairfield.

Turning out of Botany Road, he considered the annoyance of these call-outs. Still, they were no worse than when he was in Homicide, and they were much easier to handle. He and the dogs did their business and then they came home. That was it. Harry didn't want to spend any more time investigating what people could do to each other. He didn't want to work with that, or in that. He didn't want to walk into a crime scene anymore and find a woman with her head looking like a steamroller had flattened it into the lino and then spend hours with the man who had done it. He didn't want ever again to have to look at twelve-month-old twins with their matching jump suits and cut throats. He didn't want to talk to killers anymore in the soft, empathetic tone that had earned him a nickname he hated hearing from anyone these days. He didn't want to know the killers' minds as well as he did. When he spoke with them they told him things they wouldn't tell other people. They signed confessions because he seemed to understand that what had happened was not their fault. His success was partly because he could sense things about them they couldn't deny — his gift of noticing things that other people failed to see – and partly because he knew how to stage an interrogation to skew the odds in his favour. Now life was simpler, and he liked it that way. But he was tired out, and glad that it was only a factory and not a mountainside that he was heading for. Running kilometres after a dog on a hot trail became increasingly demanding with each year.

It was completely dark when he got to the factory in a suburb near Fairfield just fifty minutes later. It was even hotter here, further west. Nothing stirred in air that was sulphurous and acrid. Bunting drooped dejectedly around the used-car yard across the road. Not far from here was a place Harry remembered well from an arrest he and another young officer had made twenty years before, where they'd run on foot for over two kilometres until they'd caught and pinned the offender against the slogan-painted wall. After years in the cops, almost every suburb becomes haunted with memories of crimes and criminals.

Harry noted an unmarked Commodore parked outside the factory and parked his vehicle around the corner, out of sight. Then he got out, opened the back for Asgard to jump out, and walked over to the Commodore with the dog loping on the lead beside him, Harry pulling him away from the stench of tomcat against a garage. Asgard was nearly three, a little older than the absent Blade, and training up well.

Inside the Commodore, 'Handbags' Burgess waited in the passenger seat, nursing his beer belly. 'Took your time,' he said.

'What's the story?' Harry asked, and waited as Burgess, shirt gaping, struggled out of the car.

He looked at Asgard, then at Harry – a long look. 'Nice dog. Is he any good?'

'He's good.'

Burgess moved to pat Asgard's head but looked up. 'Does he bite?'

'Yes,' Harry lied, and Burgess snatched his hand away.

'I saw you when they busted that crack outfit near Canterbury,' said the lanky driver, nodding to Harry as he walked around the vehicle to join them. 'Coupla months ago.'

Harry couldn't help picking up Burgess' sloppy energy oozing in the area between them, so he called Asgard to attention and they stepped inside the sledge-hammered door. Harry paused there, studying the large, long area of the factory floor, about the size of an olympic pool. Asgard shivered by his side, all high-tensile energy.

In front of them, fluoro factory lights hung from a low ceiling over a long benchtop littered with plastic containers, bags and smudges of greyish powder. Down the other end of the space, near a locked Roll-a-door, was a truck stacked with industrial drums partly concealed under a tarp. Harry stood a moment, processing the raid from the evidence of his senses and from the dusty floor and surrounds: the scuffling; the punches thrown; the slide on the floor where the punch had connected; the nose bleed; the fall; people hurled to their stomachs with their arms cuffed behind them, or dragged out and cuffed, some of them wearing sneakers, one barefoot; the heavier boot prints of the arresting officers. He picked up traces of Asian and Caucasian foods and bodies, sweat, chemicals and the smell of cheap aftershave. Every human being has a distinct body odour comprised of many notes, like a dense musical chord, as complex if not as pretty as French perfume. A person's health, sex, occupation, diet, emotional state and environment all go to make up an idiosyncratic body odour. A dog can discriminate even between identical twins.

A bloody hand print near the lintel showed where someone had tried to pull away one last, desperate time. A crushed, wide bloodstain was visible on the wall nearby with a faint halo of blood spray along one side. Harry looked to the ground outside the door and noticed the smears. It was like watching an action replay, he'd tried explaining once to Meg, in the old days when she had still wanted to hear about his work. All the factors came together in his mind and he saw it almost like a film.

'You knocked them around a bit,' he said to a surprised Burgess. Asgard barked once, as if agreeing.

'Bastards tried to get away,' said Burgess. 'One was a real smartarse.'

Harry couldn't resist. 'The one you king-hit and threw out the door?'

Burgess just stared at him.

'So why am I here?' Harry said.

'We're not sure it's only speed. Could be other drugs.'

Harry nodded. He cast Asgard on his lead, like a fisherman casting an enormous fly line. 'Go and get it,' he told the dog, and Asgard was on the job immediately, signalling 'boracic acid.'

'Good dog, good dog. He's picked up the amphetamines,' Harry said.

'Great,' Burgess spat in contempt. 'The fuckin' fumes nearly killed us when we first came in.'

Asgard had unreeled about ten metres of his line and was halfway down the length of the factory's bottom floor, signalling with excitement.

'Hang on,' Harry said, following the dog. Asgard was standing barking, looking up at a tall metal filing cabinet.

'What's he on about?' Burgess asked, strolling up behind them.

'It's not boracic acid this time,' said Harry, noting that Asgard had dropped his hindquarters a little lower than his shoulders, and that they were swinging with his wagging tail. Each dog had a different body language, but Harry had worked long enough with Asgard and his handler to read this dog almost as well as his own.

'What then?' said Burgess, shoving his hands in his pockets and rocking backwards and forwards on his heels. Harry couldn't help thinking of Humpty Dumpty. 'Has he found something in the cabinet?' Harry didn't answer but glanced at the ceiling. It was lined with some sort of fire-resistant material fitted together in squares.

Burgess started pulling out the drawers of the cabinet: jars, bottles, rubbish, a kid's rubber ducky. He squeaked the toy in front of Asgard. 'Gun dog,' he said, throwing it to the ground. Asgard paid no attention to it, but Burgess failed to notice that. 'There's nothing here,' he said, angry. 'That dog's having a fucking lend of you.' He turned to the lanky driver standing near the deserted distribution counter. 'I thought you said this was a good idea.'

'Anywhere else?' Harry asked Asgard, ignoring the other man. The young shepherd pulled away again on his harness and raced over to the truck. He circled it, stood up against it on his back paws near the drums, jumped down again and barked loudly, with lowered hindquarters, a wildly wagging tail and his Alsatian grin.

'Good boy, good boy,' Harry told him, coming up to him and smoothing his ears, slipping a Meaty Treat into his mouth. Again Asgard pulled away and Harry went after him, with Burgess puffing behind.

'What is it now? Does he want to chase trucks, stupid arsehole dog?' But Asgard now stood barking and wagging at the bottom of the staircase. 'There's nothing up there,' said Burgess. 'We checked it out.'

'Right,' said Harry. But he followed Asgard up the stairs to the upper floor all the same. The lights were already on in what looked like a storage space. There were cartons and bags of chemicals, more of the big drums, and Asgard was running around, yapping at the drums in the right-hand corner.

'Is it LSD?' Burgess was getting excited. 'They often use these places to make more than one drug.' His raid was reaping more than he'd expected. 'I'm bloody pleased I called you in,' he told Harry. 'On *my* operation.' Harry noted the lie and the possessiveness.

Asgard had finished his run of the top floor and was circling around, pleased with himself, moving between his handler and the drums. He made a few nosedown journeys around the flooring just to make sure, but he'd already told Harry everything he knew. 'Thanks, mate,' said Harry, going to the drums Asgard had shown him and pulling a marker pen from a top pocket. He marked each of the three drums with a cross. His face didn't change, but he could feel the muscles considering a smile.

TWO

Hannah sat at her desk with her homework books stacked around in plausible piles, waiting for her mother to leave. Her pink walls were covered with photos of the dogs: Razor patient in socks and a beanie; Blade eating a straw hat that had slipped around his neck from the top of his head; Razor caught mid-jump, bridging a wide gap between two planks; photographs of herself straddling Razor or snuggling up to Blade. She heard her mother stop near Alison's door.

'If the hot water system blows up or anything,' Mum was saying, 'tell Dell. If she's not in, ring your father on his mobile. If you can't get him, ring the evening college. The class finishes at nine-thirty. I should be home not long after ten.'

'Yeah, Mum, yeah,' came Alison's voice.

'And make sure Hannah does her homework and has a bath.'

'Yes, I will. Bye.'

'And hang up those wet swimsuits, both of you. And the towels.'

'Yeah, yeah. Bye.'

Hannah slid out of her chair to meet her mother in the hall near the doorway and they kissed goodnight. 'What did that man say to you?' Hannah asked as her mother straightened up.

'What man?' her mother frowned.

'The father of the boy. The one you were telling Dad about.'

Her mother's face cleared. 'Oh,' she said, 'that man,' taking Hannah's hand, leading her back into the bedroom, to her desk. 'He was very angry,' Meg said, 'because I'd asked Matt – the boy – to write a list of the things he would like to see change in his family if he could wave a magic wand. And his father read it.'

'But why did that make him angry?'

'He didn't like some of the things Matt had written. They were very straightforward.'

'Like what?'

Her mother smiled and kissed her again. 'Oh you, Hanky-panky, always wanting to know everything.'

'Well?'

'Some other time, darling. I'll be late otherwise.' Then she walked down the hall, passed her husband's office and closed the front door behind her. It was a dark brick, 1930s house, similar to the others in the street. Rooms opened off a central hallway, which was decorated with an arch halfway down its length and then opened out into a lounge room and the kitchen area.

Hannah waited until she heard her mother's car fade into the distance. Then she trotted back to Alison's room to find her sister putting dark red lipstick on her mouth, her pale face framed with black hair.

'You look like a witch,' said Hannah. Ali poked her tongue out. 'Are you going out?'

'I might. Or we might come back here.'

'You've been smoking.'

'Will you have your bath and do your homework?'

'Sure,' said Hannah, laughing. 'You sound like Mum.'

Her sister groaned. 'Don't say that. I don't want to sound like her.'

'When you're a grown-up, promise you'll always tell me everything that I ask you?' said Hannah.

'Always,' said her sister. 'Now, how do I look?'

'Sort of witchy but in a nice way. Can I come with you?'

'Don't be silly, Hankers. You're eight years old.'

'You'd better be home before Mum gets home or there'll be shit.'

Ali pulled her shoes on, kissed Hannah briefly on the forehead, said 'See ya,' and then was gone.

Hannah went to the kitchen where Razor lolled in a corner. 'Come on, old fellow. You can come onto my bed.' She unplugged the telephone, replacing the line with the one that reached into her bedroom, where she plugged her modem into the computer. She clicked on her Internet icon, waited a second then entered her security password. The familiar electronic squeaks were followed by the sound of the line ringing. She logged on almost immediately, then went into the secured Kid Chat relay that her parents had vetted. Various conversations were going on, but Hannah wasn't interested in them. 'Hanx has joined Kids Chat' appeared on the screen, announcing Hannah's electronic, nicknamed arrival. The other chatters continued. Hannah waited. Maybe he was out. Or asleep. Or maybe he was having one of the adventures he'd told her about – helping the police get the men who'd robbed the bank at East Hills last week, or in a helicopter rescuing stranded skiers, or diving on shipwrecks. Her friend Richard was the most exciting secret she had ever had. She hopped onto the bed and Razor jumped up with her, even though Mum wouldn't let the dogs get on the beds.

'Just this once, Mister,' she crooned into his ears. 'You can come up because they've all left you. Poor boy. They've left you all by yourself.'

A little while later, a flickering on the monitor screen caused Hannah to glance up from the book she was reading; his nickname and the line of words she'd been waiting for appeared. 'Flakman has joined Kids Chat.' Great. He was there. She jumped up to talk to him. Razor jumped off the bed, walked around in a circle and jumped back on it again.

'Where have you been?' he asked.

'Where have *you* been?' Hannah countered.

'Out on an adventure,' he wrote. 'Let's go into a private room.'

'Sure thing,' said Hannah. The screen changed and the other conversationalists were no longer present. In the private room, she continued. 'Tell me about the adventure.'

'I can't. It's top secret.'

'I don't think kids do things that are top secret.'

'There are a lot of things you don't know.'

'Give me a clue.'

'I can't. What have you been doing?

'Nothing much. Just school. Helping with the dogs.'

'Tell me about the dogs.'

Hannah told him. But she wasn't quite honest because she knew already that Richard hated cops. So far, she'd avoided telling him what her father did.

'One day,' he typed across the screen in her bedroom, 'you and I will meet and have great fun and adventures together. You miss out not having a brother.'

'You're not telling me anything,' Hannah sent back. 'It's really, really awful around here lately,' she told Richard. 'My parents fight all the time. Or they don't talk. It's horrible when they don't talk to each other. But it's worse when they do. Mum just goes ballistic.'

'Mine was a real bitch,' said Richard.

'What happened to her?'

'She went away.'

'Didn't you even care?'

Richard answered with a silly smiley-face symbol.

'Were you glad? I would be really sad if Mum or Dad left. But lots of kids have separated parents these days. I could live with Mum during the week and go and stay with Dad at the weekends. No, I couldn't. He'd take the dogs. Anyway, it's just horrible lately. Mum's supposed to be a school counsellor.'

'What do you think about my idea?' Richard asked her.

'I think it's really cool.'

'I could post you some money,' he said. 'You could tell me what you wanted to do. We could do anything. You just have to tell me what day you want to do it and I'll meet you wherever you like.'

'Great,' said Hannah. 'I could just go off to school – ha ha – and come home at the usual time. They'd never even know.'

'They'd never even know,' his answer repeated, signing off from the screen with the smiley face again.

Hannah hugged herself with secret excitement. One day soon, everyone would be doing Maths and History and standing around in the hot playground at school and she would be off having fun with her secret friend. It was the secrecy that really delighted her. She knew that everyone had to have an important secret. Mum wasn't allowed to talk about the kids she counselled in the schools. Dad wasn't supposed to talk about his police cases either. Hannah only knew about

Alison's boyfriend because one of Hannah's school friends had seen them cuddling in his car after school.

Razor jumped off the bed and went to the door, listening and whining.

'What is it, Mister?' She knew from his body language that it was a family member coming home. If it had been a stranger, he'd be barking his warning bark and prancing at the door. Either Mum or Alison. She heard the key in the front door and it was Alison's shoes she could hear coming up the hall.

'You're early,' she said to her big sister, secretly relieved. She worried that one night Alison would not get home in time and she wouldn't know what to tell Mum or Dad. It was the same at the swimming pool. Although they went together most hot afternoons after school, Ali always left her on her own to go and sit and smoke cigarettes with people Hannah didn't know and who didn't go to school. Hannah didn't mind too much. She was a top swimmer and there was usually someone she knew to play and talk with.

Alison didn't respond and went straight to her room and shut the door. Hannah went to it and thought for a moment she might knock. But instead she turned away and went back to reclaim her bed from Razor.

Imports/Exports",' she read from the

y did at class tonight?'

g about perspective last week,' he told
ered, looking down the length of his
. She concentrated on the little bump
eft groin. She put her tongue out and
ple, giving it little bites. As she worked,
the bump start to enlarge and lengthen.
ear out of her mind. Sex would do that
he cigarette down and reached over for
rom the bottle, tilting his head back like

d drug sometimes,' she said. 'You drink

down, took another condom from the
ide table, and leaned over, cupping her
closer. 'I do a lot of things too much,'

ady made love awhile ago, all she had
im by pushing onto him with a little
n their sides, facing each other. He
ckwards then rammed forward to fill
bbed the top of her chin on his soft
gether in a gentle rhythm until she felt

,' she whispered, rolling over onto her
shing himself home and into the waves
n. He covered her gasping mouth with
silently into him, subsiding. Then he

?' she said.

THREE

Meg lay on her side, away from him, staring at the nautical painting on the wall above the stained timber desk. It was as safe and dull as the other furnishings of the four-star hotel. Max was dozing beside her. She looked at his handsome face, the lashes long on his cheeks. Things had gone very fast since that night at the end of first term, when the class had all gone out together to celebrate and he'd been sitting beside her, chatting with everyone but holding her gaze just a little too long whenever he spoke to her. And then the shocking surprise as he'd leaned over, when the rest of the group were at the snack bar, and kissed her suddenly on the mouth. She had been too taken aback to say anything. When the others had returned with their plates, there had been a new energy between the two of them, as if they were in a conspiracy. Which, she had to admit to herself now as she glanced again around the hotel room, they most certainly were. Their attendance at the art classes was infrequent. Most weeks they met at the hotel and spent the time making love. Once or twice they'd gone out for dinner instead, but this had been too dangerous as far as Meg was concerned. 'Anyone could see us,' she had said to him. 'So?' he'd challenged. 'I don't care.' And he'd leaned across the table and kissed her hard in public.

Meg knew that a lot of the heightened excitement of the affair was due to its forbidden nature, the dangers of discovery, the infrequency of their meetings, the intensity of the sexual encounters, the unreality of relationship ungrounded in ordinary dailiness. But I can't give him up, she thought to herself. Not yet.

His hair had fallen across his forehead and she gently brushed it back. His eyelids flickered and, suddenly, he was looking straight at her. There was an intriguing quality about his eyes that eluded her; sometimes she could read them, other times they were distant.

He was speaking to her. 'Have you said anything to him yet?' He leaned over to get one of the clove cigarettes he sometimes smoked, lit it up and leaned back against the bedhead. She turned around to rest against his naked chest. His heartbeat was normal again and she listened to the steady pulse, comparing it to her own faster rhythm.

'No . . . I think he knows, though,' she said, staring sightlessly at the pastel-coloured print of the *Cutty Sark*.

'How?'

'He picks things up from me.' She thought of the early days with Harry and what had drawn her so strongly to him: his exquisite aliveness, his awareness, the way he listened so intently, his acute sensitivity to her moods and even the sudden movement of her unsaid thoughts.

'Picks up what?'

'He's like a dog. He notices everything. He sniffs and sees things other people don't. He knows things. He knows when I go to say something and change my mind. I'll be about to say something, then I'll decide not to and Harry'll say, "What was it?"' It occurred to her then that Harry hadn't done that for some time.

Max looked
said. But she t
'Why?' she
The velvet i
was a flicker
she knew, thi
God, she thou
said, frightene
He looked
come away w
day. You'd ne
Meg lay lo
'There's some
'What? Do
on me.'
She put her
and eyelashes.
ran to his lips
'That's not p
there *is* some
excitement,'
to me.' He
nibbling it.
'What's th
She would
be true. It w
in the lowes
her finger a
handsome w
'You're rich
'I wish,' h
it up, runnin
be rich,' he

'"Max Wolan
card.
'Yes?' he said.
'I wonder wha
'She said some
her, and she rem
body under the s
that nestled near
started to circle hi
she was gratified to
Anything to put t
for awhile. Max p
the Scotch, drinki
a man in a movie.
'I feel like your
too much.'
He put the bot
open box on the b
left breast, pulling
he said. 'Come her
Because they'd
to do was enclose
grunt as they lay
tipped his pelvis
her properly. She
hair. They swayed
herself start to melt.
'Get on top of m
back. And he did,
of her building orga
his and she sobbed
withdrew.
'What's the matte

'Nothing,' he said. 'I just don't feel like going on.'

'But look,' she said. 'You do.'

'I want to finish myself,' he said and started to masturbate.

'Don't,' she said. 'I hate it when you do that.' She jumped out of bed. 'I told you I'd go if you did that again.'

'Come back,' he said. 'Don't go. Please.' But he was lurching and jerking around his cock, moving faster.

'I don't like it. It's not right for me,' she said. 'I'm going.'

He was straining towards orgasm, the muscles in his neck tightening as he tried to grab her with one hand. But Meg was dressing quickly.

'Don't go.' His movements now were short, brutal tugs. 'Please don't go!'

He was arched and coming as Meg slammed the door on him.

Burgess followed Harry and the dog downstairs. The driver came back inside, tossing a cigarette behind him out the door. He nodded to Harry.

'I've got a uniform organised for the door,' the driver said to Burgess. 'Did you find anything else?'

Burgess looked at Harry, unsure.

'We might have more than amphetamines,' Harry told him. He was aware of a tightness around Burgess as he leaned to smooth Asgard's ears. 'How many arrests did you say you'd made?'

'Five slopes.'

The tightness Harry could sense in Burgess was increasing in the silence. Finally he spoke to him, keeping his voice soft. 'I don't know how you want to do this. You might want to call in more backup.'

The driver looked at him as if he was unhinged. 'Backup?'

He looked at Burgess then back at Harry, who was winding Asgard's harness closer over his hand as the dog sat panting against him.

'In the ceiling above that metal filing cabinet,' he indicated 'and under the truck and under the stairs. And in the drums that I marked for you on the next floor.'

'What?' said Burgess. 'What about them?'

Harry smoothed the ears of his dog, considering.

'Why didn't you just pull it out? What's all this fucking around?' Burgess snarled.

The band of constriction Harry sensed in Burgess' chest now felt hard and dangerous. 'You want to be careful,' Harry heard himself saying to the heavy man. 'Your heart's not in real good shape.' He usually didn't let on about how he could sense things like this, and shut up, having said too much already.

Burgess' eyes widened. 'What the fuck are you talking about?'

'Like I said, I don't know how you want to do this. You might need backup.' Asgard suddenly yawned and licked his chops as his handler continued. 'At least another six people are hiding on these premises.'

Burgess and the driver stared at Harry and then at each other.

'It's your operation,' Harry said. 'I'm going home.'

Meg perched on a stool in Dell's neat kitchen and listened to the loud tick of the clock. Country and western music played softly on the radio and she could hear Dell talking with her ten-year-old, telling him it was only Meg and everything was all right. 'I'll leave the door open,' Meg heard her friend saying to Jack. 'Then you'll get the light from the hallway.'

'I'm sorry,' said Meg as Dell came back to the kitchen. 'I didn't mean to wake him up.'

'He wasn't asleep. Do you want a drink?' she asked.

Meg shook her head. 'No.'

Dell moved a pile of half-finished dresses with huge, full skirts from a chair and hung them safely away on the back of a door. 'Sit down on that, Meg. It's more comfy.'

'They're beautiful,' said Meg. 'I love that soft mushroomy pink.'

'Bridesmaids,' said her friend. 'I'm doing a wedding again. Swore I never would.' She grinned. 'It was a political decision,' she said, 'so I changed my mind. The flower girl's has a ten foot long train. I'm terrified she's going to end up strangling herself on it.' She poured Meg another cup of tea, made herself a wine and soda and sat at the kitchen table opposite Meg.

'I've got to finish it, Dell.'

Dell raised an eyebrow. 'I've heard that one before.'

'No, really. He did it again tonight.' She leaned forward so she could whisper.

'Variety?' Dell suggested.

'No,' said Meg. 'It's not for variety. His first choice is masturbation. It gives him the greatest pleasure. I just know that.'

'I'm sure Masters and Johnson would just call that sort of thing variety.'

Meg shook her head. 'Feels more like Kraft-Ebing to me,' she said.

'Who's that?' Dell wanted to know.

'Some old expert on perversion that I read in my student days. About a thousand years ago.'

'But he does want you,' her friend persisted. 'He wants you and the kids to go away with him.'

Meg sighed. 'I don't think he really knows what that means. I know he keeps saying it.'

'Why don't you try some time together?' said Dell. 'Just a few days. Before you call it off. What have you got to lose?'

Meg stood up and her friend stood as well. The two women put their arms around each other. 'Thanks, Delly. I don't know what I'd do without you.'

'Me too,' said Dell. 'But if I had a gorgeous, rich hunk who wanted me to run away with him and who didn't mind the bloody kids, I'd be off like a shot.'

The women walked to the door together. 'How's Harry?'

Meg shrugged. 'Same as usual. Doesn't talk, just looks. Sometimes I get the feeling he's sniffing me over.' She paused. 'He hasn't spoken to me in years. Really talked, I mean. It's like he's taken a vow of silence.'

'Harry the monk,' Dell laughed. 'Ken was the same. They stop talking. It's part of the job description. They only talk with each other. Then they even stop doing that. "No-one else understands," Ken used to say. I'd say "Give me a chance." But he never did. All he wanted from me was sex and cooking. Not conversation. I'd say "Why don't we ever *talk* about anything?" And he'd sit down and he'd say "Okay. Talk. Talk now."' Dell shrugged to show the hopelessness of it.

'Harry used to talk, a long time ago. But I've never forgotten that around the time we married he told me something weird. He reckoned he had a lock-up in his mind – of things he never wanted to think about again, let alone talk about.' Dell looked inquiringly at her friend. 'I asked him if there were a lot of things in there, and he shook his head. He said no, only a couple, but nothing could be done about them and they could never be let out. I used to

THREE

Meg lay on her side, away from him, staring at the nautical painting on the wall above the stained timber desk. It was as safe and dull as the other furnishings of the four-star hotel. Max was dozing beside her. She looked at his handsome face, the lashes long on his cheeks. Things had gone very fast since that night at the end of first term, when the class had all gone out together to celebrate and he'd been sitting beside her, chatting with everyone but holding her gaze just a little too long whenever he spoke to her. And then the shocking surprise as he'd leaned over, when the rest of the group were at the snack bar, and kissed her suddenly on the mouth. She had been too taken aback to say anything. When the others had returned with their plates, there had been a new energy between the two of them, as if they were in a conspiracy. Which, she had to admit to herself now as she glanced again around the hotel room, they most certainly were. Their attendance at the art classes was infrequent. Most weeks they met at the hotel and spent the time making love. Once or twice they'd gone out for dinner instead, but this had been too dangerous as far as Meg was concerned. 'Anyone could see us,' she had said to him. 'So?' he'd challenged. 'I don't care.' And he'd leaned across the table and kissed her hard in public.

Meg knew that a lot of the heightened excitement of the affair was due to its forbidden nature, the dangers of discovery, the infrequency of their meetings, the intensity of the sexual encounters, the unreality of relationship ungrounded in ordinary dailiness. But I can't give him up, she thought to herself. Not yet.

His hair had fallen across his forehead and she gently brushed it back. His eyelids flickered and, suddenly, he was looking straight at her. There was an intriguing quality about his eyes that eluded her; sometimes she could read them, other times they were distant.

He was speaking to her. 'Have you said anything to him yet?' He leaned over to get one of the clove cigarettes he sometimes smoked, lit it up and leaned back against the bedhead. She turned around to rest against his naked chest. His heartbeat was normal again and she listened to the steady pulse, comparing it to her own faster rhythm.

'No . . . I think he knows, though,' she said, staring sightlessly at the pastel-coloured print of the *Cutty Sark*.

'How?'

'He picks things up from me.' She thought of the early days with Harry and what had drawn her so strongly to him: his exquisite aliveness, his awareness, the way he listened so intently, his acute sensitivity to her moods and even the sudden movement of her unsaid thoughts.

'Picks up what?'

'He's like a dog. He notices everything. He sniffs and sees things other people don't. He knows things. He knows when I go to say something and change my mind. I'll be about to say something, then I'll decide not to and Harry'll say, "What was it?"' It occurred to her then that Harry hadn't done that for some time.

Max looked down at her. 'People can't read minds,' he said. But she thought he looked worried.

'Why?' she wanted to know. 'What's in yours?'

The velvet iris fibres of his eyes seemed to shrink, and there was a flicker of the skin of his face. She'd caught him out, she knew, thinking something he didn't want her to know. God, she thought, I'm getting like Harry. 'What is it?' she said, frightened now.

He looked away and ashed the cigarette. 'I want you to come away with me. You and the kids. You could paint all day. You'd never run out of inspiration.'

Meg lay looking at him. 'I can't work you out,' she said. 'There's something—'

'What? Don't do your bloody school counsellor's number on me.'

She put her hand up to his face and softly stroked the brows and eyelashes, the short nose, the furrow underneath it that ran to his lips, parted now and attempting to bite her finger. 'That's not possible,' she said. She paused and thought. 'But there *is* something about you. You excite me. But under the excitement,' she continued, 'there's something else you do to me.' He had drawn her finger into his mouth and was nibbling it.

'What's that?'

She wouldn't answer. Then it would be real, it would be true. It was best the way it was – just a spice, a twinge in the lowest pit of her belly, sidling near desire. She took her finger away from him and leaned over to pick up his handsome wallet. She opened it so that the bills fanned out. 'You're rich!' she joked.

'I wish,' he smiled. His business card fell out and she picked it up, running her finger over the embossed details. 'I used to be rich,' he said.

'"Max Wolansky, Imports/Exports",' she read from the card.

'Yes?' he said.

'I wonder what they did at class tonight?'

'She said something about perspective last week,' he told her, and she remembered, looking down the length of his body under the sheet. She concentrated on the little bump that nestled near his left groin. She put her tongue out and started to circle his nipple, giving it little bites. As she worked, she was gratified to see the bump start to enlarge and lengthen. Anything to put the fear out of her mind. Sex would do that for awhile. Max put the cigarette down and reached over for the Scotch, drinking from the bottle, tilting his head back like a man in a movie.

'I feel like your third drug sometimes,' she said. 'You drink too much.'

He put the bottle down, took another condom from the open box on the bedside table, and leaned over, cupping her left breast, pulling her closer. 'I do a lot of things too much,' he said. 'Come here.'

Because they'd already made love awhile ago, all she had to do was enclose him by pushing onto him with a little grunt as they lay on their sides, facing each other. He tipped his pelvis backwards then rammed forward to fill her properly. She rubbed the top of her chin on his soft hair. They swayed together in a gentle rhythm until she felt herself start to melt.

'Get on top of me,' she whispered, rolling over onto her back. And he did, pushing himself home and into the waves of her building orgasm. He covered her gasping mouth with his and she sobbed silently into him, subsiding. Then he withdrew.

'What's the matter?' she said.

'Nothing,' he said. 'I just don't feel like going on.'

'But look,' she said. 'You do.'

'I want to finish myself,' he said and started to masturbate.

'Don't,' she said. 'I hate it when you do that.' She jumped out of bed. 'I told you I'd go if you did that again.'

'Come back,' he said. 'Don't go. Please.' But he was lurching and jerking around his cock, moving faster.

'I don't like it. It's not right for me,' she said. 'I'm going.'

He was straining towards orgasm, the muscles in his neck tightening as he tried to grab her with one hand. But Meg was dressing quickly.

'Don't go.' His movements now were short, brutal tugs. 'Please don't go!'

He was arched and coming as Meg slammed the door on him.

Burgess followed Harry and the dog downstairs. The driver came back inside, tossing a cigarette behind him out the door. He nodded to Harry.

'I've got a uniform organised for the door,' the driver said to Burgess. 'Did you find anything else?'

Burgess looked at Harry, unsure.

'We might have more than amphetamines,' Harry told him. He was aware of a tightness around Burgess as he leaned to smooth Asgard's ears. 'How many arrests did you say you'd made?'

'Five slopes.'

The tightness Harry could sense in Burgess was increasing in the silence. Finally he spoke to him, keeping his voice soft. 'I don't know how you want to do this. You might want to call in more backup.'

The driver looked at him as if he was unhinged. 'Backup?'

He looked at Burgess then back at Harry, who was winding Asgard's harness closer over his hand as the dog sat panting against him.

'In the ceiling above that metal filing cabinet,' he indicated 'and under the truck and under the stairs. And in the drums that I marked for you on the next floor.'

'What?' said Burgess. 'What about them?'

Harry smoothed the ears of his dog, considering.

'Why didn't you just pull it out? What's all this fucking around?' Burgess snarled.

The band of constriction Harry sensed in Burgess' chest now felt hard and dangerous. 'You want to be careful,' Harry heard himself saying to the heavy man. 'Your heart's not in real good shape.' He usually didn't let on about how he could sense things like this, and shut up, having said too much already.

Burgess' eyes widened. 'What the fuck are you talking about?'

'Like I said, I don't know how you want to do this. You might need backup.' Asgard suddenly yawned and licked his chops as his handler continued. 'At least another six people are hiding on these premises.'

Burgess and the driver stared at Harry and then at each other.

'It's your operation,' Harry said. 'I'm going home.'

Meg perched on a stool in Dell's neat kitchen and listened to the loud tick of the clock. Country and western music played softly on the radio and she could hear Dell talking with her ten-year-old, telling him it was only Meg and everything was all right. 'I'll leave the door open,' Meg heard her friend saying to Jack. 'Then you'll get the light from the hallway.'

'I'm sorry,' said Meg as Dell came back to the kitchen. 'I didn't mean to wake him up.'

'He wasn't asleep. Do you want a drink?' she asked.

Meg shook her head. 'No.'

Dell moved a pile of half-finished dresses with huge, full skirts from a chair and hung them safely away on the back of a door. 'Sit down on that, Meg. It's more comfy.'

'They're beautiful,' said Meg. 'I love that soft mushroomy pink.'

'Bridesmaids,' said her friend. 'I'm doing a wedding again. Swore I never would.' She grinned. 'It was a political decision,' she said, 'so I changed my mind. The flower girl's has a ten foot long train. I'm terrified she's going to end up strangling herself on it.' She poured Meg another cup of tea, made herself a wine and soda and sat at the kitchen table opposite Meg.

'I've got to finish it, Dell.'

Dell raised an eyebrow. 'I've heard that one before.'

'No, really. He did it again tonight.' She leaned forward so she could whisper.

'Variety?' Dell suggested.

'No,' said Meg. 'It's not for variety. His first choice is masturbation. It gives him the greatest pleasure. I just know that.'

'I'm sure Masters and Johnson would just call that sort of thing variety.'

Meg shook her head. 'Feels more like Kraft-Ebing to me,' she said.

'Who's that?' Dell wanted to know.

'Some old expert on perversion that I read in my student days. About a thousand years ago.'

'But he does want you,' her friend persisted. 'He wants you and the kids to go away with him.'

Meg sighed. 'I don't think he really knows what that means. I know he keeps saying it.'

'Why don't you try some time together?' said Dell. 'Just a few days. Before you call it off. What have you got to lose?'

Meg stood up and her friend stood as well. The two women put their arms around each other. 'Thanks, Delly. I don't know what I'd do without you.'

'Me too,' said Dell. 'But if I had a gorgeous, rich hunk who wanted me to run away with him and who didn't mind the bloody kids, I'd be off like a shot.'

The women walked to the door together. 'How's Harry?'

Meg shrugged. 'Same as usual. Doesn't talk, just looks. Sometimes I get the feeling he's sniffing me over.' She paused. 'He hasn't spoken to me in years. Really talked, I mean. It's like he's taken a vow of silence.'

'Harry the monk,' Dell laughed. 'Ken was the same. They stop talking. It's part of the job description. They only talk with each other. Then they even stop doing that. "No-one else understands," Ken used to say. I'd say "Give me a chance." But he never did. All he wanted from me was sex and cooking. Not conversation. I'd say "Why don't we ever *talk* about anything?" And he'd sit down and he'd say "Okay. Talk. Talk now."' Dell shrugged to show the hopelessness of it.

'Harry used to talk, a long time ago. But I've never forgotten that around the time we married he told me something weird. He reckoned he had a lock-up in his mind – of things he never wanted to think about again, let alone talk about.' Dell looked inquiringly at her friend. 'I asked him if there were a lot of things in there, and he shook his head. He said no, only a couple, but nothing could be done about them and they could never be let out. I used to imagine these two barrels of deadly toxic waste lying at the bottom of the Atlantic, under about seven miles of ocean.'

'Did he ever talk about the shooting?'

Meg shook her head. She buried her face in her hands, then dragged her hair back away from her face, sitting up. 'Not to me. But by then I'd stopped asking questions. Now I think he's put me and our marriage in that lock-up too. He won't discuss it.' She paused, feeling an overwhelming sadness. 'Doesn't do anything except work and make those bloody message sticks.'

'Are they part of his Koori heritage?' Dell asked.

Meg shook her head and laughed. 'He's got no interest in his heritage whatsoever. God, I'm more interested than he is, and I'm pretty well pure Anglo-Saxon. The truth is, he first saw them at a North American Indian craft exhibition we went to with the kids, and for some reason got inspired to make one. Then he made another. And another. It's like an obsession with him. He doesn't do anything with them, just makes them. He never talks about his early life, or about his mother or his childhood. He reckons I'd start doing a psychology job on him.'

'Of course you would!' said Dell, laughing.

Meg shrugged. 'Maybe.' She almost smiled. 'Yes,' she admitted, 'I would. I might get some insight that way. The only thing he's ever told me is that his mother was supposed to be descended from some famous sorcerer – a "clever man". Some historical figure. But it might be just a story.'

'If he's told you that much he might—'

But Meg interrupted her, shaking her head. 'That was in the old days when we still talked, still listened to each other.' Her voice was low. 'You know, Dell, Harry used to listen to me so keenly that it was like . . .' she searched for the right words '. . . like huge doors opening up deep inside him to receive me. He's completely closed against me now. You know how it is.'

'I do,' said Dell sadly, divorced two years before.

'Oh golly,' said Meg, looking at the yellow and white daisy clock above Dell's country-style sideboard, 'I'd better dash.'

Meg opened Dell's front gate and closed it behind her. She headed for her own, next-door, before remembering the stuff she'd meant to bring in with her. Returning to her car, she lugged her art folio out of the boot, even though she'd have no need of it at home during the week and would have to lug it back into the car again. It made her feel less of a liar, this piece of physical evidence that she *was* enrolled in an art course, that she *did* spend three hours a week doing a mixture of life drawing, composition, oil and acrylic techniques and art theory. Some nights. She rested the folder briefly on the top step and looked at her house. It was a neat bungalow, but the front yard needed tending. Weeds grew among the gerberas along the front of the house and the box hedge around the post and rail fence was ragged and untrimmed. A few roses bloomed, but the bushes needed cutting back. The sound of an aircraft overhead made her look up. When the hot westerlies blew, the flight path for incoming air traffic was right over her place. The huge craft lumbered overhead, its landing lights flashing, seeming to hang low in the air, impossibly slow. Meg thought sometimes she could practically see the faces of the passengers through the porthole windows. She looked again at the run-down front garden. I don't have time, she thought. A family, a demanding profession as well as a house to run. Not to mention being a member of a twenty-four-hour operational police base. There's never any time to do the things I really want to do. I'm always tired. She lifted the folder again and went inside, feeling an unaccountable sadness. She and Harry had bought this house with such hope. He'd been married briefly when he was very young, just as she had been, but this was the first real home for both of them.

Razor wagged down the hall at her, speaking only once to greet her as she closed the door. Then he sniffed at her. 'Go away,' she said, guilty. He ambled down the hall and nosed open Hannah's door, vanishing inside. Meg dragged the folio into the living room and went into the kitchen to get a drink of water. A pile of window envelopes waited on the bench. Bills. She opened them, threw the envelopes into the bin and placed the bills in a pile. She went to check on her youngest daughter. Hannah was sound asleep with the light on and Razor was sitting next to a huge teddy bear. 'Have you been on that bed?' Meg scolded him.

She went over to her daughter and kissed her, covering her with the sheet. The moo-cow clock kicked its heels to jump over the moon at half past eleven on the bedside table. The screensaver on Hannah's computer continued to send silent shooting stars into the darkness of the room until Meg moved the mouse. The menu came up so she closed the screen and turned the light off. As soon as she'd left the room, Razor padded over and jumped back onto the bed and Hannah turned in her sleep to settle him down.

Meg tapped on Ali's door and opened it. 'It's late, Alison. Put the light out.'

'Okay.'

She looked at the seventeen-year-old face with the hard red on the soft mouth and heavy lines around her eyes. Alison was beautiful, Meg thought, and completely closed to her. Until last year, Ali had been an outstanding athlete, brilliant at the cross-country event, who had loved to run with Harry and the dogs. She could run the legs off her husband and keep up with the dogs for hours on end. But something had happened. Something had made Alison shut down.

'Is everything all right?' she asked her daughter.

Alison shrugged.

Oh Ali, Meg thought. What's gone wrong with us? She heard the wagon pull up and started undoing her blouse, hurrying to the bathroom. But Harry had inexplicably used the front door and suddenly he was there, in the hall. Meg pulled her blouse together and clutched the clean towel tightly against her chest.

'Meg,' he began, but the softness in his voice only increased her guilty feeling of unease, and she ducked to avoid him, going into the bathroom, leaving him standing awkwardly in the hall.

Asgard raced ahead into the kitchen and was sitting at attention beside his dish, knowing he'd done very well when Harry came in and opened a tin of pet food for him. Asgard pounced on the food the second Harry gave the order. 'Good boy, good boy,' Harry said automatically. He left the kitchen and walked through the living room, down the hallway to his office, passing the bathroom where Meg was showering. Harry took his gun off and locked it away. On the desk was the message stick he was currently making. He ran his fingers over the sanded wood. The grain of timber pleased him with its striations and curves. Termites or some sort of borer had made scribbly indentations along one side, and these were so complex that in some places it almost looked like a mysterious language of glyphs.

He had drilled holes along the wood at uneven intervals. On the longer side of the fork, he would wrap leather thonging, leaving several lengths about fifteen centimetres long and finishing them with feathers and beads. He would set crystals and interesting stones in the holes he'd made.

Finally, he would finish the job with a clear varnish. This timber was the soft fawn colour of a very young joey, Harry thought. When he came to decorating it, he decided, he'd keep to those warm colours of the eastern grey kangaroo – the fawn, the gold, the black – with some dark glistening beads, echoes of the mighty disembowelling back claws and shining eyes. Maybe some lines of red, black and white paint, a touch of earth brown. He looked at the finished one where it sat on the cupboard. This was a big shank of dark timber that he'd stained ebony so that it looked like the femur of some extinct beast from a peat bog. He'd decorated it with sombre-coloured feathers and leather thonging, adding a knob of glittering pyrites – fool's gold – into an excised pit in the wood. An ancient king might have wielded this, he thought. The phone rang and he prayed it wasn't going to be another call-out. It wasn't. It was only the Confessor.

Meg was pretending to be asleep when he climbed in beside her warm body, which smelled of soap and talc and tooth-brush. Harry lay in the dark, listening to his wife's breathing. He remembered how he'd fallen in love with her body scent, its brunette spiciness and undercurrent musk. Lately, her scent was different. She was using a heavy new perfume, not the light florals she usually favoured. He'd noticed new underwear in her drawers. But the biggest giveaway was the scent picture he'd discerned earlier in the hall – the whisky and the clove cigarettes, the acid sweat and the yeasty stink of another man's semen – now all washed down the drain.

FOUR

The huge river gum still stood on the rising land on the other side of the river. Over 150 years of growth had almost completely closed over the holes gouged in the trunk, and only the lumpy mounds of creamy scar growth, barely discernible from the undamaged areas unless an observer were to look very closely, indicated where the injuries had been. Not far from the original two-roomed dwelling of 1843, the great-grandfather and his two sons had built the double-storeyed Italianate house – in 1887, when prosperity allowed. The rise of the land protected it from the worst of the western sun and the westerly winds, and it looked quite grand from the road, with the French windows of its many bedrooms opening out onto the verandahs that encircled the house. The house faced north-east, and the land ahead of it sloped quite steeply down to the river flats, permanently watered by the property's huge frontage to a tributary of the Lachlan River. On the rise behind the house, 120 years before, Great-grandfather Wetherill had planted two ebony trees, one each for his children, but they had never been harvested for their black gold because over the years everyone had forgotten what they were. Now they were just two old trees surrounded by other exotics – copper beeches, oaks and maples – as well as the indigenous wattles, eucalypts and casuarinas. The original two-room dwelling, now used as a toolshed and storage area, contained the skeleton of the old sulky, dusty with spiders' webs among a great deal of rubbish. One day someone was going to get round to restoring it.

He passed the manager's house, about a kilometre away to the north-west, and drove up to the homestead. He wanted to get inside, do some work and get out before Ralph, due to leave in a few days to work in Queensland on another property, knew he was there. After Ralph left, the place would be empty except for himself, and that suited his plans perfectly. Underneath the tarpaulin cover on the back of his utility vehicle were more provisions and more ammunition, and he didn't want anyone around while he unloaded that.

He went up to the front door and opened it. The smell of damp and locked-up house hit him. Rain always seeped through the window frame in the large front bedroom upstairs. He had repaired it a few times but the water came in from the roof as well and that was a huge job. There was hardly any money left now in the account.

He'd sold most of the stock, and once the stud herd went the place wouldn't be producing anything except tussock grass and rabbits. Huge erosion gullies had split the paddocks, cutting their way towards the river. Sheet erosion had rendered the once-fertile river flats almost barren except for prickly weeds that not even rabbits could kill. Ninety per cent of Ralph's work was pest control.

My father would turn in his grave, he thought, if he could see the place like this. The thought made him smile.

He made his way through the house, opening up rooms and windows. It was hot outside but the interior of the house was always cool, especially downstairs. He went up the long staircase, where once highly-polished and carved rosewood bannisters still showed under the dust. Both upstairs and down, most of the furniture, spotted with mildew, was just useable. A woman's touch, he thought wryly. That's what's needed here. He walked right through the house, past the parlour, the living room, the dining room, the old back room that used to have the billiards table in it, past the two small downstairs bedrooms and finally down to the kitchen: a stone-floored area, part of the original house and redecorated by his mother in the 1950s. The cupboards were the same sickly pink and blue he remembered from his childhood. On one, there was even the mark his father's boot had made when a kick had gone awry and scraped the cupboard door instead of connecting with him. You're not kicking anyone now, you old bastard, he thought. He went straight through the kitchen to the back door, unlocked the bolts and the deadlock, and walked outside. The dark laundry buzzed with flies and an odd chattering. Something stank dead in there. He stepped inside and waited a second or two for his eyes to adjust. Folded in their membranous cloaks and hanging upside down, were twenty or thirty fruit bats. A dead bat lay on the ground, and the floor was coated with excrement. As he watched, two of them scolded and fought for a better toehold on the old lines that ran across the area just under the ceiling, held in position by a system of cleats and small pulleys. He picked up the stinking corpse and took it outside, swinging his arm, throwing it towards the family cemetery past the spot where the summerhouse and the lawns had once been. Bits of rotten bat flew off behind him as he hurled the stiff body and the crowd of flies rose in the air. The cemetery lay towards the right of the house, back from the river, tucked near a small rise. Ancient briars obscured the headstones and rusty iron bedheads filled the gaps in the hundred-year-old wrought iron fence around the family plot. He never went there. He remembered the story about the flood of 1899. How the river banks had been washed away and the ground of the cemetery so undermined by rising water that one of the newly dead great uncles had been disinterred and washed back home again to the steps of the summerhouse where he lay with one rotting arm protruding from his split coffin.

He returned to the house, passed through it again to the front door and outside to the ute. He undid the tarp and started unloading, using a trolley.

At the end of the day, the preparations were almost complete. He stood back and looked at his work, then returned to the sitting room and opened the cabinet. A woman was supposed to come up to the house once a fortnight to dust and generally keep an eye on things, but there was no discernible evidence of her visits. Dust lay along every surface and the old gilt mirror that hung above the fireplace reflected an image of himself as a misty ghost, marred with black spots. He took out the bottle of brandy, poured a drink into one of the little crystal glasses from the credenza and tossed it back, looking at the photographs on the mantel above the fireplace: his father in his uniform; mother in a studio portrait, looking less frightened than usual; grandfather in his moustache with his young bride overwhelmed by family lace. A few cameo portraits of other relatives collected dust on the marble surface where the ugly red Venetian glass vase still held centre stage. He looked at his reflection in the speckled mirror beside it, adding his own image to that of his family. 'Fuck the lot of you,' he toasted. He thought of the family he should have had. He thought of the man who had cheated him. He poured another brandy and took it back with him to the kitchen, his mind red–black with hatred. He finished it and hurled the empty glass against the door. But it hit one of the panels of patterned pink glass that ran either side of the drying timber. Glass shattered and splintered, spearing in all directions. He swore and kicked it into a pile in a corner.

Late in the evening he was in the utility and on the road again. He took the turn off the highway to the small airstrip too hard and fast and nearly skidded into the banks on the side of the road. He liked night driving. He had a huge bullbar on the front of the ute and any creature stupid enough to collide with him was skewed, already dead in the air, onto the side of the road. He liked the thump and hurl of a road kill. There was an excitement in the shudder. Stupid animals would sit by the side of the road, eyes luminous in the high beam, and then, right at the most fatal time, they'd decide to jump or run under his vehicle.

And right there in his headlights, as if he'd conjured it, was a big kangaroo. 'Move, stupid,' he said to himself. But it didn't. He drove straight ahead. Its dilated eyes were suddenly rushing towards him. He felt the huge smack and shudder as the bullbar collected the large body at speed. The ute swerved and righted as he corrected the near skid. He didn't bother to look back. Now, all he really had to do was fly back to Sydney, pay Pughsie the down payment to grab the first one, and the rest – well – the rest would be a piece of cake.

FIVE

No-one noticed the man in the dark blue sedan next evening as he drove slowly past the Dog Squad buildings and the exercise yards. The driver easily picked out Harry Doyle among the other men, slowing the car almost to a stop, watching as Harry leaned over a blond Alsatian. Then the man put his foot down, changed up to second gear, missed it, tried again and picked up speed.

Harry swung around at a noisy gear change from the road outside, but all he saw were the rear red lights of the car vanishing into the night. Training took place in a well-lit yard out at Bass Hill where the Dog Squad had its headquarters. It was still hot, and the workout was hard on the men and the dogs. The buildings, kennels and runs occupied a couple of hectares, with the airconditioned administration block and its dusty front garden giving on to the main road, and the dogs' quarters and yards at the back. There were two new man-dog units fresh out of training school and the two new dogs responded well. You don't have to train the dogs, Harry thought. Just the men to understand and support their dogs' deft skills.

He turned his attention back to the dogs as they went

through their paces, tails wagging despite the heat: up and over the smaller hurdles, urged on by their handlers, through the tunnel, up the jungle gym and across the bars at the top, over the sloping roof section, through the long pipe, up and over the section of two-metre fence, across a ladder lying prone on the ground, and up another one leaning against the wall of the training area. Light-faced Blade, the two-year-old he'd picked up from the vet that evening, sat with him and Razor, also watching. In time, the younger dogs would learn to jump through hoops, across teetering footholds, along narrow ledges. As the bond of trust grew, those dogs would pretty well go through fire for their handlers. 'Good boy, good *boy*!' and some fondling from the handlers kept the dogs keen and eager to please the man they saw as leader of the dog pack. An active dog was sometimes rewarded with a 'tug of war', playing with their handlers for possession of a toy. Police dog recruits were as rare as their handlers; only about one in a hundred pups had the right combination of boldness and aggression without savagery, gun steadiness and the desire to get out front and lead. Applicants had to pass a gruelling three-day trial. All training simply enhanced or supported the animals' natural capacities and instincts. All dogs track by nature. Tracking, hunting, and bringing the prey back to the home base is what a dog does in the wild. There is only one area where a dog's training goes against a natural instinct – and that is in the matter of food refusal.

It was the Germans who had perfected the working dog – initially not bred for beauty. Different breeds had been trialled but handlers kept coming back to the shepherd as the best all-round dog. Bloodhounds might have somewhat keener noses, but when it came to climbing, bloodhounds weren't too keen. Nor were they particularly speedy over distances. Bloodhounds were favoured by certain American

K-9 units, but almost always there was a man and a shepherd close behind, for the bite. The powerful Rottweilers, too, had their advocates. 'But,' Harry's sergeant had told him in the early days, 'after you've had to lift a Rotty over nine fences, you never really want to see him again.'

When Harry had applied to join the Dog Squad eight years before, it was not much older itself. He wanted to work with animals again, he'd told the sergeant who interviewed him. He wanted to get away from Homicide, away from murderous humans and back to animals. He liked their honesty, the way they lived in the moment, their simplicity. A good dog never gave mixed signals. A good dog never smelt wrong. The sergeant had liked Harry's strong policing background, but also his familiarity with working dogs, his childhood on the big station, his tour of duty in Vietnam. Harry was accepted and Razor the puppy was given to him to bring home on the day that Hannah was born.

A police dog lives in the home of its handler – the operational base. Twenty-four hours a day. It is a deep relationship based on the principle of the pack, with the dog perceiving its handler as dominant dog. The training works with natural instincts – tracking, hunting, retrieving – from the ancient days of the dog pack. 'You never punish a puppy for being a puppy,' he told Meg once, taking the ruined Italian sandal away from Razor, 'anymore than you'd punish a kid for being a kid. Give him something he can chew.'

A police dog pinpoints a scent using a cone-shaped pattern. After he is 'cast' in his harness, he will run around until he finds the scent, then, like an oscillating pendulum, he will swing back and forth in smaller and smaller arcs until he's homed in on the track – that place where the scent picture is brightest and strongest. The apocrine glands of the mature human being, unlike the other sweat glands, are activated only by emotion. These glands are distributed all over the body and secrete a fluid that rapidly breaks down, becoming odorous, when the person is in a high state of excitement. Knowing that a large police dog and his handler are hot on your heels creates a strong trail for a dog to follow, more especially because there is a large concentration of apocrine glands on the feet of all mammals, including humans.

As well, the dog follows a complicated weave of odours – the ground scent, which might include crushed herbage, insects and other factors, as well as the human scent. Wherever he treads, the quarry releases minuscule traces of sweat, possibly other body fluids, invisible skin flakes, and the myriad scents of his life: his workplace, his aftershave, his soap, his washing powder, his girlfriend's perfume, his cat, his cat's flea powder, his mother's medication, the smells picked up from his vehicle, the lawn he trod on earlier, the cedar chest his socks are folded in, his clothing and his nationality. Different national diets quite naturally produce different personal scents.

With young Razor, Harry learned to become a man-dog police team; or rather, he learned to interpret what Razor was telling him about tracking as Razor searched property for drugs or other substances. He started to recognise all Razor's idiosyncrasies, the way he 'talked' in his body language. After awhile, Harry barely needed to say anything; the dog picked up his intention almost at the same time Harry had the thought. In this way they became like one animal, joined together by the flexible harness line, moving and picking up the scent picture together. Harry's sense of smell, always extremely keen, became more finely tuned with Razor's tuition.

'I've worked with tracking dogs before,' he told the sergeant. 'In Vietnam. I want to do it again.'

In Vietnam the dogs detected anti-personnel weapons and land mines along the track. They hunted down the men their handlers called 'the enemy'. Sometimes, after a firefight, it was deemed necessary that no survivor should slip through to the village or the bunker system ahead and warn the others. The black labrador is a bold, keen dog and it doesn't 'speak'. Bred as a gun dog, the black labrador knows how to stalk and point, how to freeze, how to stay steady around gunfire. The hardest job, as always for the handler, was keeping up with his dog. No matter where the enemy tried to hide, the big labrador found him. What happened after that was also inevitable.

A company with a dog team slept better than any other fighting unit, knowing they had a sentry keener than any human curled up with its handler. Men shared their rations with their animals; medics attended the dogs' wounds with as much attention as they'd give a man. An injured army dog was Casevacced out just like an injured man, lifted on a stretcher and flown to safety. No-one begrudged them.

It was Blade's turn to run the obstacle course. He baulked at the pipe, refusing to go through it. And he turned away from the ladder, until Harry had practically lifted him over it. The dog was not working to his full potential, Harry knew. It was not only the after-effects of the virus. The dog was upset because of the way things were at home. It's affecting the dogs, the kids, Harry thought. It's getting to me, too. Two shots rang out and Harry jumped. Then he relaxed. The boss must have decided to do some further training with them.

Lumbering towards them from the far end of the property like the Michelin tyre man was the senior constable, unrecognisable in a protective suit. Made of similar mesh to seat belts, this fabric was extremely tough, its fibres designed to recover from the holes and bite marks inflicted on it. The constable staggered closer and fired another round from a snub-nosed .38. 'Ya bloody mugs. Try and get me. Come on, ya bastards.' It was clear from his face – the only bit of him showing – that he was enjoying his role. 'Mug coppers,' he sneered.

Blade stiffened but sat at attention by Harry until the threatening figure was less than fifteen metres away. The dog's brilliant eyes followed every move but he remained completely motionless, except for the energetic tremor running the length of his body. When the constable raised his pistol to fire again, Harry leaned forward, whispered the attack command and slipped the harness. The Alsatian leapt through the air, flying at the gunman's elbow. His jaws closed on the firing arm as he danced on back legs, growling and snarling, tearing at the arm holding the weapon. The constable shook his arm. He punched Blade with his free hand. He did everything he could to throw the dog off. Blade gripped tighter, growling deeper and more fiercely. As he spun around, Blade spun with him. No matter what he did, that dog hung on tighter.

'Throw the gun down!' Harry ordered. 'Now!'

The constable did so, and at the same moment Blade dropped off his arm and sat at attention, white fangs centimetres from the constable's crotch. 'If you remain perfectly still,' Harry said, 'the dog will not harm you.'

'It's hot in here,' the constable said. 'I want to scratch my balls.'

'I wouldn't,' said Harry.

The two figures remained motionless except for Blade's heaving flanks and lolling tongue. Some tiny flicker of movement in the constable, imperceptible to the men watching, caused Blade to jump at him again, seizing the fabric near the throat. Again the constable froze. Again Blade sat at attention. It was a rare offender who would take on jaws backed up by pressure of 300 pounds per square inch.

Harry called him back, and he came bounding over. 'Good dog, good dog,' Harry said, squatting to pet him and reattach the harness.

'That's what we want,' said the senior sergeant to the two new men and their dogs. 'From attack to docility as fast as that. An uncontrollable dog is no use to us.'

If the quarry tried to hide up a tree or a building, the dog was trained to sit beneath the hide and bark. Like all the police dogs, Blade would only attack on command or if his handler was threatened. The attack command was kept as secret as a cop's PIN number.

After the formal training was over, Harry looked up to see the senior sergeant coming over, wiping the sweat from his face. 'That young dog,' Matthews said, indicating Blade as he pocketed his handkerchief, 'he's off tonight.' Matthews was a big man who kept fit shooting feral pigs from a helicopter harness during his holidays.

Harry nodded. He opened the back of the wagon and the dogs jumped in.

'What's wrong with him?' Matthews wanted to know.

'He's okay,' said Harry. 'He's just over a virus.'

'Everything all right at home?' Matthews said.

'Fine,' said Harry.

Matthews looked hard at him, reading him. 'Our lives depend on those dogs doing what they're trained to do.'

Harry nodded again.

'See to it,' said Matthews.

On the way home, Harry decided to take the dogs for a run; not so much for their sakes, but for his own. He liked to run late in summer when it was cooler, and at forty-seven, he knew he was slowing down.

He had permission to train the dogs on partially-cleared

army reserve land that also had creek flats to provide open grassland. His night vision had always been good. He let the dogs off their harnesses and took off after them, noticing how they went over hidden obstacles. He ran easily behind them and ahead of him the bush fell silent. The scent picture was damp forested area amid residential and industrial land – the dank, uriney smell of stale water and old oil. He noticed the brief, fresh smell of fungus as his feet hit some soft rotting timber underfoot. There was a night-flowering native climber whose name he didn't know layered in the still, cooler air above the creek. All he could hear was the distant sound of the freeway and the frogs further up the creek who were not yet alarmed by their arrival. A plover shrieked and a half-moon was rising, momentarily reflected in the creek water as he ran past. He shivered despite the heat. Half-moon in water was an image he didn't like. It shone too close to the lock-up in his mind where horrors lay. Sometimes they twitched, stirred by certain images and situations.

Harry loped along in his easy style, relaxed, using only the necessary muscles. He was aware of the strength of his bones and sinews and it felt good. The dogs started the climb into the timbered area where the creek rose and Harry followed, slowing a little in response to the terrain. He needed to go bush, he thought. To get away from criminals and amphetamine factories and smoggy cities. To have a break from Meg whom he could never please these days. Maybe take Hannah. He imagined fishing at the river at Boolabimbie and passing on to Hannah all the things he'd been told in the old days when he was her age, about the river, the surrounding country and the skies. But hell, he realised, she would know all that from the Internet. That kid probably already knew more about the world than he did.

The uphill run didn't seem to worry the dogs at all. They

bounded and jumped effortlessly, picking their way with their snouts and eyes through brush and fallen timber. At the top of the rise, Harry called them and they came to sit at attention with him. He could see the headlights on the freeway, and the clustered lights of the housing estates on the other side. As he remained still, he became aware of the different scent picture here: dryer, hotter air, spicy and sharper. Ten years ago, on a night like this, Harry had gone to meet an informant, who'd promised to name names. Harry remembered the smell of eucalypt in the night air, the way the door had opened before he'd even got halfway up the path, the man in the doorway framed and backlit, and the way the man had swung around with the handgun silhouetted upwards into the firing position. In one movement, Harry had dived sideways off the path and fired.

But he didn't want to think about this now. He turned his attention to the dogs and they looked around, sensing his movement, tongues lolling. Half-moon shone on white fangs and Harry hardened his mind as he pushed another memory away. Except that in this memory the scent picture was not the spice of eucalypt and a suburban Sydney garden on a summer night but putrid tropical rainforest near Nui Dat, and next to the half-moon reflected in a swampy pool a gutted woman was dying on the ground, and someone was getting up off her.

Harry spoke a short, sharp command to the dogs and let them run free back down the hill.

He drove the wagon into the yard at the back of his place and parked it near the dogs' pen along the fence. He went round to let Blade and Razor out of the wagon and Asgard greeted them, standing on his back legs in the wire run. It was nearly eleven and Meg's car was in the carport. The dogs bounded into the kitchen with him and he went to get the Meaty Treats they liked. He was giving them the 'eat' command when Hannah suddenly appeared in the kitchen.

'What are you doing up at this hour?' he said.

'I was waiting for Blade. I want him in my room. And I'm too hot,' she added.

Harry gave Blade another treat and ruffled his ears as the last aircraft before the curfew flew over the house towards Sydney Airport. Outside, Asgard barked at it.

'Was he good tonight?' Hannah asked.

'He was the best,' her father said. 'He showed two new dogs how it's done.' He felt bad lying to her.

'Why can't Asgard come inside?' she asked.

'It's better for him to stay out there. Dogs are territorial and we don't want fighting.' He noticed the way she clung to Blade and he picked up the wave of fear and sadness that pulsed out of his daughter.

'What is it?' he said. 'Why aren't you sleeping?'

'I have to have Blade with me. He helps me sleep.'

'Why aren't you sleeping?' he asked again. 'What's frightening you?'

His daughter's eyes looked into his. 'I hate the way you and Mum don't talk to each other. And I hate it when you do talk. I can hear things in my room.'

Harry noticed how skinny she was. And it wasn't just the unfillable thinness of pre-adolescence. It pained him to think she might go the same way as Alison, and be lost to him as well. There were shadows around her eyes that a child only had when she was sick or in pain. He put his arms around her and she hugged him back.

'It's all right, Dad,' she said. 'Don't worry. I'll be all right. It's just sometimes I don't like everything.'

He felt at a loss. He knew there was a capacity in him to talk to her but he found it extremely difficult. So he took her hand and led her silently back through the house to her room.

'What is it?' Meg appeared, wrapping her dressing-gown around herself, her face pale and anxious. 'Why aren't you in bed, Hannah?'

'I'm going, Mum.'

Harry and Meg looked at each other over the child. 'She's frightened,' said Harry.

'I am not,' said Hannah.

He went back to the kitchen to lock up, stopping on the way to look around the half-closed door at the sleeping form of his elder daughter. He was uneasy about her room. Strange, hostile scents. Leather. A man he didn't know. Cigarette smoke, very faint. Brought home on her hair and clothes, other scents he didn't want to know about. When she was four, Alison had said she was going to marry him when she grew up and Mummy could be their baby. She had adored him and it hadn't mattered that she was not his child. She'd been two when he and Meg had married, the result of Meg's brief, unhappy first marriage. The ex-husband lived somewhere in Perth, remarried with another family. Alison had never known another father apart from him. Now she barely looked at him, let alone spoke to him.

Immense loneliness welled up inside him, like a swamping wave. He felt alienated and isolated from every other human being. He let Razor come in and walked outside so that Razor had to turn and follow him back out again. Asgard pranced in the dog pen along the back fence and Harry walked over to him and petted his ears. Behind them, Razor pawed at the screen door, opened it, and went back inside. 'You'll be going home soon, mate,' Harry told Asgard, who licked his fingers. The air was still and hot, filled with cooking smells from the Asian restaurants along the main street and petrol fumes from

Anzac Parade. Harry longed for the aromatic smell of a hot night in the scrub. He looked up at the sky, searching for signs of a change in the weather. The stars were dull here, on the edges of the city, not like the great cloudy masses of radiance they'd displayed to his boyhood gaze. Once he'd known the skies of his childhood like he now knew his backyard: the way the constellations moved throughout the hours of night, the way they swung in their greater migrations through the seasons of the year. The scent of wood fire, yellow box, came to him, and he could have been back at Boolabimbie, 300 kilometres away to the north-west of Sydney, in the hut with his mother and the stockman she lived with. Harry recalled the enclosed verandah that had served as his bedroom, and how he'd always positioned himself to go to sleep with a star shining straight down on him through a small hole in the corrugated iron of the roof above him. It had satisfied him in the same way tracking did. Some deep faculty in him was filled and satisfied by following the dog – even to exhaustion – to the quarry and bringing him home. It was that essential quality, only found in one in a hundred men or dogs. Both handlers and police dogs had to have it.

'That dog is not allowed on the bed.' Meg's voice interrupted his thoughts and he went back inside and locked up, checking all the downstairs windows and the front door, stopping at Hannah's room.

Meg was holding up the cable that plugged into the phone. 'What's this? You've been on the Internet again.' Harry looked at his wife, whose anger was now directed at her daughter.

'You said I could,' Hannah reasoned. 'You said I could have five hours a week.'

Meg started rolling up the extension lead. 'I don't know,' she said. 'I don't know about this Internet. I don't even have it at work. It's all going too fast. Anything in the world can come pouring into my house.'

'It's just stuff, Mum. Information. It's like a library. Just because you don't know about it, you don't have to worry about it.' Her bottom lip quivered but she wouldn't cry.

Harry went to her, picked her up and put her into her bed. 'Come on Hanka-panka,' he said. 'You're overtired.' Blade padded over to the side of the bed.

'You always say that,' she said through tears. 'Just because I'm not doing something you want me to do.' He was aware that Meg had vanished, leaving him to deal with Hannah.

'Look,' he said, 'I'm overtired too. I've had a hard day. So's Blade. He wants to go to sleep.'

'And Sarah said she doesn't want to be my friend anymore,' said Hannah, bursting into a wail.

'She'll change her mind about that,' said Harry, arranging the sheet over his daughter.

'No she won't!' Hannah shrieked in a voice that indicated she was at the end of her tether. 'You don't know what it's like to have a best friend who doesn't want to be best friends anymore!'

He sat on the edge of the bed and took her hands. She tried to pull away at first, refusing to be comforted, but eventually let her hands lie still in his.

'When I was a little boy,' he said, those magic words that Hannah loved to hear, 'my best friend was Angus. We did everything together. Like you and Sarah. We rode horses, we camped out in the bush.' Hannah's eyes were wide with listening. 'His father owned the property and my father worked for him. But Angus's father used to beat him.'

'Why?' said Hannah.

'He used to drink too much and get violent.' Harry remembered terrible scenes, terrible beatings.

'And then what happened?'

'Angus eventually got taller than his father and hit him back one time. And the old man never touched him again. Not physically.'

'Then what did you do?'

Harry smiled. 'You know the next part. We went to the Vietnam War together. Two country boys. And when we came home, everything had changed. Australia had changed. And Angus wasn't my friend anymore.'

'Why?'

'He did something that I couldn't forgive.'

'What?'

Harry looked at his daughter – her concern, her puzzled frown. He would never tell her. He would never tell anyone what Angus had done. He stood up and leaned over, kissing her goodnight. 'Questions, questions. You'll make a great cop.'

'Grown-ups are weird,' she said, turning away from him. 'You start to tell me things then you stop. So does Mum.'

'You don't have to know everything,' he said to her. 'There are things I wish I didn't know.'

'When I grow up,' she said, 'I'm going to know everything. And I'm going to tell my kids everything.' She rolled back to face him.

'Dad? Will you make me a message stick? A special one just for me?'

Harry was touched. 'Would you really like one?'

'Yes, with some beautiful purple athemist crystals on it.'

'I'll make you one,' he said, suppressing a smile. 'Complete with athemists.'

Meg could hear the low voices of her daughter and her husband as she wiped down the kitchen counter. Hannah loved hearing about the things Harry had done when he was a boy. Once she had, too. She walked to the kitchen door and went outside. Asgard was curled up on some sacking under the roof of the dog pen and he watched intently as Meg sat on one of the two swings Harry had built for the girls years ago. She swung gently back and forth, remembering times gone by when they had sometimes sat here together in the hot nights, with a beer, gently rocking on the swings and talking. She could see the dull glow of the lights of the city, five kilometres away, reflected in the night sky low on the horizon. Overhead was a turbulent sky but it hadn't rained for months and the air was charged. Meg felt immensely lonely. She sighed and stood up and went back into the kitchen. She dialled Max's number.

'Hullo?' he said in his anonymous, downwards inflected voice.

'It's me,' she said. 'I want to see you soon.'

'Haven't you just seen enough?' he teased.

Meg shook her head. 'No,' she said, 'I haven't.'

'That's easily arranged,' he said and she could hear the longing in his voice. She rang off.

Harry climbed into bed and felt his wife lying awake beside him.

'Did you go out tonight?' he asked her. Her scent picture was bland tonight.

'Yes,' she said. 'I went over to Dell's.'

He couldn't smell Dell anywhere. Just his wife's own brunette smell – the nightie, food scents, the washed cosmetic late-night smell he knew so well. Her secret scent was faintly there, too, and he turned away from her, knowing that it didn't flower for him anymore.

'I was thinking,' Meg said, 'of how you used to listen to

me once. Now you don't even talk to me.' Harry knew it was safer to stay silent.

'You should have come with me to that counsellor last year,' she continued in the dark. 'But you wouldn't.'

How often she did things like that, he thought. Just grabbed something out of the resentment box and tossed it at him. He didn't answer, just lay there with his eyes open, sensing a shift in his wife, a decision taken, something deep changing.

Perhaps I should have, he thought. But I didn't want to talk to some stranger about very private things. 'Nothing I ever do is enough,' he finally said. 'I am always a failure to you.'

'That's the longest speech you've made for about a year.' His wife's voice was hard, defensive against the pain in his voice.

'It won't happen again,' he said, further hardening his voice. He heard her eyes blinking in the darkness. I've given up, he thought.

She felt him very still beside her, as if he were watching and waiting for her next move. 'But you don't care anymore, do you?' said his wife. 'I wonder if you even care about the kids. I don't think you even care about the job anymore. All you care about these days are the dogs . . . the precious dogs.'

He turned away and closed his eyes. 'I don't know what to do either,' he said finally.

Harry was just about to pull a huge codfish out of the river at Boolabimbie when a bird started screaming at him. He'd never heard this bird in his life and he turned and grabbed the phone, instantly awake.

'Yes?'

'We've got a situation.' It was Arnold Peake, assistant to the

Area Commander. 'We need the dogs. Some crazy holed-up in a house at Strathfield. He took a few pot shots at the uniforms when they tried to go in.'

Harry got the address and hung up. In situations like this, a dog could be very helpful, and more and more patrol leaders were using them. If the offender came out shooting, as they sometimes did, a dog could disarm him faster and more effectively than a man. The subject might be bitten, but that was certainly preferable to the use of lethal force, and while the offender was dealing with the dog he was unable to deal with the police. Should he somehow elude the police, having a dog on the spot meant that he could be tracked down almost immediately.

It was 4.40 a.m. and the house had cooled down. Harry swung his legs over and sat on the edge of the bed. Meg stirred and said something incomprehensible then resettled and Razor padded in, sitting at attention beside him. 'We've got a job, mate,' he told the old dog. Razor's ears pricked and stayed up, swivelling at his master's movements.

In the corner of the bedroom Meg had leaned her major art work for the term, a brilliant abstract of light, darkness and colour. In the dimness, it looked as if tiny spirit faces peered out of the thick swirls of paint. Harry showered, washed his hair, shaved and dressed.

Blade and Razor sat by the kitchen door, already waiting for him. He decided that Asgard needed the experience but he took Razor too because the old dog was a steadying influence on the spirited blond youngster. 'Next time, Blade,' he said. 'You look after the women.'

Blade stood at the kitchen door watching the other dogs jump into the back of the wagon on Harry's command. Their gear was already stowed and he checked their harnesses and his weapon, fastening it down. The sun was rising behind him as he drove west, skirting the city, joining the Parramatta Road near Sydney University.

He had no trouble finding the place, a gracious, tree-lined parade off Strathfield Road, because the streets were cordoned off all around for a one-kilometre radius. Police vehicles formed barricades, while curious neighbours and bystanders looked on from a distance. Harry drove across the footpaths, around the police vehicles and found the man in charge. Two streets formed the long horns of Bromeliad Crescent, where the unknown gunman was holed up in number six. Harry was waved through to the small group of State Protection Group men in dark blue overalls and boots. He parked the wagon on the footpath and gave both dogs a drink from the big jerry-can. He ordered Asgard out and left the top half of the back of the wagon open, because it was going to be a hot day. Razor slumped down again and poignantly tilted his head between his paws, looking up at his pack leader. Harry touched Razor briefly on both paws in a superfluous command to stay.

Harry recognised negotiator Clive Wren. With Asgard obedient beside him, he walked over. 'What's the story?' he asked.

'We got a call from the neighbours about midnight,' Clive said. 'They thought they'd heard a shot. There'd been fighting and arguing earlier in the week and the local uniforms had been over to have a chat.'

'What did they find?'

'A woman who said there was nothing the matter. Just a routine domestic tiff.'

'Who is she?'

Clive shrugged again. 'Elizabeth May Golding. She said there'd been an argument with her boyfriend earlier but that everything was A-okay now.'

'And the boyfriend?'

'She gave his name as McEwan. He wasn't there at the time.'

'What about the weapon?'

'We're not sure yet. Some sort of semi-automatic. Black gun, maybe,' said Wren, using the M16's nickname. 'It's been too hot round here to be hunting up close for cartridges. We've got blokes in both next-door properties as well as in the house that abuts the backyard.'

'Have you made contact with him yet?'

'We had a chat on the phone. He's considering coming out, he said. But he doesn't know when. He said he needs time to think.'

'What about the other person?'

'We don't know. We don't know much yet. Her son's being interviewed. The neighbours. Usual stuff.'

'What are you planning on doing?'

Clive shrugged. 'The usual. Tell him we'll consider every request he makes. Agree with everything he says. Don't laugh at his jokes and basically bore the mad bastard stiff until he walks out. I've got a gut feeling the hostage is dead and he hasn't got a clue what to do next.'

'Where's the boss?'

'Somewhere round,' Clive shrugged again. 'He's trying to get some more intelligence on this clown. The name we've got doesn't show up anywhere. He's a cleanskin.'

Harry walked Asgard around the police vehicles until he could get a good look at number six: a large sandstone, brick and timber single-storey house in Federation style, blinds and curtains drawn, with verandahs and a small round tower with a witch's hat roof at the southern end. Dark, well-established gardens set back behind a stone wall enclosed the property. About a million dollars worth or more these days, Harry estimated. A driveway ran up to a small, closed garage on the right-hand side. Dense hedges along the fencelines, where wrens whispered, hid the house from neighbours on either side.

Harry and Asgard approached the property on the left of number six where two Tactical Control men, bulky in flak jackets, waited next to their vehicle. Harry remembered from his days with Homicide how too much police work involved simply waiting.

'I'll take the dog and go down round the back,' Harry told them. 'See what's doing down there.'

'There might be a couple of our blokes round the back,' said the heavier of the two. 'Don't let them shoot you.'

Asgard trotted ahead down the side passage of number four and Harry followed him, noticing the jumpiness. There was no doubt that the absence of his usual handler and the trouble at home was showing up in the dog. Dogs and kids, Harry thought. They pick up on everything going down – especially when no-one talks about it.

At the back of the place he found a timber-decked patio with barbecue furniture and a small in-ground pool. A Willie-wagtail dived around the pool, chasing insects, and he heard the snip of its beak. The scent picture here was ammonia, lawn clippings, blackened sausages, rust, diesel and the fragrance of cypress pines on a hot summer morning. Any early moisture was quickly drying, sending vapours away. And there was something else: a scent that teased and eluded him. He concentrated. The hairs on his forearms started rising in instinctive fear. He felt the same crawling up his spine and neck, under the sweat in his heavy overalls. It was right there, the impression of a scent memory, like the memory of a dream that dissolves in the same action of conscious mind trying to examine it. He swung around, but there was nothing. Asgard was intent on him, alert to something that was important to his handler. His intelligent hazel eyes looked into Harry's. 'Just some old something, mate,' Harry told him. An aircraft droned high overhead heading for Bankstown Airport, and the scent ghost vanished.

At the hedge that formed the southern boundary, Asgard stood up on his hind legs as Harry squinted through to number six. Do you want me to go through? Asgard's body language asked him. 'No. Stay,' Harry said. He could see a little more of the outside area of number six – the lush garden, crowded with perennials, geraniums, overgrown shrubs and a savage-looking aloes plant with thigh-thick monstrous spear leaves. Bees buzzed in a bottle-brush and he could smell honey on the wing. There could even be a wild hive around, he thought, the odour was so strong. Apart from a blue wren and two little brown females hopping through a collection of pots, nothing moved in number six. He and Asgard waited, watching through the hedge. He heard the phone ringing in the siege house as he made his way back down the side passage of number four.

'Please answer the phone,' Harry heard Clive call out in his level, steady voice. 'We can sort this out, mate. Just let anyone else come outside and then we can talk easy.'

When it happened, it was so fast that he understood only later how it had all gone so wrong.

Harry crouched, tensed in every muscle, ready to spring, because he'd noticed the front door move. He felt Asgard shudder with excitement beside him and tightened his customary hold on the harness line. Harry had a split-second glimpse of something the size of a lemon flying sideways out of the open doorway to land in front of the house; of a man taking cover behind a large elm tree; of a short, thick weapon.

'Grenade!' Harry shouted. Instinctively, he dived with Asgard behind another of the sturdy elms. 'Get down! He's lobbed a grenade!'

The explosion erupted in a vivid orange flame and black smoke. In the shocked silence, Harry and the dog raced through the smoke past the star-shaped pattern on the driveway. Harry had seen the man heading for the opposite fence and he and the dog crashed through into the sedate gardens of number eight, smashing vegetation, crushing seedlings, splashing through a small wire-covered ornamental pond. He got a glimpse of the man just before he leaped over the back fence; noted his low crouching run, and saw the armalite. Harry unfastened his holster as he and Asgard scrambled over the fence. Suddenly the man turned and stood his ground, aiming the weapon at Harry. Harry crashed rolling to the ground as he dived behind a corner. He stayed covered for a moment, then cautiously looked around. The offender had dropped into his crouching run again. Harry drew his weapon, released Asgard's line and held him by the collar.

'Stop!' he commanded. 'Or I'll shoot. Drop the weapon.' The offender kept moving and Harry was about to release the dog when he saw the glint of a knife. Asgard, too toey, didn't wait for the attack command. He shot through the air to fasten on to the right arm of the offender. The armalite fell from the man's grasp, but Harry sensed the knife thrust and heard Asgard's yelp. He charged forward, saw the offender pick up the armalite, and jumped sideways again, taking cover. Asgard dropped to the ground then staggered to get up again while the man raced towards the back of the siege house. Harry ran after him, ducking past an overturned deck chair. 'Stop or I'll shoot,' he yelled again. He stood and fired – once, twice – then continued to run after the man. The place was going crazy with shouts and orders and swearing. In Vietnam, the

air would be full of lead. But this was policing in a civi_
In a war zone, soldiers keep firing. Police cannot. 'Collaterai
damage' – the acceptable civilian dead and injured that are
part and parcel of a combat firefight – is not tolerated in the
suburbs in times of peace. Harry raced after the gunman,
who had disappeared over another back fence. Harry heard
a whimper and turned to see Asgard dragging himself across
the ground towards where the man had vanished. Harry ran
past the injured dog and crashed through the hedge, looking
each way, but all he could see were other police, all doing
the same.

'This way, this way!' Harry ran across the hedge. There was
no-one in number eight or on the footpath. Nor in ten.

'Spread out,' he could hear the boss yelling. 'He's just
here. Let that ambulance through.' Ambulance officers were
already attending to someone lying on the ground near the
fence, not far from the crater.

Harry ran back to Asgard, who was lying near the hedge,
heaving. Let the others find the mad bastard, he thought.
He squatted beside the dog, pulling his belt off, making a
tourniquet. Asgard's tail flickered in an attempted greeting.
But there was nothing Harry could do. He could hear the
whistling of a lung wound and blood bubbled from the hole
with every breath and heartbeat. A stinking jungle pool, lit
with a half-moon, rose in his mind at the agonising sound.
Another severe cut had opened up the area above Asgard's
right eye and blood poured over the snout and onto the
ground. Harry picked up the dog and ran with him, weaving
between vehicles, ducking police officers who continued to
run towards the siege house. He'd noticed a doctor's surgery
in the street. But Asgard was dead before he pushed open
the door.

*　　　*　　　*

Harry drove home with Razor, and Asgard in a body bag. The house was empty; Hannah and Alison were at school, and Meg at work. When he went round the back of the wagon to let Razor out, Blade barked from the dog pen to greet them, and when Razor ran over to the younger dog his tail was tucked under his hindquarters. The old dog was distressed. Blade seemed listless and dry-nosed, so Harry took the dog's temperature and the result decided him to take Blade straight back to Don Rawson.

'I'll keep him a little while,' said Don. 'Get this temperature down and keep the fluids up.' Harry said goodbye to Blade, who licked his hand and looked reproachful through a wire cage.

Back home, Harry gave Razor a drink and washed down Asgard's bloody harness, dreading the thought of ringing his owner.

He went into his study and locked his weapon away, brushing past the message stick so that it swayed slightly on the leather thong that suspended it from the ceiling. Any handler hated losing a dog. Asgard's name would go up on the honour roll at the Dog Squad. 'PD Asgard. Killed on duty 22 November 1996.' Something from the morning's events also troubled him: an elusive scent and the escaped offender.

He drove to the Dog Squad with Razor and pulled up near the fenced-off pen where a batch of new puppies were climbing all over their patient mother as she rested in the shade. Opposite was the row of kennels, as big as stables, where the dogs rested when they weren't out on a job, and just like stables each animal's name was painted on the door.

'Harry. What happened?' Ray Gosling came out of the office building. 'Arnold Peake's been on the phone. Wants you back to track that guy. Or will I go?'

Harry considered. Ray's dog, PD Javelin, was a first-class animal. It would be a good idea to let Ray do this. But he shook his head and went back to the wagon.

Ray followed him. 'Shit,' he said, when he saw the bloody, dead dog in the body bag. 'Ron's going to take it hard.'

'Put him in the freezer. Ron'll want to bury him. Razor and I'll go back. I've got a score to settle with this bastard.'

Back at the siege house the police presence was still considerable. Physical Evidence people were packing up their boxes of tricks and leaving.

'We lost him really quickly,' Peake was saying as Harry got out of the wagon. He went round the back, opened it, and Razor jumped down. Harry harnessed him and the two men and the dog walked into the house, past the claypan left by the grenade. Harry smelled human blood and Razor became agitated beside him. He'd picked up Asgard's scent. Razor sniffed at the spot near the hedge where Asgard had struggled to breathe. Harry let him discover what had happened; watched him, sniffing, jerking and barking around the dark stain, now drying in the sun and covered in flies. Harry squatted and soothed him.

'Only had him for a coupla blocks and then we fucking lost him,' Peake was grizzling behind him. 'The media's going crazy. Wanting to know how one man gets through the State's finest. Short of turning the suburb into a war zone . . . I told them we can't actually do that.'

Outside the house, Harry let Razor meet the people present. Running from one to another, the dog checked them all out, sorting them from the complicated scents of ambulance officers, antiseptics, explosives and stretchers. Then Harry took the dog to where he'd seen the gunman stumble after the grenade and just before he'd crashed through the fence. Razor immediately pulled away on the lead and took off. 'Good boy, good boy,' Harry told him. 'That's the bad guy.' Razor scrambled through the hedge, dragging Harry after him. A few half-circles and Razor dropped his hindquarters, sweeping his tail round and round like a corkscrew. Harry read Razor's tail. 'I've got him,' that circling tail said. 'I'm right onto him.' The dog took off through gardens and yards, hardly aware of the scared faces at windows. Within a minute or two, Harry recognised the pattern of autonomic flight.

When we are afraid, Harry thought, we all behave in the same way. You haven't got a clue yet where you're going, have you, he thought to the escapee. You're just getting the hell out of here, trying to put as much distance between you and the crime scene in the smallest amount of time. So he wasn't at all surprised to follow Razor across the road to a house nearby and make for the right-hand side, even though that side was blocked by a high gate and on the other was a nice, easy driveway. But you didn't take that, did you? he thought to himself. Because you're in flight mode on foot and following an ancient, universal brain pattern, you will invariably go down the right-hand side, even if there's barbed wire in the way. I've followed you so often. I know how you go until you start thinking again.

Razor was jumping and dancing at the gateway. Harry gave the old dog a leg up and followed him over. Down the right-hand side of the garden out the back, over the fence again. You take an initial left turn, like I saw you do at the hedge after you'd lobbed the grenade. And from then on it's right all the way. Until the next stage. And I know that, too. Razor tugged him along through the driveway and out at the front of the next house. They crossed another road and Razor made another right-hand turn into a little lane. Strathfield's gracious mansion zone had given way to a mix of housing and light industrial of a modern era. Running down the lane, Razor danced to a halt where a large exotic tree overhung the back walls of what looked like factory buildings. 'You would,' Harry cursed, and Razor scrambled up and over the fence, squeezing himself between the top of the timber and the scratchy boughs of the tree. Harry grunted and lugged himself over.

Behind him, he was aware of the thudding of the State Protection blokes, keeping up with him because they were fit as buggery. He imagined the swearing and the out-of-condition complaining of the support cops behind them. Harry dropped over the fence, grazing his right hand on the rampant thorns of a blood-red bougainvillea that was growing up the tree. Razor tracked around the tree and stopped, signalling 'He had a rest here'.

So, thought Harry. You went to ground here, did you, and had a bit of a think about things? Eighty per cent of all urban tracks terminate within four blocks. You are running true to form.

The faint ghost of memory stirred. It was a rainforest tree; he didn't know the name of it, but he'd seen them before in Vietnam, or ones very similar. The hairs at the back of his neck prickled and suddenly it wasn't a game anymore. Where did you go? Harry wondered.

Now their quarry had switched from the unconscious flight path syndrome back to his own idiosyncratic pattern. Razor, barking excitedly, pulled him towards the back of the buildings – 'Prestige Buttons and Fasteners' – running up to a door marked 'Trade enquiries only'. Harry opened the door and the dog went in, leading him through empty corridors until he stopped outside a door marked 'Men's toilet'. Harry swung around, hearing thudding feet, but it was only Arnie Peake, purple-faced, followed by another, younger man.

'Get and find the owner. Or the manager,' Peake gasped. 'Get them out of here.' The young man obliged and vanished along the corridor.

'What've we got?'

'Don't know,' said Harry, thinking of a grenade in a small space. 'But I'm not going in until I do.'

When the State Protection mob kicked the door in eight minutes later, there was no-one at home. Razor led them to one of the cubicles then sat and barked loudly, his whole body shaking. Harry looked up. The manhole in the ceiling gaped. 'Shit!' said Peake, who had come up behind him.

'We can tear the ceiling to pieces,' said Harry, 'or try and pick him up outside again.'

They ran through the building, past gaping employees in white overalls and the agitated manager who was being pacified by a police constable. 'If he came out on the roof,' said Harry, 'he's got to have either jumped down somewhere. Or . . .' he paused as he went outside into the morning again. He looked down both sides of the Prestige building.

'Or what?' said Peake, following him, extremely puffed out and pissed off. 'He can't fucking fly.'

Harry noticed that the gap between Prestige Buttons and the next building was close enough for someone to jump. If he was fit and desperate. Or perhaps only desperate. 'He started working this out under that rainforest tree,' Harry told Peake. 'That's when he stopped being unconscious. Started thinking again.'

Arnold Peake looked at him. 'I knew you Dog Squad blokes were weird,' said Peake. 'What are you talking about unconscious?'

Harry and Razor tried to pick up the trail again. But a strong wind had blown up from the west and the roads and footpaths were stinking with the smell of tar, hot metal and petrol fumes. Razor arced around, trying to locate the trail again. Then when he'd covered the area, he drooped. 'Scent's gone,' he signalled.

'Boss wants you back at the siege ranch,' Peake told him as he and Razor hitched a lift in a car. 'Wants you to check out the inside of the house.' He shook his head as if this was one of the strangest requests ever to come from a senior officer.

The siege house had been taped off around the inner perimeter of the crime scene when Harry approached. 'The ambos reckon he'll probably lose an eye,' he heard someone say as they passed through the group of police clustered round the grenade's crater.

Razor trotted up the sandstone steps and into the cool, well-furnished interior of the house. 'There's no-one here,' said Peake. 'It's been searched thoroughly.' Harry nodded. The scent picture was floral: polish, dust, expensive timbers, cedar and rosewood as well as faint traces of other things Harry couldn't identify. The two of them moved around the open-plan rooms, Razor acquainting himself with everyone there. With the gunman's scent in his repertoire, Harry was waiting for him when he signalled 'someone else'. Harry nodded. The faint fragrance of perfume was the other scent he'd noticed.

'Find her,' Harry told the dog.

Razor tugged on his lead, hot on the trail. He found her everywhere. 'She sat here quite recently,' his signals told Harry. He followed her all around the house. In the mauve and white bedroom, the bed was unmade and the woman's cream nightgown was on the floor. Harry nodded and patted Razor. They'd had a fight here, he thought. The bedside table was overturned and a lot of jars and bottles lay on the floor near the dressing-table. Dying roses lay on the floor near a vase. Harry squatted and felt the carpet. It was dry. So, not last night.

'I'm heading back,' said Peake. 'There's nothing happening here.'

'There's a woman here,' said Harry. 'A woman came here and she hasn't left the premises.'

Peake looked at him and then at Razor, who was sniffing at a corner of the room, pawing an active alert. 'She's down here,' the dog told him.

'She's down there,' Harry told Peake. Peake stared. Razor was scratching at the lavender carpet and Harry went over. He squatted down and saw where the carpet didn't quite join the cedar skirting board. He peeled it back and there it was, the neatly crafted brass ring, nestled in its housing on the top of the trap. Peake came over to look with several others as Harry pulled the carpet completely away from the entrance. 'Well, bugger me,' said Peake.

Harry lifted the brass ring and pulled the trapdoor open. There was a light down there. The scent picture was dust and wine cellar and fungus and cold, old air.

Harry let Razor race down the steps and followed him.

There was very little blood on the front of her blouse and the marks on her skirt were from the dusty cellar floor. The woman lay on the cellar floor surrounded by neat racks of wine. A naked bulb shone mercilessly into her blind and staring eyes. But the wide eyes didn't reflect back. The aqueous and vitreous humours were clouding and already the corneas' surfaces were starting to dry.

Back at headquarters Harry rang Ron, who had already heard the news about Asgard.

'I'm sorry, mate,' Harry told him. 'He was a good dog. But he jumped before I gave the attack command. There was nothing I could do.'

The afternoon was baking hot, close to thirty-eight and with no cooling breeze. Ray Gosling and PD Javelin were out on a job and a probationary constable was cleaning out the kennels. The constable sprayed the puppies in their run and they squirmed and yelped with pleasure.

In his office with its lumbering, inefficient airconditioner, Harry wrote up the morning's incident. If he'd still been in Homicide, his work would just be beginning. But he was Dog Squad now and his job was finished. Never again would he have to spend hours and hours with deadened, brutalised killers and maimers, questioning them, empathising with them, trying to experience their points of view, coming almost to understand why they did the things they did, sitting up late in small rooms with overflowing ashtrays and empty coffee cups. That was behind him forever. He blessed the dogs for this, and went home to get some sleep.

SIX

In the bedroom, he drew the curtains against the heat and turned the airconditioner full on, so by the time he'd finished his shower, the room had cooled down. He lay down in his underwear. On the wall beside the bed was one of Meg's watercolours of Nelson Bay, a delicate wash of gold and turquoise with children playing in the sand. He dozed. Sometimes, he'd start from his sleep with racing heart, unable to remember what dream figure had terrified him.

He woke to a slamming kitchen door. Hannah appeared at the bedroom door, home from school, dragging her backpack along the floor with Razor wagging beside her.

'Hullo. Where's Blade and Asgard?'

Harry swung his legs over the side and sat up. He patted the bed beside him. 'Come and sit here,' he said. 'I've got some sad news.'

'Oh no,' she said, tears springing to her eyes, knowing already. She wouldn't climb on the bed, instead stood facing him squarely with her wide eyes.

'He was too brave and an armed man killed him,' he said. 'Blade's okay. Don's keeping an eye on him for me.'

'Poor dog. Poor Asgard. He was just doing his job.' She

cried her full-throated Hannah roar at the injustice of the world and tightened her grip on Razor's fur.

'Hanx, some people don't care what they do. They don't care if they hurt people or animals. Listen,' he said, standing up and leading her out into the kitchen. 'Don Rawson said we could pick your best friend Blade up later.'

'I hope you get that man,' she said fiercely, turning to him. 'He must never hurt Razor or Blade. I need Blade to keep me safe at night. And Razor is my twin dog.'

Harry looked at her again. 'What is it?' he asked. 'What is it that you're afraid of?'

Hannah shrugged. 'I don't know. I just worry at night.' She continued to hold the big dog. 'I can't sleep. You know.'

He did and was ashamed of himself. He changed the subject. 'Would you like to come out bush with me? During the holidays?'

Hannah sniffed and rubbed tears away with her sleeve. 'That's ages away. Ages and ages.'

'It'll come round. It always does.'

She vanished from the doorway and soon he heard the soft chattering of her computer.

Hannah e-mailed her cousin in Adelaide. Her mother's sister, Ingrid, had three children, and Diane was only a year older than Hannah. 'Hi Di,' Hannah wrote. 'Thanks for your letter. We're okay here. Asgard was killed on duty. He was a dog Dad was minding for a friend in hospital. Ali thinks she's the coolest person in the world, but she's not. I've got this friend called Richard who is on the Chat line and we have fun. One day you'd better come over and we can all go out together. See ya. Love Hannah.' She pressed 'Send' and off it went, vanishing through the optical fibre at the speed of light to wait until her cousin switched on her terminal and checked her mail. Just on the chance that there might be a letter, she checked her in-tray. A few musical chords played by her computer accompanied a message 'You have new mail'.

She felt a thrill of pleasure and hit 'Open'. She read the letter and it made her feel very excited. She wanted to answer it immediately, giving her postal address so that he could send the money as soon as possible. Mum would be home any minute now and it was better that she wasn't still on the net by then. But she just couldn't bear to wait till the next day.

She hit 'Reply' and wrote: 'Hi, Richard. Thanks for the letter. My postal address is 55 Botanical Avenue, Kingsford.'

Harry dozed a bit more but the ghost memory was still stirring, drifting with him in and out of consciousness. He deliberately sat up, blinking, and got up.

It was the ghost scent from this morning's siege and the pale woman lying shot through the heart on the cellar floor of the million-dollar Strathfield house that kept haunting him.

He'd arranged to meet Gentleman Jim Coates from Physical Evidence for coffee and a catch-up that day, so he rang to check if Jim was still available. He and Jim still kept in touch about once a month.

'Sure,' said Jim. 'All the crims of New South Wales have given me their word there'll be no misbehaviour for an hour or so today. Meet me at the usual place, usual time.' It was an old habit never to mention placenames over the phone.

Harry waited for Jim at a cafe with tinted windows on Oxford Street, taking in the chaotic scent of traffic fumes, perfume, disinfectant, food with a predominance of onions, the delicious smell of coffee roasting. This place had a courtyard and an exit out the back, so that if anyone came in that you wanted to avoid there was a way to disappear.

Jim walked in and sat down. 'I heard about the dog,' he

said. 'Are you all right?' Harry nodded and they ordered coffee and cheese melts.

'That Strathfield siege,' said Harry, looking out the window at a derelict man deep in conversation with the pole he was leaning against. 'What have you got?'

'There's a lot involved,' said Jim. 'You don't get a siege, a murder and a grenade attack in one place as a rule. We're still sorting through all the bits of wire. Major Jack Baker says the grenade was an M26. Used in Vietnam. He's chasing up where it was issued. It appears that the woman had been living in the cellar for some time. There was food down there and some plumbing had been done – connected up to the drains to give her a bathroom. She had a toaster and a kettle, some tins of food, water – that sort of thing.'

'Living down there or imprisoned down there?' Harry asked him.

'Not possible to say for sure,' said Jim. 'But, yes, imprisoned more likely. Why would you live in a cellar when you had a whole house?'

The waiter came with the coffee. Harry sipped his. 'There'd been a fight in the bedroom,' he said. He remembered the dry carpet and the dead roses. 'Maybe they had a fight some days ago and that was when he decided to lock her up. Maybe the neighbours could hear her yelling from the cellar.'

'Why are you interested in a crime scene all of a sudden? And an offender? I thought you were finished with all that,' said Jim.

'I am,' said Harry.

'We had an interesting fire last week in Paddington,' said Jim. 'Antiques place. You would have loved it.'

Two youngsters walked past the window, hair dyed like rosellas and tiny rings in their eyebrows. At a table nearby, a couple sat in silence, staring at the passing parade.

'Tell me about it,' said Harry, biting into his melt while it was too hot and burning his tongue.

'He'd used an accelerant,' said Jim. 'Soon as I walked in, I could see where he'd splashed it around.'

What arsonists didn't realise, thought Harry, was that whatever accelerant they threw around, burned more deeply than anywhere else, so an investigator could clearly see the carved-out pattern of the splashes.

'But it took me a while to work out how he'd started it. He was in Wollongong by the time the fire was raging.'

'Some sort of timing wick,' said Harry, venturing the melt again.

'I found this neat little spiral of ash,' said Jim, indicating with his finger on the table. 'Completely untouched. Still in perfect order. About that big.' He drew the spiral on the table with the tip of his forefinger. 'Suggest anything to you?'

Harry thought a moment. He chewed the rest of the cheese melt and swallowed it, wiping his mouth on the paper napkin. 'Mosquito coil,' he said.

Jim beamed. 'Exactly. By the time it had burnt to the end and set the wick into the petrol alight, he was down the coast, sleeping like a baby. I did one of your tricks and pulled a mosquito coil out of my pocket when we questioned him. You should have seen his face. He practically burst into tears.'

'See,' said Harry 'they don't consider that although it might be their second or third crime, or even their twentieth or thirtieth, for us it's crime scene 200 . . . or 2000.'

'I don't like the sound of the joker who got away from you at Strathfield,' said Jim.

Harry called for the bill. He didn't either. Something haunted him, a pattern he recognised about the way that gunman had covered the ground between the house and the hedge; the way he moved. He'd talk to Jim about it later when it was clearer in his mind.

He and Hannah picked up Blade and drove home. Meg was nowhere to be seen but Alison was there, sprawled on the lounge watching a game show.

'Ali?' he said, and the pencilled eyes turned and looked straight into his.

'What?'

Harry wanted to ask her what she was so angry about but thought he already knew. What do you want from me? he nearly asked, ashamed that he didn't know the answer.

'I just thought maybe you'd like to do something on the weekend. With your mum and me and Hannah.'

Alison didn't answer immediately, simply looked at him with her cool eyes as if he had suggested the most disgusting thing in the world. 'I don't think so,' she said, turning her attention back to the canned laughter.

He had a couple of rostered days off due to him, so while he cooked tea for himself and the girls he wondered what he would do with the time. Meg rang to say Dell was shouting her a meal at the golf club, an early birthday present.

'Meg,' he said, reminded, 'I want to take you out for dinner.'

'That'd be nice,' she said. 'We haven't gone out for dinner for ages.'

Harry grunted and hung up and it rang again the instant he put it down.

'I need to talk to you, Harry,' came the thin voice. 'I killed that woman. The Archons were practising chemicals on me.' The voice almost faded away.

'Tell me about it,' said Harry, sitting on a stool next to the griller with a fork in the other hand.

'I had to kill her,' said the Confessor. 'The Archons told me.'

'I see,' said Harry.

'I didn't want to do it, but they said God wanted it done. I am but his trusted servant,' the voice wavered. 'I must carry out the will of God. We are but vile sinners who must do His bidding.'

'I suppose that's one way of looking at it,' said Harry, pulling the griller out and jumping as he was stung by hot fat.

'In His will is our peace,' said the Confessor.

'True enough,' said Harry, turning the chops, placing them in neat rows, curled together with their tails all facing the same direction.

'I just needed to tell someone about it,' said the Confessor. 'I am guilty and I need to be punished.'

'Well,' said Harry, 'I'll tell you what I'll do. I'll make a full report of your confession to me now and someone will come down shortly and take a statement from you. Where are you living at the moment?' He pushed the tray back under the griller.

'Soon I will be living in the Kingdom of Heaven?' the voice queried. 'But now I am living with my brother who has been released from Inferno land. And we are preparing for a new guest for the feast.'

'That's nice,' said Harry. 'But if you would just give me the address . . .'

The Confessor's voice changed. 'I have to go. He's coming. Goodbye.' And he rang off.

Harry put the phone down and poked the potatoes. They were ready. He drained the peas, stirred in some butter, sliced up some tomato and served the chops and vegetables onto their plates, calling out to Alison and Hannah to come and get it.

'Yum. Curly tails,' said Hannah, picking up, then immediately yelping and dropping the hot chop. Alison sat in silence and picked at the peas. Glossy, jet-black hair looped like curtains on each side of her pale face. Harry thought of a woman lying dead with a small hole next to her sternum. He looked at the older girl's gothic whiteness, the fine skin over the bones and tendons of her hands. As a child, she had followed him everywhere. Now, she fiddled with a chunk of potato, squashing it into a paste.

Hannah had already eaten one chop and was working her way through the tail of the other. She smiled at him. But his attention was still with Alison. 'You're too thin,' he said to her. 'Why aren't you eating?'

'She wants to be a supermodel,' said Hannah.

'I'm not hungry.'

'Everyone gets hungry. The bloody dogs get hungry—'

'I am not a member of a dog pack,' said Alison, turning her scorn on him. It was so exactly like something Meg might have once said to him that he was silenced.

'Well I am,' said Hannah. 'And Razor is my darling, darling twin brother.' Razor came over at the sound of his name and pushed his snout into Hannah's lap. She nuzzled him.

'Hannah, don't do that while you're eating,' said her sister.

'Don't they have mothers in dog packs?' Hannah asked.

'Of course they do,' he said.

'She means Mum's never home,' Alison interpreted, and stood up to take her almost untouched meal to the sink.

Hannah looked up and frowned at her big sister.

'You think you know everything. But you don't, Ali.' She slipped off her chair and went into her room. Ali didn't know about Richard, nickname the Flakman. Only Di in Adelaide knew about Richard, and even she didn't know much. Richard was her special secret.

★   ★   ★

Harry wiped down the sink, hanging the tea towel up to dry. Alison had vanished into her room and he could hear the head-banging rhythm of her latest CD. He went down the hallway and knocked on her door. 'Please turn that down, Ali,' he was yelling when she suddenly did so and his voice was exposed, roaring her name.

Across the hallway, Hannah looked round from the computer.

'Shouldn't you be doing homework?' Harry said to her. 'Mum wouldn't like you doing that now.'

'Mum's not here,' said his logical child. 'Do you mind too?'

Harry shrugged. His mobile rang and he went into his office, brushing past the message stick to answer it. It was Gentleman Jim.

'We've got some more on the gunman, Padre,' Jim said, using Harry's nickname from the old days.

'Don't call me that,' said Harry.

'I do apologise. It just slipped out. John Thomas McEwan. Age forty-eight. Businessman – whatever that means. The woman was shot with a pistol – a Tokarev. Neat little Russian piece. You don't see many of them around. Distinctive crimps on the cartridge. The commies used them in Vietnam. We've had the dead woman's son in here again in a real state. Reckons he's going to go after this guy.'

Harry sighed. 'You know a lot of them say that for awhile. Talk to him. Let him talk to you. He could give you a lot. What else do you know about this McEwan?'

'He's got an unrestricted pilot's licence. The address on that is Brisbane. But there's no record on him in Queensland. The deceased was a good style of a woman, from what we've got – an ex-teacher who had a small business selling cosmetics and lingerie in peoples' homes. She'd been involved with our fellow for about a year. The son only met him once.'

'Why are you telling me all this?'

'To increase your curiosity. We wish you'd come back.'

'I'm not curious anymore,' said Harry. 'Shooting Franco changed all that.' He paused. 'But there is something you should know. I saw how he moves. Tell the blokes to be very careful if they get close up. This guy's done a lot of fire and movement drill. He moves like a professional soldier. My guess is he's seen active service. You might be going after a crazy vet.'

Meg waited in the pastel motel room, staring at the floral prints on the wall, until she heard his car pull up. When she opened the door to his knock and he came in, her heart lurched because he was so good-looking, a little taller than Harry's 190 centimetres, with a tanned face and dark hair just a little too long to be neat. He put his arms around her and she pushed her face into his breast and armpit, smelling him through his leather jacket and pushing both it and his shirt away so she could lick his skin. But he put her gently to one side and moved past her, to fall on the bed.

'Get us a drink, will you?'

So she went to the bar fridge and made herself a brandy and a Scotch on ice for him. She brought the drinks over and, kicking her shoes off, joined him on the bed.

'I'm going up to Maldon in the next few days,' he said. 'And then I want you to come up and see how you like it there.' He took a long drink and put the glass on the bedside table. 'Come here,' he said, pulling her down to join him. 'I can just see you,' he said, 'sitting up in the north room. There's a huge old room upstairs overlooking the gardens and the river. French windows fill it with light all day. I'd make a fire for you in the fireplace, and leave you alone to work. Or you could sit outside on the front lawn in a shady hat. Like one of the Impressionists.' He laughed at that and she looked hard at him. He was preoccupied, edgy. His restlessness was irritating her. She looked at the handsome face and suddenly realised how little she knew him.

'Max. I . . .' She stopped.

'You what?'

'I don't know anymore. About whether I should go.'

He turned to her then and she encountered something in his eyes she'd never seen before. It vanished as she looked.

'You'll come,' he said. 'I know that.'

Meg took a mouthful of brandy. 'I think I should take some time for myself. I don't think I should just go from one man to the next.'

His laugh wasn't pleasant. 'Why the hell not? Every woman I've ever known does exactly that.'

'I meant I think I should give myself some space. I still have an eight-year-old daughter. Alison would be all right. But Hannah would have to come with me.'

He leaned over and kissed her, softly parting her lips with his tongue. Maybe, she thought, I've been too hasty. She found herself returning his kiss; his beautiful mouth excited her. I don't have to call it off right now, she thought. Soon she forgot that she was thinking of calling the whole thing off, forgot that she had decided to warn him that if he ever did that business again it would be over for good. Instead, she rolled over into him and started unzipping his trousers. Next time, she thought. I'll make a decision next time.

Hannah tried to drag the big dog higher up the bed and Razor, understanding her intention, clambered up to be beside her. She wrapped her arm around him, sniffing his good, clean, doggy smell. She heard her mother come in the front door, heard her high heels clatter down the polished boards in the hall, past their bedrooms, past the little room that her father used as an office and into the lounge area near the kitchen.

'Do you realise what time it is?' Razor sat up at the sound of her father's voice.

'Yes.'

Razor flopped back down again. Hannah turned over and pulled the pillow over her head. She kept her attention on the plan that she and Richard were making. If she left early in the morning, at the same time she normally left for school, and made sure she was back by four, no-one would know the difference. She could put shorts and t-shirt in her school bag and change. She wasn't a hundred per cent sure that Richard was a rich kid, although he said he was. But if the money came in the mail, she would know. And she would go.

'I don't know what I want to do,' her mother's voice intruded. 'If I knew, I'd do it.'

'There's someone else, isn't there, Margaret?' Razor pricked up his ears again, alert to the distress in his pack leader's voice. 'Don't even think about lying. I can smell him. I've been smelling him for months.'

She heard her mother rush down the hall into the bedroom, heard her father's footsteps following. Don't, don't *don't*, Hannah begged silently. Just leave her alone and it won't get worse. Please, *please don't*.

But her father's voice was raised. 'I've been running this family on my own for months,' he was saying. 'Cooking tea as well as working all hours with the dogs—'

'Fuck the dogs!'

Hannah was shocked. She had never heard her mother swear before.

'If you'd paid as much attention to your wife or children as you do to those fucking *dogs* . . .'

Hannah started crying, cradling Razor, covering his ears. 'Don't listen to her,' Hannah sobbed into the dog's warm body. 'She doesn't mean it. She doesn't mean it. You are a very good dog. You are.'

Then came her father's angry footsteps down the hall to her room, dragging her mother with him. Hannah shrank into her bed, fearful. Her door swung open. Suddenly her parents were there, blocking the doorway to her room. Her mother's eyes were wide with fright and anger. 'Look. Look what you're doing!' her father yelled, switching the light on to reveal Hannah sobbing into Razor's wolfish fur. 'Look at her. Look at your daughter.'

'Stop it, Harry. Stop this!' Her mother struggled to free herself from her father's grasp. 'Let me go! Stop it! Will you let me go?'

Her father swung them both round and tried to open Ali's door across the corridor, but it was locked. With Meg still tightly held, he bashed on Ali's door. 'Ali doesn't eat,' he yelled at the closed door. 'Ali's starving herself. Ali locks herself in her room and doesn't eat. You're a bloody school counsellor. Just look at these kids.'

'Harry will you stop this immediately. You're frightening everyone.'

'Frightening everyone? *I'm* frightening everyone? How do you work that out?'

Her mother broke away from her father and came into Hannah's room. She leaned over Hannah, smoothing her hair. 'Don't cry, darling. He's just upset. Please, don't cry.'

'Why shouldn't she cry?' her father was yelling. 'She's got plenty to cry about.'

'I'm only crying because Asgard is dead!' screamed Hannah.

Her mother stood up and went to the door, switching the light off, going out into the hall, her voice low and hard. 'Harry, stop this immediately or I'll take the girls and go right this minute.'

'Why don't you do just that?' he yelled back. 'Piss off with your fancy boyfriend and give me a break. You're never here anyway. You're always out.'

'Oh Jesus Christ don't you start on that one! There were months I'd go without seeing you. You and your precious bloody dogs.'

Hannah heard Ali's door open across the hall. She jumped out of bed with Razor following. 'Come on,' her sister whispered opposite, beckoning. And Hannah scuttled across the hall and into Ali's room. Ali locked the door again and Hannah climbed into the warmth of her sister's bed.

'It's okay, it's okay.' Ali got into bed and cuddled her until Hannah's sobbing decreased.

'I hate it when they fight,' she told her big sister.

'I know. I do too.'

'And I hate it when Mum gets those phone calls. You know the ones I mean.' In the darkness, Hannah felt her older sister nodding. 'But you're big,' she went on. 'You're nearly grown-up. You can go out and everything. You can even leave home soon. What will I do?'

'You can come and live with me in my flat.'

'Could I?'

'When I get one. Sure.'

'And the dogs? And my computer too? I'd have to bring that because I have this friend, Richard . . .' She hadn't intended to say all that, but the thought of leaving everything familiar jolted her.

Their parents' fight had subsided and all seemed quiet again. In the hall, Razor scratched at the door. Alison got up again and opened the door. Razor's ears and tail cast pointed shadows across the floorboards of her room. 'Oh all right,' Alison finally said. 'Come on in, you big dog.'

'He is *not* a big dog, not the way you say it,' said Hannah.

Razor climbed up on the bed with them and in the silence they heard their mother's voice from somewhere in the house. 'I remember years of not seeing you. Of doing everything on my own.' It's true, Ali thought. But why did you marry a man who was always out on the job?

'Do you think Dad worries about that man that he shot?'

Alison didn't answer.

'Ali, tell me. Do you?'

'I don't know,' said her sister. 'It was a mistake. Maybe he just doesn't think about it.'

'What about in the war?' Hannah continued. 'Do you think Dad killed people then?'

Alison shrugged. 'I don't know. What makes you want to know something like that? Why are you thinking about that right now?'

Hannah didn't answer for a moment. 'They don't ever talk about anything really important,' she finally said. 'They just talk about stuff that doesn't matter. Or they yell at each other.'

After a minute Alison became aware of the steadiness of her sister's breathing. Hannah could do this, she recalled. Just suddenly go to sleep almost mid-sentence. 'Go back to your own bed, Hanks, before you go to sleep. You're getting too heavy for me to carry back.' In her arms, Hannah was almost asleep, breathing softly again except for an occasional jagged in-breath, the last vestiges of the storm of crying.

Down the hall, Meg and Harry faced each other across the kitchen table. He was ashamed now of how he'd dragged Meg through the house, pushing her into her daughter's bedroom, trying to force her to see things the way he saw them, tossing her about with his careless strength. He knew why he dared not really think of her with the other man, why he preferred to leave it in another part of the lock-up in his mind. He only had to move towards looking at that, and his head and chest started the buildup and his hands and fingers started folding into fists. And that was the basic reason underlying all the others for leaving Homicide and the interrogations. Because he comprehended *exactly* why the murderers that he spoke with did as they did. 'You'd just had it up to here, didn't you,' he'd say to them in his soft voice. 'I know what that feels like. Little girl looking at you like that, with all her hair hanging down, screaming at you. Pretty face all screwed up. I know why you just had to stop her. Had to smash her head.' And they'd raise their heads and give him a sideways look in the eye and know he wasn't bullshitting. Now, he glanced at Hannah's school painting, showing the four of them walking hand-in-hand with the dogs. Once we were happy.

'Those years with Homicide,' Meg said. 'You were always out. You know, I thought that shooting would turn out to be a good thing in the end. For us, I mean. I thought you would have more time with the kids and me when you started with the dogs. I thought it would be nice for the kids to have a dog live with us. You wouldn't have to be sitting up all night questioning people like you used to. But it's no better. In fact it's worse. You're always on the job just the same.'

'You knew that,' he said. 'I told you that. I told you over and over. You said it was okay. You said you didn't mind. You knew it came with the job. Jesus Christ you said you *loved* me!' Harry's voice mixed anger, bewilderment and disbelief.

'That was a long time ago, Harry. We can't go on like this. I can't live with a man who's closed down.'

He knew what she was saying. He was silent about the past, about what had happened to him in his earliest days, in Vietnam, and the silence extended into the present. I don't tell anybody anything, he admitted to himself. It's like I've always lived in a war zone. I don't tell anyone about the life I live in here, in my mind, the truth about my mother and my father. I have never told these things to anyone. Of how I was taken away and put into that terrible place. My mind has no-go areas where certain things are dead and buried and I've been silent so long, I can no longer speak of them.

They sat in silence looking away from each other until Harry, leaning back in his chair, noticed where Hannah had written 'Mum's birthday' on the calendar for tomorrow's date. He closed his eyes. He'd completely forgotten. He leaned forward and Meg turned to look at him. 'Meg,' he said, 'I can book a table at Beppi's tomorrow night if you want. We can . . .'

The phone rang then and he grabbed it up, still looking at his wife. Her face had softened. Then he turned his full attention to the caller, nodded, and noted down an address, ringing off.

'Out near Bathurst,' he said to Meg. 'A woman. A dead woman and a missing child.'

'Great,' she said. 'That's really great. It's half past ten at night and you can do the bolt again and be a hero.' She slammed out of the room and down to the bedroom. Once, a long time ago, she would have cried.

Harry rang Ray Gosling and told him, picking up the switch-blade knife lying on the top of the filing cabinet while he spoke. It was no longer than his palm, operated with one hand by holding it between thumb and forefinger, developed for paratroopers who might find themselves stuck in trees with one arm out of commission. Harry sidled the blade open and shut with his thumb. When he'd finished the conversation, he slipped the folded knife into his pocket. It felt like a talisman.

SEVEN

The flight to Bathurst took less than an hour but it was well after midnight by the time Harry and Razor were met at the airport by a couple of the local cops. Dark-haired Ayoub and stocky Brennan introduced themselves, and Harry and the dog climbed into their vehicle. The scents in the car were mostly the beefy body scent of Brennan and the subtle Middle Eastern scent of Ayoub.

'I remember you,' said Ayoub. 'I heard you lecture in Sydney a few years ago. About your investigation into that little girl's death. Penrith.'

Harry nodded. He couldn't remember Ayoub, but often there were fifty people at the policing lectures.

'Then we went out to visit the government analysts' labs. You wouldn't credit it,' Ayoub continued. 'All he does, this pathologist, is cut the crotches out of women's panties and take samples. Then he makes slides out of them. That's his job. All day long, cutting the crotches out of women's panties. Piles and piles of panties. Imagine it. All day long. Snip, snip. Pass the panties.'

Brennan pursed his lips. 'What if they were wearing crotchless knickers when they got raped? Then what'd he do?'

Ayoub looked across at his mate and rolled his sheik's eyes upwards. 'I don't believe you sometimes. Crotchless knickers when they got killed.'

'Plenty of molls wear crotchless knickers,' Brennan insisted. 'I remember we picked one up last year and she was only wearing crotchless knickers and these high heels under a big coat. She'd been raped and when one of the young blokes asked her if she'd mind turning it on for us, she hit the bloody roof. Females.' He shook his head.

Harry interrupted. 'I've got a dog here. What's the job?'

'Looks like a rape murder,' Brennan turned from the wheel. 'The woman had a three-year-old child with her and he's nowhere to be found.' He turned back again. 'We don't know whether he was taken by the killer or if he's taken off into the scrub. That's why the boss wanted the dogs. We don't know what we'll find.'

'We haven't touched anything,' Ayoub added. 'The doctor's been and gone and so have the crime scene people. We can get someone to take her away once you and the dog have done your tricks.'

Bathurst lies beyond the Great Dividing Range that separates the inland from the coastal cities of New South Wales. Its wide, gracious streets, laid out by Governor Macquarie, are fronted by fine nineteenth century buildings in among the fast food outlets, many of the former reflecting the prosperity of the gold rush of the 1860s. Even now, flecks of alluvial gold turn up in the rivers and creeks around Bathurst and Sofala where graziers and small farmers run cattle and sheep, and raise crops. Harry had grown up around this area. He remembered that only several years ago two lucky diggers had turned up a nugget worth tens of thousands of dollars. Bathurst's rich grazing western plains, watered by the Macquarie River, 205 kilometres from Sydney, lie between and around undulating hills dotted with farms.

As they drove through the wide main street, the big country town was almost deserted except for a group of youngsters, hanging out at a corner cafe. They drove all the way through town until they were on unlit road, the headlights on high beam picking out the reflective trim on road posts. Occasionally, the bright reflections were the eyes of some nocturnal animal on the roadside.

'Christ, I need a beer,' Brennan muttered. 'I'm dry as a dead dingo's donger.'

'Mind if I smoke?' Ayoub asked, and Harry suddenly felt old and surprised by the new breed of young cops. He didn't answer and Ayoub lit up. They drove through the night in silence along the dark bush roads. Some desultory calls on the radio and the hum of the engine. Harry could hear Razor foxtrotting in the back, keeping his balance.

About five kilometres out of town on the Eglinton side, Brennan turned off the tar and almost immediately they were at a gate where a white-painted four-gallon drum on a straining post showed the name 'Peacehaven'.

'Here we are,' said Ayoub, turning in with the headlights still on high beam. 'The place's a bit of a madhouse,' said Brennan as they bumped up the driveway. 'Volunteer searchers and the State Emergency people have been everywhere looking for the little kid. Just as well it's not winter.'

'Is it the woman's kid?'

'Grandson. She was minding him for a few days.'

'What about the parents?'

'They were in Queensland on holidays. They're on their way back,' Brennan added. 'The woman's been living out here rent free helping out at the Schofields' house,' as if everyone, including Harry, would know who the Schofields were.

'And what about them?'

'They're straight up. Their place is about half a mile over there. They were both asleep in bed when we arrived. Heard nothing, saw nothing.'

'Who found her?'

'Her boyfriend dropped in for a bit of nooky after the pub. Says he found her like this and rang us. He's in a bad way. He was pissed as a parrot when he got here and the doc gave him some dope as well to calm him down. He passed out on us. He was a cot case. We'll have another chat with him in the morning when he's back.'

Ayoub checked in his notebook. 'Name's Faye. Murray Faye.'

'Do you think it's him?' Harry asked.

Ayoub shook his head. 'I've got a feeling. He would have had blood all over him and this guy was clean; paralytic, but clean. Whoever did this was cool. Mind you, I could be wrong.'

Brennan turned around again. 'What? I can't believe I'm hearing this. You could be wrong?'

'Just drive the car,' said Ayoub.

The lights in the house were on and the crime scene police had rigged up their own system when the three men got out of the wagon. In the distance, Harry could hear whipcracks ringing out like shots. 'Here's the dog,' he heard someone needlessly say and turned to see a group of State Protection brutes strapping up and locking on pieces of weaponry.

Harry walked blinking round the back and let Razor out, clipping the lead onto his harness. Razor instantly looked around, taking it all in, his nose and ears working full pelt. Harry stood and did the same. The glare from the police lighting hid the starry night that had overarched them on the drive out to the murder house. It was a neat timber bungalow with a front verandah and a little patch of lawn with fruit trees at the front. French windows gave onto the verandah and one of them was half-open. The scent picture here was rural: softly moving fresh air currents as the earth cooled for the night, the spice of eucalypts, a faint overlay of orange blossom and the honest smell of livestock – cattle and some horses.

'Okay, boy. Let's do some good.' Razor trotted ahead, nose down, then up, looking around. Harry stepped up onto the verandah, noting the ancient timbers. He stepped through the open French window and there she was on the floor at the end of the bed, spread-eagled in front of him, a large black pool drying around and under her upper body. The scent picture here was old house, stale fireplaces, faded meals, a woman's toiletries and the septic tank on occasions. And human blood. Her blood-soaked nightdress covered her head and upper body, and she was naked from the belly down. Harry noticed a little healing nick on her left shin, where she must have cut herself shaving. She was wearing novelty slippers – huge white fluffballs with pink fabric toes stitched onto the end, a ladylike monster's feet. Between her legs was a bloody mess. Her right arm was outflung with a plastic bag over the hand, the other was hidden under the fabric of her nightdress. He introduced Razor all round so that he could sniff, record and file the scent of everyone present at the crime scene. Then he looked very carefully around the room. It wasn't long before he noticed a few things that troubled him. On the dressing-table was an old-fashioned silver-backed hairbrush and mirror set, its comb missing three ivory teeth in a sequence he remembered perfectly, even after twenty-five years.

Harry's heart started pounding. It couldn't be. He pulled surgical gloves on and opened the drawers of the bedside table, sifting through the contents until he found a passport.

But it was. The passport photo had been taken several years earlier, but it was her all right, smiling out at him with the same slight tilt of the neck, the same expression of defiance that had always given her an edge, made her seem more attractive than she really was.

'We've got the ID already,' said Ayoub, watching him, but Harry hardly heard. He dropped the passport back into the drawer and shut it, taking a few moments to compose himself, the blood ringing in his head, before he turned his full attention to the job. He was a man-dog unit and he was here to find this woman's killer. He saw a hairdryer on the bed, still attached to the power point. He saw a lighter square of floorboard near the bed, indicating that something that had been standing there for a long time had recently been moved.

When Razor sniffed the woman, he drew back with the little start that dead humans elicited from him. But then he trailed nose down to a spot on the rug and barked loudly, indicating something exciting, turning to tell the leader of the pack.

'What is it?' Harry asked, frowning.

'Here,' Razor indicated, looking at the rug. Then he stopped barking, sniffed again, sat back and once again spoke loudly.

'Are you sure?' Harry asked him.

'I'm sure,' Razor signalled.

'Well done, good boy.' Harry went over and petted him. 'Very good boy.' He fondled Razor's velvety ears.

'What's he done that's so good?' Brennan asked, sounding like a jealous kid.

Harry took another long look at the woman. He glanced around the room again then returned his attention to the sprawled figure on the floor. She seemed so small in her silly slippers. He shook his head. Something was very wrong.

'Is this exactly as her boyfriend found it?'

'That is correct,' said Ayoub. 'The doc covered her face up again,' as if that was the explanation Harry had wanted. 'He's not used to this sort of thing. The usual bloke's away.'

It takes awhile to get used to this, Harry thought. After that it wasn't long before such a scene was the subject of black humour that was unfit for any ears except those of other cops or death professionals. Then, some time after that, somehow it ceased to matter anymore.

He squatted and leaned over and with the tip of his little finger he lifted the sticky nightdress. Her face had gone. But he recognised the shape of one delicate ear that was not completely flattened. And her dark hair, now matted and ruined by violence. And there was the little mole on the side of her neck. He let the nightdress fall again. His heart was still pounding uncontrollably. It had taken him by surprise, this deep, personal reaction. He breathed deeply and once again forced his mind to concentrate on the job he was there to do. 'Something's wrong,' he said, straightening up.

'You bet something's wrong,' said Brennan. 'A perfectly good woman's been knocked. That's what's wrong.'

Brennan is young and hasn't been to as many violent rape and murder scenes as I have, Harry thought. Must be hundreds over the years.

'And a little kid's somewhere out there frightened to buggery. Or he's already dead. Or he's with a person capable of that.' He indicated the faceless woman on the floor.

'It's odd,' said Ayoub, looking at Harry in agreement. 'Vicious attack and no sign of a struggle. Nothing upset, everything neat and tidy. My bet is we won't find anything under those fingernails.'

'And she's got her slippers on,' Harry pointed out to Ayoub. Ayoub looked at him a moment, considered and nodded. Brennan looked from one to the other, trying to work out what was going on.

Harry studied the blood spatters on the wall nearest the ruined face. 'She was on the floor when he did this. You can see the up and the down of his blows quite clearly reflected here.'

Brennan looked at the blood patterns and then looked at Harry.

'He was with Crime Scene and Homicide,' Ayoub explained.

'Find out what's been moved from there in case it's relevant,' Harry said, pointing to the lighter square of wood on the floor. 'If he's done what I think he's done, there won't be much use looking for prints, but you never know your luck.'

Ayoub nodded again. 'I'll call you,' Ayoub said, 'if we find anything interesting.'

Then Harry walked Razor through the house checking it out, making sure it was quite empty. He glanced into the three-year-old's room. The white cot with a large blue rabbit in it stood in a corner and farmyard animal prints and toys were neatly displayed on shelves and bookcases. They walked through the rest of the house, out the kitchen door, checked the area behind the house and then came back to the front lawn area.

Harry cast Razor around the front of the house and he quickly found something to interest him. He set off with Harry following in a steady lope away from the house where Janette Madden lay outraged and dead. Janette, Harry thought. Janette. He asked the dog to rest a moment and Razor sat to attention, waiting. Ayoub and Brennan came up behind him.

'We'll follow you with the musclemen,' Brennan jerked his head in the direction of the SPG men, 'in case you run into him. We don't know whether he's armed or not. We can't take any chances.'

Harry jogged along with the torch behind Razor through the scents of the early hours of the bush, following the track of little Julian Madden. Small creatures scuttled sometimes at their passing and the moon was setting low in the west. A shiver went through him despite the heavy overall and the steady pace.

Razor's nose-down movements and gestures told the story of a little child, wandering first one way then another; sitting down, perhaps crying; standing up again, walking a little way, stopping, walking again. Or was it the deliberate track of a cunning man, trying to confuse them? Harry knew that the tricks undertaken by clever quarry were always aimed at confusing the handler because there was really no way of avoiding a shepherd's snout.

Now they were moving through semi-cleared forest with tall, thin gums rising above regrowth and scrubby bushes. Here and there, the perfume of native pea flower came to him and the scents of fox and kangaroo. His torch picked up fox scat marking the side of the trail. The low night sounds of cattle carried through the still air, and they were close enough to Boolabimbie for Harry to imagine he could smell the scent picture of that place: the cedars; the huge, dark magnolias; the monkey puzzle trees that grew on the lawns in front of the house; the two ebony trees that stood at the end of the garden, planted by the great-grandfather; the rope swing over the river that young Harry and Angus had jumped onto and hurled themselves across like Tarzan.

That was a long time ago, Harry thought. It is not time to be thinking of the past. But in this night light it was unavoidable.

Harry deliberately brought his attention back to the armed men behind him who kept up with his steady pace as he kept up with Razor. They went down an incline to a little creek, crossed it and started moving up again. The country was getting steeper and wilder, low foothills with rocky outcrops and crumbling shale. Harry skidded a couple of times but Razor's four sure feet kept up their steady rhythm. Then the track went down again, towards the creek. Again he wondered if this was the frightened, aimless wandering of a lost little boy or the deliberate ploy of a murderous man.

Sometimes, he imagined he was accompanied by thin, smoky ghosts among the trees, figures that flitted in and out of his peripheral vision. In Vietnam, it was always at the peripherals that you first saw them, casting your eyes like he now cast a tracking dog, in wide arcs, sweeping the landscape, always on full red alert. Looking for the slightest movement that wasn't part of the normal sway and bend of an Asian forest nightscape. Trying to sweep the terrain each side, ahead and downwards as well, for the telltale, too-heavy 'cobweb' that meant the shine of moonlight on fishing line, used as a trip-wire attached to a booby trap. Trying to walk on the outer edges of feet swollen and throbbing from fungus infections, heat and misuse. Trying to make as little contact with the earth as possible, always expecting the horrific flame spurt and roar of the explosion that cut men in half as they stepped.

He felt the tension start building in his chest at these thoughts, and deliberately brought himself back to the present, to the hunt that was now leading him along the creek. Behind him, he heard someone trip and curse in a harsh whisper. Razor suddenly propped. Then sat and barked. 'Good boy, good boy,' Harry whispered. He strained his eyes along the creek but it vanished in blackness a little way ahead, in shadows too deep for the setting moon to penetrate. He turned to the panting detectives behind him. 'Okay,' he told them. 'About fifty metres ahead. Tell the State blokes.'

An hour later, Shane Speck, who had leopard-crawled in near perfect silence for sixty metres, his weapon at the ready, found an exhausted three-year-old boy, asleep under the ferns near the turn of the creek. An hour after that, Ray Gosling arrived with Javelin to pick up the offender's trail and Harry and Razor went home, getting a lift from a National Parks and Wildlife ranger, flying to Sydney as the new day dawned. By the time they had landed at Bankstown and collected the wagon, Harry found himself stuck in peak-hour traffic as he drove towards Sydney, arriving, exhausted, to an empty house. He took his work overalls off and stuck them in the washing machine, unloaded his .38 and locked it away in the wall safe in his workroom. He'd picked up a hamburger at Maroubra Junction for himself and he ate that while he fed the dogs.

Blade still wasn't looking too bright and was happy enough to curl up, snout to tail, in the less-favoured corner of the lounge. Harry went to bed and slept deeply. He woke with a gasp of fear. For a moment, he thought some dark figure had slipped below eye level. Then he woke properly and the dream slipped away. All he could remember was that it was terrible, it was violent, and somewhere, someone was bashing Janette Madden's head flat on the floor.

Harry slept for four hours, waking in the early afternoon. He drove back to work via the railway end of the city where he knew there was a shop that sold crystals. He parked the wagon in the shade across the street from the shop and went over to it, selecting three deep-purple amethyst crystals for Hannah's message stick. Now all he needed to do was keep an eye out for a well-shaped piece of timber.

By the time he reached Bass Hill, the dogs were relieved to get out of the vehicle and trot with Harry over to their shady kennels. Razor walked straight into his and flopped in the relative coolness. Blade wanted to play and Harry had to push him into the kennel, closing the bottom of the door behind him. He checked that both dogs had plenty of water, walked back to the office building and went down the hallway to his own room. With the airconditioning full on and the crystals shining on his desk, he spent a few hours catching up with the endless paperwork of policing.

At five-thirty the phone rang and it was Meg. 'Where are you?' she said.

'Oh shit,' he said, remembering. The silence at the other end of the line was ominous. 'I completely forgot,' he said. 'I'll come straight home and get ready. We can still find somewhere nice.'

'By the time you get back from Bass Hill it'll be nearly seven.' His wife's voice was hard. 'Harry. Let's just drop the whole idea.'

'But it's your birthday,' he said.

She rang off without another word.

He collected the dogs and drove home, calling in at a florist for an expensive bunch of white roses, elegant in shape but without fragrance, tied with white and silver ribbon.

When Harry walked in the kitchen door, carrying the roses, Meg was sitting hunched over a takeaway Chinese meal and a glass of wine.

'I thought we were going out,' he said, putting the flowers down on the table beside her. She picked them up, sniffed them, and put them down again, her fingers briefly touching their cool beauty. 'Thanks,' was all she said.

'Where are the girls?' he asked.

'Ali says she's studying at Amanda's place. Hannah's in her room. Allegedly doing homework.'

'What about tomorrow night?' he said. 'We could go out tomorrow night. It was the Bathurst thing. Pushed everything out of my mind.'

'I've got something on tomorrow night,' she said, and he felt anger starting to rise because he felt she was being perversely difficult. He was on his way to have a shower when she called after him. 'I've been thinking,' she said.

'Yes,' said Harry, stopping halfway down the hall and coming back, 'so have I.'

'It'll be the Christmas holidays soon,' she said. 'Maybe if I take Hannah and go away somewhere on my own for awhile.'

Harry felt his hands tighten into two fists. He deliberately released them but did not come into the kitchen again, standing instead by the door. 'Who's the man?'

Meg didn't answer.

'Who's the man, Margaret? Either you tell me or I'll find out. It's up to you.'

Meg looked up at him and he didn't like what he saw in her eyes. 'It doesn't matter,' she said. She started crying. 'It's over.'

Harry watched his wife. Her shoulders, her whole body shook with uncontrollable spasms. Once, he would have tried to comfort her. But not now, and not over this issue. When the sobbing had subsided she lifted her head. He suddenly saw how terrible she looked, as if she hadn't slept for days. She looked old and plain and full of grief. He didn't know what to say now.

'Maybe that would be a good idea,' he finally said. 'I thought I might take Hannah bush for awhile. But I can do that another time.' He left the kitchen where his wife still slumped at the table and had a shower. Then he went into his workroom, closing the door, imagining the house empty of his wife and younger daughter with only the presence of silent, haunted Ali drifting around. And now he had another ghost to deal with, that of Janette Madden. He put the three new crystals on the shelf above his desk and mindlessly polished the message stick he was making, while somewhere, in a silent, dream-like world in his imagination, the people he had killed swayed like sea grass – graceful, nameless Vietnamese men and women; tubby little Franco, who had made the mistake of opening his door from the first rung of his stepladder, brandishing the drill he was working with, so that Harry thought he saw a tall stranger in the doorway levelling a dangerous weapon into the firing position. And now Janette. Did she die because of her connection with him?

He put the message stick down and realised that at the moment the only person he felt any connection to in the world was an eight-year-old girl. And a couple of dogs. The gulf between himself and Meg seemed to widen and deepen by the day.

'The shooting happened because everything was different that night,' he'd said to Jim Coates before the inquiry. 'And anything different from the routine always makes me suspicious. It's not just the job. It goes a long way back.' A long way back, he thought, to when I was a tiny child, and they were coming for me.

He continued. 'We were always on the lookout for something different: silence in the jungle when there should have been the usual bird and insect noises; a different smell, or the absence of some odour that was always around. Anything different meant you could die in the next few seconds. You've got to notice if the animals are silent then sniff the air. Like a beast.' He paused then went on. 'Usually, Franco contacted me himself and I always checked with him before I went to meet him. But this time, his wife called me. That was the first difference. And when I rang to check with him, he wasn't available. That was the second. I almost didn't go at all. But I was desperate to get that second name and his wife said he was going to tell me who else was involved in the Marrickville Tab shooting. But because of this feeling of things being different, I'd automatically unfastened my gun even before I started walking up the path. Then when he opened the door and it looked like some stranger swinging a gun round to me . . .' Harry looked into his friend's eyes '. . . my response was instinctive. It was like being in a firefight again. When I'm confronted with an armed man, I'm trained to react instinctively. That's what drill is all about. I did months and months of army drill and then police drill – trained for automatic response. I acted in exactly the way my drill sergeant would have wanted. And now a man is dead because of it.'

Suddenly Franco loomed up in memory. Harry remembered the terrible cry. 'Why, Harry? Why did you do this?' Franco was such a little man, not even five feet tall, and he had seemed so much smaller then, crumpled bleeding on his doorstep, the question dying in his throat, and his outflung arm and the cordless drill in his loosening fingers.

Jim stayed quiet. He sensed his friend had something more to say.

'Once,' said Harry, 'just before we met up with D445 – that was a VC company we fought with – I smelled someone behind me and I swung around with my M16 levelled and I'm looking straight into the eyes of a young VC. He had his weapon levelled to fire at me. But for some reason he didn't. Neither did I. We both just stood there. In that moment, we were just two men. Then I shook my head. I was telling him 'Let's not do it'. And he shook his head too, like he was saying 'I won't kill you either', and he just melted back out of sight. Yet years later, I shoot Franco without thinking. I don't understand why I was so different in that situation when I was geared to war. I wonder if that VC soldier ever thinks of me. Like I think of him. I really hope he made it.'

Jim was surprised to see that Harry's eyes shone with tears. 'Do you think he'll make up for Franco?'

He turned his attention to the message stick again while its fellow, suspended from the roof by fine leather, softly moved its feathers at his passing. 'You can't imagine what it was like,' he had said to Jim, 'just sitting there waiting for the ambos, with his blood all over me and that stupid drill lying there. I had to sit with him. I couldn't leave him alone like that.' He sanded the timber a bit more, noting the wavy grain of the wood and the way it surged and looped in places like the whorls of fingerprints. In his mind, Franco dying in his blood in his own hallway triggered another memory from Vietnam of a VC soldier dying of a chest wound while Harry and a black labrador stood and waited. Harry brought his mind back to the present and the simple task in hand. Previously, he'd drilled one small and one deep hole at each end of the piece of wood. It was shaped very roughly like a bullock's femur, knobbed unevenly at each end. In his drawer was a small packet of beads and crystals that he'd gathered from different sources. There was even a small piece of alluvial gold that he'd panned from the river years ago. Now it was stored in a phial. Maybe the time had come to use the tiny nugget of pure gold on a message stick. He emptied the beads and crystal mixture out onto a sheet of paper and shook them gently so they spread around. Carefully, with a fine paint brush, he separated the blues and the whites until he had a small pile of each. Then he poured glue into each drilled cavity in the wood. He waited a little and then started to drop the beads and tiny crystals onto the gluey coating of the tiny caves. They hit and stuck. Just like a shepherd, he thought.

Although the departmental inquiry had cleared him, he'd almost resigned. 'It was like,' he'd said to Jim later, 'the whole of the fucking department was against me. I felt like I was one of the bad guys and, apart from you and a couple of other mates, the organisation just wanted to distance itself from me. All that talk of loyalty was bullshit. We're expected to be loyal, but they shaft us whenever they think we've become a problem for them. Those academics at the top, they forget. They're too far removed from the sharp end of policing.'

He heard his wife's footsteps come towards his room, pause at the door, then move on, into the bedroom. He heard her go into the bathroom and run a bath, and the sound brought him back once again to the present moment. He turned the message stick in his hands. Soon, the inside surfaces of the scooped-out holes sparkled like the insides of a thunder egg when it is broken open to reveal its Aladdin's cave of treasures. In the bigger one, and just off centre, he stuck a perfect, clear shaft of quartz. He placed the message stick carefully down on his desk to dry. The quartz crystal glittered like an ice shard.

When his mobile rang it was Ray. He was on his way back from Bathurst. The trail of Janette Madden's killer had been lost in a sudden thunderstorm that had blown up, flooding the ground with torrential rain, causing creeks to overflow their banks. 'He's got the devil on his side,' said Ray.

EIGHT

'We've got some results from last night's crime scene,' said Ayoub down the line to Harry. 'Thought you'd be interested to hear. I'm in Sydney picking up the physical evidence receipts. Let's meet.'

Harry grunted. The reason he'd left Homicide was exactly because he was no longer 'interested to hear'. Awhile later, Ayoub arrived. He wanted to see the dogs, so Harry gave him the tour. As they passed the kennels, each occupant barked and stood up at the door to greet them.

Finally, they stopped near the run where the bitch and her puppies played. 'The rug had been moved and we had a good look under its new position,' said Ayoub, leaning over the wire run where Clotho lay back and puppies tumbled and fell all over her. 'We got enough in the cracks. He'd washed that part of the floor because that's where he shot her.'

'The dog told me that,' said Harry. 'About under the rug. And then he's dried off the washed patch with the hair dryer.' He clicked his fingers over Clotho and she jumped up and came to nuzzle his hand, shedding puppies.

'That is correct,' said Ayoub, leaning over and patting Clotho's head. 'Nice dog.' He straightened up. 'Ballistics said she was on the floor when the bullet hit her. Why did he deface her? Didn't he want us to know about the shooting?'

'That's why he obliterated her head,' said Harry, petting Clotho's intelligent face.

'That is correct. But we found the hole in the wood. We dug the cartridge out.'

'He's a cool fellow,' said Harry. 'Just taking his time with the hair dryer.' They turned away from the puppies' run and went to look at the exercise yard.

'Her boyfriend could've arrived on the scene at any time,' Ayoub agreed as they walked through the yard, past the ladders and leaning timbers that the dogs used to climb and jump from.

'Do the dogs have to crawl through that?' Ayoub asked, looking at the length of ceramic pipe running across the yard.

Harry nodded. 'It wasn't a rape murder,' he said.

'How did you know that?' Ayoub wanted to know.

'When you've seen 200 violent rape murders, you know what one looks like. This one didn't look like any of the others I'd seen.'

'Yes,' Ayoub agreed. 'The bad guys should study a few hundred crime scenes if they want to set something up that looks right. He's used some heavy, blunt instrument to smash her with. Same between her legs.'

Harry nodded. 'When they smash the face like that—'

'Yes,' said Ayoub. 'I think I know what you're going to say. That the killer and the victim know each other. The worse the disfigurement, the closer the relationship.'

These are hard truths to hear, Harry thought. 'But in this case,' he continued, 'the killer might be just trying to hide the fact that he shot her.'

'Funny way to hide something,' Ayoub said. 'Making sure we'd take a closer look.'

Harry grunted. 'She opened the door to him,' he said. 'She wasn't frightened. She gets up and she puts her slippers on and walks to the door. Lets him in. He doesn't have to render her unconscious at the door. She knows him, trusts him. Seems quite happy to see him. Leads him into the bedroom. No worries.'

The two men left the yard and made their way back to the low buildings of the Dog Squad. 'But just inside the bedroom door,' Harry continued, 'he knocks her down and shoots her as she lies on the floor. And she still doesn't know anything is wrong until she wakes up on the other side.'

They walked into the meal room and Harry opened the fridge. He pulled out two cans of beer and offered one to Ayoub.

'Thanks,' said the other. He pulled the ring off and threw it in the bin. 'Do you believe in an after-life?' Ayoub wanted to know.

'I don't believe in anything,' said Harry, opening his own.

'I don't know,' said Ayoub. 'My girlfriend's into past lives. She's got some interesting things to say on the subject. She can remember living in the fourteenth century.' He took a swig on his beer. 'That's nice on a hot day,' he said.

'I can remember living on the fourteenth floor,' said Harry. 'When I worked with Homicide.'

'There might be something in it,' said Ayoub. 'Lots of people talk about past lives. Then,' he continued, abruptly getting back to the subject, 'he moves her, cleans up the blood on the floor where she first goes down, wipes it off the varnish, dries it with the hairdryer and pulls the rug over it. Then he smashes her head in to hide the fact that she was shot.'

'That's what was going through my mind,' Harry said, 'when I first suspected it was a set-up.'

'Maybe he *didn't* know her,' Ayoub offered, 'but he knows something about profiling so he wants *us* to think he *does* know her. So he spreads her head out like that knowing we'll concentrate on her nearest and dearest instead of him.'

Harry shook his head. 'If it's a set-up, he knows her,' he said. 'Otherwise there's no need to hide it. You don't go to the trouble of setting up a false story unless you don't want the true one to come out. I don't suppose there were any prints?' he added.

'That is correct,' said Ayoub. 'One of the guys went to get a drink of water from the outside tank and poured himself what looked like a glass of blood.' He looked at the can of beer in his hand. 'The killer chucked the clothes he used to wipe the floor into the tank. There wasn't much water in it.'

Harry grunted. 'What about whatever object he used to bludgeon her with?'

'We haven't found it. Must've taken it with him. Arnie's got some botanical traces as well,' said Ayoub. 'Some mortar. Some pink glass. And some organic stuff – animal shit or something. It's all been sent off to the experts.' Ayoub crushed his empty can with one hand and neatly flicked it into the wastepaper basket. 'I'd better hit the toe,' he said, glancing at his watch.

After Ayoub left, Harry drove home with Blade and Razor panting in the heat even though he had the wagon's airconditioner turned up. After attending to the dogs, he went into his office and checked his diary for the following week. 'Shit,' he said out loud. He'd forgotten he had to give a lecture to Crime Scene detectives the following day. He picked up the message stick. The glue had hardened and the little crystal spear caught the light.

He looked out the window, thinking of two dead women. One almost untouched except for a small, fatal hole in her heart. Another one over 200 kilometres away without a face. With a mess between her legs. You couldn't get two such different MOs, he thought. You couldn't get two such different kills – one short, sharp and straight to the point, the other messy and blundersome. Yet each of these men had been acceptable to the women.

He put the message stick down. The Strathfield killer had maintained a relationship for a year with an attractive, educated woman. And the Bathurst killer had been invited into a lonely house in the country at night by a woman living alone.

Next morning he went into Physical Evidence at the Police Centre in Goulburn Street – the huge, grey, concrete fastness around the corner from the notorious old 'Hat Factory', erstwhile home of the defunct CIB and built on the slope that eventually levels out at Eddy Avenue and Central Railway. There was no sign of the crazy man Harry remembered as haunting the area, who could only endure looking at the world through his cherished piece of broken green glass held up to the traffic and to passers-by.

Inside the doors, Harry nodded to the two security guards on the front desk, walked through the security gate and went up in the lift, carrying his lecture notes and box of slides. On the fifth floor, Gentleman Jim was waiting for him. 'Do you want a coffee before you start?' he asked his friend.

'Make that a Scotch,' Harry joked. He did not relish public speaking.

Jim's phone rang as he was walking out the door. He turned. 'Answer it, will you Harry,' he grinned. Harry identified himself and took the message for Jim. It was the commander from the Strathfield siege. He rang off, glancing up to read the poster on the wall, the famous statement from the Institute of Criminology in Lyons:

> Wherever he steps, whatever he touches, whatever he leaves, even unconsciously, will serve as silent witness against him. Not only his fingerprints or his footprints, but his hair, the fibres from his clothes, the glass he breaks, the tool mark he leaves, the paint he scratches, the blood or semen he deposits or collects – all of these bear mute witness against him. This is evidence that does not forget. It is not confused by the excitement of the moment. It is not absent because human witnesses are. It is factual evidence. Physical evidence cannot be wrong; it cannot perjure itself; it cannot be wholly absent. Only its interpretation can err. Only human failure to find it, study and understand it can diminish its value.

Jim returned with the coffee. He handed a blue mug to Harry.

'That phone call was Strathfield,' Harry told him. 'McEwan isn't his name. They've traced him back to a woman who knew him before he was McEwan. They found a flat he uses and some personal papers including pilot's licences in the different names. They're checking those now. So we're still in the dark about who this joker is.'

'Great,' said Jim.

'What about the physical evidence?' Harry asked.

'It's all still with the experts,' said Jim. 'Various traces. Some sort of mould.' He paused. 'The important thing is that the same glass also turned up at Bathurst.'.

Harry leaned forward. 'The same glass,' he repeated.

Jim nodded. 'In the bad old days,' he said, 'it'd tell me that one of our fellows had been present at both crime scenes with glass on his big boots. But not these days.'

'It's a link,' said Harry. 'But you couldn't have got two such different MOs.'

'Anyway,' Jim said, 'it's too early to jump to conclusions, but it's interesting.'

'It certainly is that,' Harry said. 'How's the missus?' he asked as he finished his coffee.

'I wouldn't know, mate. I only see her when I pick up the youngster. How's Meg?'

Harry put his mug down and looked at his friend. 'She's okay,' he said levelly. 'Doing art classes.'

'That's nice,' said Jim.

Harry stood up, gathering his notes and slides together. 'I'd better go and give my lecture.'

The two men walked out of the office. 'Does the green glass man still hang around here?' Harry asked.

Jim shook his head. 'Can't say I've seen him recently.'

'Does the Confessor still ring you?' Harry asked at the lifts.

'He hasn't done for awhile,' said Jim. 'I think he got to like you more than me because you used to listen to him.'

'Do you know where he's living these days?' Harry asked.

Jim shook his head. 'Why?' he asked.

'He rang me and confessed to the Strathfield killing,' Harry told him.

'He would,' said Jim. 'He used to confess to everything when he was ringing me.' The lift arrived and the doors opened. Harry stepped inside. 'It wasn't just that he rang me,' said Harry. 'He added some details that were very uncharacteristic. About himself and his brother.'

'That's a good sign,' said Jim. 'Taking an interest in family life. Maybe he's getting better.'

'I don't think so,' said Harry, and the lift doors started to close.

'I've been asked to talk to you,' Harry addressed the group of detectives in the lecture room, 'about a successful investigation I was part of some years ago.'

A technician had set up the video unit for him and all he had to do was operate the console in front of him. He picked up the folder of notes and put it down again. He'd given this talk so often over the years that he practically knew it by heart.

'About ten years ago,' he said, 'a schoolgirl, Helen Semple, was found on the banks of the Nepean with her neck broken and her head bashed.'

He looked around at his audience – policemen and women attending their compulsory lecture. Some leaned back, frankly bored, in their chairs; others stared at him as if daring him to challenge them; one or two had pens poised over notepads. He encountered the eyes of a pretty young woman in the front row and continued.

'Bob Brewer from Penrith, whom some of you might know, called me in because I'd had some success with interrogation techniques that Jim Coates and I had been working on. Bob had a suspect in the case of Helen's murder but it was all circumstantial and the suspect was denying everything. The suspect's name was Ronald Pugh and his record was mostly petty crime. Malicious damage. Theft. But he had been a suspect in a rape case three years before Helen's death. That time it was a thirteen-year-old girl. It didn't go anywhere.

'I went out to Penrith,' Harry continued, 'and met the two

detectives who had been assigned to the murder investigation. They told me that ten-year-old Helen got off the school bus after school, crossed the road, walked towards the bridge, and that was the last time she was seen alive. Several hours later, she was found along the river bank. She'd been raped and killed. Skull fractured. There was a beaten track along the river banks; not an official path, and Helen wasn't supposed to use it. She was supposed to stay on the path beside the road and cross the bridge using the pedestrian walkway. It was only a ten-minute walk to her place.'

Harry showed the first slide. Helen Semple lay on her stomach wearing her school uniform, legs gently bent, with arms outflung either side of her slim body. Her head was partly covered by the large sandstone block that had crushed it. From under the sandstone block, one fair plait, ending in a ribbon, nestled into her shoulder. Harry became aware of the focused silence in the room.

'The PM report,' Harry said, 'indicated a broken neck as cause of death. You'll notice that one shoe is on.' The coloured slide showed the other shoe near her small foot.

'Her pants were on inside out,' Harry said. 'And there was blood on them.' Harry clicked on to the next slide. 'That's the bus stop where she got off,' he said, 'and you can clearly see the river below and just make out the track she was found on if you look to the left of the slide.' There was a murmur in the room. 'We've got some television news footage here too,' said Harry, and he switched it on at the console.

The screen behind him lit up and he stepped out of the way to reveal a rough track, inclining towards the river, leading through straggly bush. 'Notice the clearing and the fireplace to the right of the track,' said Harry, over the silent film. A dreary place for a barbecue. The fireplace looked like it hadn't been used in a long time. 'There is the short cut she wasn't allowed to take,' said Harry, indicating the beaten track along the river. 'And that's where she was found.' The footage showed the river banks, covered with long, dry summer grass and police standing around. 'We did a pretty good search of this area. Bags and bags of stuff. Mostly rubbish. You can see all the grass seeds on the front of her clothing quite clearly here. Yet there was no debris on her back. What does that suggest?' he asked the group.

'That she'd been killed elsewhere and dumped,' someone called out.

Harry nodded. 'That's right. She'd been raped too. We suspected the killer had done this in a vehicle.' He switched off the news footage and clicked another slide. He paused.

'I then found out that the suspect didn't have a car. Because he'd lost his licence. Prescribed Concentration of Alcohol. When I heard that, I also wanted to know when it was that he'd lost his licence, and found that it was three years before, just after the alleged rape. Does this suggest anything?' He looked around. The policewoman in the front row spoke. 'Behaviour often becomes marked after a violent crime,' she said. 'Heavier drinking, geographical moves.'

'Good,' said Harry. 'Among the people we questioned when Helen was killed, Pugh's name kept coming up. He'd been working in the Nepean area on contract with the council, poisoning lantana and English broom. We knew he'd spoken with Helen on at least one occasion. A neighbour of the Semples remembered the incident very well because Helen had been wearing her costume for the Christmas play. She was the Christmas fairy. Little silver and white tu-tu. Little ballet slippers. A red ribbon on the top of her hair. Helen's neighbour recalled Pugh walking right down from where he was working to chat to her.

'I asked the interviewing detectives what was the first thing the suspect had said when he was asked if he'd committed the crime. And they told me. I went through the transcripts of the original interviews and checked up so as to be sure. Jim and I had started to notice a few things about lies and lying. Humans seem to prefer to tell as much of the truth as they can, as if attempting to convince themselves of their own innocence. They just leave important bits out. I particularly wanted to see what Pugh had said when Bob asked him if he'd killed Helen.'

Jim had slipped into the room and was standing down the back and Harry opened his folder and started to read. 'So,' said Harry, 'I looked up the record of interview.' He looked up. Every person was looking at him, waiting.

'"Question",' Harry read out. '"Ronald Pugh, did you kill Helen Semple?"' Harry looked up at the audience again before reading Pugh's reply.

'"Answer: There's no way I'd kill a kiddie with a rock like that."' Harry paused to let that sink in, then turned to the whiteboard and copied out the words he'd just read.

He put the marker pen down and turned round to face the room again. 'That's when my guts told me he'd done it. That he'd killed her.' He looked around the lecture room because it was clear now that he had everyone's attention. 'So then I set things up with Jim Coates.' He nodded at his friend down the back and several people turned round to see him. 'Jim,' Harry asked, 'would you like to come up and tell these people what happened next, seeing as you were there too?'

Jim came up, relaxed and perfectly at home in his world, and Harry envied him that ease and gracefulness. Jim leaned casually on the desk behind him as he spoke.

'Harry here asked me to set up the interrogation room in a certain way late one night,' he said. 'And I did as he said. There's a technique to successful interrogation just like there is for anything. Harry and I had worked out a routine together. We wanted to create an atmosphere like the courtroom does. We wanted to use what we had in order to give ourselves the best chance of breaking Pugh. No-one's going to admit to a murder unless they have to. Harry wanted one of the police exhibits from the case set up in a big carton so that Pugh wouldn't see it straightaway. I'd also created a pile of folders with different reports and Pugh's name written on them. It looked like we'd gathered an enormous amount of information on him in connection with the killing. Then I used the material we'd developed from the profilers to write up the sort of man the killer could be – on the board, so that Pugh could read it when he came in.'

Jim turned and started writing on the whiteboard: 'Male. Age 19–33. Troubled childhood, absent father, unstable mother. Work: unskilled or semi-skilled, history of unemployment, poor literacy skills, divorced or separated, problems relating to opposite sex, drifter, difficulties with peer friendships, loner, non-joiner. Local knowledge of area used as body dump. Previous records for rape, PCA, petty crime. Drives older sedan or utility.'

Jim turned from the whiteboard and faced the audience again. 'Harry and Bob Brewer brought Pugh in around midnight,' he said. 'Harry, maybe you should take over from here?'

Harry walked up behind the desk again. 'Ronald Pugh was getting very nervous by this stage,' he told the group. 'We'd driven from Penrith in a police car with him in the back with Bob Brewer. You know what this place is like at night,' he said, indicating the Police Centre. 'It seems bigger. The lighting is dimmer because a lot of the sections that don't do shift work are closed up. Nighttime is psychologically the time for secrets. Pugh was spooked by the time we got him in the room. He read the points Jim had written up on the board and the first thing he said was, "I don't have a car."' Laughter filled the room.

'I thought I was halfway there,' said Harry, 'if Pugh was this defensive this early. And the other thing I noticed was how Pugh was staring at the carton with his name on it.

'So I started on my line. Here is the record of interview. This is one of the first videoed interviews, by the way; now, as you know, it's standard operating procedure. I told Pugh I wanted to tell him a story. And this is how it went . . .'

Harry switched on the footage and sat down in a spare seat. It was eerie to see himself up there on the wall, ten years younger. Someone wolf-whistled. The room filled with his soft voice from ten years ago as he spoke to Pugh on the screen.

On the 23rd of September, a little girl called Helen Semple was walking down Airlie Drive on her way home from school. She stopped and had a chat with Mrs Saunders in number 145. Helen was wearing a cute little ballet dress that showed her frilly pants because she had a part in the school Christmas play. She had bright red lipstick on her lips the way little girls do when they're pretending to be grown-up. There was a man spraying weeds on the other side of the road and he couldn't take his eyes off this pretty little girl with her long blonde hair and her red ribbons and red lips. He made sure he was in her path when she continued on her way and he had a chat with her. He was the sort of man who didn't have much luck with women. He'd been married very briefly. But that didn't last. Of course, it was the woman's fault. She was a bitch, wasn't she? Good riddance, I'll bet. There were very few women who appreciated this fellow. But this little girl seemed to be different. She seemed to like him. She stopped and had a chat with him, too. And we all know what that means, don't we Ron? Although girls pretend that they're not interested, we know the truth about the bitches, don't we, Ron? Prickteasers, the lot of them. She was a very friendly, popular little girl and she chatted with this man. But she did more than that, didn't she, Ron? She was a real little tease, wasn't she? The video image of Pugh showed the narrow man leaning forward, listening to every word Harry was saying. *She was making eyes at the man, wasn't she? She was a real little flirt; not innocent at all . . .*

A few people in the room shifted in their chairs, uneasy.

. . . And the man knew that. He knew that very well. So on she went on her merry, flirty way and he thought he'd really like to have sex with her. Not only that, he knew that really she wanted to have sex with him. He couldn't stop thinking about her. He had fantasies about her. I know for a fact that this man played with himself while he thought about that little girl. Pugh was really bug-eyed now. He was staring at Harry. *I should add by the way that this man had already got away with one rape in another city,* Harry continued. *Or what they call rape. Probably just another lying bitch pretending that she didn't want it. Anyway, one day the following week, when this man was driving to the pub – oh, I forgot to tell you, this man didn't have a licence, so he shouldn't have been driving, but he used to borrow an acquaintance's car in exchange for the occasional joint.* Pugh was looking at Harry like he was some sort of witchdoctor. And his body was shrinking away as if he wanted to vanish, all the time with his wide eyes fixed on Harry, and this gave his body a weird and crooked twist. *When this man was driving to the pub,* Harry went on, *who should he see but the same little flirty girl getting off the school bus just down the road. Well, he knows that she's going to be thrilled to see him so he stops the car and invites her in and what do you think? She plays hard to get. But he can see just how much she wants it so he forces her into the car. It's not a difficult thing to do and that road is never very busy at the best of times. 'Where are you taking me?' she asks, as if she doesn't know.*

The man drives off the road and into a little clearing just off the track that nobody ever comes to. He makes that little girl undress and he rapes her. Then everything seems to go wrong. She's screaming and fighting and he realises there's only one way to shut her up. He didn't have murder on his mind at all. But suddenly, there it is. It's his only way out. To control the situation, he pretends he's going to let her go. This calms her down and she probably even promises never to tell anyone what happened. It was clear to see on the video that there was a little tic going very fast near the outer corner of Pugh's left eye. His face was ghastly pale. He was absolutely riveted.

Harry froze the frame on the screen. 'See how engrossed he is. Remember that. The guilty ones always are,' Harry told the equally engrossed audience. 'The innocent ones are yelling blue murder by this time at this sort of talk. But the guilty ones fall absolutely silent, mesmerised. Because they're so amazed at how you're getting the reconstruction right.'

Harry pressed 'Play', and on the screen the younger Harry was once more talking to Pugh. *So she starts getting dressed again, this little girl, thinking that she's soon going to be home and this will all be over for her. It will, but not in the way she thinks. Because as she runs down the track to go the short cut home along the river, the man follows her and looks around for something to stop her with.* On the video, Harry stood up and went over to the big carton. Slowly, he opened it, peeling back the four flaps. *There's no-one around on this track, although the man knows he's got to be quick because someone might come along at any moment. But then he found this, didn't he, Ron?* Out of the box, Harry lifted a heavy, sandstone block and put it on the table next to Pugh. The video camera easily picked up the beads of sweat that had popped out on Pugh's forehead under the lights of the interview room.

Harry turned away from his image on the screen and looked

around at the room full of detectives. They were enthralled. No-one noticed him looking at them. He turned his attention back to the screen images.

In the video, Pugh strained forward, staring at the rock as if it were about to address him. His breathing was shallow and panicky. The little tic grew faster; it was almost a perceptible squint. *The man hits the little girl on the head with this from behind*, said the screen image of young Harry. *Down she goes and one of her shoes flies off because she hasn't even tied them up, she's in that much of a hurry to get away. The rock stuns her, but she's not dead. So do you know what he does? He breaks that little girl's neck. Just as if she's a chicken in the farmyard. Then, just to make sure she's good and dead, he drops that rock on her head. Then he races back up the track to the barbecue clearing, jumps in the car and is at the pub, a little bit later than usual. And it's as if the whole thing hasn't happened at all.* Harry stopped.

In the lecture room, there was no sound, no movement. Everyone was transfixed by Harry's performance. In the video, young Harry had moved up to be very close to Pugh. His voice was almost a whisper. *You see, Ron*, said Harry, like a conspirator, *it's not a question of whether you did this or not. You know that. And I know that. We know you did this. And you know we know. We've got physical evidence which I'll tell you about in a minute. But most importantly, you told us yourself that you did it in your statement. In your own words.*

Pugh stared at him. He shook his head vigorously, but then stopped, listening again to Harry. *The thing about liars*, the onscreen Harry went on, *is that after many years of dealing with them, I've learned a few things about them. They like to tell the truth. Now, I know that sounds funny. But you think about it. When you're lying, it's always a good strategy to tell most of the truth but just leave little bits out. Like a gentleman who comes to mind told me recently, he walked into his house and saw his wife lying strangled on the kitchen floor. All of this was perfectly true. But it turned out later that he'd just decided to leave out mentioning the fact that he'd strangled her just after he'd walked into the house and just before he'd seen her lying on the floor. Telling almost the truth saves you the trouble of making something up completely. Much easier to hold on to under questioning. So when you were asked outright 'Did you kill Helen Semple?' what did you say? You said . . .* Harry turned around and picked up the original record of interview . . . *You said, 'There's no way I'd kill a kiddie with a rock like that.' That's what you said. Because you didn't kill her with the rock, did you? You broke her neck. You could proudly say, 'I wouldn't kill a kiddie with a rock' and somehow feel you were speaking the truth, because in your own twisted way you were.*

Harry froze the video, feeling awkward watching himself. 'I think that's about enough,' he said.

'No,' said several voices. 'Let's see the rest of it.'

Harry looked at Jim, who nodded. He restarted the video and stepped back to watch his younger self at work. *With blunt-force trauma . . . sorry,* he was saying on the screen, *I'll put that in layman's terms. Where something like a rock has been used, there's always blood splashes and tiny spots, too small often for the eye to see. Those spots are on your shoes, on the trousers you were wearing. We know your blood type and we know Helen's. Those shoes of yours are with our scientists. We know you did it. The only thing that's going to help you now is if I can tell the sentencing judge why you did it. Because I understand, Ron. I really do.* Here Harry's image on the screen was almost touching Pugh, they were so close. His voice was a low, soothing murmur. *You never meant to hurt that flirty little girl, did you? You can tell me, Ron.*

Ronald Pugh had collapsed over the table and was sobbing like a child. *You just wanted to have some fun. And you thought she did too. But it all went terribly wrong. She mucked everything up. Carrying on like that. Really, you could say it was all her fault. So if you sign here, when it gets to court we can talk to the judge and put your point of view across. It was an accident, wasn't it, Ron? Manslaughter. But not murder. We know you never meant to kill her.*

Pugh was sobbing. *I never did mean to hurt her. She got me into a state. All that screaming. I had to stop her. I had to, I had to.*

Harry stood up and froze the image on Pugh's face. 'Any questions?' he asked.

'You sounded like you were blaming the little girl,' said a young man down the back of the room, 'the way you were talking to that crim.'

'I have to start thinking like he does,' Harry said, 'to convince him that I really know everything he's done. And most killers want to find someone to blame. Once I started to see that, I started to see how their minds worked. It would have to be the victim's fault. I knew from his point of view it had to be her fault. I knew a few things already about the case just from reading the facts and looking at the photographs and the crime scene. And reading his transcript. I knew it wasn't planned. It was a rape of opportunity. I knew he'd never intended homicide. He'd have brought a weapon with him.'

He looked around. A woman down the back raised her hand. 'How did you know he told her that he was going to let her go?' she asked.

'Because she'd been allowed to get dressed again,' Harry said. 'She'd pulled her pants on inside out in her panic. She hadn't done up her shoelaces properly. That charade of re-dressing made her think that the nightmare was nearly over. All she would have been thinking about was how to get home as quick as possible. So while she was running away down the track, sobbing, blind with tears, her shoelaces still undone, he caught up with her, looked around, saw that sandstone piece, picked it up and bashed her from behind with it. People found her on the track. It was assumed she was taking that route home when she was attacked. But she wasn't.'

'What would an innocent man have said to the question "Did you kill Helen Semple"?' the pretty young woman in the front asked.

'He'd've said something equally straightforward like "No, I did not," or "No, I didn't kill Helen Semple",' said Harry. 'Notice how people talk when they're denying something. If it's complicated and indirect, it should alert a good investigator. Learn to notice,' he told the group.

He switched off the slide projector. 'We were able to tell Helen's mother that she didn't disobey her. She was walking home on the top road like a good girl, the way she'd told her mum she always did. She was walking home the safe way and she still met Pugh.'

'If there are no more questions,' Jim said, 'let's put our hands together for Harry Doyle.' Brief clapping and it was almost over. But the pretty young woman in the front row put up her hand.

'I've got one more question,' she said.

'Yes?' Harry asked.

'If you were so good in Homicide, why did you leave and join the Dog Squad?'

There was a silence in the room. Harry looked at Jim. 'Personal reasons,' he finally said. He saw two men down the back lean their heads together and surmised one was telling the other about Franco. For a split second, he considered making a public announcement about it, like a confession. But the moment passed and the detectives moved out of the room and Harry gathered up his things, aware that his armpits were soaked. Public speaking always had that effect on him. The challenge in the young woman's question had also rattled him.

Jim walked with him towards the lifts. 'I still think about Pugh,' he said. 'And the time we bumped into him after the case. Do you?'

Harry recalled the incident – coming suddenly face-to-face with Pugh as he was being taken from the cells beneath the Police Centre and loaded into the prison van.

'You cunt, Doyle,' he'd yelled. 'You never had a thing on me. There was no physical evidence, you lying piece of shit.'

Pugh had strained against his restrainers, his body dense with malevolence.

'I'm going to get you, Doyle,' he'd screamed. 'No matter how long it takes, I'm going to get you. I'm going to hurt you bad.'

Harry had stuck up two fingers as the Corrective Services van accelerated past him and away. 'Piss off, you sick bastard,' he'd yelled to its departing rear.

'Yes,' said Harry, ten years later. 'I think about it from time to time.'

'They all make threats,' said Jim. 'Never amounts to anything. Come back to my office and have lunch with me.'

'Give me an hour. There's something I want to do first.'

As they went down in the lift, Harry tried to recall anything he could about the man with the grenade and the armalite at Strathfield. All he could get was an impression of a soldier in a war zone – the weaving, ducking run, the practised combat manoeuvres. Then there was the matter of that odd, fleeting odour. Ten thousand different scents, Harry remembered, was, according to recent scientific thinking, a conservative estimate of what the human system could discern. Smell was the least researched sense. It was only quite recently that he'd read about the importance of the olfactory process in homing pigeons as part of their process of finding their way back home. At Strathfield he'd hit on some subtle note, but it was too slight to have registered properly in his brain.

He left Jim and went along the hall to another of the Crime Scene Support offices. He had a chat to the leader there and they made a phone call. In a few minutes, Devlin, the forensic hypnotist, walked in. Harry knew him from the old days. He'd seen the extraordinary information that could be elicited in a deeply relaxed trance state – information that had sometimes provided invaluable leads. They found a quiet room and, after the pleasantries, Harry told him why he was there.

'Can you put me under?' he asked finally. 'I want to recall as much as I can.' Harry shrugged, seeing Devlin's surprise. 'I joined the Dog Squad because I just didn't want to know anymore. But this guy's got on my wick.'

Devlin sat opposite Harry, looking steadily at him. 'Okay,' he said. 'Just take a nice deep breath. And another one. And just one more.' Harry obliged.

There was a soft knock and Jim came in. 'So this is where you got to. Can I sit in?'

Harry didn't mind so Devlin started the induction again, beginning with the muscles at the back of Harry's neck all the way down his body. He felt himself let down into a softer state. He felt his belly soften and his breathing become regular and even pleasurable. The distant ringing of the phones worked in Harry's favour.

'Every phone ringing just allows you to go deeper into a state of relaxation. In fact,' Devlin's voice softly told him, 'every noise you hear, whether it's near or far, whether it's in this section or whether it's the sound of an aeroplane over the city, will only serve to allow you to go deeper and deeper.' Harry was aware of himself folded around a place of deep peace and stillness, completely relaxed and yet poised and alert to Devlin's voice and words.

Devlin took him back to the lawn at Strathfield, the cotoneaster hedge, the door opening, the man coming out in combat mode, lobbing the grenade. Over and over the scene he went.

An impression of dark hair, an impression of age – forties, but youthful, very fit. 'He's been a soldier,' he said, his voice barely audible. 'And there's something else.'

'Would you like to tell me the something else?' Devlin's measured voice.

'There's something familiar in the scent picture.'

'What's a scent picture?' Harry heard Devlin's voice from a long way away.

'It's the term the dog people use,' said Jim. 'For the total picture of a place. All the different smells and traces. Air and ground scent.'

'Can you tell me more about the scent picture?' Devlin now asked him.

Harry shook his head. 'There's something. There's something that's important. And I just can't get it.' he shook his head. 'No. It's useless. It's too faint. It's too fleeting. It's just like a ghost. Vanishes.'

'Let's have a closer look at that smell, Harry.' Devlin's voice. 'That smell that you just can't quite get. I want you to amplify it. By ten times. Then by twenty times. Where have you smelled it before?' Devlin's voice, calm, soft and surrounding.

The scent grew stronger and stronger till it filled Harry's nostrils. 'It's like a bar late at night. It smells like something you might get in a bar.'

'Tell me more.' Devlin's steady voice. 'Is it a bar? Does it smell like a bar you know?'

Harry concentrated. He slowly shook his head. 'It's not a place,' he said. 'It's something like alcohol. But it's not any particular drink. In a crowded bar you might notice it. Or sometimes when I've interviewed suspects I've been aware of it. But mixed with other smells. I don't know what it is by itself. It's not pleasant.'

Nothing else came to him. So Devlin brought him out of the trance and Harry sat up straight, looking around. 'Well,' he said, 'that was nice. But I didn't get it. I didn't get the damn thing. Whatever it is.'

Harry went with Jim back to his office. Jim walked over to his sealed, double-glazed window and looked out, and Harry wondered what he could see from there. The Police Centre, constructed of grey concrete, proofed against civil unrest, had narrow ledges outside the windows. Jim's office was on one side of a rectangular light well in the middle of the building and there was no view. Just outside Jim's window, a pair of pigeons had made their nest and the female was sitting, brooding, eyes almost closed, while the male rested further along the windowledge.

Jim had covered the bottom of the window with a cardboard screen so that the pigeons would not be alarmed by movements inside the office.

The phone rang almost as soon as Harry walked in. It was Ayoub from Bathurst. Jim grunted and listened. 'Harry Doyle's here. I'll put him on.' He got up and went to the window.

'We've got some more on the Bathurst crime scene,' Ayoub told Harry.

'Tell me,' he said.

'The little boy couldn't help us much. Seems he was woken

up by a big noise – that's all he said, "big noise bang" – and climbed out of his cot, found his grandmother like that and wandered away. He's with his parents now. But the cartridge turned up,' said Ayoub, 'and it comes from a thing called a Tokarev—'

'—a rare little pistol that the commies used in Vietnam,' Harry finished for him.

'How the fuck did you know that?' Ayoub asked, forgetting his manners. 'Well,' he continued, somewhat deflated, 'we know it's the same gun that was used at your Strathfield scene. Ballistics got a perfect match.'

'We might be looking at two offenders,' Harry said, 'using the same gun.' He looked up at Jim who was following the conversation.

Ayoub continued. 'We've got tiny slivers of broken glass, too. The expert tells us it's a rose-coloured glass, old style, probably Victorian, no longer made, and has an embossed pattern on it.

'From his rose-coloured glasses, maybe.' Harry couldn't resist.

Ayoub rang off and Harry and Jim looked at each other. 'It's him again,' Harry said. 'Strathfield and Bathurst. Same killer.'

A Russian handgun. Rose-coloured glass. Harry leaned back in the chair, taking it all in, turning his attention to the bigger picture of two dead women and their killer. The information started unrolling in his mind. He couldn't help himself. It was just automatic, like the old days. 'He can maintain relationships with women,' he said. 'They're both killed in their own homes. He seems trustworthy. The sort of man a woman lets into her house late at night when she's alone with a small child. He knows how to be gentlemanly and well-behaved.'

'Nice to be murdered by a gentleman,' said Jim, coming back from the window and sitting down behind his desk. 'We'd better start talking to anyone who knew the dead women, and try and track down that one particular gentleman friend they had in common.'

Harry nodded. 'He shoots one woman in a cellar, clean through the heart, facing her fair and square. That's a tough thing to do,' Harry said. 'Unless you're in a state of rage.' He paused, refusing to allow a memory out of the lock-up in his mind. 'Or cold, hard hatred. Then he holes up for a while, lobs a grenade, gets away from me, kills the dog, jumps from rooftops, travels to Bathurst while all the time avoiding New South Wales' best and finest who are supposed to be right up his arse, goes to an isolated farmhouse, gets invited in, knocks the woman down and shoots her with the same gun he's used at the first murder, moves her body, cleans up where she fell, smashes her head up, smashes her up between the legs and disappears again into the bush. I want to know what's going on. It just doesn't make any sense.'

Jim raised an eyebrow and looked at his friend. 'He shoots two women,' said Jim. 'He gives it to us by using the same gun. But then he tries to make the next killing at Bathurst look like sexual assault. Why?'

'Maybe it was,' Harry suggested. 'Maybe there was a sexual element. We can't know what was in his mind while he did that. Even though there's no semen showing up. Maybe he's a nearest and dearest staging things to look like a stranger.'

'Maybe he's a stranger staging things to look like a nearest and dearest.'

'But she let him in,' said Harry. 'She put her slippers on and she let him in. She turned her back on him. She felt comfortable with him. I want to talk to her boy-friend. I want to know if he knew there was another man on the scene. I'll talk to Ayoub again and line that up.'

Jim nodded, but he was pursuing his own thoughts. 'He creates two completely different murders, but uses the same gun,' said Jim.

'It's now you see me now you don't,' said Harry. 'He's playing.'

'What have you got so far?' said Jim, like in the old days.

'Highly organised,' said Harry as the information came to hand. 'Older person. Military training, obviously. Combat experience in Vietnam so that'll give us an age group. I'd be looking for an officer.'

'How do you work that?'

'You said there were pilot's licences in different names. Okay, they're bodgy, as we know, but I'm pretty sure it means our man actually *is* a pilot. And that he does have an unrestricted licence. That indicates to me someone who is not only intelligent,' said Harry, 'but someone who can apply himself to long study commitments. And complexity. Ever had a go at aviation navigation?' Jim grunted.

'He's skilled in the use of weapons. So far, he's used a handgun, an assault rifle, a knife and a grenade,' Harry continued. 'He was able to do a spot of bush carpentry in that cellar. So he's an allrounder. Could have grown-up in the bush or spent a lot of time in the bush because that's where he headed. He's probably got a good employment history. He could run his own business. He's well-built, presentable. But this part's cheating,' he added, 'because I've seen him.'

Now Harry stood up and went to the window. The brooding pigeon fluffed up her feathers and resettled. 'But he's hard to read,' he said. 'He's a real odd one. This is not a serial killer. He knows his victims very well.' He paused. 'I'm thinking of the way he flattened her head at Bathurst,' he said to Jim eventually. 'I don't think in the end he was trying to hide the bullet wound with those post-mortem injuries. Maybe that's what was in his mind at first, but then I think smashing her up felt so good it became part of his gig. And you know what that means. He's escalating. Getting more practised at it. The violence is increasing.' He considered a moment. 'I think you'll find he has or had a very difficult relationship with his mother. That his mother tried to dominate and control him. And that he hated her.' He briefly thought of his own mother, but put her out of his mind straightaway. He made a decision. 'I've got a couple of days due to me. I want to go back. I want to talk to Janette Madden's boyfriend. And I want to take the dog back to the Bathurst crime scene. We might pick something up. You've got my mobile number. Ring me when you ID him.'

'What's happened to the man who doesn't want to know anymore,' Jim said a moment later, 'about killers and why they do it?'

'This is different,' said Harry, and hesitated for a moment. 'There's something you should know.' He was aware of Jim's gaze, intent on him, listening like a good cop.

'Janette Madden used to be Janette Doyle. For about eighteen months. The marriage broke up not long after I got back from Vietnam.'

'Shit,' said Jim. 'I didn't know you'd been married before.'

'It was a long time ago,' said Harry, sitting on the chair opposite his friend.

'Two dead women,' said Jim. 'And one of them your ex-wife.' He paused. 'When did you last see her?'

Harry considered. 'I haven't seen her for twenty-five years. There were some letters around the time of the divorce. We didn't have any property. Then I lost track of her entirely. I heard she'd gone to New Zealand to live with her second husband. That must've been eighteen, twenty years ago.'

'And since then?'

'Since then, absolutely nothing.' He noticed his friend's shrewd eyes, observing him. 'It'll be very easy to check my whereabouts at the time of the murder. I was at home.'

Jim's face relaxed. 'Harry. You know how it is.'

'The nice way of putting it is to say "We need to eliminate you from our enquiries".'

'Yes,' said Jim. 'But I wasn't going to try that on with you.'

Harry stood up.

'We need to stop this bastard, Jim. It'll be three dead women otherwise.'

'You said "we", Harry,' Jim pointed out. 'Just like the old days.'

He said goodbye to his colleagues in the city and drove home through the worsening Sydney evening traffic. The sky was dull with pollution and he could smell hot metal, exhausts and petrol fumes, mixed with food odours and hot tar. He could smell the dogs and their gear. He could even pick out a little bit of Hannah and the green and red frog sweets she liked. But the lost scent still eluded him.

When he got home, he checked Blade and found that his temperature was normal. He gave the dog a dose of vitamins prescribed by the vet and then packed up the wagon. Razor wagged around after him, like a kid.

When he was ready, he rang Matthews, the senior sergeant back at the Dog Squad.

'Is your other dog operational yet?' Matthews wanted to know.

'Another few days should see him ready for work. I've got

a few days owing. I want to go back to that Bathurst crime scene,' he said. 'Ask a few questions. Sniff around a bit.'

'Bit late for a dog. It was washed out.'

'It's good exercise for the dog. I want to look around. This bastard owes me.'

He rang off. The unfinished message stick lay along his desk like a trophy from some alien war and he briefly touched its smooth surface on his way out. There was some gear he needed to pick up from the Dog Squad.

Meg opened the little, low gate next-door on her way home from work. The afternoon was hot and the light summer dress she was wearing stuck to her armpits. She walked round the back of the neat weatherboard in its quarter-acre garden, and past its above-ground pool. Jack wasn't around. She opened the flyscreen. 'Dell?'

'In here, hon,' called her friend. Meg heard the sound of a sewing machine and walked into Dell's tiny sewing room, crowded with fabrics, patterns, tins of beads and pins and the bulging albums Dell used to record and display her work for potential customers. Meg picked one up and opened it at a bridal party. She closed it again. A tall fan kept the hot afternoon air moving, and lifted the layers of the fabric her friend was stitching. Dell wore little white cotton gloves, so with the billowing clouds of fabric swirled and folded around her she looked a bit like the cat who ate the cream.

'It's gorgeous,' said Meg, not touching it, aware of her hot, sweaty hands.

'Yes,' said Dell. 'It's gorgeous. Over a hundred dollars a metre. If they spent as much on pre-marriage counselling as they do on the dress and the reception, they'd have a great life together. But, you don't know that at the time, do you?'

Meg went into the kitchen and put the kettle on. She

sighed. 'You can't know until you know.' She came back to the doorway of Dell's little sewing room. The fan lifted a swathe of lighter fabric that Meg supposed was for lining. 'Harry's going bush for a few days. And I'm almost sure I've decided to call it off with Max.' She wanted to cry but couldn't.

'Meggie, you won't be cross with me if I tell you I've heard you say that before.'

Meg shook her head. 'I know I'm indecisive. But I don't know what's going to happen next. It's not just a question of Max or Harry – I mean it's not just a choice between men – I feel I'm at a real crossroads.'

Dell looked up. 'Does Max know you're thinking like this?' Meg shook her head.

The kettle started murmuring and Dell got up and went to the kitchen, pulling her white gloves off, with Meg following. Dell took the tea things out, opened the fridge for milk, put the good cups on the tray because she had a visitor.

'I'll tell him next time I see him. He didn't show up for our last date. I waited at the hotel and he didn't show.'

'Something important might have come up.'

'I don't care how important. You can always leave a message at a hotel. Always. That's what hotels are *for*. Maybe he's dead. Anyway, it's not only that.'

'I'm sure you'd have heard if he was dead,' said her practical friend, making the tea. 'Look,' she said, 'you and Harry could make a go of it. He's not a drunk and a womaniser like Ken was. You've just let things slip, you two.'

Meg sat on a stool and Dell passed her a cup of tea, sitting opposite at the kitchen bar. 'We've hardly spoken for the last few years,' said Meg. 'I mean apart from stuff like who's going to pick up the kids, or who'll be home first to take something out of the freezer. He's just closed down on me. I was so pleased when he got out of Homicide – until I realised what the Dog Squad meant. It hasn't made him happy.'

'Men close up on women because women keep poking at them,' said Dell. 'I know that for a fact. My father closed down like that and Mum never let up on him. He just went silent. Harry's like my dad. Maybe that's why I went for the fast-talking sexy ones like Ken.' She sipped her tea, put the cup down and raised an inquiring eyebrow. 'And maybe Max?'

She went back into the sewing room and came out with part of the bodice and a strip of seed pearls. She put her white gloves back on and started stitching by hand.

'I don't know,' Meg said. 'That's the truth. I must have been crazy to think I could just go off with him like that. I don't know what I was doing. But it seems like a dream now.' Sitting in Dell's ordinary kitchen with the sound of distant traffic and Indian mynah birds squabbling outside, the affair with Max seemed an impossible dream, a film script she'd got mixed up with.

Dell continued to sew tiny seed pearls in a strip onto the bodice of the dress, frowning with effort. 'I don't know why I ever thought dressmaking would be an easier way to make a living than nursing.' Then she continued with the previous conversation. 'A womaniser,' she said, 'usually doesn't want the woman *and* her kids to move in with him. Quite the opposite.'

'I don't know if he's a womaniser,' Meg shrugged. 'What do womanisers do? What do men do, or want? The kids are hurting. I'm supposed to be a counsellor, know how to deal with this sort of thing. When I talk to Alison she looks at me as if she dislikes me. And I have to be honest and say I often feel the same way. I sometimes wonder if I should

have been a mother. I didn't have the foggiest clue about it.'
She finished her tea.

'It's always easier with other people's problems than with
your own,' said Dell. 'Everybody knows that.'

Meg nodded, looked away then back again. 'I feel better,
having made the decision to finish with Max. God, I'll miss
him. My body is in love with him. You know how it is. I
haven't felt a thing for Harry for ages.' She suddenly started
sobbing and Dell dropped the strip of seed pearls, got up and
put her arms around her friend, holding her, smoothing her
hair. After a few minutes, the shuddering spasms eased and
Meg pulled a man's hankie out of the pocket of her dress and
blew her nose.

'You could sort it out with Harry,' said Dell. 'You could.'

'I don't know anymore. Feels like the relationship between
us is dead. Dell, there are things *I* want to do. A portrait of me
and Hannah. Go to Florence. For Christ's sake, I'm forty. I'm
tired of living on a twenty-four-hour operational police base,'
said Meg. 'It's too much. Even on an oil rig people get time
off. It's impossible, living like this.'

'Have you talked to Harry about this?'

'I tried the other night.' Her eyes flashed. 'You know what
he said? We'd have to take several things into consideration
if I wanted a separation. You know why?' She made a sound
that was half bitter laugh, half contempt. 'Because of the *dogs*.
The bloody dogs.'

A few minutes later, she opened her kitchen door and
stepped inside. The white roses drooped in their vase because
the water level had fallen, and a listless Blade came over to
greet her. She topped up the rose water and blew her nose.
Hannah ran out at the sound and dropped down beside
the dog.

'Dad says I have to keep an eye on him.' Then she looked

at her mother. 'Mum, what is it? You're *crying*.' This was so shocking that Hannah stood frozen, staring at her mother.

Meg shook her head, blowing her nose again. 'It's nothing. It's just . . .'

Hannah couldn't speak. They looked at each other uselessly. 'Please don't cry, Mum. You mustn't cry. I'll tidy my room. Right now. You come and look in a minute. It'll be really tidy.' Hannah turned and raced away down to her room and Meg could hear the explosion of energy as doors and cupboards opened and slammed and furniture was straightened. Meg went to the door of her daughter's room and looked in. Hannah was wildly hurling things around, slamming drawers shut, blindly pushing things out of sight. She went to her daughter, bending down, and caught her mid-shove.

'Don't, darling. It's okay. It's got nothing to do with you. Truly.' Hannah moved into her arms and Meg slipped onto the floor, leaning against the bed, rocking the two of them, as if Hannah was a baby again. She wondered where Max was, and tried to imagine what she would say to him.

'Mum, I've got a friend.'

'That's nice.'

'He wants me to . . .'

Meg heard the phone ringing. Max. She just knew with every cell in her body that it was Max.

'Hang on, darling. I'll get the phone. Then tell me.'

It was him. 'I'm so sorry,' he said. 'Something came up. I must see you. Tonight. Meet me tonight at the hotel.'

Meg considered. I can't do it over the phone, she thought. It's too brutal.

'Max,' she said, and her voice faltered, 'you stood me up. You can't do that to people.'

'I tried to get a message to you,' he said. 'I was out of range.'

'Aren't I important?'

'I'll explain,' he said. 'I promise. You'll forgive me.'

'I just don't think things are working out between us,' she said, feeling like some idiot player in a daytime television soap. How on earth could things 'work out' between a man who couldn't be pinned down and a woman who already had a husband and two children? But she didn't say that. At the other end of the line she had the sense of something huge opening up, the way she sometimes thought she could hear the unfathomable depths of coaxial cables swinging in blackness at the bottom of the sea. 'Max?' she said. 'Are you still there?'

'Yes,' he said. 'I'm thinking.'

She heard Harry pull up outside. 'I can't talk now,' she said. 'Harry's just arrived.'

'I don't care,' he said. 'I'll deal with him. Maybe if he knows the truth—'

'He already knows, for heaven's sake,' said Meg. 'Don't make everything worse than it is.'

'Worse? How can I make it worse? You're having a change of heart. This doesn't change anything,' he was saying and she thought he must be mad. 'I'm coming round as soon as I can. We've got to talk. I just couldn't get to ring. I felt dreadful, knowing you were waiting for me.'

'I've got to go,' she said. 'Goodbye.' And as she put the phone down, her husband walked into the kitchen.

Harry looked at Meg's face and wondered why the blood had drained away from it.

She was only wearing a sarong loosely around her body and her dark hair spread out over her shoulders behind her.

He wondered what she was thinking about, and knew that it wasn't of him. The airconditioner rattled in its housing. 'I'd better go,' he said.

'You want to get away from me.'

'There's that,' he said. He yearned to be able to say something more, something that would be true and satisfying. The phone rang and he picked it up and barked, 'Yes?'

'The Archons are up to something,' said the Confessor. 'They're buying new clothes. Little angel dresses. He's expecting a visitor,' said the voice.

'Not now, Milton,' said Harry. 'Ring me tomorrow.'

'You should know,' said the Confessor. 'It's your business too.'

'How do you work that out?' Harry asked.

'I know your name,' said the Confessor, 'and so do the Archons. They want to practise more chemicals on me. And more electricity. They want to practise something on you, too.'

'Milton, I can't talk now.' Harry hung up. He went into Hannah's room where she was sitting at the computer. Razor was lying against her legs while she worked and Harry could see she was upset.

Hannah clicked the mouse and the screen went blank. She pushed Razor away from her legs. 'You're too hot, Mister,' she said.

'What are you doing?' he asked.

She shrugged. 'Just talking on the net.'

'Who do you talk to?'

'Lots of people. All over the world. World Wide Web chat.'

Harry shook his head. 'Do they say anything worthwhile?' he asked.

'Yep.' He could tell she didn't want to tell him anymore,

that she was holding something back. He noticed her beautiful profile, her soft full lips, the top lip like her mother's.

'When I get back—'

'Where are you going?'

'I want to borrow my dog back again,' he told her. 'Just for a day or two. If that's okay.'

She smoothed the side of her face against Razor's glossy neck. 'He's my beautiful twin brother with extra serves of ears. And he loves me.' She rubbed Razor's ears between her fingers. 'Why do you want to take him?'

'There's a matter I want to look into.'

'You are talking like a cop,' she said, tightening her hold on Razor. She suddenly thought that maybe what she was planning was not a good idea. Maybe Richard should meet her family first. Maybe the time had come for her secret friend to become a family friend. She felt uncomfortable, holding this huge secret.

'Dad—' she began.

'What, Hanks?'

But she didn't say anything. Maybe soon, she'd tell Dad. 'Dad,' she said instead, 'you can take this good dog. And tell me what you were going to say – about when you get back.'

'I was going to say we'll have a good talk. About things in this family.'

Her eyes looked steadily into his. He saw gratitude and relief. 'That would be good,' she said. 'I hate the fights and when you don't talk.'

'We'll sort it out. I promise you.'

She threw her arms around him and he was alarmed at the vehemence of her hug.

He went into his office and called Bathurst to leave a message with Ayoub that he'd meet him the following morning, then turned around because he sensed Meg standing behind him in the hall doorway.

'Harry?' she said. 'What are we going to do? About us?'

'We'll talk about it when I get back,' he said. He put out a hand towards her, hoping for some sign of truce. Her face was hard and lined and it was difficult for him to recognise the sweet woman he'd teamed up with all those years ago. 'It's not me who's otherwise—' he stopped short, thinking better of making the remark, letting his hand drop to his side again.

'Where will you stay?' she said, a little softer.

'I'll sleep out,' he said. 'I'll take the mobile. But I might not always be in range.'

'You've never been in range, Harry,' she said. 'Never let anyone get close.'

It wasn't true, he thought to himself, remembering his boyhood and Angus and the days at Boolabimbie before Vietnam.

'Meg,' he said. 'We'll talk when I get back.' But his wife turned her back on him and walked away.

It was dark by the time he drove through Lithgow and he stopped at Mount Lambie to give Razor a break and a drink and to buy a hamburger.

When he reached Bathurst, he took the Eglinton road and made his way back to the property where Janette had been killed. As he passed, he noticed there were no lights. He would have another look in the morning. He wondered briefly what would become of the tiny boy, and his memories of what had happened in the house at Bathurst. He had seen something so horrible that night that he had preferred fleeing in the darkness to staying with his murdered grandmother. What nightmares would he suffer all through his life and never really understand because stupid and well-meaning adults would presume that he was 'too young to remember?' The suffering caused by one murder rippled out from the central violent act, he thought, into other lives, harming many people. What business did the killer have with the women? he wondered. What relationship was there that brought them into collision? Why had he tried to set it up to look like something it wasn't? He hadn't bothered at Strathfield. Two dead women linked by a Russian handgun and near invisible shards of rose-coloured glass.

He drove a little way past the property and discovered a bridge over a meander of the Macquarie. On the other side picnickers had made an ad hoc trail along the grassy river bank. He took the wagon down off the road and drove a little way along the river. He looked around and saw a good campsite further down, where the steep banks opened out onto a smooth area, like a small beach. Harry estimated he was about five kilometres north of the farmhouse where Janette had been murdered. The fragrance of stringybark filled his nostrils. The headlights showed the opposite bank about twenty metres across a barely flowing river. He unlocked the back and Razor jumped out, bounding like a pup down the bank. Harry pulled out a groundsheet and a sleeping bag, a gas ring and a billy. He locked the vehicle and made his way down the slope to the grassy clearing. Stars shone on the surface of the river and, as his night vision started to restore itself, he squatted, listening and sniffing. The frogs were silent. The scent picture was dry grass and dew beginning to form on surfaces. From off the river came a movement of air, too light even to be called a breeze, a stirring that raised the smell of wet clay soil, ducks, freshwater fish, newly cut lucerne, the distant highway and the smell of cattle. Small crickets chimed in the grass and a plover shrieked from the river flats on the other side. Harry could hear the tearing of grass and chomping of a large herbivore – a horse from a paddock nearby, its scent mingling strongly with that of fresh cropped grass.

When his eyes were accustomed to the night, he stood and went towards the edge of the river. Razor was running up and down along the water's edge, sniffing and tripping on all the different odours. Harry pulled out his torch and flashed it onto the damp soil near the water. He saw the tracks of a large goanna that had come down to the river to drink. Nearby was a graceful, plait-like track that he remembered as the mark of an echidna. It was a good watering spot, although a little too exposed for the smaller, more vulnerable creatures. He dipped his billy into the water and rinsed it, then half-filled it. As he stood up, he stopped and squatted down again. Just over from the marks left by the other animals were the tracks of a huge kangaroo, bigger than he'd ever seen in his life. He judged it to be a male from the length of the clear print of the back foot: nearly thirty centimetres. He estimated it would have to stand over two metres high, taller than a tall man.

Sitting in the silence of the evening and reading the ground like that turned him back to Vietnam and the tracks that indicated the passage of enemy soldiers burdened with heavy materials; the way he would distinguish tracks made by fresh walkers from those made by exhausted walkers. This was helpful in calculating whether they'd hit on a group that lived nearby or one that had penetrated the area from another region. It was easy to see whether the quarry was running. He learned to study the water that gathered in a footprint, calculating how fresh or how stale it was depending on the cloudiness or clarity of the fluid.

The scent of cigarette smoke drifted down from the road, bringing him back to the present. Cigarette smoke is detectable up to 400 metres away. He looked around but didn't see anyone.

In Vietnam, Harry could smell the enemy – their latrines, their cooking, their cigarettes – much earlier than anyone else on his patrol. Different diets make different shit. And even before his nose had sensed it, he would be aware of the sudden influx of flies that indicated death nearby or enemy latrines. In Vietnam, Harry had learned that stealth was their greatest ally, a stealth made easier, despite the encumbrances of their heavy equipment and painful feet, by the fact that to make a noise could, and did, result in sudden death. He'd learned to notice that rust spots appeared on opened tin cans within about twelve hours; learned to judge the severity of a wounded man's injuries as much from the way his footprints moved and the way his blood fell onto the jungle plants as from how severe the bleeding was. Heightened by the dark exhilaration of combat and the adrenalin of terror, of never knowing whether the next breath might well be your last, Harry had learned to notice, to see and to smell. From these visual and olfactory clues, his mind had started making pictures in his head, a bit like the cinema, of who and how many enemy soldiers had moved through this pathway, and how long ago, and whether they were sweating with exhaustion and heavily burdened, or whether they were fresh and carrying only their arms. It was like an automatic process. He didn't have to make it happen. His mind just filled with collated information and he was very rarely wrong in his projections. It was a skill that had become invaluable in the days he worked with Homicide at crime scenes.

He went up the bank a little and spread his groundsheet on a level area. He lit the gas ring and put the billy on it to boil. He lay back on the groundsheet and looked at the stars. The Pleiades shone in the northern sky, near Orion.

He knew them also as the seven sisters who had fled from a warrior bent on ravishing and had jumped up into the sky for safety. A hazy circle round the moon meant rain in about three days, according to his calculations. The river made soft sounds that were at first inaudible but, as his senses stilled and opened out, became quite clear. A fish jumped. A bull called out in the distance. He made tea in the billy and pulled out the cooked chicken he'd purchased in town. After he'd also had his tea, Razor curled up beside the leader of the pack. Harry pulled out the sleeping bag and lay on top of it, legs crossed, looking at the stars, thinking that he hadn't felt so good, so peaceful, for a long time.

NINE

At five-thirty next morning, Harry was making billy tea by the hushed river. The sun was shining over the horizon, making pink swathes of early-morning radiance on the long dry feed that edged the hills and in the soft mist that covered the river further downstream. On the other side of the river, upwind, Harry saw a young fox trotting along the ridge. It froze and stared at him, then turned away and trotted out of sight. In the same moment, Razor caught its scent and barked ferociously.

He made his tea, and bird calls, silenced by Razor's voice, once again filled the air. Harry identified noisy miners, magpies, pied butcherbirds, lorikeets and the high-pitched piping yelp of a brown hawk. By the time he was drinking his tea, dew was already steaming and vanishing. He squatted, watching it. He felt the best he'd felt in years. His mind had calmed and straightened out. The bush always did that for him. As he gazed around, he noticed a perfect piece of timber for Hannah's message stick: a piece of eucalypt branch fallen off a tree. He went over to it and broke off the smaller branches, leaving a well-shaped 'S'-bend about a foot long. As he put it on the floor in the back of the wagon, he thought of his children and how they would grow away from him, as indeed one already had. And that was as it should be. In the long run, he thought, I am only responsible for myself.

Back at the campsite, he jettisoned the last mouthful of leafy black tea, watching it arc in amber droplets and hit the ground. He looked up and saw that the hawk had perched in the eucalypt nearby. The smaller birds cried out as they flew from the clump of flowering mistletoe where they'd been feeding. The bird of prey sat alone now in the tree and the clean scent of morning made Harry hungry. He swiped the side of his face; the flies were already a worry.

After packing up, Harry drove into town and had a hamburger for breakfast. Then he picked up Ayoub from his flat and the two of them drove to an address across the railway line. A flatmate of Janette Madden's boyfriend answered the door when they knocked, scratching his balls through his jeans, saying they'd better come in and not to worry about the mess. In the lounge room, Harry took in the scent picture: stale cigarettes, alcohol, and the closed-in smell of three untidy young males living together.

'He's just coming out now,' said the man. And there it was again, as he spoke – something that reminded Harry of the ghost scent he'd touched on at the first crime scene; the odd, sharp something in the air. Just as suddenly, it was gone again.

'What do you coppers want?' Murray Faye had come in with a cup of tea from the kitchen. 'I still can't believe it,' he said. 'Who would hurt her?'

Faye gave them more details. He'd been employed as a storeman at a Sydney supermarket but had been retrenched and decided to come up to the country for awhile. He and Janette Madden had met six months ago at the local pub. Although she was quite a bit older than he was, she was a very attractive woman and they had become intimate quite quickly.

'She housekept for the Schofields in lieu of rent for the cottage and worked part-time at Karrawonga. That's the name of a property out of town. On the river. Janette used to cook for them a few days a week.'

'Yes,' said Ayoub. 'We've made a few inquiries there already.'

'Did you know of any other boyfriends she might have had – or maybe used to have?' Harry asked.

'Her ex,' said Faye. 'I think he visited once or twice. Stayed awhile at the house. But that was before I knew her,' he added.

'What was his name?'

Faye shrugged. 'Dunno,' he said. 'Businessman of some sort. They were on together when she lived in Sydney. Before she came up here to get away from it all.'

Now you are really away from it all, Janette, thought Harry, with your earrings and your tilted head and smart mouth.

Faye had his head in his hands. 'Christ, I really can't believe it,' he said. Harry looked around the messy room, at the motorcycle posters on the walls, plates and cushions on the floor, the tumbled surroundings of undomesticated males sharing a house. 'She didn't talk about him. Not to me, at any rate.' Then he looked up. 'She did say he was a pilot so he must have had a quid, that one.' Something in the inflection and grain of the voice alerted Harry.

Faye was a good-looking young man, tanned skin and exceptionally vivid green eyes. Harry looked at him more acutely and noticed something about the nose and forehead. 'You're Koori, aren't you?' he said, but it wasn't a question.

'You're a cop, aren't you?' Faye snapped back. 'So what?'

'What brings you here? Into this town?' Harry persisted.

'I can go where I like.'

'I'm not arguing about that,' said Harry. 'I simply want

to know why here. Why *this* town? Why Janette Madden?'

Murray Faye looked hard at him. The vivid eyes were narrowed now. He lit up another cigarette, looked at it, realised he already had one going, lying on an ashtray, shook his head slightly and decided to talk to Harry.

'I come up here with a couple of other young blokes. Karrawonga's a sort of halfway house for urban blacks who want a break from the filth of the city. I come up here to get some clean air. Do some hunting. Fishing. Get away from the pub life. The cigarettes.' He looked wryly at the cigarette in his hand and the other one burning into a long ash on the glass ashtray. 'Father Bill runs the place. Janette worked there a coupla days a week helping out with the cooking and cleaning.' He suddenly stopped talking as grief choked his voice, then collected himself.

'I used to know Father Bill,' said Harry. 'He must be a hundred years old now.'

Murray suddenly grinned. 'Yeah, about a hundred. He can still break up a fight, that one. Mean left for an old fella.'

'Thanks for talking to us,' said Harry. Murray looked at Ayoub and then back at Harry with his level, green-eyed gaze. 'I only talked to you,' he said.

At ten that morning, Harry called Razor back. The dog was going round in circles, stopping and sniffing at various interests. They'd gone back to the house where the murdered woman had lain spread-eagled on the floor in her novelty slippers. Razor had picked up something there and followed it to the river banks, about two kilometres from the cottage, where the trail stopped. Harry reeled the dog in and they went back to his vehicle, parked behind the house. Harry drove back to a bridge and crossed the river. A fire trail ran up the ridge on the hill that overlooked the river and he took it, occasionally getting a glimpse of the murder house across the wide expanse of brown water. He left the vehicle, harnessed Razor, and the two of them walked downhill back to the edge of the river. Harry and the dog patrolled the river banks, going east and west along the water's edge. Razor picked up on different interesting animals, but none of his body language signalled recent human tracks.

At 10.47 Harry pulled into Bathurst's main street. He left Razor in the wagon and went to the police station. Neither Ayoub nor Brennan were in. Ayoub was expected back after lunch.

'He's out at the retirement village,' said the desk sergeant. 'Suspicious death.'

Harry decided to drive out and meet Ayoub there. The desk sergeant gave him directions.

The Lady Joyce Cahill retirement village was set on twenty hectares of what had been pastoral land, foothills country about a kilometre from the outskirts of town. It had its own nursing home as well as units, dormitory-style accommodation and a communal dining and activities centre. Harry followed the signs along the driveway to Reception and found a parking spot in front of dense old camellia bushes that would shelter Razor from the increasing heat of the sun. He walked up the steps, across the black and white marble verandah, and stepped through the grand entrance into the airconditioned interior. Reception was housed in the original homestead, since renovated and partitioned into serviceable office spaces. The scent picture here was complex, with top notes of flowers and disinfectant, and an underpinning odour of urine and old, worn clothes. There was also the unmistakable hospital scents of polish and methylated spirits.

Harry went to a doorway signposted with a little street sign and walked into a comfortable room. Large bay windows gave on to the gardens and elderly people sat around tables, reading newspapers or chatting. Gracious marble fireplaces now housed sensible slow combustion heaters, and the carpet reminded him of an RSL club.

'Can I help you?' asked a wispy woman who had been bending over a table close to an old woman.

'I'm looking for a police officer, a John Ayoub, who I believe is on the premises.'

'And you are?' Her thin eyebrows rose and stayed aloft until Harry answered and showed his warrant card.

'He'll be around with the doctor. In unit eleven. I'm Mrs Lindgrun.'

Harry followed her out of the building through a side exit, across a small rose garden and into a modern-looking wing, where tiny units with even tinier garden patches ran in a long, low building, like a motel. He stepped inside, following Mrs Lindgrun. He could hear Ayoub's 'that is correct' almost immediately and they turned into a unit where a very old woman lay dead in her bed, her white hair drawn into a knot on the top of her head. Ayoub nodded at him as Harry stepped inside and the doctor was packing her bag up, about to leave.

'She had an early visitor,' said Ayoub. 'And he left. A staff member found her about two hours ago. The doctor says she's only been dead a few hours.'

The doctor put her bag down. 'Look at this,' she said. She turned the sheet down and revealed the old woman's neck. Dull purplish bruises could already be seen on the fragile skin. 'Living to ninety so that somebody can strangle you.'

Harry made a non-committal response. This was nothing to do with him. The world was a nightmare and he knew this more than most people. He became aware that the doctor was speaking, looking at him intently – a pretty woman in her forties, with short, glossy hair. 'The first time I ever had to pronounce someone dead was in a room like this,' she was saying. 'I sent all the relatives out and put my head on the woman's chest. Then I wasn't so sure. I thought I could still detect a faint heartbeat. I listened. And then I noticed a ceiling fan going round, making a slight click each time. I didn't know what to do. I didn't want to make a mistake and then have to call all the family in and say, by the way, your grandmother's not dead after all.' She suddenly stopped, as if embarrassed that she'd said so much to a stranger. People did this with him, Harry knew. Told him things like that.

'In this case?' he said to her, indicating the still figure of the old woman.

'No doubt at all,' agreed the doctor. 'She's going over to the PM man now.'

He was just about to follow Ayoub out of the room when he noticed the name on her locker – Vera Wetherill. 'Auntie Vera,' he said, without meaning to.

'Pardon?' said Ayoub. 'Nothing,' said Harry. 'I used to know someone with that name.'

'There are a few Wetherills round here,' said Ayoub. 'Used to be a big name in the district.'

Harry nodded. 'Yes,' he said. 'I used to know one or two of them a long time ago.'

'They seem to come to grief a bit more often than other people,' Ayoub said.

Harry considered. 'Big families often do,' he said. 'More of them to get into trouble.'

Harry looked at the dead woman again and remembered Auntie Vera forty years ago. At fifty, she had been an imposing figure, stout with dyed red hair in a frizz, contained by tortoiseshell combs. Angus had hated her. She would come and stay when his mother was incapacitated or sent away to 'have a rest'. Like her brother, Aunt Vera controlled and dominated everyone around her.

Harry suddenly heard Razor barking, and excused himself. When he got to the vehicle, Razor was causing a commotion in the back of the wagon. Several staff members stood around, not quite knowing what to do. He was jumping and dancing against the window, barking like crazy, his tail whizzing round in the circular twist that meant 'I'm onto something important'.

'What is it?' Harry asked, opening the rear to let the dog dance out of the back of the wagon and onto the ground, his nose honing in on a scent. Harry frowned and clipped the harness onto him. Razor was charging back up the steps and into the entrance of the hospital. Harry ran after him through the reception and office area, across the ugly carpet and onto the lino of the corridor. He hardly noticed the surprised faces, or the secretary who came up to him. I don't believe it, Harry thought, as he ran to keep up with Razor, his mind racing too as he tried to make sense of what was happening.

'You can't bring that dog in here,' the secretary said as Harry and Razor ran past. Down the hall they went, back into the room where the dead woman lay, and where Ayoub and the doctor were still talking near the doorway. Razor's nose vacuumed the floor past them and went right up to the bed where the old woman lay.

'Really?' said Harry. 'You sure?'

Razor sat and barked. He couldn't be surer. Then he jumped up, standing against the bed, nosing the sheets near the woman's neck.

'What's going on?' asked Ayoub.

'Get this animal out of here,' demanded the secretary from

the doorway. 'Animals are forbidden in this section. Please. I must insist.'

But Harry and Razor were out the door, straight past her, and down the hall again, Razor pulling hard on his harness, his tail indicating the freshness of the trail he had hit. Out the front door again, and down the steps, around the side of the long dormitory wing to a section of gravelled roadway signed 'Visitors Parking'. Razor went right up to a spot and stopped. Right damn slam in the middle of the parking area. He whined and cried and went round and round in circles, looking up and whimpering with frustration. Then he sat and barked while Harry stood panting. He was starting to get the picture.

That same morning, 205 kilometres away in Sydney, Hannah woke excited, because today was *the* day. She pushed Blade gently off the bed before Mum could wake and knelt up to look out her window. The sun was shining through next-door's flowering cherries, the red leaves glowing next to the robinia's acid lime green. She hopped out of bed and opened her drawers, taking out a new pair of shorts, her favourite t-shirt with the dogs' photo on it, and her smart sunshade. She squashed them into the bottom of her backpack then ran to have a wash.

At breakfast, Mum was quiet and Dad's chair was draped in one of Alison's cobwebby shawls. Alison herself was still in bed. She never ate breakfast with them. Hannah could hear her heart beating in the silence. She took a guarded look at her mother's face. You could see, she thought, that Mum had been crying a lot. But at least she'd stopped now. Hannah hoped that whatever terrible thing had happened to make her mother unhappy would go away. Maybe she was sad because Alison was so thin. Or that she herself was troublesome. She felt guilty about her plan for today, the meeting at Circular Quay where Richard would be waiting for her, the surprise he'd planned. He'd promised that she'd be back in plenty of time to catch the bus back home, just like any other day.

'I'm going shopping straight after work today,' Mum was saying. 'So you come home on the other bus with Alison, will you?' Her mother looked at her. 'Did you hear what I said?'

'Yes,' said Hannah.

'What are you so down in the mouth about? I thought you liked coming home with her.'

'I do,' she said. 'But the big girls won't talk to me.'

'But you'll have Ali.'

Hannah nodded. It didn't make any difference to her plan, really. As long as Mum didn't notice that she would be first getting off the city bus to join the regular one. And Mum would hardly notice that, because both bus stops were round the corner and down the road.

'Aren't you going to work this morning?' she asked her mother.

Her mother sighed. 'Not till later. I had a meeting with a family but they cancelled. Said they'd rather deal with it themselves.' They got themselves into this mess, she was thinking, by dealing with it themselves. Maybe this family of mine needs help, too. I am a trained counsellor with a degree in psychology, she told herself, competent in and practised with many therapeutic techniques. We can deal with this, she told herself firmly. It will have to start with me.

Hannah slid off her chair and took her plate to the sink.

'Don't worry about doing that,' said her mother. 'I'll do it before I go out. Bang on Ali's door when you go past, will you?'

Hannah did, then opened the door and peeked in. Only

Ali's dark hair could be seen spread over her pillow in wild skeins. Hannah withdrew and closed the door, banging on it again. There was a groan from the bedroom and eventually Alison came out, dragging herself to the bathroom, and Hannah could hear her coughing and splashing in the shower.

Hannah put on her uniform, school shoes and socks, cleaned her teeth and brushed her hair. She slipped her gold locket into her pack, and her see-through plastic purse with the ten-dollar note in it and some coins, and the forbidden drop earrings. She could change out of her studs when she had her shorts and t-shirt on. She zipped up the backpack. Her small unsmiling face stared back at her from the photo on the bus pass attached to the straps. Blade stared at her while she made these last-minute arrangements. She hugged him and he wagged back and woofed a couple of times, just like his old self.

'Bye, Mum,' she called from the front door.

'Bye, darling. Remember to get Ali's bus.'

'I will, Mum. Bye.'

At Circular Quay, Hannah went into the Ladies and changed her clothes. Her school shoes and socks didn't look too bad with her shorts. She put the earrings and the sunshade on, her hair cheekily pushed back by the sunshade and the earrings bouncing as she moved. Maybe I'll be a model, instead of Ali, she thought. If I lose some weight. She was thrilled to think that in a little while she'd be meeting her good Internet friend and e-mail correspondent, Richard, age thirteen, already nearly two metres tall, dark eyes and hair, interests – surfing the waves and the net, films, computer games and having fun with other kids.

Hannah left the Ladies and crossed the road, waiting,

according to their plan, in the first bus shelter. It was just nine-thirty. Richard couldn't miss her in the dogs' t-shirt and sunshade that she'd told him she'd be wearing. Excitedly, she scanned the passing faces. But they were all grown-ups and, of course, they didn't notice her. Grown-ups only notice kids, Hannah thought, when they're doing something the grown-ups don't approve of. Or when they don't stand up for them on buses. Or when they're very tiny and cute – they like to pat us and carry on. One boy who might have been thirteen was firmly in the grip of his mother, and he was fair. Hannah waited.

Meg agreed to meet Max at the motel they'd used a couple of times before finding a hotel that pleased them more. She had to whisper on the phone, worried that Alison might hear. Her older daughter shambled out of her room and into the bathroom as Meg hung up.

'You're very late,' she said. But Alison was busy in the bathroom and either didn't hear or decided not to respond. Meg made herself a cup of coffee and stepped outside in the backyard with it. The wisteria and grape vines were at the height of their summer tangle and the pergola was sagging under their combined weight. The little garden needed watering and Meg picked up the hose. My house is in disorder, she told herself. She turned the water on the daisies and lavender bushes and a wave of fragrance was released as she did. Blade bumped his way out of the kitchen door to see what she was doing. He's a young and vigorous dog, she thought. In his prime. Unlike me. She walked to the end of the yard dragging the hose and looked back at the house. It was undeniably shabby. Paint blistered and lifted along the timber of the pergola that adjoined the kitchen. The grape vine had become completely uncontrollable and was flourishing over the roof, obscuring the tiles. Then Alison wandered out, still in her underwear and with her hair still wrapped in a towel, and paused to rub Blade's fur with her foot.

'Put some clothes on,' Meg said and immediately regretted it. It seemed she never said anything to her daughter lately that wasn't critical or interrogatory.

Alison looked straight at her. 'I don't want to go to school anymore,' she said. 'I hate school. I want to leave.'

'And do what?' said Meg.

'I don't know,' said Alison. 'It's so boring. None of the teachers like me.' I'm not surprised, thought Meg, and then was ashamed of herself. 'What's the point of all the bullshit we learn? How is it going to help me in my life?'

'You'd have to get a job,' said Meg.

'Where?' shrugged her daughter. 'There aren't any round here'.

'What do you plan to do then?' Meg was feeling the anger mounting. 'You can't just hang around here, sleeping all day like you do in the holidays.'

Then an awful thought occurred to her. She put together Alison's antisocial ways, her secretiveness, her lack of appetite. 'Alison,' she said, 'you're not on drugs, are you?'

She was surprised at her daughter's burst of contemptuous laughter. 'Really. I can't believe I'm hearing this. How pathetic,' said Alison, wrapping the towel tighter around long hair and disappearing into the house.

Meg followed her inside. 'Why is it pathetic?' she demanded to know.

'Because,' said Alison, turning around to face her, 'this whole family's fucked and all you can think of is that I must be on drugs!' With that, she went into her room and closed the door.

Meg stood in the kitchen. Her daughter had said something that, painful as it was, came uncomfortably close, and she put the untouched coffee down and went to Alison's door. She tapped. 'May I come in?' she asked. 'I only want to talk with you.'

'No,' said her daughter. 'You start off just wanting to talk and next thing you're yelling at me. Go away.' Then she added, 'Please.'

'Alison,' said Meg, feeling foolish talking to the timber panels of the door. 'I don't know how to talk to you anymore. I don't know what to say to you. I feel I don't know you.'

The door suddenly opened and Alison stood there in her black weeds, her tangled hair and dark red lipstick and the strange scent she used, smelling of witchcraft. 'You've never bothered to find out,' said her daughter. 'You think you're so perfect with your school counsellor stuff. So how could you know what to say to a stranger?' Then she stepped past her mother, slung her school backpack over her shoulder, walked down the hall and left the house.

Meg ran to the front door, wanting to say something to help, but she couldn't think of anything.

Meg went back to the kitchen. God, what am I going to do? she asked herself. I'm supposed to have wisdom and I don't know what to do with my own daughter. Why is she so difficult? She sat at the table and flung her arms out, laying her head on them. She tried to remember how it had been for *her* at seventeen. Not very good, she remembered, and at least she'd known her father. It must be so hard for Alison, Meg realised anew, to have an unknown father somewhere in the world who made it very clear, day after day of a lifetime, how unimportant his child was to him. She wondered briefly if she should try to contact him. But what realistically could a stranger offer Alison after all these years of neglect? Maybe she should talk to her daughter about Jeff, discover what Alison's feelings were. It would be something. A line of communication at least.

An hour later, she drove to the motel in a nearby suburb. It was far enough away, she hoped, for her not to be recognised by anyone she knew, because it was used primarily by visitors from the country.

She parked her car next to Max's dark blue sedan. The mid-morning shimmering heat was oppressive here, only a few kilometres from the coast. She went into the reception area, feeling guilty, adulterous and clumsy. An enamelled receptionist with hard red nails and black eyebrows glanced up at her.

'Mr Wolansky?' Meg asked.

The receptionist flashed a false smile. 'Suite six. To the right.' And Meg went down the pastel hall, with its pastel prints and armchairs that nobody sat in, to the door and knocked.

'It's not locked,' he said. He was already in bed, waiting for her.

Meg came in and closed the door, staying away from him. 'Max. We've got to talk.'

'Yes,' he said. 'Later. Come here.'

'No, now,' she said. He heard the tone in her voice and sat up, patting the space beside him.

He looks very tired, she thought. Tired and sad. Like me. She wanted to run to him, snuggle up to him and make love and forget everything that was in her mind. But she stayed where she was.

'I want to say good bye,' she said. 'I want to say that this is the last time I'm going to meet you.' Then she burst into tears. He didn't move, just lay there, looking at her, watchful.

She pulled a handkerchief out of her pocket and blew her nose with it.

'It seems that all I do these days is cry,' she said.

Max sat up in the bed and regarded her. She was too distressed to notice his expression. 'I've offered you a new life,' he said in a soft voice. 'A chance most people never have. These tears of yours are completely optional,' he said.

'You are very naive,' she said. 'You don't think I could just turn my back on my whole life and run away with you to some fairyland where we'll be happy forever? This is the real world,' she said.

'Ah. The real world,' he repeated, swinging out of the bed. 'The real world is what you make of it. I've been working towards this real world for many years. You wouldn't know about that. You've just drifted through your life like most people. Letting things happen to you. First one thing, then the next. No plan. No bigger picture. Passive, weak, pathetic—' He grabbed a handful of clothes and pulled his trousers on. 'And now that you've had a play around with me, and I've become an inconvenience to your horrible suburban life, you're getting scared and you want to get out. So you come here and make the grand announcement. "This must stop."'

'Max, I—'

'I don't want to hear it.' He turned to her while he pulled his shirt on and she was stunned at the rage that blazed in his eyes.

'Max, you said – right at the beginning – no strings, remember? I told you I was married with two children. "Just a lighthearted affair" – they were your very words. No promises, no conclusions. *You* said what's the harm in an artistic affair? Then you seemed to become more deeply involved. And I did, too. For awhile. You wanted me to leave my marriage. Now you're changing the rules.'

'Life changes the rules,' he said bitterly, coming closer to her, leaning over her. 'You can't do something like this without changing everything. Did you really think you could have an affair with me in a neat little box—' he grabbed her hard between the legs '—and not let it affect the rest of your life? The rest of your family? You don't know who I am. You know nothing about me. Who's naive now?'

Meg turned to go. She was stunned at the anger and hatred in his face. She couldn't bear to be there a second longer. She went to the door and opened it.

Max swiftly came over and slammed it shut again, grabbing her arms, pressing her up against the door. His face was distorted and much too close.

'You don't know anything,' he hissed. 'Nothing, Meg Doyle.'

With all her might, she pushed against him. 'Stop it. Let me go,' she said. It was hard to breathe, he was pressing so heavily against her. In his variety of mood changes, she'd never seen this dark violence before. 'Max. Please.' Then her own anger overrode her confusion. 'This is an assault,' she heard herself say and it sounded stupid.

'You bet it is,' he said in her ear, pinning her two wrists above her head, shoving the fingers of his left hand between her legs, hooking up into her body painfully hard through her clothing. 'Now,' he snarled, releasing her as suddenly, 'get out.'

She almost fell to the floor but managed to scramble to her feet again. She couldn't bear to look at him and, wrenching the door open, she was out, running down the hallway, past the blonde with the raised black eyebrows, and back to her car, trying to control the sobs, until she finally unlocked the door and climbed in. She sat there, shaking and sobbing, tears running down her face, until her hands were able to start the ignition and drive home.

TEN

Harry cast Razor all around the car park and its surroundings. But it was clear that whoever Razor had hit on was no longer in the environment. Razor was sharp enough to follow someone in a car if all things were equal. Harry had tested him years ago on a colleague with a half-hour start who was picked up mid-paddock by a trailer and then driven a kilometre and a half away to the nearby farmhouse. Razor hadn't missed a beat, staying nose down after the trailer's tracks straight to the front door of the farm. But here in this car park, there were too many cars, too many cross tracks, too many people.

Harry ran lots of information through his mind and tried to sort it out as he took the dog and went back to his vehicle. He installed Razor who stood panting in the back, looking at him, circling and whimpering.

Ayoub was standing waiting on the step of the reception area as Harry came up.

'The dog was onto something,' said Harry, 'but we lost it in the car park. I want to know who was visiting this morning. Is there some sort of visitors' book?'

Mrs Lindgrun heard him say that and smiled. 'It's not a club,' she said. 'Only the staff have to sign on. But I usually know who's coming and going.'

'I want to know who was Mrs Wetherill's visitor this morning.'

'She rarely had visitors,' said Mrs Lindgrun. 'Apart from the clergyman.' She was flicking through a card index. 'I didn't notice the visitor this morning. Ask Sonia. She looks after the comings and goings of that wing of the building. The next-of-kin is a grand-nephew. Lives in Sydney. He's never come near her as far as I know. That's families for you.' She sniffed her disapproval. 'The first time he'll hear from us about her is to hear that she's dead.'

Mrs Lindgrun called for Sonia, who arrived at the reception area within minutes. 'I didn't really pay much attention,' she said. 'All I can say is that it was a man.'

'Tell us anything you can remember.'

'Colouring? Age? Height and weight?'

Sonia shook her head. 'I was going round with the medication trolley. I was concentrating on my list. I just said good morning to him like I say to anyone I pass in the corridor. I barely looked up.'

Ayoub took her details and she promised to ring him if she thought of anything else that might be helpful. 'No matter how tiny,' said Ayoub. 'And my suggestion is that you improve security around here. These people are very vulnerable.' He turned to Harry. 'I'll go back to town and alert the hospital.'

Police in surrounding towns were already on alert, Harry knew, and the main roads east, west, north and south were all being checked in what was building to a State-wide manhunt. But this man was a pilot and it was harder to police the air roads. The two men walked out together. 'I believe it was the same man,' said Harry. 'The killer from Strathfield and Bathurst.'

'What?' said Ayoub. 'What are you talking about, the same killer?'

'The dog,' said Harry. 'The dog was very excited. He knew that smell in the hospital room from recent experience. He picked it up.' Ayoub looked at him with a frown as they walked towards their vehicles. 'We already know he varies the MO. A shooting, a bashing and now strangulation.'

Harry sighed. 'I should tell you,' he said, 'that there's a connection between these women. Janette Madden used to be my wife. For eighteen months in 1972. When I was in Vietnam.'

'I didn't know you'd been to Vietnam,' said Ayoub.

'I don't tell people these things,' said Harry, 'because in my estimation they're not relevant and happened a long time ago.'

Ayoub pulled out his notebook and jotted something down. Then he looked up again. 'You said a connection between these women,' he said, waiting.

'The woman in there,' Harry said, indicating the long building of the nursing home where the dead woman lay, 'I used to know her when I was a kid.' Ayoub waited patiently. 'I grew up about a hundred k's from here, on a property near Boolabimbie. My family worked for the Wetherills. That woman was a relative. Used to stay at the homestead sometimes, when Mrs Wetherill, the squatter's wife, was taken away for a rest.'

Ayoub considered. 'So they're connected through you.' Ayoub's sheik eyes narrowed under their heavy brows. 'A connection to one victim is odd. But two . . .' he shook his head. '. . . two is nearly the trifecta.' He noted something further on his small pad. 'Why didn't you mention this at the first crime scene? That you'd been married to her?'

Harry considered. 'At that stage I wasn't seeing it as anything more than the sort of nasty coincidence that happens in our line of work. You know – young bloke called out to a motor vehicle accident and it's his wife and kids mangled in the car? I'm only telling you this now in case it means something later.'

'Like what?'

Harry laughed. 'We won't know till later, will we?'

Ayoub went round to the driver's side of his car and opened the door. 'And you reckon the dog has suggested to you that this might be the same bloke that did Strathfield and Bathurst?' Harry nodded. Ayoub didn't look convinced. 'I don't know if a dog's word is good enough,' he said, getting into the vehicle. 'Can dogs take the stand?'

'By the time we get this joker to court,' said Harry, 'we'll have a mile of evidence. The dog won't come into it.'

Ayoub nodded to him and switched on the ignition. 'Harry,' he said. 'I know you're a good cop. But this is my turf and until I find hard physical evidence to say otherwise, there's no reason to think this woman's death has anything to do with Strathfield or Bathurst. Leave this to us. You're Dog Squad now.'

'I trust my dog's responses,' said Harry, 'like I'd trust a partner's. It's like my partner told me something. I have to pass it on to you or I have to follow it up myself.'

'Yeah, well, thanks,' said Ayoub. 'You better do that.' He looked for a moment as if he was going to say something more, but then Harry sensed him change his mind. He backed the car out, and drove away.

Harry drove back to the river bank just a little upstream from where he'd camped the night before, parked the vehicle under a yellow box that gave some shelter from the sun and walked towards a picnic area with low timber seats, a fireplace, and a bronze council plaque set on a square of pebblecrete. *On this site in 1878*, he read, *Troopers Daniel Scroggie and Edward*

Templeton were killed by the outlaw Paddymelon. Underneath this were the names of those who'd erected the memorial, the local aldermen and the Mayor, Gregory Edward Templeton. So you got a couple of troopers before they finally got you, Paddymelon, Harry thought, because it wasn't the first time he'd heard about that man, outlaw to one tribe, hero to the other, and Harry's ancestor, according to his mother. He heard another car pulling up, heard the voices of Mum, Dad and kids. Harry wanted to be alone, so he went back to his vehicle, nodded to the family group who were noisily spreading a picnic over a rug on the ground and covering it with plates. He drove a little way along the bank, towards his earlier campsite. Behind him, he could hear the kids from the picnicking family splashing and yelling, their voices carrying along the water course.

Where he now sat, the river in the early afternoon was still and silent, a paler brown than the dark rivers and streams of Vietnam. The birds were silent in the midday heat, conserving their energy for the twilight feeding session. Cicadas and grasshoppers filled the summer air with fizzing sound. He let Razor out of the back of the wagon to roam at will while he sat under a huge river gum and dozed in the singing heat. He could smell the hot metal of his own vehicle and there was a whiff of Razor, who needed a bath. The scent picture here was midday summer: pungent with eucalypt, fragrant with a nearby pepper tree and, somewhere, the scent of hay-cutting – all contributing to his reverie. Something in the layout of the river and the trees that overhung it reminded him of the swimming hole at Boolabimbie, a hundred kilometres to the north-west. His unconscious swiftly did the rest, and a memory filled his mind.

'That Paddymelon, he was a clever man.' He could almost hear his mother's grainy, throaty voice. 'A real run-away bugger. His real name was Mungiebah. In those days before the Law was pretty well finished, the missionary says to him, "God tells all men are equal and you must become equal to us whitefellas." That Paddymelon tells him "You don't want me equal, you want a servant." And he just rides away with some other wild young fellers. He killed some bullocks belonging to the old boss, Hunter Wetherill. (Our people used to call him 'Cockatoo Nose' because he had a nose like a galah.) All the good eating animals – the kangaroos, the wallabies, the emus – were killed or driven away for the old boss' cattle to use the grass. Those bullocks were good eating and there are so many of them. They brought the kidney fat on their spears to give to old Cockatoo Nose and his sons in the way of saying thank you for the bullock feed, but Cockatoo and his sons started shooting them out of the house so they all rode away again. And some of them got killed. Cockatoo Nose and his two sons they rode out with the policemen and killed a lot of people for eating the bullocks. Take them out in the bush and just do 'em in. And they killed the women and the little babies too. Down in the river-hole near the waterfall. Only one little girl got away. Paddymelon's little girl. She told what happened at the waterhole to the old people. When she grows up she tells her children about that terrible day. The stories come down that way, you know that. And we never forget them. We don't write it in books, we keep it here. I've shown you the marks on those trees the bullets made. Pretty well closed up now, but my old auntie and uncle they saw those marks clear when they were little children.

'In those days they were trying to quieten down the bush blacks, bring them in, but the policemen never found old Paddymelon because when they chase him, all they see is a big kangaroo, biggest one they ever see and he just hops away from them. They made plenty of threats against him,' his mother used to say, 'but they never got him because he was a sorcerer, what we call a "clever man". My grandmother, old Wanda, she used to say that Paddymelon was her father. Might be he'll always look after you. The police say they killed him dead. But I don't know about that. Maybe that's old Paddymelon over there.' And Harry remembered staring in wonder at the kangaroo his mother had spotted, almost invisible in the long grass among the tree stumps, with only the outline of its ears betraying him. 'They say they shot him dead. But they never got him,' his mother had said. 'Not his spirit. Always they were threatening him.' Sadness again filled his heart.

He shifted mental and physical gears. Threats are something all coppers have made against them, he knew. The only one he really remembered as having some sort of serious weight behind it had been the child-killer, Ronald Pugh. He could see the face and figure of the man and remembered the dramatic collapse that he and Jim had engineered all those years ago. In fact, he thought, this spot was very like the river banks on which little Helen had died. Same long dry grass, same barely discernible track along the banks, following the curve and wind of the river. As he became quieter in himself, he became aware of a sound that made him immediately think of Vietnam and hot, stinking jungle days. It was the distant buzzing of swarming blowflies. He stood up and looked around, hearing Razor bark.

'Where are you, boy?' he asked, following the sound from the clearing towards a steep section of the river banks. Then he had to climb down, leaning ridiculously backward to maintain his balance on the slope. It seemed Razor had found something interesting about a hundred metres away from the big river gum, and Harry stamped through the long grass and came up to the spot. At first, he thought it was a bundle of rags, because all he could see at first was some yellow and blue fabric, with a nursery print of ducks on a pond. But even before he came up closer, he could see the cotton was stiff and stained with dark, dried blood. Razor was circling and dancing, but as soon as the pack leader came up he sat and was silent. The object lay on a bald patch of earth surrounded by a few woody weeds. Harry poked the fabric with a stick and hundreds of blowflies rose and resettled. The fabric covered something solid but quite small, about the size of an old-fashioned flatiron; exactly the size in fact, as Harry discovered when he lifted a piece of blue material on one side to reveal the curving edge of the rusted antique. His memory jumped back to the empty cot in the nursery where Janette Madden's grandson had slept. This was a sheet from the cot, he realised. And here, he was certain, was the weapon that killed her. Harry felt a shiver of fear run down his back, starting at the base of his skull, and he looked around startled, because he knew that bloody bundle hadn't been there last night when he'd camped there. The killer must have dumped it that morning, because otherwise Razor would have warned Harry during the night. He reached for his mobile.

Later on in the afternoon, Harry stood with Ayoub and watched while the photographer framed up shot after shot of the bloody bundle on the ground. 'The Schofields said there were two old flatirons in the house,' said Ayoub, 'and we could only turn up one. Now we know where the other one got to.'

The sun was lower now, and the worst heat of the afternoon had passed. Flies still swarmed and Harry was continually waving his hand in front of his face, while Razor sniffed around.

'I suppose he dumped it from a vehicle,' said Ayoub,

looking around at the grass. It was flattened from being used by campers and picnickers over the years. 'No-one'd take any notice of him. People are always stopping at that picnic area a bit further back.'

'You'd wonder though,' said Harry, 'why he'd take the trouble to carry the thing away with him and then come back and dump it here.'

Ayoub grinned. 'You're the expert. You work it out.'

Ayoub, the photographer and the weapon went back to Bathurst together, leaving Harry and Razor working the area where the dumped weapon had lain. Razor cruised around, sniffing, returning and moving away again until he picked up something very definite. His tail started its distinctive corkscrewing and his hindquarters dropped in concentration.

'What is it, mate?' Harry murmured to him, taking up the slack on the harness, trotting along behind him.

It was an easy trail at first. Harry had no difficulty keeping up and Razor loped along, nose down, tail signalling that he was covering the track easily. Harry was cautious. Somewhere, and not too far away at the other end of this trail, linked to him by subtle ground scents, was a man who had already killed three women. Others may not think so, thought Harry, but I'm certain it was the same man. Razor knew.

As they trotted along through the scrub, Harry tried to make sense of the man he was tracking. He knew that there was no such thing as a 'random' killing. Human beings never do things without a reason. It might appear random to an outsider, with some, unlucky stranger targeted by a lunatic. But when you got right down to it, Harry knew, there was always the killer's own logic. He might not be aware of why that particular person was selected. In fact, if he *were* aware, he'd have access to such self-understanding

182   Gabrielle Lord

that murder would probably not be necessary. One of the things Harry had come to see in his time in Homicide, and in his discussions with Meg in the days when they discussed such things, was how killing was the most extreme form of acting out. So why had this killer targeted these three women? And how important was it that two of the women had a connection with him, Harry Doyle?

ELEVEN

When Meg arrived home with the shopping, it was half past six and the house was hot, still and quite empty except for Blade who had padded in behind her. She put him out again and he wagged over to the open door of the pen, flopping down in the shade of the grape vine.

'Hannah? Ali?' Her voice echoed. But there was no-one home. The pool, she surmised. If I hadn't had such a difficult day, dealing with Matt's angry father, reassuring him that Matt's 'wish list' was not a personal attack on his father, nor had such an attack been encouraged by the school counsellor, Meg thought, I might have the energy for a swim myself.

Meg heaved the bags onto the kitchen table and collapsed in a chair for a moment. She was grateful for this time to herself after the unexpectedly awful scene at the motel. Remembering the hatred and the contempt of Max's voice, his face, his gestures, brought tears of anger and humiliation and made her heart beat faster. She went to the fridge and poured herself a long drink of iced water, taking it into the living room where she lay on the floor in the relative coolness.

It was over. Really finished now. No possibility of re-seduction, of reconciliation. Not this time. She lay on the floor staring at the pattern on the ceiling, feeling relief that it was over, and for the very first time allowing that the spice underneath her attraction to Max was *fear*. It had always been there, and she had always known it, but she had never wanted to examine it, nor take it to its logical conclusion: that lust and fear combined in her to make of her affair with Max an exciting, glamorous and dangerous cocktail. A woman is allowed a little indiscretion, she told herself. But Max was more than that. He had touched something deep and dark in her. And some of the things he'd said, although hard for her to hear, had come very near the bone. She had wanted excitement, a little spice in her life. Just a little danger. Sex is always dangerous, she knew that. Anything can happen once those boundaries are crossed. Worlds wobble on their axes, rules are smashed. Some extraordinary piece of cosmic machinery swings around into a new place and an unnoticed ratchet engages an alien gear. The compass needle flickers. Nothing can ever be quite the same again. She should have known that. She *did* know that. And yet she'd played it out like a naive schoolgirl, thinking that she could have the excitement of the affair and not have the consequences that sex, of necessity, brings with it.

But now it was over. Why is it, she wondered, that we human beings always end these things in pain and rage? Why can't we just be reasonable? Maybe, she thought, Harry and I can work something out. But she had no energy right now. She felt drained and emptier than at any other time in her life. I need to heal, she thought. So does this family. She thought of her husband, of his silence and his reliable, everyday *thereness* that had seemed so boring once she'd met Max. On the table, the white birthday roses were now fully open and Meg couldn't remember if she'd even said thank you for them.

She got up, went to the phone and dialled her husband's mobile. The cool recorded female voice told her that the mobile was switched off or out of range. Like Harry, she thought. Like us. Like me. I have been switched off from him for a long time now.

She went into the kitchen and started preparing tea for the three of them, unpacking the vegetables. It's been my blind spot, she thought, that's been keeping me from realising that any problems in Alison are really problems in me. And in Harry. This truth was so basic to counselling children that she almost laughed at the way she'd been unable to see it. With some humility from me, she thought, the divide between myself and Alison might be healed. And then, when Harry comes home, there might be a flow-on effect.

Meg started washing lettuce and rocket. She sliced tomatoes and cut her finger, standing at the sink sucking the wound. Then she walked around with her finger stuck up in the air like an idiot as she opened drawers with the other hand, trying to remember where she'd last seen the bandaids. Finally she found one. She wrapped it around the cut and wiped the drops of blood off the floor. It's just as well Harry's not here, she thought, to make some injudicious remark about bloodstain patterns.

Meg opened the freezer and made sure that there was a packet of fish fingers, which for some unaccountable reason were the ultimate favourite food of her youngest daughter. Alison didn't have any favourite food at the moment. She seemed barely to eat at all.

The phone rang and she picked it up, expecting Ali's voice. 'Yes?' she said.

'I need to tell Harry something,' said the thin voice. 'It's urgent.'

'Who is this, please?' asked Meg.

'I can't talk to anyone else,' said the voice. 'I must talk to Harry Doyle.'

'Harry Doyle is not available. Can I take a message?' The sound of sobbing on the line surprised Meg. 'I'll take a message,' she said. 'I'll make sure he gets it.'

'Have they practised chemicals on you?' the voice asked her, and Meg suddenly realised who it was.

'Do you want me to give him a message or not,' she asked impatiently. But the sobbing caller had hung up.

This house is impossible, she thought angrily, dropping the phone again. It's not only a twenty-four-hour a day police operations base, it's also a phone-in centre for the alienated. Meg went back to the sink and dried the leafy greens in a clever German whizzing bowl. It was while she was waiting for the centrifugal spinning to stop that she noticed the things on the line. She felt a small coldness in her chest. Underwear and the two swimming costumes, the two big beach towels. The girls weren't at the pool.

She left the salad and ran next-door, hardly bothering to knock. 'Dell, Dell,' she called. Her friend looked up from the lounge where she was sitting with Jack, watching the early news.

'Have you seen the girls?'

Dell got up and shook her head. 'No,' she said. 'Jack?'

Jack looked up from where he was sitting on the floor. 'They didn't come home yet,' he said. 'I was waiting for Hannah to go to the shop with me. They might have gone straight to the pool.'

'No. Their things are on the line.' Meg's voice was harsh. 'They're not at the pool.'

There was a terrible silence filled only by the television reporter's voice telling of a new sporting world record. Meg felt the terror then. Where are they, my daughters?

She ran out of Dell's house and back into her own with Blade barking outside, having picked up the charged atmosphere in his territory. She looked around the kitchen and the living room for a note. She went into Alison's room and the chaos there. Nothing. Hannah's room also gave nothing away. She ran out the front door and stared up and down the road, which showed nothing but its normal late-afternoon face: suburban, blazing red and scarlet callistemon blooming on the nature strips, a few cars. She ran back inside and tried to ring her husband again but the same cool female told her the same cool message. 'Damn you, Harry!' she screamed, slamming the phone onto the counter.

Dell was suddenly there. She put her arm around her friend. 'Listen, calm down,' she said, putting the kettle on. 'You're over-reacting. Stop being a cop's wife. Stop imagining the worst. They're probably just out somewhere doing something.'

'Where?' Meg demanded. 'Doing what?' She realised how irrational she was being and how her concern for the girls was also fuelled by the ugly scene with Max. And she was aware of the guilt. Bad mother guilt.

'I'm sorry, Dell. You're right. I'm upset. I already was upset. And then they go and pull this stunt on me.'

Suddenly there came the sound of the key turning in the front door lock. Meg wheeled around in relief. 'That's them now,' she said, running down the hall.

Alison came in, turning to close the door behind her. One look and Meg knew.

'You're drunk,' she said. 'Where's Hannah? Where have you been?'

Alison's eyes widened. The alcohol had flushed her face and the whites of her eyes. 'With someone who cares about me.'

'Where's Hannah?'

'How should I know?' said Alison, and that carelessness combined with Meg's own frustration and rising fear caused Meg to raise a hand and slap her daughter very hard across the face. Alison's head jerked with the force of the blow. She caught her breath and stood, eyes wide with horror and shock. A red mark was already starting to become visible across her cheek and Meg's own fingers stung with the force of the slap. Alison burst into tears, pushed past her mother, ran to her room and slammed the door.

Meg could hear the sound of violent sobbing. She ran to the door. 'Alison, please. I'm sorry, I'm sorry. Ali, please. I didn't mean it. It just happened. Please, Ali.'

She became aware of Dell's hand on her arm. 'Come on,' whispered her friend. 'Leave it be for awhile.' Shocked, Meg let herself be led back into the kitchen where Dell had made tea. Still in stunned silence, she sat on a stool while Dell poured her a cup.

'Where is she? Where's Hannah?'

'Have this, and then we'll go and make a few inquiries. Come on. Drink this up.'

Meg realised her mouth had dried up completely. She moistened her lips and drank some tea. 'There'll be a simple explanation,' Dell was saying. 'She's probably off playing in someone's yard.'

Meg slid off the stool. 'I'll go and ask Alison if she was on the bus.'

Dell put an arm out and intercepted her. 'I'll do that,' she said. 'You stay here.' Meg did as she was told and waited till Dell came back. When she did, her friend's face was oddly pale.

'What is it?' Meg asked, the fear rising up again.

'Hannah didn't go to school today, Meg. So she doesn't know.'

'Where did she go?'

'She doesn't know.'

There was a knock on the back door. It was Dell's son Jack leading a little girl by the hand. 'Come in, love,' said Dell to the two of them.

'Um,' he said. 'I was talking to Sophie and she wants to tell Mrs Doyle something.' The little girl nodded. Jack looked at her again. 'She said Hannah wasn't on the bus this afternoon. Didn't you, Soph?'

Sophie nodded. She seemed quite overcome.

'Maybe she got a different bus. A later one,' said Meg, wanting to shake the silent child. But Jack and Sophie stood there, wide-eyed, looking at the women.

'Sophie said she wasn't on the bus at all,' Jack reported. 'Not in the afternoon and not in the morning.'

'Sophie, is this true?'

Then Sophie looked up and the expression in her huge eyes would haunt Meg for years to come. 'Mrs Doyle,' Sophie whispered with great effort, 'Hannah wasn't at school today.'

Meg covered her ears with her hands. Someone was screaming 'No! No! No!'

TWELVE

Harry followed the gently sloping terrain towards the foothills, holding Razor's line. The dog ran along ahead of him, twisting his tail in its distinctive chase pattern. The trees cast long thin shadows behind them as the western sun blazed low in the sky and, although the afternoon was still hot, the air already had that inland softness that denotes evening isn't far away. In the bush, birds were making the most of the daylight. Harry saw a tiny fire-tail finch dart away from him and realised it was years since he'd seen that particular bird. The scent picture here was much dryer than down near the river flats, with the dusty smell of rocky hillside, woody weeds and eucalypts. He noticed a small leguminous red and black pea flower trailing vine-like across the ground in places, and many of the native shrubs displayed their tiny creamy blossoms, fragrant only in the quieter air of twilight. He stopped for a break, to catch his wind. It was suddenly very still, very silent. There is an eeriness that descends on the bush in the brightness of late afternoon, a special haunting that people from northern countries might not understand. It is a hushed waiting in the heat.

Then he decided to press on. After another ten minutes, he turned and looked back the way he'd come. Although he couldn't see it for the timber, he knew that the river was now hundreds of metres beneath them. A crow jeered as it flapped overhead and Harry instinctively looked around for its mate. Crows always move in pairs, he knew. Then he turned back to the trail again because Razor had run on ahead and was barking loudly with excitement. Something's changed, Harry thought when he heard that particular tone in the dog's voice. He paused and unfastened his holster. Then he went forward.

He didn't know this country at all and it nearly cost him his life. Just ahead of him the track suddenly stopped at an open area of dusty earth, with just some low scrub, leading to a slightly raised rock formation, boulders piled on top of each other like giant's blocks. Razor had unwound all the line and was invisible, although Harry could hear him just beyond the tumbled rocks. Harry leaped up onto the tallest of the rocks and then jumped sideways and back in shock. Instinctively, he gripped the rock, peering down. He had almost jumped into thin air. Beneath him, an abyss opened. He was standing right at the edge of a cliff that dropped away in a sheer fall, to the densely wooded forest far below. Razor was running backwards and forwards the length of his line along the edge of the precipice, indicating that the trail stopped. He danced again a bit too close, and dislodged a shower of tiny stones that fell and bounced over the cliff, falling silently hundreds of metres to the valley floor. Harry called the dog to sit beside him, back from the edge. Keeping his centre of gravity low, Harry cautiously climbed forward onto the rocks again and looked down. Perhaps his quarry had made the same mistake Harry had almost made, and stepped over those rocks, and dropped into eternity. He craned over as far as he dared, very close to the edge. Vertigo threatened and his mind started to do a spiral dance. He edged back to feel a little safer. He could only see the walls of the cliff down to a depth of about twelve metres then it fell away underneath him in an invisible concavity. But perhaps, underneath the very spot on which he was standing, his quarry was hiding even now, waiting for him to go away.

Harry looked along the edge of the cliff to his right, then looked closer. On one of the rocks of the tumbling formation that hid the drop was what looked like a scrape mark shining on the surface of the rock. He crawled to the spot to examine it closely. He thought he could discern just the barest mark, such as might be made by the steel tip of a boot. It was not impossible that the man he was hunting had eased himself down over this precipice and somehow managed to climb down to disappear underground. Or the scrape mark might have been the last desperate flailing of a man who had lost his balance and was already doomed to plummet over the cliff.

Two hours later, Harry sat with his back safely against a big leatherjacket tree, resting. It would be much easier and safer for the offender, Harry conjectured, to climb a little way down that cliff, wait until the police were off his heels, then climb back up the way he already knew, than attempt a descent down that cliff wall. Harry decided he would wait here with the dog. What goes down must come up.

A three-quarter waning moon was starting to rise through the tangle of boughs and leaves and Harry shivered despite the mild evening. Razor lay resting, occasionally twitching his snout. Harry was thinking of a story that had haunted him when he was a boy, of a man waiting through the night for a deadly cobra to rise out of nowhere in the night. Then his memories were back in the jungle near Nui Dat and sitting waiting in the pissing rain. Those operations were from four to six weeks in length, with a week in between. Day after day of creeping through the dripping, stinking country, with blistered, festering feet and chafes and rashes covering almost all his skin. Scrub-bashing had its own pattern: moving for about fifty minutes, a brief rest to send a locstat, and then on again. If the halt was for any longer than five minutes, there was a security drill that became automatic, with the lead section spreading out and covering from ten o'clock to two o'clock, the middle section covering from ten to six o'clock, and the rear section taking care of the area from six to two o'clock. Machine-guns and sentries were posted. 'If you forget that this war is a war without fronts or flanks, if you forget – even for a second – that this war surrounds us like the jungle surrounds us, you will die,' his trainers had told him over and over again. 'Stay alert, stay alive,' he'd been told. He had been drilled, over and over again, in fire and movement battle drill until it had become automatic; the same drilled movements that had made him recognise a combat survivor in the man from the Strathfield siege.

In the end it was like second nature to be always searching his arcs of vision, ready to fire in whatever direction his eyes were following. Harry recalled the way the rain had just dropped out of the sky at the same time every day, so that a change of clothes was a waste of time, the clean clothes looking exactly like the discarded ones in minutes. He remembered the leeches, which had seemed untroubled by the repellent they all used to douse trousers and socks. He remembered one man waking up screaming with revulsion because a leech had somehow slipped through the seam of his closed eyes during the night and gorged itself under his eyelid.

He recalled dragging himself through the driving rain and the chafing of the weight on his back, exhausted, slashing the grass that formed walls ahead of them. He recalled how they used to pool their rations, he, Angus and Max, and make a half-decent meal out of Australian bully beef and American dehydrated chile rations and rice. He remembered how you'd had to dig a scrape and shit in front of whoever was on the machine-gun, the sudden firefights that had happened even if you were in the middle of having a shit, and the instinctive dive into mud; or if you were on patrol and fully loaded when you dived, how the weight of the pack would almost knock you out as it slammed into the back of your head as you hit the ground.

When the artillery was called in by the signaller and their own shelling started, Harry would lie low until it was quiet again, not wanting to die in friendly fire, being bounced off the ground by the reverberation of the shells when they hit. He remembered the screams for a medic in the sudden, shocking silence once the firing had ceased, then the automatic defence formation they would make around the medic and the badly wounded man; the constant strain of never knowing what had happened until after it had stopped happening; the way he would attempt to piece the story together, working it out, step-by-step.

The scent of the beads of red resin that bled through the bark of the leatherjacket brought him back to the present and he wondered why he was going over this old, dangerous ground again. Why this, suddenly and now? Then he came to see that squatting here, keeping an eye on the rim of the cliff, was stimulating his memories of the abandoned bunker systems he and the black labrador had sometimes entered, following the trail of a wounded enemy soldier. The VC soldiers were aggressive, brave and formidable enemies who were able to move at what seemed an unbelievable pace despite their squatting stance, like martial arts experts, firing all the while. He thought of the afternoon they'd suddenly come upon a group of five heavily loaded men and a woman and their group had cut down the woman and four of the men. Then Harry had taken the black dog and followed the trail of the wounded man he'd seen staggering into the buffalo grass. He remembered finding him almost at the same moment as the dog, nearly walking on top of him. Seeing how things were with the VC soldier, it was not in Harry to take any further action. He and the dog had simply waited for the enemy soldier to die. All the man's attention and remaining energy were being expended in trying to breathe, despite the huge leaking hole in his chest. It bubbled and sucked as his ribcage heaved with effort. Harry and the dog waited. The man's exhausted eyes flickered up to Harry's face. The fingers of his right hand moved. Was it a last desperate search for a weapon? An attempt to speak? The bubbling breath went out in a long sigh from which there was no return. As the face of the enemy soldier had stilled in death, Harry had felt something happen in his own mind. In that moment, Harry had felt that he had no idea about what he was doing, or even who he was. It was like some huge weird turn of the entire universe, with this event at its centre, so that he thought that nothing would ever be the same for him or for the world again.

He remembered trying to write about this to Janette – about this man's death and what an important event it had been for him. It was as if a light had flashed on somewhere in his mind while the VC soldier died, had shone briefly so that in that space of time he'd suddenly understood everything, then as suddenly the light had gone out again, leaving him once again in the dark – in the stinking mess of an abandoned bunker in a war zone in an alien land. 'Weapons,' his instructor had told him, 'are designed especially to be used against the three targets: armoured vehicles, aircraft and people in green baggy skins who hide.' He had found himself thinking of the weapons' designers and manufacturers safe in their engineering shops in the civilised countries of Europe, designing and making these things, going home to luxury houses, luxury women and unmaimed children. He had wondered if they ever considered the works of their hands. Harry had prayed there was a special place in hell for arms' manufacturers. But he couldn't talk about things like these; not with anyone, far less a woman. It had not been possible to write about these things to her and the tone of his letters had always been false and superficial, as if he hadn't wanted her to know what things were really like over there. He'd found her letters the same. The rain had spoiled a picnic at Nielsen Park, she'd write. She'd been getting hassled by people who were anti-war, so she'd stopped saying where her husband was. She'd just say he was away working.

He thought of the two days' steady drinking in the bars of Vung Tau, and the bar girls, and the way the adrenalin-charged shivering of excited terror was merely replaced with the tremor of drunkenness. There was no relief from the feelings engendered by their daily combat activities; no outlet for the fear, the horror, the perverse, awful things that happened day-by-day. Or the equally terror-filled days and nights out on patrol in which often nothing happened, but anything could. And these two terrors operated all the time, month after month. There was no release. No relief. Men used tranquillisers and alcohol, pushing the horror down further into their bodies and minds. Some men became walking time bombs. Almost all stopped caring. The questions went through Harry's mind and tormented him. Am I going to be able to handle the next contact? Will I panic? Will I disgrace myself in my own eyes and the eyes of my comrades?

Please don't let me fall to pieces, he remembered praying to the nothingness.

He remembered shy Max Wolansky and the way he treated the bar girls as if they were his mates' sisters back home. He remembered his first shock on discovering the cruelty in Angus and the way he mistreated the women, buying them and abusing them. And further, the shock of the day Harry had discovered Angus reading Janette's letters. 'They should be for me, these letters,' he had said as Harry snatched them away from him. And that's how Harry had discovered that Angus had been in love with Janette – the accusations of treachery, charging Harry with betrayal; the fist fight in the bar that followed as Angus's seething resentment finally broke out. 'You've taken everything away from me, Harry Doyle, you bastard. You've taken my woman from me.' And Angus pulling a knife and being dragged off him by Max and the others.

He remembered the only other time Angus had spoken to him after that, just before they were flown back to Sydney. Angus looked up from a book of Roman history he was reading as their company waited for the transport to arrive. 'Do you know what the Romans did to traitors?' he asked, looking around at everyone except Harry. 'They put them in a sack with a dog and a snake and threw them over a cliff.'

After they'd come back to Sydney, Harry had never seen Angus again.

Was it the loss of his boyhood friend and not just the crazy hell of combat in Vietnam that had changed him into the closed-up man he had become? Or did his secret, closed-up self come from an earlier time, from the terrible days when the government agent had searched the place for him and found him covered by a blanket under the bed, and had driven him away screaming with his mother running along behind the car, sobbing and calling his name and falling further and further back along the road until the dust hid her from his terrified eyes? They were cruel days and nights in the institution for children like him. He recalled the brutality, the lack of love. No wonder he had withheld himself from both women and men all his life. He'd increased the barrier between himself and Janette when he'd come home from Vietnam. He didn't tell her about the terrible enmity that now existed between himself and his childhood friend. He couldn't bring himself to think about the appalling thing Angus had done, let alone talk to anyone about it. He couldn't tell her about the moment when he'd seen one of his mates cutting down a tree, the axe slipping accidentally and hitting the ground so that a hidden Claymore mine was detonated. Seeing a man you'd just shared a joke with disintegrate, right before your eyes, in a three-metre blaze of flame, earth, vegetation and nails is something that is hard to forget. Claymore mines are very good at their work. Weapons that maim are as highly regarded in warfare, he had learned, as weapons that kill. One dead man is one dead man. But a maimed man is very bad for morale. He screams. He is mutilated. He is hideously obvious. He strikes fear, terror and horror in the hearts of other soldiers. And best of all, he requires another two men to carry him out of the arena. Three men are no longer available for the fighting. Helicopters have to be called in; fighting is interrupted; the patrol's whereabouts pinpointed.

I have good reason to be silent, Harry thought. How many men have stood and waited for another man to die and looked into his eyes? How many men have shot someone and then had to sit with him, as I had to do with Franco, till the ambulance came? Then there were the disbelieving questions while the Physical Evidence people photographed and videoed his dead informant and the bloodstained hall, the cordless drill and the fallen stepladder. It will take a very big explosion, he thought, to blow the safe of my mind.

I *know* I should be more open with Meg, he thought, but knowing something and knowing how to actually carry it out are two very different tracks. Harry realised he'd been holding his breath, and exhaled. He allowed his mind automatically to begin processing information about the case in hand, blotting out the memories of the war and the death of Franco. The facts were that he was hunting a killer who was well presented, intelligent; a killer, whom he believed, despite Ayoub's scepticism, had killed three different kinds of women in three different kinds of ways; a killer who was contained and controlled enough to fly aircraft and study navigation; who had smashed a woman's face to pulp; who, despite the risk of being discovered, had held on to the weapon he'd killed with, only to come back, a mere river-crossing from the scene of his crime, to dump the bloody thing; a killer who had a strange acidic odour that Harry remembered from somewhere but couldn't place; who contaminated crime scenes with Victorian rose-coloured glass. A killer with combat experience, and who used an unusual handgun favoured by the communist forces in Vietnam just to tease interest; who had visited his ex-girlfriend in the country and had made himself familiar with the local countryside; who had known all the time about this sudden precipice and its underhang, and of how he might use this to his advantage. A killer to whom Harry was in some way linked, through a murdered ex-wife and a boyhood 'auntie'.

Harry shivered again, because something was starting to come together hazily in his mind. No, it couldn't be, his brain said. It couldn't be that. He wouldn't do that. But his mind kept up its relentless processing and suggesting. His scalp started crawling as the information unscrambled itself and started to fall into an orderly pattern. And then the memory of Angus raping the dying woman in the jungle rose up like a hideous ghost, and the horror of his erstwhile friend's action and of the whole war seemed to explode into an idea about the identity of the person he was following, so grotesque that it shocked him into making a funny little sound out loud, like a sob. He remembered the time he'd wet his pants near Nui Dat when something jumped out of the jungle at him. Because chill fear poured like dark smoke through his heart. A killer who might deliberately lay a trail for someone pursuing. A killer who knew the pursuer would be Harry Doyle. A killer who wants to take me away from my base and separate me from backup. And in that terrible moment, Harry Doyle knew who it was; knew who he was up against. Oh Jesus, he almost whispered, while the universe yawed sickeningly. Oh Jesus no.

In the same moment he saw how he'd been manipulated by someone who knew exactly how to send out mixed signals; first this, then that, knowing that any intelligent investigator would be fatally intrigued and fascinated, would be drawn in even closer. He tore the mobile off his belt and switched it on, yanking the aerial out. 'No service,' he read.

A bitter scent touched his senses. He swung around, heard Razor bark suddenly in alarm and went for his weapon. But it was too late. Something crashed down on his head. The day stopped.

THIRTEEN

Nine p.m.

The mobile phone you are ringing has been switched off or is out of range . . . Meg slammed the unit down on the counter again. 'He's still off somewhere being a hero while his daughter goes missing,' she screamed. Then she turned to Dell who stood helplessly near the window. 'Where is she? Where is my child?'

Dell remained silent. Earlier, she'd gone into town with Meg, who'd wanted to get moving and had insisted, late in the day though it was, on talking to Jim Coates in person. It'd given her something to do, something to focus on that seemed helpful. Now, there was just this waiting. Every friend had been contacted, every conceivable person and place where Hannah might have just possibly – no, *im*possibly, because she was always loathe to leave the dogs, even for a night – decided to sleep over. Alison was still walled up in her room, refusing to come out, refusing to talk to anyone. Dell ran between her household and Meg's next door, fielding the phone, calling people who might be helpful and trying to comfort her inconsolable friend.

'Where can she be? Who's got her?' Meg whirled around the room, unable to be still, the agitation and the frustration building until she was almost demented. 'What's happened to her?'

'Listen to me,' Dell finally said. 'These questions are not helpful. We can't know any of this. You're only torturing yourself asking questions like that.'

The phone rang and Meg pounced on it. It was Kathy Gore, mother of Celia, Hannah's best friend at school. 'Celia wants to tell you something,' Mrs Gore said.

'I'll put her on.'

'Mrs Doyle?'

'Yes, Celia. What do you want to tell me?'

'Well, see, Hannah was teasing me and I knew she was going to do something because she said she would have some very big news to tell me on Friday. And I begged her and begged her but she wouldn't tell me anything else. She said I'd have to wait but she gave me a clue.'

'What was that?' Meg's heart jumped.

'She said "CQ". That's all she would say. She wouldn't tell me anymore because she said it'd give it away.'

Meg thanked Celia and hung up. She turned to Dell. '"CQ",' she said. 'That's what Hannah told her.'

'Are they someone's initials?' Dell asked.

'Celia didn't know.' She thought. 'We don't know anyone with a surname starting with "Q".'

Meg went into Hannah's room for the twentieth time. She looked through books and boxes of papers and toys. She opened drawers and looked at their contents again.

'She never intended going to school,' she had told Jim Coates. 'She must have taken her dog t-shirt and her earrings in her school bag, because they're missing from her room. She's planned this all the time. But where would she go by herself like that?'

'Maybe she made a plan with a friend,' Jim had said. 'At

her age, they like to have secrets and plan things together. Tomorrow we'll check with the local schools. She may have made friends with someone from another school – on the bus or at the local shops. It happens.'

Meg had rung Hannah's class teacher, Miss Webb. 'Yes,' said Miss Webb, 'there were three children absent from the roll today: Hannah, Debbie Lahood and Matthew Shapiro.' It didn't take Meg long to track them down. But both children had been at home sick all day, according to their mothers; nor did they know anything about Hannah.

Now she waited with Dell. Jack sat cross-legged on the floor, watching television, occasionally turning to look at his mother and her friend with wide, worried eyes.

'There must be something I can do,' Meg said, wiping silent tears away. 'I can't stand this sitting around while my little girl's missing. Where could she have gone? Why didn't she go to school?'

Jack turned around to look at her. 'Auntie Meg,' he said.

'Yes?' Meg said, hardly noticing the voice of the child who was not hers.

'Hannah must have been going to meet someone. She only wore her earrings when she was going somewhere really special.'

Meg looked at him. His serious ten-year-old face was intent on her. 'That's right, Jack,' she said. 'Someone. Someone special.'

'And,' said Jack, 'she must have been meaning to come home at the ordinary time.'

'Why do you say that?' asked his mother.

'Because,' said Jack, 'she told me we'd go to the shops when she got home from school and she was laughing. And I think she was laughing because she knew she really wasn't going to school at all.'

'So maybe she's just got lost,' said Meg. 'Maybe she went somewhere and she got lost.' But the tears welled up out of her eyes and spilled down her cheeks. 'But who? Who would she go with? She knows the rules so well.' Meg noticed that Jack's eyes had shifted from her and were now looking at a point just past her. She turned around to see her older daughter, ghastly pale, standing in the doorway.

Despite her fear and grief, she was appalled at the sight of Alison's suffering. She stood up and went slowly towards her. Alison's eyes were red from crying and her face was splotched and swollen. Meg could still see the angry red mark her hand had made on her daughter's face.

'Mum,' Alison whispered, 'I'm sorry. I didn't know.'

Meg threw her arms around her daughter. 'No, I'm sorry,' she told her, and they stood together, each trying to comfort the other.

'I didn't go to school either,' Ali said. 'I didn't think Hannah knew. I didn't think she'd copy me. It's my fault.'

'Who?' demanded her mother, not hearing her. 'Who do you think she'd go with?'

Alison shook her head. 'I don't know. She didn't tell me.' Then she left the room and Meg could hear her moving things around in Hannah's room. Then she crossed the hallway to her own room and returned with the fat, pink diary with a locked golden clasp. 'I think you should look in here,' she said. 'Hannah used to often write in this.'

Meg slowly took the book from her older daughter's hand. She'd forgotten about the pink diary. 'Where was this?' she asked Alison.

'In my room,' said her daughter. 'Hanks asked me to mind it in my locked box. She was scared you'd read it.'

'Why?' Meg's voice was nearly a scream. 'What was in it?'

'You know,' said Alison uncomfortably, 'kids' stuff about life and parents.'

'Did you read it?' asked her mother. Alison shrugged and started crying again. Her sobs became uncontrollable and Meg found herself to be unaccountably angry, wanting to shake her to stop. '*Why?*' she said. 'What's in it?' But Alison kept shaking her head. The pink diary seemed to be burning Meg's hands, until she looked down at it and saw that she was crushing her fingers against it in a compulsive grip that was hurting her.

Alison's sobbing subsided. 'It was so . . .' she stammered '. . . so *innocent.*'

Meg started tearing at the book, cutting another one of her fingers on the unfinished metal of the now-broken lock so that blood smeared the false gold. She opened it and sat down to read it. She started with today's page, but there was nothing written on it.

She turned back to the previous day. Nothing there, either. She flipped through until she came to a section towards the front. She started reading it.

I hate it when they fight. I hate it when they don't speak to each other. I just want them to love each other. I wish they wouldn't fight. I wish Mum wouldn't be so horrible to Dad always nagging him. As she continued reading it, her heart almost broke. But she forced herself to keep going. *I hate it when she is always so angry with him and with the dogs too. It is not their fault because they are only dogs and they can't help being police dogs and Dad can't help being out all the time and working with the dogs.*

Meg closed her eyes and pressed the book against her body, rocking with sorrow. Please, darling Hannah, she prayed. Please be safe. Please come home and be safe and I promise I will never be horrible to anyone ever again. 'Would you take this,' she whispered to Dell. 'I can't bear to read it just now. Just tell me if there's anything that might be helpful.'

'There isn't,' said Alison. 'I already went right through it. She only wrote in it for a few months after her birthday. Then it just stops.'

Dell quickly went through it, turning the pages until she'd finished. She closed it.

'It's mostly about the dogs,' she said. 'Mostly family stuff. You know, personal.'

Meg clutched the diary again. Jack had crept up closer to the television screen until his nose was almost against the glass. His silhouette was outlined against an American sitcom.

'The other night, when you and Dad were . . . um . . . arguing with each other,' Alison began, 'she came into my bed.' Alison glanced across at Dell and then at her mother as if to check whether this was allowed, under the circumstances. It was, so she continued. 'She said something about when I moved into my flat.'

'What?' said Meg.

Alison looked helpless. 'We often used to talk about how she could come and live with me.'

'Live with you?' Meg's eyes widened. 'Hannah wanted to go and live with you?'

'What I'm trying to tell you,' said her daughter, 'is that she asked could she bring her friend to visit. I think she said his name. I think it was Richard.'

There was a profound silence, broken by stilted, canned American laughter from the television. Into this whole new world that Meg knew nothing about, a world where children made plans she knew nothing about, where they wrote down their pain but couldn't tell her, was now another unknown – a stranger called Richard.

'Who is he?' Meg said. 'Richard who?'

'I don't know. She only said Richard.'

Meg cast around in her memory. 'We don't know a Richard.'

There was another silence. 'She did,' said Alison.

It was a terrible night. Meg wandered around making cups of tea that she couldn't drink, and even after taking the sedatives that Dell pressed on her, she only dozed for a couple of hours after two in the morning. Alison kept waking and walking round the house. Meg tried ringing Harry over and over, until she became almost hysterical and Dell had practically confiscated the mobile. Dell and Jack stayed overnight, snuggled together on the double airbed in the lounge room, and there was a second or two in the early morning when Meg looked at her sleeping friend and her safe ten-year-old son and found herself hating them. All night she'd been thinking of someone called Richard.

She rang Jim Coates at six, knowing that he'd be at his desk.

'It's something,' he said, noting the name. 'We'll ask around the schools again. You never know.'

At seven, Alison came out. 'Mum,' she said, putting her arms around her mother, 'I'm going to help you find her. I'm going to ask everyone she knows in the world about this Richard.' Meg tightened her hold. She couldn't speak for fear of the uncontrollable sobbing she could feel at the back of her throat, threatening to explode. She just kept nodding and blinking. She picked up the phone and dialled a number she didn't ring very often.

'Dad?' she said when he answered. As decently and briefly as she could, she told her father the news and promised she'd keep him informed. She imagined him going into his shed and mixing up some more paint and painting the already immaculate fence yet again. Or going round pruning bushes that were already perfectly shaped. No wonder I married another man who doesn't say anything. The thought of Max jumped into her mind, hurting with a series of 'if only's as the thoughts ran away with her. If only I'd decided to take Hannah and go to his place, she'd be safe now. Or if only I'd decided to move out and spend some time on my own in a flat or unit. Hannah would be safe now and none of this nightmare would be happening.

Dell and Jack had gone back to their place for showers and breakfast and the house was horribly empty without Hannah there in the morning. Blade kept going into her room and tracking her smell round the house.

'Why didn't we track her?' said Alison. 'Get one of Dad's mates? We should have done that yesterday. Maybe we would have found out what bus she went on.'

Alison grabbed Blade's harness and he sat still while she put it on. Then they ran down the hall together, out the front door, out the front gate, Blade's nose on the ground and his hindquarters the way he slung them when he was hard on a hit.

Outside, he went up and down the street, up to the bus stop, past it, taking Alison with him, until he'd reached the stop across the road where the city bus left. His hindquarters straightened. He stood up and looked around, then dropped his nose once more. But he'd lost it.

Alison took him home. 'Blade says she went on the city bus yesterday,' she told her mother. 'The city bus,' was all she could say.

Late in the morning, Alison made them some toast and tea and sat at the table, watching her mother staring at the telephone. When it rang, Meg nearly knocked it to the floor.

'Harry?' she said. But it was Jim Coates.

'I think you should come into the city,' he said. 'I want to talk to you. A woman's coming in this morning who thinks she might have seen Hannah yesterday.'

'Where?'

'At Circular Quay. She's coming in to look at the photograph. You should be present. Eleven-thirty. Have you heard anything from Harry?'

'Harry? No, I haven't heard anything from Harry. He's not here. He's never here.' There was a silence at the other end of the line and Meg allowed her angry breathing to subside. 'Eleven-thirty,' she said. 'I'll be there.'

Meg and Alison took the lift to Jim Coates' office. Jim was waiting as the doors opened, and escorted them with his security card through the various doors until they reached his section. In a bag, Meg had brought some of Hannah's clothes, a pair of shorts almost identical to the pair she'd been wearing the day before and Alison's t-shirt with the dog print on it, exactly the same as Hannah's, except for size. Hannah, Meg prayed. You must be all right. You must be safe. You must be. And she willed her strength through the world to wherever her daughter was.

When they got to his room, Jim took the bag of clothes, put his arm round Meg in an avuncular gesture and ushered her and Alison in to where there was a woman already sitting. Fortyish, soft ginger hair and a pair of white plastic earrings. Meg's eyes fixed on the upside down photo of Hannah lying on the desk. 'Meg, this is Maureen Mackie. This is Meg Doyle, Maureen. And her elder daughter, Alison.'

'I'm so sorry,' said Maureen Mackie. 'It's terrible about your little girl.' She looked at Jim. 'I've told him what I can remember.'

Meg stared at the woman. She was trying not to scream out *Tell me. Tell me what you know. Tell me right now.*

'Tell us,' Jim invited in his gentle tone. 'Tell us what happened.'

'Like I said to you,' Maureen Mackie said, 'I was waiting for the bus and I noticed this little girl—' she nodded towards the photo '—standing waiting. I thought, why isn't she at school because she looks the same age as my Sarah. I'd just missed the bus so I had to wait twenty minutes. The little girl kept looking out for someone. You know how you can tell when someone's waiting for someone. Anyway, I saw her looking at any kid that went by and thought, maybe she's waiting for a brother or sister and I stopped even thinking about it until this man came up to her.'

'A man?' Meg's voice was barely audible.

'And he says, "I'm Richard's father and you're both in a lot of trouble." That's exactly what he said. Then he went on to say that she had to come with him and he was going to take her home to her father and she'd be in trouble for wagging school.'

'What happened then?' Meg's voice, again barely there.

'She started crying and she went away with him.'

Meg could contain herself no longer. She'd been sitting on one of the other chairs, next to Jim's desk, but at these words she collapsed onto the desk and the sobs ripped out of her. All she could say was her daughter's name, over and over, broken by the terrible sobs. Alison knelt beside her, holding her, rocking herself in her own pain. 'Oh Mum, please. Please. Please, Mum.'

Jim stood up and ushered Maureen Mackie out of the room, closing the door behind her, coming back to wait patiently, pulling a box of tissues out of his drawer, no stranger to despairing tears. He didn't have to wait long.

Meg blew her nose vigorously, wiped her eyes and sat up straight.

'Sorry,' she said.

'You don't have to be sorry,' said Jim. He went to the door and called out to someone to do him a favour and bring in three cups of tea.

'We got a reasonable description of the man. It's gone out everywhere.' He looked at Meg then at Alison. 'Why isn't Harry here?' he asked.

Meg lowered her head and was silent a moment. Then she raised her eyes to Jim. 'He's gone out bush for a couple of days. I've tried phoning him. He's out of range.'

Jim turned to Alison. 'Alison, would you mind leaving us alone for a minute? I want to talk to your mother in private.'

Alison stared at him and then at her mother. 'Why?' she said. 'Why shouldn't I hear what you're going to say? Hannah is my *sister*.'

'What I'm going to say isn't about Hannah,' said Jim. 'It's . . .' He stopped and spread his hands on the desk. A young clerk came in with three styrofoam cups in a box trailing tea bag strings, together with a container of milk and packets of sugar. 'It's personal. That's all,' Jim said.

'What?' Meg said. 'What is it?'

Jim got up and went over to close the door behind Alison. 'Meg. You should know that Harry's missing. The Bathurst police found his wagon early this morning but there's no trace of him – or the dog.'

'*What?*' Her voice was a stifled scream. Jim sighed and sat down. Behind him, one of the pigeons' heads bobbed along the ledge outside, above the makeshift modesty board of cardboard.

Meg's mind wobbled. She tried to fit this in somewhere but

there was too much distress concerning Hannah. She shook her head. 'What are you telling me? It's Hannah who's gone missing, not Harry. Am I going crazy or are you?'

Jim was patient. 'Meg. Listen. Harry's wagon turned up outside Bathurst. We don't know where he is. The local cops searched the area around the vehicle. There's some very dangerous, cliffy terrain and he may have fallen. He may be injured or worse. Or something else.'

'What do you mean "or something else"?' Meg heard an odd tone in her own voice that sounded unfamiliar.

'With your daughter going missing at the same time, there could be a tie-in. Do you see what I mean?'

Meg was still unable to respond. Hannah. Harry. What was happening? She tried to fit the two things together. 'Are you trying to say that Harry has something to do with Hannah going missing?'

Jim stood up and walked over to the window. The female pigeon was brooding on the nest and the male sat dozing further down the ledge, the surface of which was covered in bird shit and embedded feathers that fluttered in the breeze. 'What we've got to look at is whether the two disappearances are linked in some way.'

Meg's voice was at first angry. 'Why would Harry want to take Hannah when he's got her all the time? It doesn't make sense.' Then contemptuous. 'He's out with that dog. He's not missing. He's out doing some hero routine. How can a man with a *goddamn police tracker dog be missing?*' Her mind was spinning. The hysterical edge to her voice had shocked her.

'Are you all right?' she heard Jim say from a long way away as she stared sightlessly at the metallic sky behind the pigeons, dazed with pain.

'No,' she said softly through the darkness that pressed

around her, 'I'm not all right. The only thing I care about right this moment is getting my daughter back safely. Damn Harry Doyle.'

Then she burst into tears again and Jim Coates put his arms around her and held her. Alison opened the door suddenly and Meg turned to her. 'Ali,' she said, and her daughter ran to her.

'What was the private conversation about?' Alison asked her on the way home. Meg stared straight ahead, driving the car through the traffic. 'Your father,' she said steadily. 'He's missing. According to Jim.'

Ali's clear grey eyes looked straight into hers. 'No he's not. Hannah is missing. Dad is out in the bush with Razor.'

'That's what I told them.'

'Mum,' wailed Alison, sounding like a little girl again, 'what are we going to do?'

When they arrived home, Dell had made a late lunch for them but neither Meg nor Alison could eat. The three of them sat, mostly in silence, waiting for the long afternoon to be over. Outside, the world was filled with the ordinary late-afternoon noises of the bus changing gears down the road to negotiate the corner, the everyday suburban sounds of children playing and arguing in the playground near the bus stop, the familiar afternoon calling of local birds before they become silent as the twilight deepens. But inside Meg's head, turmoil and confusion whirled. Maybe Harry *had* taken Hannah, as Jim suggested, in some psychotic state. It happened, she knew, but it still wasn't credible. Parents don't kidnap their own children when they live with them every day.

She rang Jim Coates. 'There's no way,' she said to him over the phone, private in Harry's study, 'that Harry has anything to do with Hannah going missing. Why would he take his own child? He just wouldn't do that. I know Harry.'

Jim didn't say anything, just let the silence itself echo her words until Meg felt the shame herself. She didn't know Harry just as she didn't know Max. Just as she didn't even know herself.

On the television news, Meg could hardly bear to see the mockup model of Hannah that the police had set up in the bus shelter at Circular Quay and the curious passers-by who variously stared at it or ignored it altogether. *Police are following several leads*, the newsreader said, looking up conspiratorially.

'What leads, you damn fool!' Meg yelled and got up and switched it off.

'"C.Q." is Circular Quay,' she said, as it dawned. 'Hannah had arranged to meet Richard at Circular Quay. She wasn't lured away. It was all set up.'

FOURTEEN

The phone rang and Meg knocked it to the floor in her eagerness to snatch it up.

'Yes?' she said.

'Watch the television,' came the thin voice. 'You'll see her. The Archons told me.'

'Who told you what? Who will I see? What are you talking about? Tell me! Answer me! Hello? Hello?' She slammed the phone down again.

'Who was that?' Ali asked.

'Some damn lunatic,' said her mother, 'who rings Harry up all the time and confesses to everything. He told me to watch the television.'

Alison jumped up. 'Mum, he might know something,' she said. 'What else did he say?'

'Just rubbish,' said Meg. 'He's a paranoid schizophrenic. Delusions, obsessions. I can't deal with him at this stage.'

'But maybe he knows something,' said Alison, grabbing at a straw.

Her mother's look was enough, although Meg went on to explain. 'They're part of every police force. Crazies and weirdos who either confess to everything or offer to give assistance.'

Alison jumped up. 'I can't stand this just sitting around when I could be doing something,' she said. 'I'm going out.' She longed to see the man she was in love with and ask him what to do, until she suddenly remembered that Mick had a brother called Richard and her mouth went dry. She sat down again, weak in the legs.

Meg looked at her pale daughter. Her family had been halved. Now there is only Ali and me, she thought.

'Mum?' Alison's voice interrupted her. 'I know a Richard. He's at school. He's . . . he's . . .' She was about to say something more, but there was too much of a charge around the words, so she let her voice taper off.

'We'll have to tell Jim,' said Meg. 'I'll ring him now. What do you know about this Richard?'

Meg and Jim stood on the doorstep together. 'Just don't say anything,' said Jim. 'I'll introduce you and that's it. Let them make any assumptions they want to.'

He rang the doorbell.

Mrs Blunt, in white shorts and tennis shoes, answered the door. 'Yes?' she said, hesitantly, looking from one to the other as Jim introduced himself and Meg and showed his warrant card. Mrs Blunt was a pretty woman with a tanned face, bright blue eyes and soft, fawn-gold hair.

'We'd like to have a chat with you, Mrs Blunt and maybe talk to your son Richard.'

'Why?' she said, frowning and alarmed. 'Is something wrong?' But she ushered them into the comfortable house with picture rails and floral carpet and a wipe-over satin-finish lounge suite in gold.

'We're looking for anyone who might be able to help us with our inquiries into the disappearance of Hannah Doyle.'

Mrs Blunt nodded. It was clear she knew about Hannah.

Meg's heart missed a beat at the formal sound of her child's full name. Most people in Australia know that name now, Meg thought, and her eyes brimmed with tears.

'We believe,' Jim continued, 'that your son Richard might be able to assist us. Could we speak to him?'

Mrs Blunt looked scared. 'What could my Rick have to do with that? What do you mean "assist"?' But she turned and called out, 'Rick? Could you come here a minute?'

Richard Blunt came into the room and Meg stared at him. Is it you? she wondered to herself. Are you Hannah's friend?

Richard Blunt was a podgy sixteen-year-old whose brown eyes slid away from any eyes that attempted to engage them. It was an odd trick he had, Meg thought, of moving his eyes almost into contact, but then slipping away, in a wave-like motion. It was, Meg knew from her own work, the behaviour of a shamed child.

Jim went through the introductions again and Richard sat beside his mother whose tanned legs were primly placed straight together.

'Do you know Hannah Doyle?'

Richard nodded.

'How do you know her?'

'From the school bus,' said Richard. 'She's one of the little kids. She's got an older sister, Alison.'

'That's right,' said Jim, glancing to see if Meg was handling this all right.

'And how well do you know her?'

Richard shrugged. He looked up at Meg then at Jim.

'Answer Mr Coates,' said Mrs Blunt, and Meg could hear the hidden tears in the woman's voice.

'She's just a little kid that goes to the primary school. What do you mean?'

'So there's no special friendship between you?' Meg couldn't help asking, and Richard Blunt shook his head. Meg couldn't decide if he was just very uncomfortable at being questioned, or if he was lying. There was something else going on in the boy's mind, she guessed. But he seemed genuinely perplexed by the questions.

Mrs Blunt stood up and left the room for a minute. When she came back, she was crying. She held out a little plastic wallet and key ring in front of her. She couldn't look at her son. 'I found this,' she said, handing the wallet to Jim, 'in Ricky's room yesterday. I didn't know what to do. Ricky, tell me. Tell me how you got this.'

Meg's heart contracted. She tried to swallow but her mouth had dried up. Jim studied the plastic wallet and then handed it over to her. It was Hannah's: a key ring at the end of a clear plastic container in which Hannah had a photograph of herself and Razor. Meg looked at the podgy youth with the bad skin. She flew at him. But before she could grab him, Jim had firmly restrained her. 'What have you done with her?' she screamed at Richard.

The youth shrank back, even more pallid. 'I didn't do anything. I just found this and some money in Mick's car. I just found it. I never saw Hannah, I swear.'

'Who's Mick?' Jim wanted to know. Richard looked at his mother then at Meg. Then he looked at Jim.

'Mick is my other son,' said Mrs Blunt. 'Richard washes his older brother's car sometimes for pocket money.' She looked more closely at Meg. 'Who are you?'

'Tell us,' Jim repeated, still holding Meg firmly. 'Tell us where we can find Mick.'

Richard indicated Meg with a half-lifted hand, but didn't address her directly. 'Her other daughter,' he said of Meg. 'Her other daughter's going out with him.'

'But Mick's married.' Mrs Blunt looked as if she were about to burst into tears. 'He can't be going out with anyone. Sally and him, they've got a lovely little baby. They're happy together.'

Richard looked defiant. 'He meets her down at the pub. They go to a mate's place. Sally doesn't know. Nobody knows. Except me. And now you do.' Mrs Blunt sat down suddenly.

'What do you mean? My other daughter?' said Meg, not taking it in properly, focused only on Hannah.

'I need your older son's address,' Jim said and wrote it down. Then he turned to Meg. 'I'm taking you home now,' he said to her. He made a call to the detectives who were investigating Hannah's disappearance. They would arrive at Mrs Blunt's house within minutes, he was told. 'In the meantime,' he told Mrs Blunt, 'get your other son over here to wait for them. It will be less embarrassing for him than if we go to his house. We need to know how he came by this.' He slipped the key ring photograph into an envelope and put it in his pocket.

In the car, Meg sat trembling in the passenger seat. 'I shouldn't have taken you with me,' said Jim. 'It was completely out of order.'

'Everything's out of order,' she said. 'Everything's rotten. I can't bear how it is. I wish I was dead.' She felt dead, she thought, except for the great gaping hole where her daughter was missing. She cried and rocked herself.

'Don't you dare speak like that,' she heard Jim's angry voice. His strong arm pulled her towards him. She could feel his fingers digging into the muscles of her upper arm. 'We *need* you. We all need you. We've got to find out who's got Hannah. With Harry missing in action at the moment you're all we've got. So for your little girl's sake, no more talk like that.' He released his rough hold on her and Meg sat up. She found she was shivering despite the heat. The cold she was feeling came from her heart.

Alison and Meg sat at the kitchen table. Blade curled in the corner, pulling his head in tight, like a reined-in horse, to lick his chest. He turned to attack a flea on his back, pulling his nose back in wrinkles to bite it.

'Stop that snuffling!' Meg screamed at him, and Alison put her hand gently on her mother's arm. Blade suddenly barked and ran out of the kitchen down the hall, skidding in his greeting of someone he knew. Meg ran after him and opened the front door. But her heart sank again as Jim Coates, who had pulled up outside, shook his head, indicating he had nothing positive to tell her. She stepped back to let him in and followed him down the hall to the kitchen. 'I've just come from talking to Mick Blunt,' he said and looked at Alison, who had gone bright red. 'Do you want to tell your mother what's going on with you?'

Alison froze, looking from one to the other, then she slowly nodded.

'Tell me what?'

'Mick Blunt,' said Alison. 'Um. Mick is . . . he's, well, he's my boyfriend.'

'Do you mean you're having sex with him?' Meg said finally. 'A married man?'

Her daughter nodded.

'Oh,' said Meg.

'He says you dropped your bag in his car last time you were together and everything spilled out,' said Jim.

'Yes,' said Alison, remembering, 'that's true.' She remembered too how Mick hadn't been able to get rid of her quickly enough that time. Now she felt completely ashamed.

'Alison,' said Jim quickly. 'Do you have anything to do with Hannah's disappearance?'

The shocked silence that met his words and Meg's and Alison's stricken faces made Jim wish for a moment that he had never been in the job. Alison's face had gone from red to white. 'Of course I don't!' she screamed. 'She's my little sister.'

'Jim, what are you saying?' Meg said, grabbing his arm. 'It's not like that with those two. It's never been like that.' She hugged her sobbing daughter in her arms, kissing her hair, soothing her. 'It's okay, darling. It's okay.'

'Sometimes I have to ask real bastard questions. It's my job.' Alison's outraged response was exactly what he'd have expected from a loving sister. 'We've got to cover every possibility. Are you okay, Alison?'

Angry eyes glanced momentarily into his, and he walked over to the window, turning towards the two women, leaning against the sill. 'I don't think Richard Blunt's got anything to do with this. I think he just held on to the key ring because it's a handy thing to have. His room was full of the usual stuff that horny sixteen-year-old boys are interested in. Big, busty women. Not little girls. He's not the Richard we need to find.'

'But why would you have had Hannah's key ring?'

Alison shrugged. 'I don't know. Our stuff gets mixed up sometimes. I might have used her keys ages ago and kept them ever since. She can always get in using Dell's if she gets home and no-one's here.' Then she started to cry again. Meg moved towards her and they embraced, brought together by their common need. 'I'm so sorry, Mum,' sobbed Alison.

'Me too,' said her mother.

Alison struggled to find a tissue. 'Here,' said Gentleman Jim, 'use this.' And he proffered his big man's handkerchief.

'Why is it?' asked Meg, using the handkerchief after Alison, 'that men's handkerchiefs are huge and they never cry and women's handkerchiefs are tiny useless little scraps and we cry all the time?'

'Some men cry,' said Jim.

'Mum,' said Alison. 'Jim?'

They both looked at her. 'I know that crazy people ring you police all the time with advice and stuff, but I think we should tell you that Mum had a phone call from a fellow who rings Dad and wants to confess. He rang just when the bit about Hannah was on the Channel Nine news.'

Jim looked at Meg and she nodded, agreeing with Alison. 'If it's the one I think it is, I know him too,' said Jim. 'He took a shine to me years ago, then preferred Harry because Harry used to listen to him. I'll chase him up. It could mean something that he rang when that news item was on. It means he knows that Hannah is connected to Harry.' He made a note to himself on his notepad.

'And another thing,' said Alison. 'You've got to try the Internet. Hannah was always chatting on the chat lines,' she said. 'That's where you've got to look. That's where you'll find Richard.'

Meg looked at her and then at Jim who knew very little about the Internet.

'Great,' sighed Jim.

An hour later, slim, tanned, designer-dressed Travis from ADU Technology, looking very much at home despite the surroundings of an eight-year-old girl's bedroom, scrolled through the contents of Hannah's computer. Meg sat beside him, watching without comprehension as he manipulated data on the screen. Travis kept up a stream of consciousness chatter under his breath, with occasional verbal peaks breaking through. 'Yup,' he said from time to time in a colourless voice, tinted with American values. 'Okay, okay. Yup.' And his words would drop into the unvoiced and only his mouth would silently move. Jim sat on the other side of the monitor and Blade sat at the door, his head to one side, watching every move. Dell brought in cups of tea and Alison stretched out on Hannah's bed, pressing a big white bear to her face, crying into its fur.

'I should have talked to her more, done more things with her. She was my little sister.'

Meg looked over at her daughter, hidden behind the white bear. 'Ali, don't blame yourself. If anyone should have spent more time with Hanks, it was me. I'm her mother.'

'Give it a rest, girls,' said Jim, uneasy at the conversation and trying to concentrate on the fast-moving screen.

'Yup, yup,' chanted Travis. 'Here we go. Faves, faves, faves.' He seemed to speak a completely alien language in his all-purpose accented voice. Meg stared at his glossy hair and handsome tanned profile, unable to tell what nationality Travis was, nor whether he was straight or gay. His Ken-doll features were oddly unlived in as if, despite his beauty, he had no soul but was a self-invented presentation; gymmed, saunaed, buffed, dressed by advertisers, hair done by whoever was the most modish and expensive coiffeur. Beside him, Gentleman Jim looked a little rumpled and beautifully real. Meg wondered why she'd never noticed what a good-looking man Jim Coates was. Then immediately felt guilty that she could think such a thing at such a time.

'Meg,' said Jim, turning away from the screen, 'we are worried about Harry. We're treating his disappearance as suspicious.'

Meg stared at him. 'If you knew what things had been like round here,' she said, 'you'd know it isn't.'

'Isn't what?'

'Suspicious.'

'Yup, yup yup,' Travis interrupted in his soft little voice. 'Okay, and okay. I've got her bookmarks, you betcha.' Then he got the Chat Line entrance up on the screen and a cursor blinked in a window. Travis turned to the women. 'Does anyone know her password?'

Meg stared at him blankly. Alison shook her head.

'Does she have a nickname? Sometimes people just use a known nickname.'

'We sometimes call her Hankers, or Hanks,' said Alison, with tears breaking her voice. 'And Hanky-panky, sometimes. Panks, Pranks. She's had heaps of names. Dad used to call her "Joey" for awhile. And then when she started getting taller, "Roo".'

Travis started out. But each time the computer growled at him. 'Invalid password', the screen reprimanded.

'It's so typical that Harry's taken himself off at the time we really need him,' Meg said and blew her nose to hide the tears that threatened her.

Travis didn't miss a beat. 'Here we go,' he said. 'I tried different spellings and variations. Her password is "Hanx". And here's a list of the faves. We might find something here.' The computer showed that she'd only dipped into a few, favouring the Kids Chat over all others. 'Yup,' he said. 'Okay. The "Richard" person might well be on one of these. He could have told her during a chat that Richard was his real name, or they might always have chatted under nicknames. That's what people usually do.'

'I don't know what people usually do,' said Meg. 'I don't know what's happening.'

She wiped her eyes and stared at the screen. Travis had called up a column of names in a vertical box – Hannah's chat lines. 'Kids Chat, Cool Dudes, Play School, Baywatch,

K-9 Klub,' she read. She was aware of Ali and Jim also leaning forward to look. She stared harder.

'Hanx has joined Kids Chat,' the screen said as Travis entered the chat show. The line of chat moved quickly down the screen. Meg tried to read it but it was going too fast and made no sense, as other chatterers contributed. At the moment, it seemed Batto and Funster were swapping what looked like insults in chat-chic language, incomprehensible to newbies.

'There's no Richard here,' Meg heard herself say. 'There's no damn Richard here!'

Her voice rose to a scream. Ali grabbed her and hugged her, aware of the tension in her mother's body. 'What are we going to do now?' Meg was saying. 'There's no Richard here.'

'Does your daughter use e-mail?' Travis asked.

Meg looked at him. 'I don't know,' she said.

'She does, Mum,' said Alison. 'She e-mails Di and Abby in Adelaide.'

Meg suddenly had a surge of hopefulness. 'Maybe that's where she's gone. She loves Diane. She used to say that Di was her sister but they mixed the babies up in the hospital. She might be trying to get there right now.'

'Mum,' Ali's voice was gentle, 'Hannah wouldn't do that.'

'Yup, yup, yup. I'm going to check her e-mail now,' said Travis. 'Okaaaaay.' And he hit a few keys and the screen changed to the e-mail In/Out tray. He started checking it, letter by letter.

Jim put a hand on Meg's shoulder. His voice was deep and steady. 'We're going to check it all out,' he said. 'Anyone who's contacted her. We'll trace them through their providers and we'll talk to every single one of them.'

'But she said "Richard",' said Alison. 'She told me "Richard" and the Mackie woman heard that man say, "I'm Richard's father".'

'You must realise,' said Jim, 'that we suspect that whoever took Hannah is no kid. The eight-year-old daughter of a policeman is not going to go away with a stranger. We believe the man who claimed to be Richard's father is actually the person who took her. We believe that line was just to get her into a vehicle. Soon we'll have a computer face ready using Maureen Mackie's description. I want you two to come in and have a look at it. We're matching it against pictures of any crims that Harry had a hand in putting away or that might otherwise have a grudge against him.'

'I've got a grudge against him,' said Meg.

'Mum, don't.' Alison's voice touched her, with its love and its tremor, and the harshness of her voice softened.

'This whole family,' said Meg, sinking down onto a chair because her legs would no longer carry her, 'we're all over the place. We're a mess. I knew that yesterday before all this happened. I knew this house was in disorder. All these secrets. All these clandestine relationships.' She turned on Alison, fuelled with new anger. 'You're out half the day and night having something you call a relationship with some bloody married man. Hannah's off talking to I don't know who. Your damn father is away God knows where.'

There was a long silence. Ali finally raised her head and met her mother's eyes. She looked her full in the face, no longer a child but an equal. 'And you, Mum,' said Ali levelly. 'You, too.'

It was a shock to see the knowledge in her daughter's eyes. 'You too, Mum,' Ali continued. 'You have someone else. And Hannah knew about it, too. We both knew, although we never said anything.'

Meg sat stunned. She became aware of Jim looking at her in a very particular way. 'I think,' he said slowly, 'that we need to speak in private, Meg.'

'Who's Diane?' Travis asked as he opened up and scrolled through the e-mail file. The atmosphere in the room changed. Meg and Alison remembered again that there was a stranger in their midst. 'That's our cousin that Mum was talking about,' Alison told him, because her mother was sitting with her head in her hands, silent and ashamed.

'And Mardi?'

'I didn't know she wrote to that bloody woman!' said Meg, suddenly sitting up. 'Is she writing to her?'

'That's Mum's stepmother,' Alison said. 'She married our grandfather.'

'Cool grandma,' said Travis. 'Not many grannies I know who are into using e-mail.'

'She's not a grannie,' said Meg. 'And she is not my stepmother. She's a sharp little go-getter who married my father.'

'What happened to your mother, Meg?' Jim asked.

'It could be Mardi,' Meg said. 'I didn't think of her. Maybe that's where Hannah is.'

'What about your mother?' Jim repeated.

'She was discarded, like so many women,' said Meg. 'And now she's dead.'

'I don't see,' said Ali, suddenly angry through her tears, 'how you can be so horrible and judging of Mardi when you've been doing the same thing. You want to discard Dad. I know you do. You know what it's been like round here lately.'

Meg, stung, was about to answer when Jim stood up. 'Alison,' he said, 'please stay with Travis and help him with the e-mail letters. Meg, let's step outside for awhile.'

In the kitchen, Jim stood near the back door where Harry liked to stand and look out at the weather or the stages of the moon. Meg sat hunched in a chair. She'd caught sight of her reflection in a small round mirror that hung near the doorway to the lounge room and she was shocked at how dreadful she was looking. She thought she would die of the pain of loss as it welled up from deep within her and flooded her again. If my beautiful Hannah is not returned to me, I will suddenly be an old woman and die. Harry, what have you done to us? It seemed to her that it was her husband who had caused all this misery somehow. It all seemed to be his fault. Damn you, Harry Doyle, she thought. Where are you and what are you up to?

She became aware that Jim was asking her where the drinks were and what she wanted, and she somehow managed to tell him and he opened the cupboard and brought out the brandy. He poured her one and put it down in front of her, returning to his position near the back door.

'Now,' he said, 'I think you need to tell me a few things.'

'Max wouldn't have anything to do with this,' she said from a long way away. 'He couldn't be less involved.' It seemed to her that the whole Max affair now belonged to some other woman who lived far away in another country, or was just someone she'd read about once in a book.

'Anyone who is involved with any member of this family could have something to do with this,' said Jim. 'You of all people must appreciate that. Especially anyone involved in an adulterous relationship.' Meg winced at the word. 'It gives us a motive straightaway. You can see that. Did Harry know what was going on?'

Meg raised her eyes to his. She nodded. 'He knew there was someone. But he didn't know the name.'

'I find that hard to believe,' said Jim. 'Knowing Harry. He would have made it his business to find out.'

'You don't know Harry,' she said. 'Nobody knows Harry. There are some things he just doesn't want to know.'

'Name please, Meg.'

'It's over,' said Meg, choking over a superstitious feeling that the words she was saying might pertain to Hannah's life. 'It's finished.'

'Name, please.' Jim had taken out his notebook. He had the sad, tired look around the eyes of the long-serving detective – eyes that had seen too much for one lifetime. He looked like a stranger to her now, just another interviewing cop.

'His name,' she said finally, 'is Max Wolansky.'

'Address?'

'He stays in motels when he's in Sydney,' said Meg. 'And he has a property in the country. A small place near Maldon. I never did pay attention. Jim, it was only an affair. I always had misgivings.' She heard the lack of truth in her words and felt ashamed of herself. She hadn't always had misgivings, she reminded herself. At one stage she had been seriously considering going off with him. It seemed incredible to her now.

'How can I get in touch with him?'

'Look, I don't have his number. He always used to ring me. Or he'd give me different numbers where I could contact him. He was always travelling. He's a businessman.'

'What's the name of his business?'

'Same as his. Max Wolansky Imports/Exports. I've got his business card here somewhere.' She looked around as if the card might suddenly come to light.

'How did you meet?'

'We met at art class.'

'Which art class?'

'Meredith Park High. Adult education runs them using the classrooms at night.'

'They'll have a roll,' said Jim. 'I'll pick it up from there. Did he ever make any threats – remarks – about Harry or any member of your family?'

Meg shook her head. 'Of course not. He said he was going to take me away from a man who didn't appreciate me. But that's hardly a threat.' She could hear the defiance in her voice.

'Go on,' said Jim, and Meg continued. It was good to have something else to focus on, to get angry about; something that was not the terrible pain of Hannah's absence.

'He said I could bring the children with me. He'd take care of us all. He said he just wanted me to be happy.'

'I see,' said Jim.

'He told me he'd never had a family,' she said, 'and he wanted us. He said he loved me.' She felt embarrassed and stupid now, quoting these soap opera words. 'He said he'd never met a woman like me in his life and he wanted me.' Adding this extra part didn't help.

'So he wanted you to leave Harry. You wouldn't happen to know his date of birth?'

'I do,' said Meg. 'I do. He was born in 1947,' she said. 'Eighth of November. He's a Fire Boar.'

Jim stared at her.

'Dell asked me to find out. She's into Chinese astrology.'

'I see,' said Jim and noted it down. Then he looked up. 'You said it was over. What happened?'

'I told him I didn't want to see him again.'

'Why?'

'I changed my mind. I realised I didn't know him. I was living in a dream. I came down to earth.'

'What was his reaction when you told him this?' asked Jim, sensing blood.

'He . . .' But she couldn't say.

'Go on.'

'He was really upset. Very angry. He pushed me around,' she said finally, ashamed, 'when I met him for the last time.'

'What did he do?'

But Meg shook her head. She couldn't bear Jim hearing about the humiliation, Max's fingers jabbed between her legs. 'He just pushed me against a door. He was angry. Understandably. I'd just called it off.' She realised she was defending her ex-lover and she stopped.

'From what you've said, we most definitely will want to talk to Mr Max Wolansky,' said Jim, flicking the notepad closed and pocketing it.

Alison's voice called from the other room. 'Mum. Come here.'

Meg and Jim both went to the bedroom. Travis was sitting at the screen beaming away. He had a wide, dimpled, white-teethed puppet's grin. 'We got him good,' he said. 'Yup, yup, yup. We've got Richard for you. She must have done what he told her because there's only this one letter left, but at least we've got that. And that's all we needed to get his e-mail address. Here's Richard.'

Meg threw her arms around him and kissed his android cheek while Jim looked at the screen and read: *Hi, Honey Hanx. Thanks for writing to me. Now I can write to you and you can write back. But you must always delete my letters. And your replies to me, too. Is that a deal? We don't want to leave our letters lying around for nosey parker parents to find in our systems. Write to me soon and I will reply. Bye bye from your good friend, Richard.* And there was his address at the top: 'Rix@Netserve.com.au'.

'Got him!' said Jim. He grabbed his phone.

FIFTEEN

Harry was aware of a huge pain behind his eyes and the sense of being jammed up against some large warm object. His mind was coming and going in waves, with an odd ringing and echoing sensation like moving out of anaesthesia and returning to consciousness. More and more of him was waking up to extreme discomfort. His nose was filled with the stench of dog and he realised that the warm object pressing into him was Razor, and that the two of them were being bumped along. As he came round even more, he thought at first he was paralysed. He couldn't move. Then the tightness all around him, and the fact that he could barely move because of compression, the smell of rope or hemp, the harsh weave pressing hard against the skin of his face, made him realise that he and Razor were wedged together in a large sack. They seemed to be lying on the back of a moving truck or ute, with something else, perhaps a weighty tarp, covering them. Harry groaned. His mind tried to piece together what had happened. He remembered hearing Razor's sudden yelp of pain. He remembered knowing to stay back from the dog, even though instinctively his body had started in a forward movement towards his partner. Then as he was swinging around with his gun in his hand, something had hit him on the back of the head, something that must have come upwind behind them. Now, in this confined and painful place, he was starting to become aware of every part of himself. Blood itched sticky on the back of his head. I should be dead, he thought to himself. Then he passed out again, only to return, aching and terrified. There was nothing on his right hip; his weapon was gone. Then a horrifying realisation hit him and sweat broke out all over. He's taking me to bury me. This bastard thinks I'm dead, too. He's knocked us both, me and the dog, and he thinks we're both dead and he's loaded us into the back of a utility and he's taking us to another, desolate place where he'll dig a shallow grave. In spite of the bleeding and the pain of his head, Harry started struggling. That was when he realised his hands were immobilised. He felt panic start in the pit of his guts. A new cascade of blood rushed from his head. He passed out again.

The utility came to a halt near some earthworks. A sign that had been used as shotgun target warned trespassers not to enter, that this was the property of Rio Blanco Mining Ltd. Hills and mounds of dull grey subsoil loomed in towering walls, dwarfing the ute and the driver as he got out of the car, leaving the ignition running. He went around to the back of the ute and dropped the back tray. He climbed up into it and heaved and shifted the heavy, blood-stained sack in the back.

'Here we are, Harry. This is where you get off.'

He pulled the dead weight to the very edge of the tray, so that the heavy sack hung over the back. He climbed back into the ute and manoeuvred it back and forth until the back of the tray jutted over a deep gouge in the earth. He jumped from the cab and peered down the shaft. Blackness. He picked up a stone and held it over the mine's entrance.

Then he dropped it. He craned to hear. Finally, a slight but very satisfying sound, perhaps a splash, from thousands of feet below. He grinned. He jumped back up onto the tray. The sack lying near his feet moved and made a muffled sound. But the words were indistinct because the sack was squashed up against the side of the ute. The man leaned over the moving sack and gave it one mighty heave. Then he booted it with a foot. It rolled off the tray and disappeared into the gaping mouth of the shaft.

SIXTEEN

The State manager of Netserve, once the right channels had been cleared, gave Detective Inspector James Coates the physical address of Rix@Netserve.

This turned out to be a serviced office space in a building in Kent Street. Jim took the lift to the fourth floor, a long corridor with frosted glass office doors variously described as housing podiatrists, a clockmaker and repairer, an office supplies agent, a spiritual healer and a travel agent. Jim's heart sank as he saw number eleven, the door behind which Richard Fellowes was supposed to have his registered office. Old mail lay around on and under the doormat. It didn't look like anyone had been there for some time. Jim found the manager of the office suites and his heart sank even further when he was told that Richard Fellowes had done a moonlight flit and hadn't been seen for several days, although he owed three weeks' rent.

'I don't think Fellowes was his real name, either,' said the manager, opening the office with a skeleton key.

'You surprise me,' said Jim as he pushed the door open.

The manager switched the lights on and the two men looked around the small room. There was a desk, two grey filing cabinets, both empty, as Jim quickly discovered, and one easychair in a corner. A stack of magazines were piled beside the chair. Jim pushed the top one aside with his shoe to reveal pornography. 'Business must have been slow,' he said. 'What sort of business did he have?'

'He was supposed to be providing office services – photocopying, faxing, laminating, binding, resumes, that sort of thing,' said the manager. 'But who's going to come up to the fourth floor for that? Needs a good clean up,' he said, looking around. A dirty coffee mug with a ring of dried, flaky coffee at the bottom sat on the desk with bills and newspapers from several weeks ago. Jim looked round and found a plastic bag with some old takeaway cartons in it. He fished out the plastic trays and the spoon and put them in a plastic bag, together with the coffee mug and the unopened mail. 'I'll take these,' he said. 'Do you want a receipt?' The manager laughed.

Back at the Police Centre, Jim handed the plastic bag to a junior offsider, Gary Stokes. 'See what you can get off these,' he said to Gary. 'Fingerprints, whatever. Any leads from the bills.'

Gary looked displeased, then, seeing the look in his boss' eyes, nodded reluctantly.

Jim started his search for Max Wolansky. He could find no police record. He spread his net further. There were several 'M. Wolansky's in the phone book and he noted them down. He was on the phone to the RTA when Gary Stokes walked into his office.

'I'll get back to you,' his contact at the RTA said, 'when I've chased him up.'

Jim rang off. 'Will you ring the witness, Maureen Mackie, and ask her to come in? I'll tell the forensic hypnotist we'll be needing him.'

'Sure thing,' said Gary, leaving the room as Jim picked up the phone to ring Devlin.

SEVENTEEN

M eg had turned Harry's office upside down. The message
sticks were thrown to the floor, the drawers pulled out.
She went through his papers like a wild thing. Alison stood
in the doorway, shocked.

'Mum,' asked Alison, 'what are you doing? What are you
looking for?'

Meg straightened up. She saw that she had handfuls of paper
clutched in her fists. She wasn't sure what she was doing. I
need to collect myself, she thought. My little girl needs a sane
woman. She dropped the papers and sat at the desk, slumped.
They both jumped when the phone rang. Meg picked it up.
'Hullo?' she said, hoping it might be Harry. When she heard
who it was, she looked guiltily at Alison.

'Please forgive me, Meg,' he said. 'I was crazy at the
thought of losing you. I just lost it. I've never cared about
any woman the way I care about you. I've heard about your
little girl. I'm so sorry. Please let me help you find her.'

Alison had stood up and was walking out of the room. But
her mother beckoned her back. She stood in the doorway,
undecided.

'I know a lot of people, Meg,' Max was saying. 'People
who hear things and know things. I could help if you'd only

let me. I could help you get your family back together again.'
Meg felt a wave of relief. She had an ally. She had a friend.
She was not alone anymore.

'Max,' she said. 'Oh Max.' She thought of his strong arms
and reassuring heartbeat. His intelligence and sharpness. His
lazy worldliness. She could deal with his temper later, she
thought. For a second she couldn't speak. Then she composed
herself. His earlier actions seemed only a peccadillo, given the
extremity and hugeness of her present emotional pain. 'Please
Max,' she said. 'Harry's gone off somewhere. I don't know
what to do. The police want to talk to you.'

'Of course they would,' he said, as if it were the most
natural thing in the world, and his reasonable voice calmed
her somewhat. 'Because I'm involved with you they'd need
to talk to me. I'll contact them straightaway. Then let's get
together and work out a way to get your little girl back to you.
I've got money. I can organise a reward. Someone must have
seen or heard something. I'll be with you as soon as I can.'

'When's that?'

'Tomorrow. At the latest.'

'Hannah could be dead by then.'

Meg heard the pitch of her voice and was startled.

'Meg, Meg. It's going to be all right.'

'How can you say that?' she screamed.

But he'd rung off.

EIGHTEEN

The phone rang in Jim Coates' office and he hurried back from where he was waiting for the lifts just in time to catch it.

'Physical Evidence?' the voice asked.

'Yes,' said Jim.

'It's John Ayoub from Bathurst. I believe Harry Doyle used to work in that section?'

'Yes,' said Jim. 'Have you had any news of him?'

'Do you know him?' asked Ayoub, 'from the time he worked there?'

'I know Harry well,' said Jim.

'No news of him,' said Ayoub. 'But he said something that's been on my mind. I wanted to pass it on now that his daughter's missing. Any news on that?'

'Nothing,' said Jim.

'We had a murder here,' Ayoub said.

'I know,' said Jim. 'The physical evidence has been sent on to the experts.'

'I'm not talking about that one,' said Ayoub. 'An old woman was killed in a nursing home up here yesterday morning. Looks like strangulation. Harry Doyle had come out looking for me and he and the dog happened to be there at the crime scene. The dog went apeshit. Ran all through the nursing home and then out again.'

'I'm not involved in that case' said Jim. 'I can put you on to the bloke in charge.'

'No,' said Ayoub. 'I want to tell you what Harry said. He said that the dog told him the person who strangled the old woman in the home was the same person who did Janette Madden. At the farmhouse.'

'Harry said that?'

'That is correct,' said Ayoub. 'And I told him I could see absolutely no reason for him to assume that.'

'But the fact that he said this is worrying you now?' said Jim.

'That is correct,' said Ayoub. 'And Harry Doyle's vehicle is still out there near the river. That's over twenty-four hours. I think he's tried to track the nursing home killer with the dog. Maybe he's got into trouble. Had a fall.' He paused. 'And I spoke to his sergeant at the Dog Squad. He said there'd been domestic problems.' Ayoub was silent awhile and Jim waited. 'It's been on my mind,' Ayoub finally said.

'It's also possible he connected with the killer,' Jim said.

'That's been in my mind, too,' said Ayoub. 'You see, he once was married to Janette Madden.'

'I knew that,' said Jim.

'And the woman murdered in the hospital – Vera Wetherill – she had some sort of association with Doyle, too.' Ayoub paused. 'Two women he knows get knocked and then Harry goes missing. And then his little girl. Looks very bad.'

Jim didn't like it one bit. 'Could you organise a search party?' he said. 'With your local blokes?'

'I'm half of them at the moment,' said Ayoub. 'And I'm flat out like a lizard drinking. This area is terribly under-manned. Everyone is flat strap with their own work plus this state-wide search for Janette Madden's killer. Otherwise I'd take a bit of time and ask around.' He paused. 'Even though I didn't really see any connection myself I can't get it out of my mind.'

Jim considered. 'I can't possibly come up myself,' he said. 'We're throwing everything at the kidnap down here.'

'All I can do up here,' said Ayoub, 'is widen the terms of the search so that we're not only looking out for the offender but for Harry, too.'

'The name,' said Jim with his pen poised, 'of the dead woman again?'

'Vera Wetherill,' said Ayoub and rang off. As Jim put the phone down, Gary Stokes knocked at his door and came in.

'Fingerprints couldn't get anything useful from those things you found in Fellowes' room,' said Stokes. 'Few half-prints, nothing conclusive.' Jim felt himself slump in disappointment; the night had suddenly become darker. There were good reasons to be worried. The offender might have switched his attentions from women Harry once knew to Harry himself. And then to Harry's daughter.

Jim got up from his desk. If this dark interpretation of the facts wasn't correct, there'd been several times in Jim's career where he'd been summoned to the body of a colleague, dead by his own service revolver. He peered over the cardboard strip that hid the pigeons. The female huddled on the nest with the male snuggled up beside her. Pigeons knew how to do it. Humans had much more trouble, Jim thought. It was the reason why he lived alone these days, with an aviary and a garden. He went to his locker and took out his clothes, then went down the hall to the showers.

Under the steaming water, he tried to make sense of it all. If Harry is right, we're dealing with someone who has killed three women; and who is still out there, despite a large-scale alert; and who may well have tangled with Harry Doyle; who may well have taken eight-year-old Hannah. Jim decided to take it to the brass.

Forty minutes later, he drove up to Harry's house. All the lights were on in the house as if Meg were defying the night. Jim walked up the path and from inside the house he heard Blade's half-bark; Blade knew Jim quite well. Meg came to the door before he'd knocked, with Alison close behind her.

'What is it?' called Meg, noticing the slowness of his walk, the way he moved. 'No!' she screamed. 'No!' Blade barked sharply.

'It's okay, it's okay,' Jim said, grabbing her hands. 'We haven't heard anything more about Hannah. But we've done some follow-up on Rix@Netserve.' He followed her and Ali through the hallway, the lounge and into the kitchen.

Meg looked ashen in the bright light, neglected and sick. 'And?' she was saying. 'And?'

'We've got a name: Richard Fellowes. We're checking that out. We're getting a description of the car and the man from the witness. Devlin will use hypnosis to try and get a better picture of him. We're getting closer to him, Meg.'

'I want my daughter back. I want my little girl. Oh, Hannah.'

Meg buckled at the knees in front of him. Jim grabbed her and held her tight. Alison clutched her and the two of them clung together, contained in Jim Coates' strong arms.

'Meg,' he said, once he'd got her sitting down, 'we're worried about Harry, too.'

Meg turned to look at him. Jim had seen many women's eyes in his day, read many conflicting emotions and stories in them – of love and hate, contempt and hopelessness. But what he saw in Meg's eyes was exhaustion; a don't-care-anymore despair.

'What about Harry?' she said.

'He may have gone after a violent killer.'

'That's his job,' said Meg, and her voice was dull. 'That's what they pay him for.' Then angry life flooded it. 'If Harry Doyle puts his job before his family – as he always has done – that's something for him to look to. If it's got him into trouble, it's not before time. Jim, I've got enough to bear right now. I can't even think of Harry at the moment. By all means, do whatever you think is best about your buddy. But you get out there and you do everything on heaven and earth to bring my Hannah back to me.'

She saw Jim to the door, then let Alison take her back to the kitchen and make another pot of tea which she didn't drink. She sat, staring into nothing, saying nothing. Alison sat with her.

NINETEEN

Harry ached back into consciousness. He felt as if he were hanging suspended between heaven and hell, and the stench of dog piss filled his nostrils. He blinked his eyes open but everything was still black. A huge pain, located somewhere on the back of his head, was opening and deepening with every throb. Full consciousness returned and he started to realise certain things. The two of them were squashed up together hanging somewhere, perhaps caught by tree roots or jagged rock. He realised, too, that Razor was not the only one who'd pissed himself.

All around him was silence and blackness. Even the night is full of sound and scents, he thought. This deep silence was terrifying and, despite the sweat of fear that covered him, he shivered. There were none of the night noises that he would've expected and the scent picture was disturbing: a damp, metallic, very cold subsoil smell; a smell that he associated with the continuous absence of sunlight. He imagined a thick grey mud stratum would smell like this, cold and dead. Or ancient rocks, formed millions of years ago and laid down before the dinosaurs. When he strained his ears, he thought he could hear a humming, but it might just have been his own system, the blood still circulating in his injured body, the spinal fluids ebbing and flowing up and down and around his bruised brain.

And then suddenly he integrated all the information and understood where he was. Not long after he'd joined the Dog Squad, he and Razor had been winched down a mine shaft to search for a small girl, and this dank absence of sound and ground smells was the scent picture of a mine shaft. He remembered the little body Razor had led him to, not far from the vertical entrance shaft, and how he'd attached the dead child to a stretcher and sent her up first, waiting in the torchlight with Razor to be winched up again.

Harry despaired. His pinned arms hurt like hell in some places, were numb in others; rope seemed to have been wound round and round his body, pressing his arms into his sides, so that he was squashed in an absurd attitude of military attention. His belt had been stripped of weapon, torch, ammunition and cuffs. All that remained were his useless keys on their ring. But, he thought, if I can somehow bend and wriggle a hand into the pocket on my right shin, I might be able to get hold of that little one-handed knife. Flexibility was not one of his strong points, and under these conditions it was even more difficult to manoeuvre. Almost the moment he went to move his body in an effort to carry out the plan, he had to stop. The bag they were in had slipped a few notches. He froze with fear.

'Razor? Mate?'

Razor stirred and Harry felt the warm heaviness against his leg. Then the dog whimpered. Harry tried stirring again, but the same heart-sickening lurch of the bag that contained them stopped him dead again. He imagined them hanging over an abyss, held only by a tiny natural ratchet, where any movement endangered their stability and moved them closer to the final death-plunge. Then he realised that Razor had started chomping and shaking at the bag, attempting to chew himself out of their prison.

'Just go easy, mate,' Harry begged the old dog. 'Real easy or you'll have us go the big drop.' Razor's biting movements continued and their container slipped another few centimetres. 'Still!' Harry commanded, and Razor froze at the command.

Harry thought about their situation. Angus had wounded the two of them, thrown them in the bag, then driven them to this place, wherever it was, and dumped them down a mine shaft, as if they were a weighted bag of kittens. That odd, fleeting odour that had eluded and teased him he now recognised as acetone, the smell of someone who drinks too much, whose body is always processing too much ethyl alcohol through the breath and through the sweat glands. It is a smell that Harry had met in bars and clubs. He'd met it in people. Janette had sometimes exuded it. He'd noticed it most recently in Murray Faye's flatmate. Angus had already developed that acrid note to his personal scent picture in Vietnam. And over the years it had become stronger. So strong that Harry's super-sensitive nose had noted it, but not been able to classify it, outside the Strathfield siege house as Angus had taken the police by surprise with his grenade attack and his smart, practised combat manoeuvres. Angus Wetherill, his childhood friend turned murderer. Rapist and murderer. Harry remembered the curses. He recalled Angus screaming at him in Vung Tau that Harry had 'taken everything' from him; Angus trying to kill him with his bare hands.

'*Angus!*' he shrieked in the blackness. '*Don't do this!*' He realised it was madness, this yelling into nothingness. But it relieved some need.

'You murdering bastard!' Harry roared into the blackness.

'—*ring bastard, ring bastard,*' echoed the blackness around him.

Something had started Angus on a hunting and killing expedition. First, the woman at Strathfield, whose death had been the bait; then Harry's first wife, the woman he believed should have been his own; finally, Vera Wetherill had died, as an act of revenge on the Wetherill family, a stand-in killing for Angus's father, for he was unable to murder the already dead. And he'd made this trail of death unique enough, weird enough, to intrigue Harry Doyle, leading him away from home into the bush. Away from his family and his base.

Razor had started chomping again and Harry froze anew as the bag started jolting. Then he felt Razor go very still. 'What is it?'

Harry put it together. Razor has worked it out, he thought. He's got his head out and he's realised that his head is sticking out of a bag suspended above nothing in a crevasse to nowhere. Razor is taking it in. He heard his dog whimper in the darkness. 'Okay, okay,' Harry said. 'Just cool it. Don't do anything rash.'

He'd managed to get to a crushed kneeling position in the bag by moving with great care. He strained and strained, but couldn't get his hand into the pocket. It was hopeless. Gravity squashed them both down, almost immobilising them by their own weight. They would just hang there until they died of dehydration. Already Harry was feeling the pain of thirst. The bleeding had eased but he'd lost a lot of fluid. It would be better to die quickly, he thought, by moving until whatever is holding us breaks or slips. At least it will be quick, not drawn-out like this, hanging in nowhere, slowly dying.

He thought of Hannah, his darling, of Alison who used to be, and of Meg who no longer loved him. He wondered if he and Razor would ever be found, and thought it was most unlikely. Australia had thousands and thousands of secret, shallow graves, Harry knew. Under brush and under fallen timber, murderers dump their kills, perhaps digging a token scrape in the hard soil, more usually just pulling fallen scrub and tree branches over the stiffening body. Within minutes, insects gather. In just a few days, weeks, scavenging animals have stripped it of its identity and sex along with the flesh and skin, until nothing but rag and bones remain, slowly taking on the hue and texture of their surroundings until they too become invisible to the casual observer. The chances of him and Razor ever being found down here were minuscule.

He thought again of his family – of Hannah, of Alison, of his wife. Would she be sad or relieved? Would she take up again with the man she'd said she was 'over'? What would happen to his children? Tears pricked his eyes as he thought of Hannah. He thought of Alison when she was a little girl and his heart nearly broke. He remembered the way Meg used to look at him, drowsy with love, after she'd just melted down in his arms, and the way he used to kiss her on the forehead, resting with her a moment before his own climax. It was so long, he thought, since they'd made love like that. What a mess I'm leaving, he thought. What a mess I've made of it all. I never meant it to happen like this. I didn't think my life would end up like this. This is it.

He hadn't really thought about death much. Sometimes he'd wondered if he'd be killed on the job. But he knew he'd be more likely to die in a motor vehicle accident than die working. He thought of the men and women he'd killed in Vietnam. He remembered the VC man whose eyes he'd looked into as he'd waited for the man to die. He thought of little Franco and his stupid Black and Decker cordless drill. It seemed that their spirits were here, not with mockery or menace but with inevitability. You are joining us now, Harry

Doyle, as each person born onto this earth must join us. Harry felt tears run down his face. It wasn't really grief so much as anger and frustration that this was how it was to end.

And then on top of that, something else occurred to him. Angus would go after Meg. Angus would take Harry's wife just as he thought Harry had taken his. If he went after Meg, he'd have to do something about the girls. Harry felt the chill of horror as the realisation became stronger. He wants my family. He wants the things he believes I took from him. *I've got to get out of here.*

An extraordinary surge of strength rippled through his bound body. He stretched and strained and was suddenly able to get two fingers down into the pocket in his overalls. He prayed that Angus had overlooked the flat little knife, not much bigger than a bottle opener. He reached until he thought his arms would come out of the socket, then felt a thrill of triumph. His fingers touched the top of the little one-handed knife.

Razor was biting again at the fabric of the bag, pulling and shaking his head, like a shark. 'Sit still,' Harry commanded. Sweat poured from his cramped body. The effort of moving those fingers and getting the knife in the right position was the hardest work he'd ever done. He was grateful for the weekly workouts with the dogs, the long endurance trails they'd covered over the years, the fast sprints, the steep inclines, the sheer hard work of the sort of policing with which he'd been involved. Slowly, touch by touch, he turned it with the tip of his fingers until he'd coaxed it into position between his thumb and forefinger. He pressed down with his thumb until he felt the blade unfold and move into its armed position. Now he had hold of it in one of his bound hands. His body shivered with effort. He must get free. He must. His family would die if he did not. But his hand, tied against his flanks, couldn't move into a working angle. Harry groaned aloud. He must get away yet he couldn't move the hand that held the knife. Somehow he would have to shrink his body so as to loosen the ropes. He expelled his breath, deflating his lungs until they were emptied. Then he started to push against the bonds, continuing until he felt nauseated from the chafing and the effort. The rope didn't seem to be yielding at all. He wanted to cry. Instead he roared with frustration. The sound and movement of his body shifted the bag and loosened some small stones that rattled away until, a long time later, the faint sound as they hit their final resting place came to his ears. He rested a little more then strained again. Nothing gave; the bonds seemed as tight as when he'd first become conscious. The knife in his hand was useless to him.

Razor started howling in dejection. It was a terrible sound, echoing in the darkness.

TWENTY

Hannah huddled in the darkness. There was no way out of the cell she was in. She wasn't sure how long she'd been locked up here in the secret cupboard, nor how long it had been since he'd tricked her into the car, pretending he was taking her home. First they'd gone to a house and sat in the car and beeped the horn until another man had come out and joined them in the car. The other man had called Richard's father 'Ron'. Then they'd all come to this other house.

'Where's this?' she'd said when they pulled up outside a house in a road somewhere under the Harbour Bridge.

'Come on, young lady,' Ron had said, 'we're going inside to get Richard.'

It wasn't until it was too late, and Hannah had hesitantly gone inside, looking around, that she'd sensed there was something very wrong in all this. The other man they'd picked up had gone and sat down in the kitchen of the old house. Hannah could see there was something wrong with him, too, although in a different way. He'd stared at her, said 'Hullo', but after that had been silent, had just sat there, watching what happened as Ron seized her and easily overpowered her. 'Help me!' she'd screamed to the other.

'Help me.' But he'd just stared at her with a funny look on his face. Then she'd really known the truth: that she'd been stolen away by a man with evil in his mind and brought here to this place with a crazy man. Then he'd locked her in this horrible little cupboard.

She'd started to scream.

All that seemed ages ago. She had been allowed out of the cupboard to go to the toilet and Ron had given her a sleeping bag in there and she'd even been able to sleep for awhile.

She must get away. She was very hungry. Maybe it was past lunchtime, maybe even dinnertime. Her tummy rumbled and the thirst was starting to dry her mouth. She could hear the noises of traffic and of aircraft overhead. She knew that just a little way away was the ordinary world, where people came and went, crossed at the green man, went into shops and chatted on buses. This place she was in was like another world, a terrifying dream world.

She wondered now if there had ever been a Richard at all, or if Ron had tricked her from the very beginning. She knew that there were men who did dreadful things to little children. She knew that Ron must be one of them. Everything she'd ever heard her father say, everything she'd ever read about, all her own instincts told her this. She must plan and plot. She must scan for any opportunity to get away, to take them by surprise.

She started to cry. I'm only a little girl, she cried to herself. Only gleams of light filtered under the door and through the side between the hinges. It wasn't much, but as her eyes acclimatised it was something. How can a little girl get away from big men? she wondered. It was quite hopeless. But the minute she'd come home from school, she knew, Dad would get the dogs and be after her. But it would be very hard by now. The bus would've had hundreds, perhaps thousands of different scents on it. She started crying at the hopelessness of it. She slept a little, nodding off, coming back into the nightmare of the cupboard. I have to get away, she thought. Whatever else, I have to get away from these men.

'I want to go to the toilet,' she called out. There was no reply. She started bashing on the door, crying and yelling. 'Let me go to the toilet! Let me out of here! Can't you hear me? I want to go to the toilet.' She slumped back. She felt around. If they didn't let her out, she'd just pee in their bloody cupboard and they could clean it up. 'I'll do it in here if you don't let me out,' she told them through the door.

Now she could hear the other man talking with Ron. Their voices were raised as if in argument, but she couldn't hear what they were saying. The silence that followed was terrifying, then she heard someone at the door of the cupboard. She tensed with fear. He was coming back.

The door of her prison opened and Ron peered around to see where she was. Hannah gathered up all her strength. She prayed to Razor. 'Help me be a police dog. Help me be as fast and strong as you are.' She was shuddering with energy and terror and the desire to be free, all curled up ready to spring. She flew at the crack of light as it widened, leaped up and pushed past Ron. She made a dash for the doorway but his huge hand grabbed her and she was caught, crushed against his body, her head at the side of his face.

Hannah screamed in fear and frustration. With all her strength, and without even knowing where her mouth was in relation to the man's head, she used the most powerful weapon at her disposal and closed her strong teeth around his ear, biting with all her strength. His shriek nearly deafened her. He dropped her and again she made a bolt for the kitchen door. The other man was still sitting at the kitchen table, just shaking his head and saying something. He didn't try to stop her. Hannah was out through the kitchen door and halfway down the hall when the shrieking man behind her pounced on her again.

'Let me go! Let me go!' she cried. He slapped her hard over the head and dragged her back to the cupboard, despite her wild kicking. He pushed her in savagely and slammed and locked the door.

'Little bitch!' he said. 'I'll teach you!'

The seated man watched as his brother rushed back out again, hand clapped over one ear, blood pouring down his face and chin, wetting his shoulder. He looked in horror at his red hand.

'Little bitch, *little bitch*,' Ron was shouting. 'She bit me.' Indeed, half his ear was hanging down in a bloody flap against his face and he danced in pain around the room. 'I'll have to go to a doctor. A hospital. I'm *disfigured*.' The seated man remained still and watched, as he always did since he'd moved in with his brother. 'Look at all this blood. She's spoiled everything.' He slammed out of the kitchen and was gone. His brother remained in his chair and waited.

'Please?' Hannah was pleading through the locked door, having heard Ron's departure. 'I promise I won't try and run away. Please let me out. I want to go to the toilet. Really. This time I really do.' But he was too scared of Ron to do anything. Then he looked over and saw a little pool starting to spread out from under the door. The little girl had wet on the floor. Ron would be so angry, he thought. With them both.

'They've been practising chemicals on me,' he told the child behind the locked door. 'The Archons are moving. The Archons are very angry. They will destroy anyone who stands in their way. They practised chemicals on me and they will hurt you too.'

'Let me out!'

The muffled voice from the cupboard touched him, but he dared not do as she asked. The Confessor stood up. He shuffled over to the telephone. He picked it up and dialled Harry's home number again. No-one answered. There was no-one home, he thought.

TWENTY-ONE

At the Police Centre, Meg looked at the artist's picture of the suspect, drawn from Maureen Mackie's description; the likeness of the man who had taken Hannah. She looked at the staring eyes and the down-turned lips, the scraggly hair. It looked like all the faces of all the crims she'd ever seen. She studied it for a few moments, then shook her head. It meant nothing to her and she handed it back to Jim.

'I don't recognise him either,' said Jim. 'It might be someone Harry worked on by himself, but we were almost always partners.' He put the picture down on the desk.

Then Jim was ushering them out of the office and the three of them started walking down the hall to the room where Devlin had set up his interview.

'Hypnosis,' Devlin was telling the woman as they came to the door, 'is no more than a state of deep relaxation. There's nothing magic about it. There's nothing special about me. I don't have any strange powers. I'm just here to facilitate you as you enter a state of deep relaxation.'

Maureen Mackie was now sitting in a reclining chair with Devlin seated opposite her. Jim ushered Meg and Alison into the room behind the woman, where they sat close together. Alison had her arm around her mother. Jim

Coates remained standing, leaning against the wall near the doorway.

Devlin moved his chair to be a little closer to the woman, while maintaining a respectful distance. Clipped onto both their collars were small microphones. Except for those, and the fact that one of the detectives from the Crime Scene Support Unit was sitting with a video camera not far behind him, Devlin, in his long-sleeved shirt and navy and maroon tie, could have been the manager of a small business about to have a heart-to-heart with a staff member.

'All I do is speak to you,' he said. 'I offer you words – suggestions – and you accept them if that is what you want to do.' Devlin was starting the induction process already, Jim realised, with his subtle leaning forward, and his slight emphasis on the phrase 'deep relaxation.' 'I don't have control over you,' Devlin continued. 'I'm just an ordinary man who has certain skills that may help you achieve total relaxation. Do you have any questions?'

Maureen Mackie leaned closer to him as if she were about to say something.

Devlin noticed. 'There's something worrying you,' he said in his soft voice. 'Let me put your mind at rest. What is it?'

'It's just that . . . well, I've never been hypnotised before. And you hear such stories about it. I'm worried that I might—' She stopped.

'Yes?' Devlin's steady non-reactive voice.

'I was waiting for someone at that bus stop. Someone my husband doesn't know about.'

Devlin nodded. 'Are you worried,' he asked her, 'that you'll say something in hypnosis about this person, or in some other way give away secrets?'

Maureen Mackie looked very relieved. She nodded.

'Maureen,' said Devlin. 'Hypnosis isn't a truth drug. You won't say anything more to me than you would if we were having the same discussion without hypnosis. The only difference is that you will be deeply relaxed and in this state you might recall tiny details that could be helpful to our search for a missing child.' His voice had slowed down noticeably. 'But you will only tell me what you want to tell me. You will only tell me details related to our inquiry. That is why you are here. Nothing more. Your secrets are safe and will continue to remain safe.'

Maureen Mackie leaned back in the comfortable chair. 'As I count you down into a state of deep relaxation, Maureen,' Devlin's hypnotic voice intoned, 'you may notice certain things. Your eyes may start blinking. They might start watering. This indicates that you are relaxing deeper and deeper. You may wish to close your eyes so as to experience this beautiful state of relaxation even more fully.'

Maureen Mackie's eyes blinked several times and then closed. Her eyelids flickered. Devlin counted her down from one to ten, describing what might happen to the large muscles of her back, neck and head if she relaxed. The woman leaned more heavily into the fabric of the chair. When Devlin was satisfied that she was deeply in trance, he started his questions. He took her right back to the day before she went to Circular Quay. He asked her to describe what she was doing. It was going to be a long session.

Someone tapped Jim on the shoulder and he turned. Gary Stokes gestured him outside. 'Call for you,' he said. 'It's someone from the RTA.'

Jim left the hypnosis session and went to his office. He picked up the phone.

'Jim Coates here.'

'Darren here, mate. No joy for you on Max Wolansky. Magda Wolanski is the best I can do.'

'Thanks anyway,' said Jim. He rang off and went back to the room where Devlin and Maureen Mackie were going through the events of the morning before she left on the train.

Half an hour later, Maureen Mackie's mind was again waiting at the bus stop at Circular Quay. 'What can you see?' Devlin was asking.

'People. People going here and there. Standing around waiting.'

'What else? What do you notice that draws your attention?'

'A car.' The woman's voice was almost inaudible. 'A car is pulling up.'

'What do you notice about this car?'

'I don't notice much at first. I feel a bit cross that it's pulling up at a bus stop.'

Behind her almost inaudible voice, a tape played soft ambient music. Her head hung to one side; her hands lay on her lap. She looked to be deeply asleep.

'Tell me about the car,' Devlin's soft voice matching the woman's.

'It's a dark colour – a dark green.'

'A dark green,' Devlin repeated. 'Can you tell me anymore about this dark green car? What state is it from?'

'New South Wales.'

'How do you know it's from New South Wales?'

'I can see the number plate.'

'Tell me more about the number plate.'

'I can't really make it all out. I'm more interested in watching the little girl and the man now.'

'Right. We'll talk about that in a moment. But just now, we want to know about the car. That car. The registration.'

'I can't see the letters.'

'Start where you can.'

'I think there's an eight,' she said. 'And a one and a seven. I think it's one, seven, eight at the end. Yes. One, seven, eight.'

'One, seven, eight,' Devlin repeated. 'Anything else you can tell us, Maureen, about the registration of that car?'

'Now I can see the letters. There are three letters in front of the numbers.'

'Good, Maureen. That's really good. Just relax now and take a deep breath.'

'That bastard,' she said softly. 'I know what he's done.' Her breathing became hard and she shifted uneasily in trance.

'Just relax, Maureen. You're doing very well. Tell us anything more you remember about that car's registration.'

There was a silence. Meg realised she was gripping Ali too hard. She loosened her hold and Ali looked at her. In that moment, with all the agony about Hannah and the fury about Harry, Meg found herself looking into her daughter's eyes. I don't think I have ever consciously looked into Ali's eyes like this in my life, she thought. Not since she was a baby. Not since she became an adolescent and difficult. I have never really looked. It was as if she had never seen her older daughter until this moment. She tightened her hold on Alison again.

'I can't get hold of the letters,' Maureen Mackie was saying. 'Round letters. Maybe a "Q"? An "O"? I don't know.'

Devlin's cool voice steadied her. 'Let's leave the number plate for awhile, Maureen. Let's concentrate on the man you saw with Hannah. Can you see him in your mind?'

'Yes, I can,' she said. 'I can see him right now.'

'Good, Maureen. Now I want you to freeze the image of that man in your mind. Take a photograph of that man's face. Can you do that?'

The woman sighed. 'I've got him now. He's got a baby face.'

'You can help us find that baby face. In a minute I'm going to ask you to look at a television screen we've set up here. There'll be a blank face on that screen and features to choose from: hair, forehead, eyes, nose and mouth. I'm going to ask you to start choosing features that are most like those of the man you saw with Hannah. You can use the mental photograph you've taken of that man to select the features that are most like his. Take your time now. We can start any time you want.'

'Let's start now,' said Maureen Mackie.

Jim beckoned Meg and she followed him out of the room, away from Devlin's soothing voice and the blank face on the colour monitor.

'This could take awhile,' he said. 'You should go home now. I'll let you know the minute we know anything.'

Meg wanted to stay, but she looked at Alison. Her older daughter was exhausted, with dark rings under the eyes and a grey tone to her face. 'Yes,' said Meg. 'We'll go home. But you must ring me the moment you . . .'

Jim put his hand on her arm. 'I swear. The minute we've got a face, I'll ring.'

As soon as he'd organised a car for her, he went back to his office and opened some of the mail in his tray. There was a certificate from the expert botanist who'd analysed some of the material from Strathfield and Bathurst. In his opinion, some of the fragments of leaf matter came from an exotic tree – the ebony tree.

★   ★   ★

The phone was ringing as Meg opened the front door. She rushed in and picked it up. 'Jim?' she said. 'Is that you?'

'I think I took the little girl,' said the thin voice.

'Who is this?' Meg's voice was a shocked whisper.

'I couldn't let her out,' said the voice. 'She made a wet on the floor. I'm sorry. The Archons are too strong for me.'

'Stop ringing me, you crazy!' she screamed and started to cry. 'Get off this line. My little girl's been stolen!'

'Please,' said the voice, and in spite of her own pain and anger Meg took in its pleading tone, 'Please get your little girl. He's gone to the hospital. Please get her before he comes back.' Then there was a click and he was gone.

'Come back!' Meg screamed. But all that answered her was the long engaged beep. She slowly put the phone down and turned to Ali.

'What, Mum? Who was it?'

'Oh Jesus,' Meg whispered to her daughter. 'I think he knows something. I think Harry's mad old Confessor knows something. I think he knows where Hannah is. I think he wanted to help me.'

She grabbed the phone again and rang Jim. She told him, word for word, as well as she could remember, what the Confessor had just said.

'Listen,' said Jim, 'we'll get a trace on your line. If he rings again, the security people in Telstra will get onto him. You'd better stay there in case he rings again.'

Jim put the phone down, then called a mate in Telstra who said he'd do the job straightway, pending the relevant warrant. Jim went through the records. He was hoping that somewhere he'd see something, or make a connection that would be helpful. But he couldn't remember the Confessor's real name. He called out for Gary Stokes but he was out checking recent releases from psych units and prisons, so he put young Kerryann Fish on the job.

'We're looking for someone whose nickname is "the Confessor",' Jim told her. 'He's more of a pest than anything. I don't know if he's got a record. We want his full name. His first name is . . .' Jim paused. 'It's an unusual name. Some famous writer's name,' he said. 'Like . . . I don't know – Dante or something. It's urgent.' Kerryann nodded and started work.

Jim went back to the interview room down the hall and opened the door. Nobody turned to see who it was because Devlin and the Crime Scene detective, who had left his seat behind the video camera, were focused on the printer. Everyone was waiting for the result of Maureen Mackie's description to materialise in the printer tray. Maureen herself, now out of trance and alert, also stood watching as the first edge of photographic paper inched out. Dark wispy hair was all that could be seen at first; then the forehead; then wrap-around sunglasses; the nose, fleshy and curved; the area between the nose and lips, completely covered by a thick, Stalin-type moustache. Only the outline of the bottom lip could be seen.

The printer stopped and Devlin scooped the portrait up. He turned it right way up. Maureen Mackie stared at the podgy-faced man.

'Is this like the man who drove the green car?' Devlin asked.

Maureen Mackie was slowly shaking her head and Jim felt himself droop in disappointment. All those hours wasted, resources that might have been put to better use. But then he saw the expression on Maureen Mackie's face. The woman was shaking her head in amazement and disbelief. 'I can't believe it,' she was saying. 'It's *exactly* like him. It's exactly like the man who took the little girl.'

Jim stared at the face. 'I've got a feeling I know this joker,' he said, picking up the picture. He stared at it and his mind raced through the different men he'd interrogated, trying to find a match.

While Devlin escorted Maureen Mackie downstairs to organise a car for her, Jim took the picture and the registration number down to media liaison. 'Get this out to everyone,' he told them. 'Someone apart from one woman waiting at Circular Quay must have seen this bastard.'

He went back to his office, passing the open area where Kerryann Fish was sitting in front of the monitor, checking out nicknames, but she shook her head at him to show that she hadn't yet found anything helpful. Jim went through into his office and stood for a moment, leaning his forehead against the glass of the window. The two pigeons huddled together on the ledge. Somewhere out there, in the city, was this man who had taken Hannah. And he was presently, if the Confessor was really on to something as Meg believed, at any one of the various hospitals around the city. But at least now they had a face and a car registration.

Jim rang the Dog Squad and eventually tracked down the sergeant in charge. He spoke of his concern about Harry and felt a bit better when he heard that Ray Gosling was already on his way to the Bathurst area to see if he could get a lead on his missing colleague. Jim rang off. Two men, Jim was thinking. One somewhere in the bush with Harry Doyle quite possibly on his trail and another one, somewhere in Sydney, possibly at a hospital. Or are they the same man? There was nothing he could do, right at this moment, about Hannah. About Harry. He recognised that he was exhausted. Maybe his brain would work better after a rest. He sat on his chair and leaned back. He had no trouble sleeping anytime, anywhere. He'd dozed beside hideously mutilated bodies as he waited for colleagues to arrive at crime scenes. Jim was asleep in seconds.

TWENTY-TWO

Harry strained again and this time the pain from his chafed wrist made him roar. But the ropes were looser. He'd been chafing himself and wriggling and straining for what seemed like ages because the image of Angus harming his family had given him some sort of preternatural endurance and strength. This time when he gripped the knife again, he found he was able to push his hand up in an awkward angle and touch one layer of the rope that secured him. He wriggled his toes and ankles to bring some life back to feet and legs grown numb from the pressure. He could only make a tiny movement with the knife, no longer than fingertips. But it was a movement, and it would, he hoped, eventually wear down the rope, strand by strand. But the injuries to the skin of his wrists were militating against him, becoming hot and inflamed. Once the tissue swelled, it would make movement impossible. He scraped harder and harder. Razor whimpered from time to time or gave voice to a desolate howl. Every now and then a shower of little stones would fall from above his sacking prison, to tumble into the silence below. When that happened, Harry froze for a moment before resuming his persistent scraping.

He continued to saw away with the little one-handed knife

in this almost impossible fashion. If I do get free, he thought to himself, what do I do then? Do I try and cut myself out of the bag? Do I hold on to whatever projection it is that is delaying the free fall of this sack? Will Razor make it or will he plummet as I free myself? Razor, perhaps picking up his pack leader's thoughts, wriggled around and howled anew, a sad, penetrating sound that echoed through the shaft. Again, Harry squeezed ankles and calves together, wriggled his feet up and down, trying to encourage more circulation. Then he froze. The bag had slipped another notch on whatever was holding it from the yawning mouth of the shaft. Surely it would give any minute. He had to move quickly. He sliced away at the rope, only stopping now to strain against it, filling his chest, pushing with all his might against the constraints of the bonds. One last time. Nothing happened. Harry slumped in despair. He strained to make another tiny scraping motion, stopped, tugged hard against his bonds and his hands separated.

Harry roared with exhilaration, a hoarse, primitive sound. He pulled one arm up and tugged at the rope that still twisted around his body, trying to unwind it. His other arm felt cold and dead, lacking circulation, and with his free arm he rubbed some life back into it. Eventually he was able to shrug the rope lower and his hands were free. With the little knife, he made a careful opening high up in the bag, where he hoped the weight of himself and the dog would not cause the fabric to rip, and pushed his face through the hole.

It was such a relief to have this small freedom that he felt tears come into his eyes. He felt triumphant. But this feeling quickly ebbed as he blinked and looked around with eyes that were very keen now, having been in darkness for so long. High above he could see the opening of the mine shaft, almost a pinhole, showing the paler grey that was the sky. Down here, and all around him, he could see the ancient timber hoardings that must have formed the housing for the now-vanished platform lift, in whose space he and the dog were now suspended. Cautiously, he cut the sacking a little more. It started to rip and he roared in shock. But it stopped as suddenly, having hit the strength of a seam. Now he was hanging half out of the sack, clinging to the fabric for dear life, and Razor was scrabbling at his knees, trying to claw his way out. 'Sit still,' he shouted. *Your life could depend on the obedience and response of your dog,* he heard his training sergeant say from long ago. Razor obeyed immediately. 'Good dog, good dog,' he said. Cautiously, he put a hand down and petted Razor's big ears. Then he put his arm out and reached above the sack, over his head. By twisting around and feeling along with his fingertips, he could feel that he and Razor weren't caught on some tree root or jagged rock but on some sort of metal frame. He continued to creep his fingers along until he could get a handhold on what felt like flaky, rusted metal, gradually increasing his pull on it, testing its strength. Finally, he let it take almost all his weight. The sharp corrosion cut into his hand, but the metal held firm. Somehow, he had to get himself out of the sack, lift himself up, get himself into a safe position and then try to get Razor to safety. Then he had to find a way up out of the shaft. He had lost his torch somewhere in the engagement with Angus. His weapon, cuffs, baton and dump bag had all been removed from the rings on his belt. All he had was himself, his dog, a useless set of keys and the little knife.

Harry started to consider the plan of action. He had already had all the luck due to him in this lifetime with the rusty metal projection that had broken their fall some way down the mine shaft. Slowly, he raised one arm again and took hold of the metal projection that supported the sack. Beneath him, he felt the fabric of the bag start to tear again. He froze. With great care, he raised his other arm. It was almost impossible to manoeuvre, and he was thankful for a lifetime of chin-ups and push-ups, of constant running after dogs, of being forced over fences and gates and through thick brush, of having to lift heavy, unwilling dogs high up over fences. His daily work demanded that he keep up with a dog. Now, he realised, this daily endeavour to stay as fit as a police dog just might save his life.

He felt the throbbing pain of the wound on his head and the burning sensation in the skin of his bloody wrist. It seemed to Harry that he was in a combat zone again and he felt the adrenalin rush of battle. Angus had wanted to take him alive. Had wanted to throw him in a sack with his dog. And toss him alive down the mine shaft. 'You bastard, Wetherill,' he cursed. Razor whimpered and pawed at his legs.

TWENTY-THREE

The Confessor couldn't bear to hear the little girl anymore. 'Stop it!' he called to her. 'Just be good. Just be quiet. Be good or I'll have to punish you.' But the little girl would not be quiet. She kept yelling out, begging him to let her out. The Confessor stood up and looked at the locked door and remembered how it was to be locked up like that. They used to do it to him all the time in the hospitals. Two or three nurses would grab him and drag him down into the time-out cellar. People were always locking him up, since he was a little boy. 'Stop that noise,' *she* used to say in the Home. 'You shut up or in you'll go, my fine sir. Into Matron's cubbyhole until you're a good boy. You must learn to be a good boy. It's for your own good,' *she* used to say.

The Confessor shuffled a little closer to the door. 'You must learn to be a good boy,' he said to the door. The little girl was kicking the door. But it was a good strong door, he knew that, and he'd never been able to get out either.

'It's for your own good,' he told the door. He put his hands over his ears because she was crying again. He could not bear to hear her crying like that. 'Stop it!' he yelled. 'You must stop it!' He shuffled away towards the kitchen door. I will go away, he thought, and this noise will stop. He opened the door and went out, locking it behind him.

The cries could not be heard out there in the street. Ah, that was better. The Confessor sighed with relief. But the Archons stirred in his mind. 'Useless, stupid good for nothing,' they started telling him. 'You're fit for nothing. You're just rubbish. What are you? *What are you?*' 'Rubbish,' he muttered to himself as he made his slow way down the street. 'Rubbish is what I am. Must learn to be a good boy.' He was pleased that the terrible noise had stopped. He might go back to ward seventeen again and stay there for awhile because these days they didn't lock up. They gave him pills and he could be unconscious or dreamy and the voices of the Archons sometimes left him alone when he was there. There was that freckled young nurse who listened to him. Harry Doyle and the young nurse on ward seventeen were the two people in the world who listened to him. The Confessor felt in his pockets for loose change because here on the corner was a public telephone and he could tell everything to Harry Doyle. But Harry Doyle was not home. Only his angry woman was there. The Confessor reconsidered. He decided to go to ward seventeen and make the phone call from there.

TWENTY-FOUR

The ute rattled over the roads. All he needed to do now, Angus thought, was meet up with Pughsie and pay him the rest of the money. He remembered his nine months for assault and the good luck that had put him in with Pughsie, who liked to boast about the long sentence he'd almost served and then torment other men with his constant reminders that he was coming up for release. In the prison print shop, where they'd worked for the state for twenty-four dollars a week, it hadn't taken long for Angus Wetherill and Ronald Pugh to discover that they both had issues concerning Harry Doyle. Angus recalled Pugh's ugly down-turned mouth glistening when they'd talked over the plan. Jail was a great place, Angus had discovered, for hatred to harden into vengeful action.

Soon he'd have half of the Doyles accounted for. That left only the woman and the older girl. The older girl, Angus knew, wasn't a Doyle by birth. Maybe he'd let her off. Maybe he wouldn't. This must be how God feels, he thought. I'll take you, and you. But perhaps not you. Then again, I just might change my mind. Angus smiled. That left the woman, he thought to himself. The woman is definitely mine. The stupid, stupid bloody woman. He noted the kilometres to Sydney. He put his foot down.

TWENTY-FIVE

'I can't stand sitting around like this,' Meg said. 'I've got to do something.'

She and Ali had dozed fitfully, still fully dressed, sleeping in the living room next to the telephone that would not ring. Meg hoped Max would ring again, or better still arrive, beautiful and remorseful, to help her in this desperate hour. But she accepted that Max was not reliable. 'I'll be there as soon as I can,' he'd said and that would have to do.

Blade uncurled from his rug behind the kitchen door and ambled in to greet them, tail low and barely wagging, and Ali ruffled his ears absent-mindedly. He was almost recovered from his viral infection.

They'd woken well before dawn and sat in aching silence as the east lightened and then pinked. Not a breath of air stirred; it was going to be another hot day. Meg sat sipping the coffee that Ali had made for her, ignoring the toast on the plate beside it. She looked across at Alison sitting in the big armchair next to her and put her hand out to take her daughter's. Too many emotions tangled inside her, leading to tears.

'Ali. You've been so good to me. And I've been such a shit of a mother to you since you stopped being little. I sort of ignored you because I didn't know what to do. I gave my attention to Hannah because she was easier, littler. I don't understand why I did that. I just wish I'd had the wisdom to know what to do. But I didn't, Ali. I didn't know what to do so I'd yell at you instead. I've been a hopeless mother to you.'

Ali's eyes filled with tears. 'Don't say that,' she said. Meg leaned over and kissed her and they rocked in each other's arms.

'I've got to do something, Ali, to bring Hannah home. I can't bear this sitting around. I can't sit and wait like Jim says. I've got to do something to help my girl. I'm her *mother*.'

'Like what?' Ali put her coffee down and went into the kitchen to find something to eat. Meg followed her and leaned over the kitchen sink, washing her face in cold water. She straightened up and Ali passed her a towel. Meg rubbed her face. She seemed to have lost weight, Ali thought, almost overnight. There were shadows around her mother's mouth and eyes which she'd never seen before.

'I'm going to ring around the psych hospitals,' said Meg. 'Track down the Confessor. He knows about Hannah. If he hasn't got her himself he knows who has. He said "He's gone to the hospital. Please get her before he comes back." Maybe he's talking about himself; giving us a hint. Did he take Hannah and is now telling us that he's giving himself up?' Ali looked at the cereal and milk she'd poured in a bowl, then pushed it away. 'Maybe,' Meg continued, 'it's his crazy way of connecting with Harry. Taking his child.'

'I wish Dad would come home,' Alison suddenly said. And Meg had to bite her tongue because she'd been about to say something thoughtless like 'He's never here when I need him'.

'Do you think something's happened to him? Why doesn't

he ring?' Ali was yearning, Meg could feel, for reassurance and tenderness. I have been so hard, she thought to herself. Preoccupied lately with myself and my messy life. 'I don't think anything has happened to him,' she said in a level voice. 'I think he just needed to get away. Maybe he's thinking about a divorce.'

Alison turned to face her mother fair and square. 'And don't you even care?' she said. Meg bit her tongue and the 'not much' that was ready to trip off it. 'I am thinking about Hannah at the moment,' she said, and got away with it.

A little while later, Meg had made a list of phone numbers. She dialled the first one.

'Hullo,' she said when they answered, continuing almost without hesitation, 'this is Detective Sergeant Margaret Doyle from Child Protection.' She saw the look on Ali's face as she went on. 'We're looking for an informant whom we believe may help us in our inquiries about a missing child. Hannah Doyle.' Her voice cracked on the last two words and she collected herself quickly. 'We only know him by nickname: "the Confessor". He has no criminal record. It's important that we know his whereabouts.' Ali watched as her mother talked a little more then rang off.

'The woman I spoke to had heard of him through other staff members,' Meg told her daughter, 'but he's never been admitted to that hospital so there are no records there.' Her heart had lightened just a little because she was taking action, on the trail.

'Mum, it's an offence to impersonate a police officer.' Alison looked down at her fingernails and then back up at her mother. Meg left the phone and went to where Ali now sat, hunched and sad and anxious, on the edge of the sofa, and sat beside her, putting her arms around her older daughter. Alison had picked up some nail clippers and was cutting off her witchy black nails.

'I've been a member of a twenty-four-hour on-call specialist police unit,' said Meg, 'for nearly ten years. I deserve the rank.' Alison smiled. 'I swear,' said Meg, 'to do everything in my power to bring Hannah safely home, and that makes me a sworn officer. I'll do anything, Ali,' she said.

Ali nodded. 'Yes,' she said to her mother. 'Me too.'

'What are you doing?' Meg suddenly noticed as Alison clipped the last one.

'There,' she said, examining her hands. They were short, square hands, capable and strong. 'I don't need them anymore,' she said. Then the terrible thought she had previously dared not entertain forced itself into her consciousness, demanding. 'Mum?'

'Yes?'

'What if Hannah is already dead?'

Meg's heart contracted to hear the words, but once they were out in the air, they seemed to lose just some of their terrible, tormenting energy, and instead of being charged with unimaginable horror, now seemed to be laden with the deepest sadness.

'If that is the case,' said Meg, aware of how tightly she was holding herself against the pain, 'we'll get the person responsible and they will pay.' She looked out the window at the suburban scene and the bougainvillea flourishing purple blooms. 'They will pay,' she repeated.

Two hours later, she had a name and an address. 'It's only the last known address,' the night supervisor told her, 'and it's pretty old. Psych patients tend to move around a lot. But it might give you another lead,' she said. Meg noted the name and address. Soon, she would track this crazy man down. She would be reunited with Hannah. 'You've got to ring Jim,' said Alison. Meg rang and Jim wasn't there but she left the name and last known address of the Confessor with Gary Stokes.

'Jim's gone home,' he said. 'For a sleep. He's worked nearly three shifts in a row. But I'll get onto this,' Stokes promised.

Meg put the phone down. 'Ring him at home,' Alison said, and Meg tried but there was no answer.

'He might be dead to the world. He might have pulled the phone out. He might be anywhere.'

Meg went into the bedroom and pulled out a light tracksuit in a dark blue colour. She put her walking boots on. A new energy flowed through her, activating her. Her heart throbbed and she felt better than she had at any time since Hannah's disappearance. Then she went into Harry's office and unlocked the gun safe. She drew out the little steely automatic .45 that Harry always kept at home, fishing around in his desk drawers until she'd found the ammunition. She loaded the magazine and pushed it home into the butt. She put the weapon on 'safety' and carefully placed it in the pocket of the tracksuit.

She went outside and into the shed where the dogs' harnesses were stored, glancing at the empty place where Razor's gear usually hung, wishing she had a more experienced dog to work with. Blade was flighty and not fully trained, she knew, and only just over a viral infection. But he was courageous. She pulled his tackle off the wall and came back inside.

Blade, keen to work but somewhat puzzled as to why the dominant bitch was harnessing him, sniffed the air for enlightenment.

'Let's go,' Meg said. And they did.

*   *   *

Jim had been asleep for only a few hours when he was woken by his mobile ringing.

'Yes?' he said, rubbing his stinging eyes and trying to hear properly despite a head echoing with exhaustion. These sorts of hours were too much for him these days, he thought.

It was Gary Stokes. 'Boss? Brian from Fingerprints wants to talk to you. He's coming in now.'

'I'm on my way,' said Jim. One day, he thought, I'll get out of the job and I'll play golf and go to the club for lunch and have dessert. 'Anything on Harry?' he asked.

'No. Nothing. His boss said he'd had words with Harry about the family situation last week. Harry told him he was going bush for awhile. Harry's wife rang. We've got a name and the last known address of that crazy who used to ring you. You were spot on about it being the name of an author; it's Milton – Milton Pugh.'

'Milton,' said Jim. 'Not Dante.' And he wondered how Meg had done it.

'Come again?' Stokes asked.

'I can't do anything about it just now. Get someone to drop round and check it out.'

When Jim got back to his office, he made coffee. His phone rang and it was Security downstairs telling him that Brian Foveaux was on his way up. Jim checked the pigeons. One egg had rolled out of the nest and lay broken on the ledge; the female sat on the other two while the male huddled asleep.

Jim knew from his colleague's face that it was bad news the moment Brian walked in.

'I was on my way to an interview at College Street,' he said, 'so I thought I'd bring the results in person. It's about as bad as it can be.'

He opened a folder and took out several enlarged photographs of finger- and partial thumb-prints. 'We got a lot of points of similarity,' he said, dropping the photographs on Jim's desk. Jim picked one up, noting the ridges and whorls, the swirling pattern of human skin. 'Richard Fellowes turns out to be a geezer with a very nasty record,' said Brian. 'I reckon you can kiss that little girl goodbye. His real name is Ronald Vincent Pugh. Mean anything to you?'

Jim gripped the desk. 'Jesus,' he said. He knew there had been something about that face. Brian Foveaux stared at him. Jim was remembering the late night scene at the Police Centre ten years ago, and the training video he almost knew by heart with Harry talking in his soft, complicit way to Pugh; the almost hypnotic trance his voice created as he reconstructed the last few moments of little Helen Semple's life on the banks of the Nepean River. Then another scene almost immediately came into his mind, of the underground car park and a handcuffed man, his baby face distorted, being pushed into a Corrective Services van, screaming vengeance and hatred. he picked up the phone to ring Meg. Ronald Pugh. Milton Pugh. He put it down again.

'Harry Doyle put him away for a long time for the murder of a little girl,' said Brian. 'I checked with Corrective Services. He got out last month.'

Jim sprang into action. He called Gary. 'What's the latest address we've got for this bastard?' asked Jim, handing him the photographs. Gary Stokes vanished. Again, Jim picked up the phone and dialled Harry's number. Nothing. Just the answering machine. Jim put the phone down, ashamed of the relief he felt. But then immediately concerned. Why wasn't she by the phone?

Gary came back. 'Ronald Pugh gave his mother's address. Little Windmill Street, Millers Point.'

'Let's go,' said Jim, grabbing his jacket. 'Get as many people down there as we can. You come with me,' he said to Stokes. 'Tell Kerryanne to keep trying to get onto Meg Doyle. Someone line up an ambulance.' He put his jacket on. 'No sirens.' He grabbed a shoulder holster and went to the safe for his gun.

TWENTY-SIX

M eg parked down the road and on the opposite side to the
address she'd been given for Milton Pugh. It was a small
weatherboard cottage in a street in Mascot. Aircraft roared
overhead and the heat rose from the tarmac in shimmering
mirages.

'That's it,' she said. A low brick fence ran across the front of
the yard, where several old rose bushes struggled to breathe
in air filled with the fumes of Avgas. 'You stay here, Ali,
with Blade. He might be frightened of dogs.' Alison nodded
and looked up at her mother, her hair pulled back and no
make-up on her face, like a little girl again. Meg walked up
the path and up a couple of steps to the front door – timber
and frosted glass and cobwebs. She knocked and waited. Nothing
happened. She knocked again, and this time she discerned a figure
moving down the hallway towards the front door. The door
opened a little way and a face peered at her. It belonged to a
middle-aged man with pale blue eyes and waxy white skin like
a nun's. Meg had the impression of a hidden child, terrified and
waiting.

'I'm looking for Milton Pugh,' she said.

'Yes,' the man answered.

'Does he live here?'

'Yes,' he said again, but the door remained in the same

position, almost closed with the frightened, white face staring around at her.

'May I come in?' Meg asked.

'Yes,' he said without moving.

'The door,' said Meg. 'You'll need to open the door.'

'Yes,' said the other, opening the door.

Meg hesitated then stepped through and started to walk down the hallway. The house was very dark inside, and then Meg realised it wasn't just because she'd come in from bright sunlight. Meg could see a little way into the three rooms that opened off the hallway and each room was filled with boxes and piles of groceries, stacked floor to ceiling. Similar boxes lined the hall on either side, only leaving a narrow passage through the middle. It was like some crazy supermarket, filled with unwieldy piles of breakfast cereals, biscuits, tinned foods, boxes of tins, cake mixes, packets of sugar and flour. She turned around and the man stood uncertainly in the doorway behind her, staring at her.

'I'm looking for Milton,' she said. 'You told me he was here.'

'Yes,' he said again, clutching at the front of his shirt with a thin, pale hand.

'Are *you* Milton?'

Again, the man nodded. 'Yes,' he said. He stood slumped, silhouetted against the cloudy glass, head bowed.

Meg had entered the lounge room. All around her towered more hoards of food. Now that she was closer, she could see that many of the boxes were rotting or chewed and the contents spilled in little pyramids on the ancient floral carpet. She felt confusion, frustration and anger all mixed together.

'You rang my husband's phone,' she said. 'Harry Doyle. You said someone had gone to the hospital and that I should come and get my little girl before he got back. You spoke to me. Don't you remember?'

'Yes,' he said.

'For God's sake!' screamed Meg. 'Can't you say anything else except "yes"?'

'Yes,' he agreed, and Meg suddenly realised with shock that he could not.

There was a noise from the front of the house and a very fat old woman in a purple dressing-gown suddenly squeezed between two towers of ancient groceries.

'And who are you?' she demanded. She had the same waxy indoor complexion as the man at the door.

'I'm looking for my little girl,' said Meg, almost in tears. 'I was told Milton Pugh lived here. He rang me. And so I came here. I want to talk to him because he might know something about my daughter.'

'Poor dearie,' said the old woman, and her face was suddenly soft. 'Families are such trials, aren't they? But Milton doesn't live here anymore. He and my nephew Butterscotch here used to fight all the time.'

'Did he say where he was going? Do you know where he lives now?'

The deafening roar of a low-flying aircraft rattled the house and Meg stood in the dark room, among the ruined stores of food, hopes completely dashed.

'He was here, day before yesterday, just for a visit,' Butterscotch's aunt finally said, as the thunderous noise eased. 'But he left yesterday morning. I don't know where he was going.'

Meg looked down the hall to the door where the defeated man was still standing, uncertainly holding the door.

'You wouldn't have any idea where he might be, where he might go?' Meg asked as she walked to the door.

The old woman considered. She pulled her dressing-gown around her and followed Meg down the hall, opening the door wider, allowing Meg to go out.

'I think he usually stays at his mother's house.'

'Do you know where that is?'

'Good heavens, no,' she said. 'Somewhere. He wanted me to send his mail on.'

Meg felt she couldn't take another step. She'd had a taste of hope but now there was nothing but this dead end of old groceries, eccentricity. She couldn't bring herself to say goodbye, simply turned and made her way down the cement path to the car.

Alison saw her mother's face and put a hand over her mouth as Meg walked around to the driver's side and got in. 'What are we going to do now?' she asked.

Meg closed her eyes against the tears she could feel building, and took up the car keys. 'I don't know, Ali. Go home and wait, I suppose. There's nothing we can do.'

She had no energy. Even putting the key in the ignition and starting the car seemed inordinately hard to do.

She was pulling away from the kerb when she noticed the purple dressing-gown flapping out of the house and the fat woman running onto the footpath behind the car. The old woman clutched the purple fabric together with one hand, awkwardly waving a small white paper in the other. 'Stop! Stop!' the woman was calling. Meg slammed on the brakes, the car jerked to a stop and Blade fell in the back, slipping and sliding to regain his balance.

Meg jumped out of the car and ran back. 'This is the forwarding address,' said the woman, waving it. 'I remembered where I'd left it.' And she put an envelope with an address on it in Meg's hand. Meg looked at the painstaking letters, a little spidery, as if the hand that formed them had trembled as it wrote. Nineteen Little Windmill Street, Millers Point, she read. The address of the Confessor's mother.

'And will you tell Milton something for me?' said the old

woman, wrinkling her face up against the hot sun. 'Tell him no mail ever came. Not one thing.'

Meg thanked her and ran back to the car. Her heart was beating hard.

Meg had passed the house in Little Windmill Street three times, driving round the block to get a good look from all angles. It was a nineteenth century terrace with a back entry giving onto a narrow lane. It had a run-down paling fence on sandstone footings, with a rotting wooden gate almost covered by a choko vine.

Meg and Alison pulled up a little way down the road from number nineteen and on the opposite side. Meg reached for the mobile and rang Jim.

'We're on our way!' he yelled when he heard where they were. 'Stay in the car!'

'Sure,' Meg lied and rang off. She turned to her daughter. If this house was as weird as the one she'd just left, she didn't want to take any chances. 'Listen, Ali. You take Blade,' she said, 'just in case, and wait outside that back gate in the lane.'

'Just in case of what?' Alison asked, alerted by her mother's manner.

'Just in case it's helpful to have Blade out and ready. You'll be safer than if you had a gun. Blade will go for anyone who even thinks about touching you. I'll go in the front,' she said. 'But I want to be first in there. I want to know first-hand what he knows about Hannah. I don't want any police frightening him or pushing me away from the scene.'

'I don't know the attack command,' said Alison, almost in tears. 'I wish Dad was here. Why isn't he here?' Blade was pulling on his harness.

'Trust the dog's judgement,' said Meg. 'Blade will know what to do. He won't let anyone hurt you. Just hold tight to

the harness. He's trained to protect whoever is holding him.'
The two looked at each other.

'Let's go,' said Meg. 'Let's get our baby back.'

She jumped out of the car. Alison took hold of Blade's line and he dropped out of the car, looking around, sniffing, immediately interesting himself with the job. Meg watched as Alison disappeared round the corner. She gave her daughter a moment or two to station herself at the back of number nineteen, then she opened the rickety gate and walked up to the front door.

The house looked neglected. Vines covered the rusted iron of the front verandah and paint peeled from the exterior walls. She peered through a window to the left of the front door. Inside, she could see an untidy bedroom, old cheap furniture, a naked globe hanging from the ceiling. She wondered what she'd say to the Confessor, how she'd communicate with him, while she banged on the door. 'Open this door!' she yelled. And then she heard it. Hannah's wail. Unmistakably the sound of her daughter's voice. Meg's heart turned inside out. Hannah. My darling. '*Open this door!*' she screamed, bashing the door panels with all her strength. 'Hannah! *I'm here!*'

'Get him away from me!' she heard her younger daughter cry. 'Somebody help me! Get the police. Get my father! Get me away from him.'

The voice was suddenly stifled. Meg's heart pounded in her ears and her whole body was suffused with some red-hot, then white-hot energy. It burst through her body, triggered by the terror in her daughter's cry. It channelled down through her spine, electrifying her legs. Meg didn't know how it happened until later but she had smashed through the glass of that dirty window, arced off the bed like an Olympic gymnast and was on her feet running down the hallway. Somewhere, she was aware of Blade going crazy out the back.

'*I'm here Hanks!*' she screamed at the top of her voice. 'Where are you?'

'*Mum!*' screamed Hannah. '*Mummy!*'

The terrible note in the last screamed word made Meg draw the weapon. She fumbled to take the safety off. If I see him, I'll kill him. But when she did see him, he was coming out of what seemed like a dark cupboard, grabbing his trousers at the front as she came into the kitchen. Meg stopped short, panting. She raised the weapon instinctively in front of her, because now he was shambling towards her. Half his face was bandaged and he held his head stiffly to one side so that he looked like something from a horror movie.

'Stop right there, you bastard!' she screamed. 'Stop or I'll shoot.' She levelled the pistol at him, using her other hand to support her trembling grasp. 'Hanks!' she screamed. 'Are you all right? Where are you?' But the bandaged mummy kept coming at her, his black eyes boring into hers, smoking with hatred and rage. Then Meg became aware of a horrible noise coming from him. His heavy little red mouth was open and he was growling like an animal. In spite of her charged state, the guttural snarl froze her. Meg was aware of the hackles of her neck and spine rising. And in that moment of immobilisation, he had somehow evaded her, springing sideways to vanish out the kitchen door.

'Mum!' Hannah was running at her and Meg barely remembered to drop the gun before catching her daughter up in her arms – laughing, crying, sobbing, choking all together. 'Mum, oh Mum. I'm sorry, I'm sorry!' Hannah was sobbing.

'It's all right, it's all right,' was all Meg could say, choking and crying together. She held her daughter tightly as they walked, almost falling over because Meg had completely gone in the legs. Out of the kitchen they went, down the dirty hall and into the sunlight as Jim Coates' car, blazingly white in the sun and followed by two others, screeched to a halt outside.

Ronald Pugh stumbled out of the kitchen and down the overgrown flagstone path, ducking to one side to avoid colliding with the clothes. A thorny lemon tree scraped the bitten side of his head and neck and he yelped with pain. As he reached the back fence, he could hear someone in the hallway of the house behind him, yelling out his name. Pugh grabbed the bolt lock that closed the wooden gate in the back fence and slid it open. He was still growling and holding his bandaged ear as he shoved the gate open, knocking Alison to the ground. Alison screamed, recovered, and slipped Blade, who leaped at Pugh's throat.

Pugh bellowed and punched out, hitting Blade viciously. Blade's teeth closed on the bandage, ripping it off before he dropped, stunned by the blows. Pugh kicked out at him, shouting, and Alison ducked, rolling over the ground to get away. Meanwhile Blade, confused and in pain and with his handler sprawled out on the ground, flew through the air again, sinking his fangs deeply into Pugh's neck, the momentum throwing them both to the ground. Pugh struggled, kicking and punching, but Blade danced like a fighter, savaging the neck, growling through his clenched fangs, maintaining his grip. Alison got to her feet, shaking and shocked, as a brilliant sheet of arterial blood arced out from Pugh's neck onto the fence, painting the grey timber transparent crimson. Pugh's racing heart pumped his body empty through the severed carotid artery, so that by the time Jim Coates had run through the backyard and appeared at the gateway in the fence, Blade was sitting at attention beside the prostrate figure like a good dog, Alison was shaking and ashen-faced but firmly holding Blade's line, and Ronald Pugh was dead.

TWENTY-SEVEN

'But I don't want a doctor to look at me,' Hannah wailed as she sat in the bath. 'I'm not sick. And I want Dad and Razor to come home now. Why isn't he here? I want you to get Blade back from the dogs' hospital. I want him tonight.'

Meg dribbled warm water down her younger daughter's back and Alison sat on a stool. 'Okay, darling,' said Meg. 'No doctor. And I promise we'll get Blade back tomorrow. Don just wanted to keep him in overnight because of the deep bruising where that man kicked him.'

'Why didn't Dad come and get me?'

'He's away, darling,' said Meg, feeling the anger at her husband building again.

'That horrible man was going to hurt me. He locked me up in a dark cupboard. He didn't even care. But he didn't do anything to me,' she continued, 'because I bit him and then you got there. But he was going to. He kicked Blade. I was so scared, Mum.' The tears ran down her face again. My beautiful girl, thought Meg, and her heart ached. I have failed to protect my child.

'I knew when we got to the place,' Hannah was saying, 'I knew he wasn't Richard's father. But he was too strong and he pushed me in that cupboard.' She burst into tears again. 'I thought he would kill me. I thought I was going to die and I would never see you or Ali or Dad or the dogs again.'

Her wail filled the bathroom and Meg grabbed the towel and wrapped her daughter in it. 'Oh Hannah,' she said. 'I'm so sorry. I'm just so sorry.' She held her child close to her heart. 'I don't know what I would have done if anything had happened to you.'

Hannah pulled away and looked at her mother, her expression outraged and stunned. 'He came back again after I bit his ear nearly off. He was all bandaged and he was trying to get me. I just punched and kicked and I didn't care what I did to him. I got very strong. But I was so frightened. Because he was much stronger. I hate him. I'm glad he's dead. I'm glad Blade killed him. Now he can never hurt me again.' Hannah looked so small and sweet with her hair flattened on her head and her wet eyelashes in points like stars. Meg felt the love rise up in her. And the fury that anyone could want to hurt her.

'Where's Dad?' Hannah demanded again, as if she'd forgotten he was away. 'I was waiting for Dad to come and get me with Razor.' She started crying again, wailing heartbroken sobs, and Meg held her and soothed her. She dried and powdered the small, shaking body, the round bottom and the slender back.

'There, Hanky-dory,' said Alison. 'You're all iced and ready to eat.' But Hannah continued to wail, refusing to be comforted by their old icing sugar game. 'Dad's gone bush for awhile,' Alison attempted to explain again.

Hannah looked from one to the other. 'Why?' she asked. 'Doesn't he even care that I was kidnapped? Doesn't he even care that a man was going to rape me and kill me?'

Alison looked over her sister's head at her mother. Meg looked stricken. All she could do was put her arms around the distressed little girl and hold her against herself until the sobbing subsided.

'He does care, darling,' said Meg. 'He just doesn't know. He's out of range.'

'He's my father and he should know,' sobbed Hannah. 'I want Dad,' she cried over and over. 'I want him to come home.' Her grief was enormous and seemed to Meg to contain all the suffering of her life.

Later, when she'd cried herself out, Hannah told everything again to Jim. 'And the other one, the funny one,' said Jim.

'The Confessor,' said Meg. 'I'd forgotten all about him. I wouldn't have been able to get Hannah back if it hadn't been for him. I owe him the life of my daughter. I want to see him, Jim.'

'I never realised the Confessor and Pugh were connected,' said Jim. 'Looks like Ronald was sick and violent and Milton was sick and mad.'

'Happy families,' said Meg, and not all the bitterness was aimed at the Pugh brothers. I must get my own house in order, she thought to herself.

'I've got a whole lot of stuff my blokes collected from the crime scene in the car,' said Jim. 'I want to get it sorted out as soon as possible. There may be something we can do for poor old Milton now that his brother is dead.'

Hannah didn't want to go to bed, but finally they persuaded her.

'I don't want the computer in here,' she said. 'I want you to take it out of my room. And I want to sleep in the big nubbler.'

Meg and Alison looked at each other. Hannah hadn't used that name for her parents' double bed for years. 'Okay,' Meg said. 'In you go.' And they put her to bed in her parents' room with the light on and the door open, so that they could hear her if she called out.

Dell had come in from next-door and she and Jim were chatting quietly on the couch. 'I think we could do with a drink,' said Jim and Dell went to the sideboard, pouring the brandy into four glasses, finding ice in the freezer and bringing them out. Meg put her arm around Alison, and her daughter cuddled up to her.

Finally, Jim stood up. 'I'm going home,' he said. 'I'm going to sleep for ten hours. We can do your statement tomorrow.' He kissed her briefly, patted Alison's arm and stood up. 'Meg, we want to leave someone here with you, twenty-four hours a day.'

'No way!' she said. 'I'm not having some other cop in my house clumping around in his big boots. It's bad enough being married to one.'

Jim tried again. 'Meg, unless the experts prove that Pugh is our man, I have to assume there's a man out there who's already killed at least two women, probably three – two of them connected to Harry.'

'Look, Jim, I don't believe Hannah's disappearance had anything to do with the deaths of those other women. Ronald Pugh is good and dead. And I'm exhausted and I'm having a bath and going to bed.' Jim went to speak again and Meg stopped him. 'I've got a nice little automatic .45 that I know how to use, and tomorrow I'll have Police Dog Blade back on the job.'

Meg put Jim out the door and peeped in on Hannah on the way back. She was asleep, with her mouth slightly open and one hand, like a salute, on the pillow.

Alison and Meg stretched out on the floor, leaning their backs against the lounge room furniture. Meg closed her eyes and gave thanks that Hannah was safe at home. I have been impossibly lucky, she thought.

'Mum?' Ali said.

'Yes, darling?'

'Do you think you and Dad will stay together?'

Meg caught her breath. 'I don't know,' she said. 'I haven't really thought about it just lately.'

'What about your other man?'

Meg raised her knees and sat straighter against the lounge. 'My other man,' she said, 'was someone I met at art classes. He is no longer my other man.' She looked away. It felt indecent, talking like this to her daughter. 'You know things haven't been good between me and your father for awhile.'

'It's been awful for us, too,' said Alison. 'Me and Hannah. I think—' But she stopped and Meg was alerted, knowing that her daughter had stopped talking in order not to say something that might hurt. 'Tell me,' she urged. She remembered Alison's bravery and reliability of the day, taking the young dog like that, guarding the back entrance of Ronald Pugh's house of horror. 'I want to hear what you think.'

Alison drew herself up too, and wrapped her arms around herself. Then she reached for her glass. 'I think Hannah only got involved with that creep through the Internet because of what was happening here.'

Meg felt the truth of what her daughter was saying and it hurt. Tears filled her eyes. She picked up her drink and sipped it.

'When I was waiting there at the back of the house,' Alison said a little while later, 'I was really scared. Even though I had Blade, I was scared. But once that man came out and kicked out like that, something happened in me. I wasn't frightened. I was just exploding. I can't explain it. I just knew what to do. How to slip Blade, how to get out of his way. Mum,' she said, and there was concern as well as pride in her voice, 'I really liked that. It was an amazing moment for me. I think I want to do it again.'

'When Dad comes home,' Meg said to her daughter, 'we're all going to sit down and talk. Talk about what we want. What's important to us. But this time, we're all going to listen to each other. No arguments. Just listening. No trying to be right. No trying to make someone else see another point of view. None of us know each other. I don't know you, Ali. You've never told me about you. I've just assumed I know you and Hannah. But this time we're all going to listen to each other and hear what it's like for you to be you, for Hannah to be Hannah. And for me to be me.'

A slight noise made them look up. Hannah was standing in the doorway in her pink and white spotted pyjamas.

'What is it, darling?' said Meg, getting up from the floor.

'And Dad too,' said Hannah. 'Dad has to tell us all the things he won't tell us. And Dad has to listen to us, too. And you have to let Dad talk, and not fight against what he says like you always do. You have to listen too, Mum.'

TWENTY-EIGHT

H arry crouched on the rusty framework. Once out of the sack, he'd been able to haul it up, even though Razor had seemed heavier than it was possible for a dog to be. Now Razor huddled near him, whimpering from time to time. 'Stay quiet, boy,' Harry told him. I'm weak, thought Harry. I need water badly. I need to eat.

He rested as he tried to work out what to do next. Towards the top of the shaft there was a little light and he could make out the bricks that lined the sides. He could see their irregularities and he hoped and prayed that these continued all the way down, because they were his way out of this place. Then it was no longer possible to see any lower down the shaft because the light cut out. He put his hand out, but he couldn't touch the side. He moved as far as he dared, never knowing if and when the projection that they were caught on would hold fast. He would have to feel his way.

He had done worse jobs than this. He remembered the time he'd had to climb under the foundations of an old house to bring out a suicide and how searching about in the blackness with the appalling stench of decay all around him, his fingers had pressed into too-soft human flesh, sickeningly warm from the activity of maggots. There was a chance he could climb out of this pit. The alternative was to sit there and starve to death.

Or slip over the edge and into the depths below. He looked up. Right in the middle of the entrance to the shaft, all those dozens of metres above, a single star shone down. Harry felt his eyes fill. The star wobbled and swam as he looked at it. It took him back to the memory of his childhood bed, after his mother had found him again and brought him back home, those days he would not let himself think of, far less talk about. He remembered his mother showing him the star as she tucked him in, now that he was safely back. She told him the story of the seven sisters who had jumped up into the sky to evade their pursuer and how they shone down still, safe forever from capture.

'And those people, they won't ever get you again, either,' she'd whispered. 'You're safe here. We're safe here. This is a good place. This Joe Doyle, he's a good man and a good worker.'

His mother's face came into his mind: her too-rare joyous smile; her laugh; her courage; her grief; her warm, shy goodness. The way her face would squeeze up when she yelled at him, which she often did.

I have to get out of here, he told himself anew, from this pit, while a killer stalks my people. He thought of his wife, thought of how things were no longer good between them, and vowed to change that. He would make peace with Meg. He thought of his daughters. If he got out of there, he would ask them what they needed from him. Then he felt around and found that there seemed to be absolutely no handhold for him.

His helplessness washed over him, disarming him, and he sobbed – the deep, tearing sobs of a man who hasn't cried since he was a child, the creaky sounds of unused chords and ligaments moving stiffly. Help me, he asked his mother. Help me to get out of this place and go home. I have to get home. He wiped his face, crouched down again and started taking off his boots.

TWENTY-NINE

M eg was exhausted. She and Alison were nearly asleep on
the floor. 'Come on, possumpants,' she said to Alison.
'It's beddy-byes for you.' She supported her sleepy daughter
down the hall to her bedroom.

'Tuck me in, Mum,' said Ali. 'Like when I was little.'

When Meg tucked her in and kissed her, Alison suddenly
grabbed her. 'Mum,' she whispered. 'I keep seeing that man
with Blade jumping up on him and tearing his throat. All
that blood. I can't get the picture out of my head.'

Meg held her. 'It must have been terrible for you to see
that. Ali, I wish you hadn't seen that. I wish none of it had
happened. To you and Hannah.'

Alison put her arms around her mother. 'It's okay, Mum.
It's okay.'

Finally, Meg kissed her again and stood up.

'Do you want something to help you sleep?' she asked.

Alison shook her head and Meg was about to close the
door when Alison called out, 'Leave the door a bit open,
Mum. And leave the hall light on.' Alison hadn't made that
request for many years.

Her own body was about ready to drop, Meg realised, but
her head was still spinning like Alison's with crazy, strobe-like

images from the day: of Hannah in that filthy cupboard, running towards her, screaming; of Pugh's eyes blazing and the inhuman growling that rasped in his throat as he came towards her in that nightmare moment.

Meg ran a bath, took a sleeping tablet and lowered herself gratefully into the hot water. In awhile, she started to experience the effects of the drug. I'd better get out, she thought, before I drift off in the bath and catch my death. But despite the agitation in her mind, there was a new understanding. Since Hannah's kidnapping and return, it was as if her whole world had swerved about and realigned itself. She wasn't sure if it was only an effect of the sedative and the lavender oil in the bath, but a new softness now seemed to fill her heart so that she could almost imagine herself getting it together with Harry again. She did not share Jim's concern about her husband's absence; long-serving detectives always have a dark view on the world. There was no way Harry would suicide. Of that she was entirely certain. He'd gone off like this once or twice before, she remembered, in the early days of their marriage, when he needed to get clear about something. He'd just go bush and return days later, freer and refreshed. When he came home – *if* he came home – she would listen to him. Maybe he would listen to her if she dropped her long list of complaints and sued for peace. Maybe right this minute he was wondering, just as she was, whether there was any point in continuing with a marriage that had become nothing more than a prolonged battleground. Maybe quite soon, she imagined, she would be living only with the kids, like Dell; maybe starting to go on dates with men again. This made her giggle into the washer. Then she felt the giggle change to sobs. She cried a little while and then splashed warm water over her face. She decided that whatever happened with Harry, she was going to tell him the truth – about herself, about the affair she'd had, about her life and what she wanted, what she needed. Not in the old angry way of wanting him to do something about it, but in a new gear, just so he'd know the truth about her and she could get on with it. She was thinking of him when she heard the doorbell go. She heaved herself out of the bath and wrapped a towel around her dripping body. 'I'm coming, I'm coming,' she told the door, sure it would be Harry, deciding that there would be no talking that night, but tomorrow, after a good night's sleep, it was essential that they work out what they were going to do, whether the marriage could continue.

She opened the door. 'Oh,' she said. 'It's you.'

As Jim turned into his street, he suddenly felt wide awake. He knew it was the adrenalin charge of exhaustion, but he also knew there was little point in him going to bed. He knew this state of his – physical exhaustion chafing against mental agitation. His concern for Harry was growing. The events of the afternoon and evening hadn't dulled that. The late Ronald Pugh had most likely been planning his revenge in jail for over a decade. Now Pugh was dead. That was that. Hannah was safely home and the pressure had eased. But he would have to make sure whether or not there was any link between that and Harry's disappearance. Pugh might not have acted alone.

He pulled up outside his block of flats and sat a moment, considering. The building was in darkness apart from the downstairs hallway light and the little glowing rows beside each flat number on the security intercom. He rubbed his eyes and blinked. A couple walked past, entwined, and Jim sighed, indicated, changed gear and swung his vehicle around again, heading back to town. If he couldn't sleep, he might as well start on the physical evidence collected from the house at Millers Point and start writing up the events leading to the death of Pugh. In the morning he'd ask Meg and Alison to come in and do statements. And he'd have to track poor old Milton down and try to make sense of whatever he had to say. It was clear he'd known something about the kidnapping.

He drove to the Police Centre, nodded to the security desk, used his card to get through to the lifts and rode up to his floor, carrying the various bags and envelopes with him. The corridors were dimly lit and he was the only person on his floor. Jim opened the security door of his section with his card, switched the lights on and went into his office.

He put some music on and looked over the cardboard strip along the window. The male was on the nest, brooding. The female was nowhere to be seen. He pulled on a pair of thin, white rubber gloves and started going through the papers they'd found at Ronald Pugh's place: bills, letters, large exercise books filled with clippings, pornographic magazines, a couple of knives, and videos without commercial packaging which promised to be interesting if you liked that sort of thing. Jim didn't.

He grouped the collection in various piles on his desk. He glanced through the papers. As he sorted, he noticed a message lying in his in-tray which Gary Stokes must have left for him: 'Max Wolansky,' he read. 'DOB 8. 11. 47. Killed in action, Vietnam, 6.7.72.' Jim stared at the name and read it again carefully.

He put the piece of paper down, his mind racing to work this through. As he did, he noticed that one of the envelopes taken from the Millers Point house had a name and telephone number scribbled on it. Jim picked it up because it was the name that had drawn his attention. He dialled the number scribbled beside the name.

'Hullo, Martendale Hotel,' a professional telephonist's voice answered him. 'How may I help you?'

Jim identified himself. Meg had told him that she and Max Wolansky met at hotels and motels. 'I'm looking for Max Wolansky,' Jim said. 'Is he staying with you?'

There was a delay while the receptionist went to look. It was just possible there were two people born on the same date with the same unusual name. Otherwise, Meg had been having an affair with a ghost. The unease in Jim's guts grew stronger. It was not uncommon for criminals and others who wanted well-documented aliases to use the details of the dead to obtain a legitimate birth certificate. Who, then, had Meg been involved with? Jim's mind processed possibilities. He wanted to ring Meg straightaway but the clock on the office wall showed 1.45 a.m. This was not a good time to ring anyone, particularly Meg, and not about this particular subject.

His mind started putting it all together. Ronald Pugh had the phone number of a Max; Meg had been involved with a Max. There was nothing necessarily criminal about using another name, unless there was proven intent to defraud. Bedding another man's wife could hardly be called that, thought Jim, or a lot of the male population of the country could be prosecuted. But Jim's sixth sense would not stop nagging him.

'Hullo?' said the receptionist. 'Mr Wolansky isn't with us at the moment. But he does stay here from time to time. We could take a message and give it to him next time he stays. I couldn't give you the address over the phone. Security reasons, sir. But you could come in with your ID and talk to the manager.'

Jim thanked her and rang off.

If Pugh had been involved with the same Max Wolansky,

it meant a nasty connection to Harry's family that Jim did not like one bit. He cursed himself for not having insisted on protection for Meg. He moved fast to the lifts, down to the car and drove up out of the ramp onto the streets. There was little traffic except for Oxford Street, where people thronged and shops and clubs were open. A man with acid-yellow spiked hair, fantastically clad in lime green lycra, put out his tongue lasciviously at Jim as he made the right-hand turn up towards Taylors Square.

Jim drove towards 55 Botanical Avenue, his anxiety increasing with every kilometre. As soon as he turned the corner and started the drive down to Harry's house, all his sense jumped into red alert. Meg's car was parked out the front and light streamed onto it and onto the lawn of 55 because the front door was wide open. Jim swung to a halt, jumped out of the car, raced up the steps and inside.

'Meg? Meg?' There was no reply. Jim went through the house, looking and calling, checking the rooms. Hannah was snoring with her arms around a huge teddy bear. Alison also was soundly asleep but stirred as he looked in. There was no sign of Meg.

'Where's Mum?' Alison called, coming out of her room, pulling on a long football jersey. 'Maybe next-door,' she suggested to Jim. 'Maybe she's with Dell.'

But Dell, alarmed and wrapped in her green towelling dressing-gown, shook her head when the two of them knocked on her door and asked her. Jim ran back to his car and called the local police. 'I'll get some people round here straightaway,' he told Alison. 'To do a thorough check and stay here with you.'

'But where is she?' screamed Alison.

Jim took hold of her shoulders. The young girl was shaking

uncontrollably. 'What's happening to my family?' she said. 'Where's my mother? Where's my father?'

'I don't know,' he said. 'But we're going to do our damnedest to find out. Wherever she is, she hasn't been gone long. We'll find her.'

'I'm going round to the vet,' said Alison, gulping down sobs and straightening herself up. 'And I'm going to get Blade back. I want to know where you're going. I want to go with you.'

'Alison, that's impossible. You know that. Stay with Hannah. She needs you.'

'I can get Dell to stay with her,' said Alison. 'I mean it. I'll wake up Don Rawson. I'm getting the dog and I'm coming with you. I'll take Mum's car.'

Jim started to say something. Then he went back to the car and radioed for the address of the Martendale Hotel. While he was waiting, Alison came out of the house, down the steps and stood by his car.

'Martendale Hotel,' said the operator, 'corner of Blackett and Darlinghurst Roads.' Jim noted it down. Only a few suburbs away back towards the city.

'I want to come with you,' said Alison. 'I know where that place is.'

'Not possible, Alison. You know that.'

'Okay,' said Alison. 'Okay.'

Meg didn't know where she was. She was lying in the back of a utility vehicle with a tarpaulin over her, jolting over roads at high speed. She could smell the bush. Her mind replayed the scene of only a few hours ago, at her doorstep. 'Oh,' she'd said. 'It's you.' She'd been so surprised she couldn't speak and the effects of the drug had slowed her responses.

'I got held up,' he'd said. His handsome face was clouded

with tiredness. 'But here I am. I'm completely at your disposal. You look very beautiful in that towel.'

Meg had stood there, not knowing what to do, what to say. She knew now she was a thousand light years away from him.

'Aren't you going to ask me in?' he was saying, with his slight smile. But Meg had looked steadily at him.

'Max,' she'd finally said. 'I don't want to see you again. I told you that. Your behaviour at our last meeting was unforgivable. Unacceptable. It's over. You've got to accept that. It's late. I'm buggered. I got Hannah back. Everything's changed. Too many things have happened.'

He'd pushed his hair back as he stood supplicant on her doorstep and she caught his personal scent – a sharp, male sandalwood. 'Please, Meg,' he said, 'I couldn't get here any earlier. I had this deal happening. I just couldn't get away.' His dark eyes looked into hers. 'You are beautiful,' he said. 'I want you.'

Meg said nothing, her stomach fluttering and her breathing edged with excitement.

'You *were* pleased to hear from me, on the phone. You can't deny that. I could hear it in your voice.'

'I don't deny that, Max,' she said. 'My little girl had just been stolen. I was desperate for some help, some support. Harry was God knows where. But you didn't show. You offered all this help from your exalted position, your friends, your money. The grand gesture. But you didn't show, Max. I got my girl back by myself. With the help of my other daughter. I tracked the kidnapper and we went in there and brought Hannah back ourselves.' She thought his face darkened, but blinked again, trying to clear her mind of the tranquilliser.

'But Meg, remember the things you said,' he was pleading now, 'the experiences we had together . . .'

She thought of the nights of lovemaking, the delirious excitement, the crazy way she'd abandoned herself to this man. Her traitor body quickened. 'I had great sex with you,' she said. 'But sex is only sex and life is much bigger than that.'

She saw his face change as he started to see she really meant it this time. She drew the towel closer around herself and prepared to close the door. She didn't like the way his expression was hardening. She remembered their last meeting, his contempt, his assault on her. She put her hand up to the doorhandle, ready to close it. 'I'm sorry I got involved with you,' she confessed. 'It was a mistake. I was naive and vain. I didn't know myself and I feel I was a fraud. What you said the other day hurt me but it was the truth. My motive was mere adventuring. Curiosity, excitement. It wasn't love, and you know that as well as I do. I am very sorry if I've hurt you.'

She saw the anger drawing his brows down, saw the way his handsome mouth had started to curl. She couldn't resist a parting shot. 'Max,' she said, starting to close the door, her mind surprisingly active despite the leaden relaxation of her body, aware that she wasn't really angry with him, that she was already detaching from him, 'Max, you're a fraud. You say grand things. But you don't follow through. Any woman who got involved with you would come a poor third – no, fourth – to your Scotch, your exotic cigarettes and your business deals.' She thought of his sexual preference and smiled. 'Max,' she couldn't resist saying, 'you're a wanker.'

She remembered Max putting his foot in the front door as she was closing it, grabbing her, flattening her agaisnt the wall, one hand over her mouth. Then he'd done something painful to the side of her neck and she must have blacked out because the next thing she knew, she was in the situation in which she now found herself, jolting along, lying on an old rug, with her hands and feet bound and her mind half stupefied with narcotics. 'Max!' she screamed. 'Let me out! Let me go!' But her voice was lost in the noise of the engine and the rush and bump over rough roads, the occasional sounds of other vehicles and the roar of passing trucks. '*Max!*' she screamed again. '*Stop this! Let me go!*'

THIRTY

Harry dozed for awhile, on and off, trying to build up a bit of strength after his ordeal in the sack. He rested leaning against Razor, taking some comfort from the old dog's warm flanks. Later he woke, stiff and sore, to see pre-dawn light shining down the shaft. He could see the mossy bricks up the top and, by feeling around and stretching out as much as he dared, he managed to find a fingerhold and then a toehold. Now, he was a metre or so higher than the rusty surface where Razor whimpered. The dog would have to wait until Harry could bring back the necessary equipment to winch him out.

'Mate,' he said to the dog. 'I'm going to climb up out of here and then I'm going to get help for you. I'll be as fast as I can. Wish me luck.' Razor barked sharply, sensing a parting. Harry hauled himself up further. He found a fingerhold, dug into it, and then was filled with fear as his fingers slipped off the mossy brick. For a second, he swung there one-handedly, until he could bring the other arm up again. Painfully, he hauled himself up until he could find another toehold. Beneath him, Razor whimpered again. 'It's okay, boy. Just sit. Wait.' He knew the dog was thirsty, hungry and exhausted. He knew it from his own experience. Somehow, he had to find the reserves of strength to claw his way up and out of this place. The thought of Angus Wetherill harming his family gave him an extra burst of adrenaline-charged strength.

Harry continued to inch up the bricks, toehold by painful toehold, sometimes almost losing his footing on the slippery surface. He willed himself to cling to the mine shaft walls. Sometimes there was good purchase for his searching fingers; at other times, only the slightest surface angle presented itself. Whenever there seemed to be no hold at all, Harry rested, staying where he was, recovering what remained of his strength. Then, by feeling around on each side, he would find some small irregularity on the brickface and, inch by inch, Harry Doyle slowly made it towards the top. After he'd gone some way up the shaft, Razor started howling somewhere in the darkness beneath him. Harry knew how he felt.

At the Martendale Hotel, Jim showed his warrant card and badge. 'It's a very serious matter,' he said. 'The kidnapping of a little girl.' The purple-lipped redhead behind the long polished counter responded by calling the night manager, very dapper with his shaven head and earring. 'We saw it on the telly,' she said. 'That poor little kid. She's one of the lucky ones who come home.'

Jim waited while they consulted the records.

'I'll also want a list of any phone calls he may have made while he was here, too,' said Jim. 'Print out all his details for me. I'm quite happy to wait.'

Within half an hour, Jim had what he wanted. He thanked the young woman and the night manager and left.

Alison put on the blue overall in her father's office. In the living room a young police officer sat reading a magazine.

The overall was far too big for Alison's slender body, but by rolling the sleeves back and tucking the surplus length of the trousers into her bush-walking boots, and by tightly belting the zipped up waist with a plain black belt of her own, she was able to make it fit. Blade sat and watched her. She picked up his harness from the desk.

Earlier, the vet had handed him over with a scolding. 'I want to see your father in the morning,' he said. 'It's not like him to push a dog like this.'

'He's not my father,' said Alison. 'Blade's needed for a job.' The police officer, summoned by Jim, had arrived at her house just as she was bringing Blade home.

Now, Alison pulled her hair back from her face and pinned it up. She looked at herself in the mirror in the bathroom and thought she still looked ridiculously young. If my real father were here, she wondered, what would he do? What would he say? All she really knew about him was that his name was Jeff Kruger and she had a photo of him and her mum in which he looked a bit like a young Michael Douglas. Mum had told her that her father had sent money for a few years after she was born.

Alison walked down the hall to her parents' bedroom and found a jacket of her mother's to wear and the car keys from the bedside table. Blade followed her into the room and sat beside her while she picked up the phone and rang Mick's house, something she had never done before.

'Hullo?' he said when he came on the line.

'It's me,' she said.

'Oh Jesus,' he said. Then his voice dropped. 'What are you doing ringing here at this hour? What am I supposed to tell Sally?'

'I don't know what you're supposed to tell Sally,' she said.

'I need someone to help me do something really important. I need your help, Mick.'

'Don't be silly. I can't talk now.' She heard his voice change. 'Yes, yes,' he was saying. 'I'll get straight onto it the minute I get to work. I'm so sorry you've been inconvenienced.' Then he hung up.

Inconvenienced, Alison thought. She wanted to cry but she put the phone back gently and looked at herself in the mirror. If I were a dog, she thought to herself, I'd go round to your place, Mick Blunt, and I'd jump at your throat. The shocking scene of Blade savaging Ronald Pugh replayed itself through her mind and she had to sit down suddenly. The shaking in her legs subsided and she stood up and went back to the living room where the young police officer looked up from reading a double-paged spread in a magazine with the headline *I poisoned my sister and married her husband*.

'I'm taking the dog for a walk,' said Alison. 'I'll take him in the car to the oval.'

'I don't think that's a good idea,' said her minder. Her stern blue eyes encountered Alison's as the two young women considered each other.

'I'm safe as houses with this fellow,' said Alison, turning as she spoke. 'And you can't stop me.' But as she walked down the hall and out the front door, she could hear the young woman speaking to someone on her portable. So she moved quickly to open the door for Blade to jump in, climbed in and started the car, leaning over to strap Blade in with the seat belt. She switched on the head-lights, backed out of the driveway, buckled her seat belt and took off. She drove till she came to the Martendale Hotel and parked some way down the road and on the other side just like she knew Harry would have done. Jim's car was outside the hotel and Alison switched off the ignition and the lights and waited.

★   ★   ★

Harry dragged himself up, his fingers reaching for the next irregularity. He didn't think he had much more energy left. His head was whirling with pain and dizziness. The injury throbbed in time with his racing heartbeat. Sweat ran down between his shoulder blades and itched on his sides. Far beneath, he could hear Razor whimpering but he didn't have the strength left to waste on words. Above him, the dawn was breaking, flushing the sky a pink gold.

He thought he was hallucinating because he seemed to hear whispered words in a language he no longer understood. Soft voices seemed to urge him on. Sometimes he even dared to try turning his head, so sure was he that there was someone behind him. Sometimes he thought he saw flashes of light and lifted his head painfully to look up. But it was only the sky, moving from pink to gold to amber to the harsh white light of day that shone in a block of light above him.

His nose caught the scent picture above the ground – the smell of kangaroo, of eucalypts and fragrant heath. A blowfly stormed his sweating face and he spat it out. Then another. The decay of the brickwork was worse the further up he got, more exposed to the weathering elements, and he was forced to stop time and again to pick out the least treacherous path. Sometimes there seemed nothing to hold on to, nothing to take the weight of his blundering foot or desperate fingers as they tried to find a supporting surface before it crumbled away. He'd discarded his boots so that he could use his toes for maximum grip, but they were city feet now, unused to the exposure of bare skin, and he was sorry he'd discarded the protection of his boots. He knew he was leaving a trail of blood behind him and each step was almost impossibly painful.

It was the sounds that helped him. He could hear laughter

and people talking. If I can just keep going, he thought, if I can just make the last few metres out of this pit, those people will have cars and phones. I can get the muscleheads from the SPG. I can get Jim. I can get the works and throw them at this bastard. The dogs, the whole damn pack of us, can come down like a ton of bricks on Angus Wetherill.

The people's voices were getting louder up there. He could hear the squeals of children and laughter of women. Half-remembered words and phrases came to him. Harry craned his neck to look up at the opening of the shaft. He had to blink the sweat away. Hot sun streamed down towards him and it was the most beautiful thing he'd ever seen in his life. He talked to Razor who wasn't there; he talked to his kids, to his wife. 'I'm nearly there,' he told them, as he lifted swollen and bloody hands to haul himself up the last section. 'Help me,' he called to the people. 'I'm here. I'm down here.' But they couldn't hear him.

Using the last of his strength, Harry hauled himself up to part of a timber construction that formed a shelf not far beneath the opening. He lay there, drenched with sweat, every muscle aching, his head splitting. He gathered his resources for the last bit. It was easier going here. Now he climbed awkwardly through masonry and soil until his head and shoulders lifted above the opening of the pit.

The people were suddenly quiet. I must have frightened them, thought Harry. He looked around. There was no-one there. It was a desolate, grey landscape that lay around him, smoothed by machinery years ago and dotted with weedy regrowth and heaps of mullocky rock; a desert of subsoils, clays and rubble. Beyond that was bush. He looked around again, wondering if the people would come over to him from their hiding place. As he lifted himself out and rolled onto terra firma for the first time in many hours, he thought the whole earth shifted. Then, exhausted and injured, he lost consciousness.

When he finally woke, the sun had crossed the sky. He sat up and looked around. There were no people; there never had been. He'd been hallucinating and now his head had steadied to a dull ache behind the eyes. He needed water badly. He needed a dog. More than anything, he needed backup and a weapon. A voice somewhere in his mind said *This battle has no fronts, no flanks. One lapse in security and you're dead*. He needed clarity, not this dull muddle in his mind.

Harry looked around. There was no jungle here, just dry, dusty bushland. He studied the ground around him. Dead country. Old mined country. Now that he had no dog to lead him, he tried to read the country the way he had in his youth. For the first little while, it was like picking up a book in a language he used to know but hadn't spoken or read in years. Then, as he looked and observed, bits and pieces started coming back to him: the phrasing of trees, the sentences of landform, the punctuation of a fire trail and clearings made by humans. The whole picture seemed to waver in front of him, then settle into place. It was as if he'd been looking at some chaotic 3-D image but now had his focus perfect, so that an amazing picture was taking shape before him. He noticed the marks of hundreds of animals, the trails of insects, lizards, and saw the scuffle where a hawk had taken a goanna. He noticed the random action of the wind in the dust, where it bent grass stalks over like compasses to draw tiny arcs on the topsoil. He saw in his mind the wombat blundering along the road, head down, nosing along. He saw the tiny kite-like marks of bird tracks, and started to read their cuniform language: parrots and magpies on the ground. He saw the characteristic conical holes dug by bandicoots. He saw the base of a tree, burnt by the constant urination of feral dogs, then he noticed the tracks of two wild dogs and, from the width of the straddle, surmised how fast each animal had been moving. He saw the long marks left on saplings by the teeth of rabbits or hares. He noticed the tiny scats of different creatures and then started to become aware of the movement of the creatures themselves in trees and hollows. He noticed the way the wind moved the leaves and lifted the soil in blurred ridges on the clay.

Clearly now, he saw the recent tyre tracks of the utility, nice and clean in the soft surface dust, showing on top of all the other marks and scratches in the sand. He saw the double tyre track where it had driven over itself and then away, and his eyes followed the track past the dusty arena and into the straggly bush. He followed it to the edge of the mining area and into the surrounding bush. The scent picture here was poignant and familiar. Behind the spicy smell of dry sclerophyll forest, was another smell.

Harry sat down again, cut lengths of fabric from his trousers and tied this around his feet. They were a mess of cuts and abrasions, but swaddling them gave some protection. It was many years since he'd been able to go across this sort of country barefoot. Following the utility was easy. As the land-reading skills came back to him, he could almost see it in his mind's eye, the way he could reconstruct a crime scene, bumping along the road just ahead of him. He saw where it had pulled over to the shoulder and stopped. He saw where Angus Wetherill had climbed out of the cabin in his boots and walked over to a big eucalypt, placed his legs apart, made himself comfortable, and pissed against the ground at the base of the tree. The soil under the tree still clearly showed the pool that once had formed there, soaked in then dried. He saw Angus's boots walking back to the ute, climbing in, and saw the ute start to move away again, back into the centre of the dusty fire trail. Angus had taken off too fast here, Harry saw, because the back wheels had spun in the dust.

The land sloped away from the dirt track and Harry left the fire trail and the ute's tracks to follow the slope. As he stumbled through the straggly bush, he saw the tracks of many animals and he knew that water must be close by. He thought he could even smell it. He noticed the track of a huge kangaroo and wondered if it was the same fellow he'd noticed at the earlier camping spot. Once, his eye had been keen enough to distinguish individuals. *Backup*, an internal voice warned. *Don't do this alone. Get to a phone. Get to a dwelling. Organise backup*. But the knowledge that this was familiar territory silenced the insistent voice.

With his inner eye, he saw the shy marsupials sneaking along the ground, going to the watering place, cautiously sniffing the wind to pick up the scent of any predator. Harry looked around, smelling fox strongly. Then he noticed the narrow-straddle red fox track ahead of him, leading down the slope. It was getting very steep and now he could see water lying below him – a narrow creek that had cut its way through the hillsides aeons ago. It was only a few more minutes before he was there, on all fours like any other creature, the marks of his knees and hands obliterating the other tracks, drinking and splashing his face, washing his hair back, taking in as much as he could. He looked around for Razor and it took several seconds for his mind to recollect. Razor would be thirsty too, but he was in the cool depths of the shaft and if he stayed still, he'd be all right for awhile. If he was smart, he'd know to lick any moisture off the brick walls.

Harry made his way back up to the fire trail again. His head was spinning with effort. He picked up the ute's tracks again and started loping along in their wake. As he went along, the fragments of physical evidence fell into place in his mind and started making up a picture of the crime scene he was heading for; the pinkish mortar that mad old Wetherill had mixed one day to mend the crumbling stonework that supported the western verandah; the bats that used to fly in at night to eat from the fruit trees of the century-old orchard; the ebony trees; and the pink Victorian glass of the old kitchen door where he'd often waited until Angus was allowed to come out. The smells all started coming together in his mind: the orchard, the tall glossy English hedge, the pastoral and agricultural smells of the house and the 1840 cottage used as a storehouse for ancient equipage, the sulky that rotted in a corner.

Backup, warned the voice again. *Get to a base. Organise security.* But all the scents and odours and esters that went to make up 'home' converged on him. Despite his exhaustion, he felt euphoric. This was the safe place his mother had found for them. He wanted to cry; he wanted to laugh because even though he had no strength, his spirit wanted him to run and shout for joy. As he loped over a rise, the valleys spread out before him began to take on a startling familiarity. The remembered scent picture was overwhelming. It was calling him. In a flash, he had it all in his mind. Memories of his childhood were so strong that they pushed everything else away. He could hear the mysterious whispering again. Compelled, he followed the ute's tracks, knowing where they were leading.

THIRTY-ONE

When Security rang from downstairs to say there was a technician from Telstra waiting to come up, Jim went down himself to greet him. 'We got that trace on for you,' Wayne said. Jim nodded. 'And we got the names and addresses matched up for you,' Wayne added, eyes smiling through a pink birthmark that stained the upper part of his face 'of the calls made by your party at the Martendale Hotel.' They stepped into the lifts. 'Here they are,' he said, passing Jim some pages of computer printout.

Jim studied the list. The doors opened and he and the technician walked out.

'Come in,' he said to the technician as he went into his office. 'Take a seat.' But the technician was staring at the cardboard rampart running along the windowledge, then walking across to peer over and see the pigeons.

'Oh that,' said Jim. 'It's to stop everyone gawking at them.' Wayne drew back and gave Jim a look.

Jim sat at his desk and turned over the pages, glancing down the numbers. He wasn't surprised to see the name and number of Elizabeth Golding, the woman murdered at Strathfield. Nor was he surprised to see Janette Madden also showed up. There were records of several calls to an address at Boolabimbie. And calls had been made to 55 Botanical Avenue, Harry Doyle's house.

The technician was tapping on the glass, wanting the pigeons to look up at him, when Jim called in Kerryann Fish and asked her to escort Wayne downstairs. Then he rang John Ayoub at Bathurst.

'What do you know about a property at Boolabimbie called Maldon Downs?'

Jim waited on the phone while, 200 kilometres away, Ayoub asked around. Then his voice returned to the phone.

'Hullo?' he said. 'Boolabimbie is about another hundred k's northwest of here, near Cowra. Maldon Downs is a historic property and it's been in the same family since settlement. Family called Wetherill. The present owner discourages contact. Very run-down and usually uninhabited except for the manager, but he's usually away. There's been some activity there lately, according to local gossip. The house itself can't be seen from the road. It's pretty isolated.'

Harry had walked until it was too dark to make sense of any tracks or landmarks then taken shelter for the night beneath a small rock overhang. In the morning he'd woken stiff and hungry but with the same relentless urge driving him on.

For the first few kilometres the trail rolled on over the scrubby hills, then dipped down to follow the course of a dry riverbed. The steep banks hid the surrounding country from view so effectively that for awhile Harry began to lose his bearings. Then, suddenly, the tyre tracks veered up and over a rise and the house was right there before him, its cluttered memories and scents crowding his exhausted brain. I'm home, he thought. After all this time.

Harry circled the house. The ute wasn't there, just as he'd known because he'd noticed fresh tracks, doubling over the ones he'd been following on the driveway, this time heading away from the house towards the front gates. Angus had come here, then left again. But Harry kept low just the same, his ears tuned for the sound of the ute.

The house was smaller, meaner and more crumbling than the image in his memory. He had imagined the grand sweeping driveway with exotic trees lining it. Instead, although many of the trees were still growing, in front of them was only a dry patch of open ground, overgrown with weeds and thistles, beyond which the house rose darkly. The place was neglected; stones were being gradually blown away back into dust. The timber frames of the top verandahs were decaying, sections of them fallen away like missing teeth in a mouth. He went round the back and noticed the stench of bats and their droppings. *Call for assistance*, warned the inner voice. *Do it now.* But Harry was heedless as he made his way painfully past the homestead and towards the station hand's house where he'd lived as a boy. Broken windows, the front door half hanging off and the verandah piled with rusting tractor parts didn't deter him as he walked inside. Light streamed from the ceiling. Much of the sky shone in now where once only a star had been visible. He walked into his mother's room. He saw the wallpaper the station hand had pasted up for her on one wall only, never getting around to finishing it, done in a fit of remorse – sprigs of lily of the valley, against a soft grey background. Now it was stained and peeling. Although he was exhausted, grief still hit him hard and he had to lean against the crumbling wall. I've pushed all this away, he thought to himself. I have denied myself. This is where I grew up. This is the place that made me, he thought. This is the place she brought me to after she'd stolen me back and I want to see her again. I want to ask her about my father.

He hobbled out of the cottage and towards the back of the

homestead of Maldon Downs. The stone-fruit trees in the old orchard were heavy with rotting fruit and windfalls steamed in piles underneath, glistening with busy flies.

The back kitchen door had been smashed, as he knew it would be, and shards and spears of rose-coloured glass glittered on the ground. Carefully, Harry reached in through the broken glass and pulled the bolt sideways. The stench of petrol hit him then. He opened the door, grinding it over powdered glass. Someone had kicked most of it into a corner but he was careful all the same. He went further inside. *Get to the phone*, said the voice. *Call Ayoub for backup. Do it now.* But he felt he was in some sort of dream, a protected, sacred space, with the past and the present merging into this moment, coming together in him. He made his way through the kitchen and into the main body of the house where he could almost hear old man Wetherill stamping down the staircase with his heavy, angry tread. He could almost hear Mrs Wetherill's clipped little high voice, asking him if he'd like a biscuit. It was still as he remembered it, but meaner, smaller and oddly dark. The smell of petrol was overpowering; the scent picture obliterated by the fumes. Someone must have spilt a lot of it in here, he thought. He cautiously went towards the centre of the house and towards the hallway, moving through the two little rooms, probably maids' bedrooms a century ago, that lay between the kitchen and the grander rooms of the front of the house. Again he wondered what was obscuring the light. Then he came to the back side of the stairwell and, ahead of him, the hallway led to the large parlour and dining room.

Harry stood still. Because now he could see the hallway and into the rooms on each side of it. What he saw chilled him to the bone, while the stench of petrol nauseated him to the point of faintness. In every room, sheets hung from the ceiling, spilling like sails hung up to dry from the manholes, falling to the ground where they were heaped in piles or twisted into ropes to snake along the floor, out the doors and into the hallway, to return through another door. In the lounge room, with its two doors that gave onto the main hallway, he could hardly move for the shrouding sheets that hung everywhere. There was a four-gallon drum in the centre of the room and someone – Harry had no doubts now who that someone was – had swathed the drum with the long, rotting curtains dragged off the dirty windows, so that the old curtains made contact with the looping sheets. He went back out into the hallway again and looked upstairs. The bannisters were draped with mildewed bedding, blankets and sheets. Along the hallway, wallpaper bowed off the wall onto the floor. He walked carefully up the stairs, and saw where petrol had been splashed and soaked on all the old mattresses that rotted in the several bedrooms whose doors stood off their hinges. He went back down again on stairs that threatened to give way with every step, noticing the muffled footprints he'd left with his bandaged feet on the bare boards each side of the worn carpet runners in the centre of the hallway, following the doused sheets back into the dusty parlour where mad old Wetherill, his wife and Aunt Vera looked down at him from their portraits on the wall.

The long curtains around the French windows, rotting into strips, all fed onto the twisted up sheets that in turn ended up in a bucket of petrol. *Okay*, said the inner voice. *Move now. Get backup. Give your location.* He looked around for something to use as a weapon, an instinctive and useless gesture considering he was standing inside a huge, primed bomb. Behind another hanging sheet he saw the telephone and, pushing the grey fabric aside, he picked it up. His head was ringing from adrenalin and petrol fumes. As he dialled emergency, he thought he heard a sound. He looked up and lifted a corner of the sheet. Nothing. Just the slightest movement of the shrouds hanging down from the ceiling near the doorway to the hall. As he waited for the operator to answer, he noticed his own footprints smeared in the dust of the hallway boards. Harry's heart contracted in shock and fear. Because beside his own blurred prints were the fresh tracks of sharply defined boots, the same boots that he'd seen on the fire trail road. Almost at the same nanosecond that he made the connection, someone spoke.

'Put the phone down, Harry.'

Angus Wetherill stood in the doorway, holding the neat little Russian Tokarev in one hand and a cigarette lighter in the other. All he'd have to do was flick the lighter where he stood, Harry knew, and the volatile fumes suspended all through the house would explode around them both. Harry froze with the phone halfway down.

'Can I help you?' said the emergency operator's tiny voice. 'Hullo? Hullo? Hullo? Is there anybody there?' There was a pause and she squeaked again. 'I cannot hear you and I am terminating this call at 0–eight–hundred hours and twenty-seven minutes.' There was a click and the bleat of the engaged tone on the line.

He and Angus stared at each other in silence. Harry found himself taking a deep breath. Somewhere, he'd always known they'd have to see each other again. Angus still looked remarkably youthful, as if life hadn't touched him. With one hand, he pushed thick hair back from his forehead in a gesture Harry remembered well. Slowly, Harry put the phone down.

'Good,' said Angus. 'That's the way.' He relaxed and lowered the lighter. 'You're tough, Doyle. Anyone else would be dead. But not you, you black bastard.'

Then Harry heard an odd noise. It sounded as if it came from far away. Perhaps it was the hallucinations of his climb coming back to him. It sounded like a woman, but a great distance away. Almost under the ground, under the earth, trapped and wailing. He immediately thought of the Strathfield house and the dead woman in the cellar. 'Who else have you got here, Angus?' Harry asked, dreading the answer, knowing he'd left his home base unguarded.

'Guess,' said Angus and Harry didn't have to. 'She's here with me, Harry. She was ready to leave you and come with me. But then she changed her mind. Just like Janette did. Women. You can't trust them. Just like you can't trust best mates.'

'What are you talking about?' Harry said.

'We had great sex, Harry. Me and your wife. You should ask her about it sometime. If there is any time.'

Harry felt the rage rise up in him. Rage and fear together, adding to the fumes already in his head. He practised staying as calm and quiet as he could. 'What do you plan on doing, Angus?' he asked.

'I'm going to ask you to come down to the cellar with me,' said the other. 'Everything's ready. I had planned on having your little girl here, too, but that didn't happen after all. You can't trust rock spiders.'

The silence between them seemed to open out into something deep and ancient in that crazy house with the hanging sheets and the petrol fumes. Harry's mind rallied and gathered itself. This was life and death.

'You can't think you can do this and get away with it,' he said in his old soothing voice. 'You'll get caught, Angus. You'll rot in prison.'

'I've already rotted in prison. You saw to that.'

'How do you work that out?'

'If I'd married Janette, my life would have been different. None of the other things would have happened,' Angus said. 'After I'd got back from Vietnam, things would have gone right for me – the things that went wrong and ended me up in prison. You stuffed me right up from the start.'

'Angus,' he said, trying to make a little time, 'you're not thinking straight. You're not making sense.' Harry remembered conversations he'd had with old crims. 'You do the crime,' they used to say, 'you do the time.' Do the crime, do the time. But some people never seem to notice that they do the crime.

Harry's mind was racing. If he could muster enough strength, he might be able to take Angus with a tackle and grab the lighter. But Angus, as if reading his mind, had taken a throwing knife out of his pocket, and Harry remembered how good he'd been with those, slicing lizards in half on the walls, impaling frogs; he remembered the sudden death of Asgard.

'Come on,' said Angus. 'She's waiting for you.'

He came up closer, but not too close. 'Turn around and go back to the kitchen,' Angus ordered. 'Slowly now, very slowly.' Harry did as he was told, pushing his way past the hanging sheets out into the kitchen, wincing at the petrol fumes.

When he got to the kitchen, he thought of making a run for it. But then what? And he couldn't leave Meg here alone in this place.

'Now lift the handle of the cellar door,' Angus was saying. 'Remember, Harry, how we were never allowed down there because the old man kept all his booze there?'

'Yes,' said Harry. 'I do remember.'

'Lift it up,' Angus ordered. 'Nice and easy.' Harry leaned over and did so, kicking shards of pink Victorian glass to one side. He noticed without interest that he'd left a smear of blood from his ruined foot on the flagging of the kitchen floor. As soon as the trapdoor opened, the scent picture came up to him: dead air, cold and still, with the scent of mould and mushrooms and dusty spiders' webs. And something else. Meg's scent drifted up.

'Max, please,' her voice from the dim cellar. 'Please let me go back to my children. Please, Max. Don't do this.'

'Climb down, Harry,' said Angus.

Harry climbed down, trying to think, trying to find a way out. At the base of the ladder, he looked around. It was a low-ceilinged bunker, much larger than the cellar at Strathfield, and a naked low-wattage globe shed sickly light on shelves of storage. There was an earthen floor, and an open drain had been dug along the length of the area, following the slight natural incline of the land. Angus had made four rough, square frames, a bit like bedsteads, raised some way off the ground, with a trench cut beneath them.

Harry's heart contracted in horror. Human being frames, he realised; like coffins for the living, to confine people in, with holes cut beneath them to take waste away, a further refinement on what Harry now realised was the practice run at Strathfield.

Meg was already cuffed to one trestle and only her left hand was free. 'Harry,' she said. 'Harry.' She was past crying.

Harry stood there, shocked at the sight of his wife.

'I'm so sorry,' Meg was saying before she turned away from him. 'He's crazy,' she said. 'He planned to take us all away, me and the kids, and kill you.'

'You were going to come with me, Meg, of your own free will.' Angus's voice was hard and triumphant behind Harry. 'To start a new life, away from a man who failed to appreciate you. Don't you remember?

'I want you to get into that nice little structure I've made for you, Harry, and cuff yourself in.'

'I won't do it, Angus,' he said.

'Yes you will. I'll hurt your wife if you don't.' He went across to where Meg lay like a sacrifice and grabbed a handful of her hair. She winced and closed her eyes. Then they were wide open again.

'Why are you calling him Angus?' said Meg. 'Do you know him? Is this Angus?' Her eyes were dilated with fear and horror. 'Are you Angus?' she said. She strained but there was no escaping.

'Get down, Harry,' said Angus, ignoring her.

Again, hopeless, Harry did as he was told, climbing onto the coffin frame.

'Snap on the cuffs. First on the leg, then the arm. That's the way.'

This is breaking every rule, thought Harry. Never allow yourself to be immobilised. He despaired.

Angus leaned over and snapped the cuffs around Harry's other arm. 'Good,' he said. 'I always wanted a happy family. But you betrayed me. You stopped me having my own.'

'That's absurd,' said Harry. 'People like you can't have happy families. You bring your own shit with you.' He was surprised at his own words.

But Angus wasn't listening. 'If I'd married Janette . . .' he was saying.

'You murdered Janette!' Harry roared. 'And the woman you lived with at Strathfield. And old Aunt Vera. Some family man.'

Angus continued to ignore him. 'So I've had to make do with yours. I was going to set you all up down here, in a nice little bunker where you'd be safe. I put food away for you all. I was just going to keep you all for awhile until I worked out what I'd do next. But then things changed. The woman changed her mind. Just like Janette. She wouldn't come. I don't like losing control of things I've planned. The kid got away from Pughsie.'

'A dog tore his throat out,' said Meg. 'And all the time you pretended you were concerned. You offered your support. And I believed you. How can you talk about "betrayed"?'

'I think it would be better for you to be quiet now,' said Angus. 'Both of you.'

'Can't we talk about this a little, Angus?' Harry asked, in his soothing voice. 'Surely we can talk, man-to-man, and leave the women out of this. This is between you and me.'

Angus turned on him, looking down at him. 'Yes. It is between you and me. You are the person who destroyed my life.'

'Oh, for Christ's sake,' Meg couldn't help herself. 'You can't blame other people for your miserable life.'

'You did, you bitch,' he said, swinging round on her. 'You did *exactly* that. You were waiting for the handsome rich man who would take care of you. And you thought you had him for awhile. I remember some of the things you told me about Harry. You blamed him for your miserable life.'

And Meg was shamed into silence.

There must be something I can do, Harry was thinking, desperate and helpless. Something.

'You always judged me, Harry,' Angus was saying. 'I always felt those eyes of yours. Those bloody eyes looking at me, judging me, always making me wrong. I'd look up and I'd see your eyes.'

'If you're talking about what happened in Vietnam,' said Harry, 'these things happen. You could still get help. Even though you've killed people. Post-traumatic stress disorder. You might find that you could get help and not be held responsible for all this. You might end up doing your time in a hospital.' He tried to indicate the surrounding situation with his cuffed hands. 'I would even take the stand on your behalf. I know what you suffered when you were a kid. I remember your father, remember the beatings.'

'Suffered? What are you talking about? My father was a great man. And my mother was a saint. My father taught me to be a man. He taught me how to be tough.'

Angus started walking away towards the ladder. 'I don't need help. I just want to be free of your judgement. I was going to go down with the ship but I've changed my mind. I'm flying to another state. There are other dead men's names I can use. I've kept some money. Dealing with you at last will change my luck, Harry Doyle. I know it. I've been planning this a long, long time.'

Then he climbed up the ladder out of the bunker. Just before he closed the trapdoor he leaned in, crazily upside down. 'By the way,' he said, 'I've got another M26.' Then he was gone and the trapdoor slammed down.

He must have hidden the ute down the road, thought Harry, watched me until I'd gone inside the house and then crept in on foot behind me, knowing the petrol stench would cover him. He closed his eyes briefly. He was exhausted. Then he rallied. 'My keys,' he said. 'On my belt. See if you can reach them. My handcuff key.'

Meg strained and stretched, but it was useless. Harry and his key ring were impossibly out of reach. 'I can't,' she sobbed, falling back, closing her eyes. Then she opened them again. 'What's an M26?' she asked.

'A grenade,' he told her. 'This place is a bomb. He's primed it with petrol. He'll throw a grenade in from outside.'

'And then?'

'Then the whole place goes sky high.'

'What about us?'

Harry opened his eyes. 'If we're not killed in the explosion, we'll burn. If we survive that, the sheer size of the blaze will suck up all the oxygen down here. We'll asphyxiate.' His mind filled with images of all the dead and all the ways of dying he'd investigated in his time.

'We're going to die, Harry.'

Harry could see no way out of this one and tears pricked his eyes.

Meg noticed.

'You're crying,' she said. 'You've never cried in your life.'

'Not in front of you,' he said, and that silenced her. She looked away again. 'I'm thinking of old Razor,' he said, 'who will starve to death down a mine shaft.'

'Where were you, Harry?' Meg was saying. 'When I needed you. When Hannah was taken?'

'I was on the job,' he said. 'I was tracking this bastard. But he got me instead.'

Meg started crying then, deep sobs, a sound that tore Harry's heart. He thought of Alison and Hannah whom he'd never see again.

'The girls,' she said, as if reading his thoughts.

'I've got to find a way out of here,' he said.

'There is no way out of here,' she said. 'This is it. Talk to me, Harry. Tell me something about yourself.'

'I used to tell you once,' he said. 'But you wouldn't listen. You criticised me. Tried to make me over. So after awhile, I shut up.'

'That's too easy, Harry.'

'That's why I never tell you anything, Meg. You can't help yourself. You can't hear me. So I shut up.'

'Here we are still squabbling,' she said bitterly. 'We're

about to be blown to bits but we're still fighting about who's right. That's marriage.'

'That's *our* marriage,' he said.

There was a silence.

'Tell me what happened with Hannah.'

Meg told him the full story of how she and Alison and Blade had got Hannah back. He turned to look at her, his brave, amazing wife who wouldn't love him. And in turn, he told her about Angus Wetherill and this place and the war.

'That name – Max,' said Harry. 'That was the name of one of our company who was blown up by a Claymore mine.'

'He used a dead man's name,' said Meg. 'And I fell for him.'

'He must have set you up,' said Harry. 'Joined the art classes to get to you. Done a deal with Pugh to get Hannah. All the time working on revenging himself on me.'

Meg closed her eyes. It was all so awful. It was all so insane. 'I brought him into our lives,' she said. 'It was my doing.'

'He would have got in somehow. It was his lifetime plan. He said so.'

'No,' she said. 'All this mess . . . I caused it. Instead of looking at the ninety-eight per cent of a person that's good, I only look at the two per cent that I think should be different. I did it with you. I did it with Alison. I would have started doing it with Hannah once she got to the stage of wanting to be different from me.'

Harry wasn't listening. 'He did something in Vietnam. He raped a woman. When she was dying. I saw it happen and I could never speak to him after that.'

'He's going to win,' said Meg. 'All that cruelty and vengeance is going to win. And I helped.'

Harry looked across at her. She wasn't far away. He stretched his fingers out to touch her, and she turned and saw what he was doing and stretched out her free hand, but their fingers, no matter how hard they stretched, just failed to meet.

'Maybe we should pray,' said Meg. 'But I don't know how to. Harry?'

'My mother used to pray,' said Harry. 'She taught me some prayers.'

'You've never talked about her,' said Meg. 'Why?'

'I was ashamed of her,' said Harry.

'Why?' she asked.

'When I was little, I didn't worry. About being Koori. Her grandmother was one of the Achumenra people, she used to tell me. And she was descended from a famous "clever man". I used to like hearing that. But as I got a bit older, I just didn't want to know about it. I went to the little school at Maldon, the nearest big town from Boolabimbie. We learned all about the brave explorers and the noble white doctors and missionaries who tried to help the primitive, treacherous blacks. I didn't want anyone to know what I was. People have thought me to be all sorts of different things over the years – Black Irish, Spanish, Maltese, Greek – and I let them. Once I got away and went to Vietnam I never went back home. I just kept quiet about it. Never told anyone. After awhile it was like it was someone else's story. I thought it didn't mean anything to me anymore.'

'Where is she now?' asked Meg.

'She married some old bloke years later and moved away to Maldon. She didn't want to go too far from her people's country. But I never visited her.'

There was a sharp, flat crack somewhere above them. Harry recognised the sound. The other grenade. Now he could smell the fire upstairs. He imagined the blazing sheets, taking the fire to the roof, the huge updraught billowing into the sky. Was the air thinner down here already?

'I'd do anything to see her again,' said Harry. 'Speak to her. Ask her forgiveness.'

'I'm sorry, Harry,' Meg was saying. 'So sorry for all the hard things I've said in our life together. I failed to do the thing I advise other people to do. I didn't listen.' She smiled weakly. 'I have to be chained up in a cellar in a house that's about to blow up before I can see a few things.'

'I'm sorry I was so closed down. And I'm sorry I failed to protect you and my family,' said Harry. 'He planned things so that I'd follow him away from all of you. And I did.'

'Cops and school counsellors,' she said, 'see the world in a completely different way.'

'They'd have to,' he said. 'They come at the world from different directions.'

'Worlds within worlds,' she said. 'Like you and me. Never the same world. The same bed, but a different world.' The scent of burning was getting stronger, the roar of the fire above them like an approaching aircraft.

'Harry, I'm really scared. My whole body is shaking.'

'So is mine.'

'What were the prayers your mother taught you?' she asked.

'I can't remember,' he said. 'Meg, I'm sorry.'

'My children,' she said. 'I will never see them again.'

THIRTY-TWO

Ray Gosling sat up in the front of the wagon with Jim as passenger and Police Dog Javelin dancing and circling in the confines of the rear. Behind them, in the other car, were Ayoub and Brennan and two other officers from nearby Maldon. As they turned off the road and into the driveway of Maldon Downs, Jim leaned forward.

'Step on it,' he yelled as they bumped over the uneven surface. He could see smoke over the rise, the black smoke of an accelerant.

Ray was driving as fast as he dared and the second car was bouncing along almost on their tail. As the wagon topped the hill, Jim's heart sank. In front of them, the homestead of Maldon Downs was blazing. Rolls of black smoke unfolded around and above the two storeys. Fire tongued out of the downstairs windows and curled upwards. The wagon skidded to a halt close enough for Jim to feel the heat on his face. Ray jumped out and opened the back for Javelin, snapped the harness on and the two of them raced away around the side of the building towards the back. As the second car pulled up behind them, Jim could hear Ayoub yelling to base to hurry up with the Fire Brigade.

The fire roared at the front of the house and the temperature was horrendous. But the back section of the house was still undamaged; the fire hadn't taken hold yet where there were flagstone floors and granite walls. Ray and the dog disappeared round the back of the house and Jim ran through the heavy black smoke after them, aware of the sound of another car coming down the driveway. As he turned the corner, he saw that the back door to the house was open and Ray and Javelin had vanished inside. Jim followed them.

'Harry!' Jim yelled as he went in as far as he dared. 'Are you there?' Past the kitchen, he could barely see through rooms dense with smoke and the roar of the fire was deafening. 'Is there anyone here? Ray?' he shouted. 'Where are you?' Jim had to turn away, the heat from the centre of the house too intense for him to stay.

Ray and Javelin suddenly appeared beside him out of the smoke and Ray's brows and hair was scorched. 'I can't go any further,' Ray yelled over the noise of the blaze. 'There's nothing we can do. Get out of here.'

In the house, fire zipped along the floor of the hallway following the petrol-drenched fabric, past rooms where flames were burning through the ceiling joists to the next storey, flaming up the sheets into the manholes. A jet of flame jumped the staircase and exploded in the air of the landing. Another fiery runner blazed along the hallway towards the back of the house out to the kitchen. It turned into the flagstoned room and ran along the floor, lapping at the paintwork of the cupboards. It filled the doorway from the hall with its blistering radiance.

Outside the back of the house, Ray and Jim watched.

'I think we should get a long way back,' said Jim. 'It's going to go up like world war three.' They found a place to stand near the derelict orchard, with the heat still burning their faces. Fruit bats squeaked and flew past them, blundering in the smoke.

'What if Harry's in there?' said Ray. His anguished face tried to see through the pall of smoke and the hectic light of flames.

Black smoke was rolling and spreading all around them. Through the noise of the blaze Jim heard Ayoub yelling, 'Hey! You can't go in there! Come back. Stop! Stop that woman!'

Jim was horrified to see a slender figure running with a dog towards the same door they'd just exited. Then he realised it was Alison running with Blade, holding her arm up in a futile attempt to shield her face from the inferno. For a second, her slight figure was backlit by deadly light. Then she vanished into the house. Jim started running towards the kitchen again, screaming her name.

Inside, Alison took no notice. Smoke blinded her. '*Mum!*' she was screaming. '*Where are you?*'

In the kitchen, she was almost overcome with smoke and she screamed as the glass door of a cupboard suddenly shattered.

'Mum!' she screamed again, blinking, eyes stinging, frantically peering through the smoke. The roar of the inferno was terrifying, and the heat penetrated the thick fabric of her overall. Blade went nose down straight to the trapdoor ring and Alison dropped to her hands and knees, following his cue. Around her in the kitchen, the fire was starting to take hold. Flames danced on the painted surfaces of the cupboards and played up towards the ceiling. Blade whimpered at the trapdoor ring. Alison was tugging at it, trying to pull it back, when suddenly it gave way. As she opened it out her mother's voice penetrated the roar of the fire.

'We're down here. We're cuffed. Please get us out of here!'

'Mum! I'm coming,' screamed Alison. She stumbled down the ladder, looking around as she did, and her mind, pristine with terror, immediately comprehended the situation. Black smoke was spilling down past the ladder, moving into the cellar from the opening where Blade barked furiously.

'Darling, it's you,' sobbed her mother as Alison ran to them.

'The keys on my belt, Ali!' yelled Harry. 'Get them.'

Alison grabbed at Harry's belt, trying to pull the key ring off. But her fingers weren't working. 'I can't get it off!' she screamed. 'It won't come off!'

'Take it easy,' said Harry in his soft voice. 'Just squeeze and lift.'

Alison pressed the clasp open and pulled the bunch of keys away from the black mesh. She knew the cuff key and her fingers closed on the narrow needle of steel.

'Get your mother out of here,' said Harry as she separated the cuff key from the others and stooped to free her mother. As Alison's fingers fumbled with the key, Jim and Ray suddenly appeared at the top of the ladder. Hellish light shone above them as the fire claimed the kitchen. Blade's barking became hysterical and, somewhere, Javelin joined in, howling.

'Thank God,' said Meg,' She freed her hand and snatched the key. 'Get out of here now,' she commanded. 'I'll do the rest.'

'But Mum—'

'Do as you're told!' Harry roared. 'Get Blade and get out.'

Alison scrambled up the ladder, turning once near the top. 'Hurry,' she screamed at them. '*Please!*' Then she disappeared.

Meg scrambled out of the frame and had Harry free in seconds. Jim grabbed her, and Ray helped Harry up and the four of them raced over to the ladder with Jim in the lead. 'Follow me,' said Jim. 'Stay close behind and move quickly.'

Jim put his head out of the trapdoor to confront a solid wall of flame. He hauled himself out, feeling the terrible heat on his skin. Smoke filled his lungs. He coughed, then held his breath, grabbing Meg's hands, lifting her and swinging the two of them out the door in one movement. Behind them, Ray and Harry scrambled low along the floor, crashing through the door to the outside a half-second later.

The four raced past the blazing laundry building and, as they did, there was a deafening roar and the little huddle of people, with the reflection of the flames flickering in their eyes, turned and watched transfixed as the entire length of the roof collapsed. No-one spoke as the back section of the house, including the kitchen they had just vacated, disappeared under a rolling, roaring wave of flaming roof and masonry. Maldon Downs homestead had disintegrated.

THIRTY-THREE

M eg, Alison and Blade stayed the night at the local motel,
courtesy of the owners, with Blade allowed a special
place in the laundry. Meg attended to the blisters on her
daughter's face and fingers and ordered food that they left
almost untouched, quite unable to eat. Ray Gosling and
Javelin dozed in the wagon outside their unit, keeping an
eye on things. At Meg's insistence, Harry spent the night in
the local hospital where his shredded feet were dressed. Jim
Coates dozed in a chair beside him.

In the morning, Harry's boss rang. 'Take a few weeks off,'
Matthews said. 'Spend some time with the family. Look after
yourself.'

Meg and Alison arrived and, together with Jim, helped
him out of the ward and down the corridor. He was limping
between his wife and Alison, with Blade trotting behind,
when Ayoub and Brennan pulled up outside in Harry's
wagon. With them was Razor. They had worked with
a couple of local rock climbers who'd gone down the
mine, secured Police Dog Razor and winched him safely
back up. Then they'd fed, watered and washed him. When
Ayoub lowered the back of the wagon, Harry squatted and
Razor flew into his arms. Then Razor and Blade caught

up with each other, sniffing, circling, barking in delighted reunion.

While Meg, Alison and the two dogs waited for the men in Meg's car, Harry took Jim aside for a word. 'While Angus Wetherill is on the loose,' he said, 'I want twenty-four-hour protection for my family.'

'It's already been organised,' said Jim. 'Hannah and Dell are having a four-star holiday, courtesy of the state.'

Harry gripped his friend's arm. He didn't have to say anything.

During the drive back, the state-wide search for Angus Wetherill was in evidence. At two roadblocks when Harry showed his warrant card, they caught up with the latest. No-one had seen Wetherill since he'd left town, heading west. Police searching the burnt-out property had found the original set of registration plates from Angus's vehicle but were still pulling over all fawn utilities as a precaution. It seemed, however, that Angus Wetherill had slipped through. All reports of stolen vehicles in the area were being checked out. 'I know Angus,' said Harry. 'I know what he'll do. He'll lie low. He's a good bushman. Wait till the heat is off. Then make his move.'

Jim drove into the underground car park of the serviced apartments in Darlinghurst and Harry followed in Meg's car. Jim and the family went up in the lift, while Blade and Razor were fussed over by the concierge's wife downstairs. Hannah and Dell were waiting for them and Hannah's joyous welcome when her father, mother and big sister walked into the room almost knocked Meg off her feet. 'Mummy, Mummy,' as she snuggled her face into her mother's breast. Then she hugged her father.

'Where are the dogs?' she wanted to know.

Harry told her.

'You must never go away again, Dad,' she said, 'because you nearly lost me and then we nearly lost Mum.'

They all had lunch together, sitting in the building's private courtyard with the dogs flopped out under the table. Meg went out shopping with Harry while Jim stayed at the apartment. When she came back, she made the kids' favourite lasagne and Harry sat with a rare beer.

There was no sign of Angus Wetherill and, after two days, the family moved home again. As Harry got out of the wagon at 55 Botanical Avenue, he thought the scent picture had never smelled so good. A gang of honeyeaters, perfect with their black and yellow markings, was disturbed by their arrival and rose from the top of a large grevillea.

He let the dogs out of the back and reached in to pick up the S-shaped piece of timber for Hannah's message stick.

'I'm going to make a vegetable garden,' Meg announced as she walked right through the house and out to the back. 'And a flower garden. I'm going to fix up this yard. I could plant something lovely over the dog pen and soften the whole look of the place.'

She looked around at her family and her heart filled with love. Harry saw something in her face and was touched. He leaned across. 'Come inside,' he said. 'There's something I want to show you.'

'Oh yeah?' said Alison. And Hannah giggled. Razor went to follow Harry, but Hannah grabbed him for a hug.

'In here,' said Harry, as they walked down the hall and Meg followed him into his study. As they walked in, the phone rang again and Harry picked it up, putting the piece of timber down, hesitating just a fraction, aware that Angus Wetherill was somewhere on the planet.

'He doesn't live here anymore and the Archons told me you were dead,' said the Confessor.

'No, Milton. You see that I'm not.'

'Can I speak to him?' Meg was signalling. Harry nodded and passed the phone to her. 'Milton?' said Meg. 'I'm sorry I called you crazy last time we spoke. I was out of my mind with distress about my little girl. I want to thank you for your help. I wouldn't have found her without you.'

There was a pause on the line. The Confessor's voice changed from the thin, hesitant voice she knew. 'I am a person,' he said in a man's strong voice. 'A human being.'

'Yes,' said Meg, handing the phone back to Harry. But the Confessor had gone.

Overhead, the sound of an aircraft approaching and the whiff of benzine resolved Meg to buy a thankyou card for Milton and send it to the address where no letters had ever been forwarded.

Harry picked up the uncompleted message stick and took out the phial with the tiny gold nugget in it. Meg watched as he dropped strong glue into a small hole he'd drilled some time previously. Carefully, he picked up the small shiny lump, where it sat for a moment, golden on his fingertip, then he dropped it onto the glue, where it settled and sank into place immediately. Harry carefully put the message stick down again on his desk.

'I didn't tell you everything back there,' he said, and she shivered, remembering the hours she thought she was going to die alone, unforgiven, unheard and never see her girls again. 'The saddest thing about me being ashamed of my mother,' he said, 'was this.' He looked up and Meg saw that his eyes were soft with tears. 'Fair skinned children like me were taken away when we were little kids.'

Meg looked at him in astonishment. 'You?'

'I was taken when I was two or three – I don't even know how old I was – from where we were living in New South Wales and shipped interstate. Kidnapped by the government agent. Put in an orphanage in South Australia. They wanted to separate us completely from our families and make us into useful labour. For the first time in my life, I knew what it was like to be hungry and cold. It's where I first experienced cruelty. And hatred. Maybe one day I'll be strong enough to look at what else happened in that place. My mother – she must have only been about nineteen or twenty at the time – she walked all the way across the country somehow with her sister. That's where she met the stockman, Joe Doyle, and he was allowed to visit me in the orphanage and take me out for a walk. The warders wouldn't let us go with our mothers. It was against the law. But a strange white man was considered all right. My mother and her sister were waiting for us near the edge of town and the four of us went on the lam. I'll never forget the moment I saw her face again after all that time. I can only remember bits and pieces of that time. We moved back to New South Wales and Joe and my mother got work at Maldon Downs. That was the place I always felt was home.'

'I had no idea,' she said. 'I thought you'd always been at Boolabimbie.' She went to the window and looked out. The honeyeaters were chiming in a bunch on top of a red callistemon. She turned back to her husband and her voice was low. 'I don't know much about the people I claim to love, do I? Even though I know that to love someone is to know them. I don't know much about you,' she said. 'About anything.'

She touched the message stick and was surprised at how smooth and soft the polished timber felt under her fingers. She looked into her husband's eyes and out the window again.

The honeyeaters had gone, but a nectar-laden breeze wafted into the house from the brilliant callistemon blooms.

'I thought I was going to die yesterday in that cellar, Harry. I'd got Hannah back only to die down there.' She looked at him and felt tears soften her own eyes. 'It's like I've been given another chance. And not just me. This whole family has been given another chance. To really live. To learn about each other. And you and me, too.'

Harry took her two hands in his and she gazed into his eyes. 'That place they sent us little kids,' he said, almost in a whisper. 'It was a terrible place. That's where I first learned silence. There was no-one to hear me then. It became a habit. It wasn't just the job. Maybe my silence drove you towards another man.'

'Maybe,' she said. 'But I have to say that much of it came from my own restlessness and lack of satisfaction with myself.' I need to learn more about myself, too, she realised.

'Can you let the business with Max go?' she asked after a moment.

Harry released her hands and went over to the window, staring out. 'That was Angus Wetherill, not Max,' he said finally. 'Max was a good man.'

'Harry. I don't know if I can forgive myself right now for that, but I could learn to listen to you,' she said. 'Just as you are. Not try and change you.'

'I've got some time off,' he said. 'Maybe we could all go away for awhile. I want to track down my mother. I want to spend some time with her.' Meg nodded. 'And I want to find out about my real father. I never knew him. I want to know his story. His country. Why he deserted us. If he's alive or dead. What happened to him.'

Meg looked at her husband in surprise. 'That's amazing,' she said. 'So does Alison. She told me this morning. Would you mind?'

Harry shook his head. 'I'll help her,' he said. 'That's something we can do together. It's important to know these things. Where we came from. What sort of people made us. What their stories were.'

Meg saw the goodness in her husband's face, the kindness in his eyes that she'd stopped seeing in the years she'd judged and blamed him. She remembered something a lecturer had said years ago; that the potential of a human being is unlimited. It had sounded impossible to believe then, but she was starting to understand. Human beings are designed for deep connection, she thought, and if we fail to get that, we go mad. I went more than a bit mad, she thought. And Alison was going that way too, until I learned some humility. And Hannah. Reaching out to strangers instead of her parents. She understood the softness that lay behind her husband's guardedness; realised that his lock-up defence system had been completely appropriate.

'What now, Harry?' she asked. 'You and me?'

'No more secrets,' he said. 'Let's be fair like Hannah says.' He took up the message stick again and the feathers lifted softly with the movement. The tiny nugget of gold looked as if it had been there forever, washed into the seam of the timber by some archaic flood.

'Yes,' she said. 'It's the unsaid things that haunt us. The unsaid and the unknown. They still have power to hurt us. Generation after generation.'

'This is for you,' he said, giving her the varnished stick with the alluvial gold in it. 'Because you are a good woman, and because you are my wife.'

Later, they went into their bedroom and made love like they hadn't for a long time.

Just as Harry was gently kissing Meg's forehead, the phone rang. For the first time in his life as half of a man-dog unit in a twenty-four-hour a day operational police base, Harry decided not to hear it.

Six hours later, he and Jim and Razor sped west along the highway. A suspect utility and a driver answering the description of Angus Wetherill had been seen by a sharp-eyed constable in a small town not far from Maldon, buying fishing tackle. It was dusk and the evening was closing in with the sharp fall in temperature that occurs without the influence of the coast.

In the township of Durham, they talked to the young constable. 'There's really only the highway,' he said, pointing to the map on his desk. 'These little roads here only go to small towns. If he takes the back roads he still has to get back on the highway if he wants to get to a major centre.'

'He's arsey coming back so close to Boolabimbie,' said Jim.

'No,' Harry shook his head. 'It's exactly what he'd do. It's the last place anyone would think to look for him.' He's going to ground, Harry thought, where he feels safe, while he waits to make his next move. 'He's probably booked on a flight at a major centre,' he said. 'He'll wait till he thinks we've got bored checking airports for some other dead man and then he'll fly out of the country.'

'Where do you think he might hide out?' said Jim, thinking of the burnt-out shell of Maldon Downs.

'He liked to fish when he was in strife,' said Harry. 'He'd go down to the river and he'd set up a few lines. Sit on the bank and have a whisky. Sometimes, he'd keep casting a spinner, over and over.'

'Where're the best fishing spots around here?' Jim asked.

Harry looked at the map spread out on the counter then at his colleague. 'Come on,' he said. 'I know where they are.'

Jim drove along the highway, following the wandering Boolabimbie river. Harry maintained a sharp look-out for any sign of a possible lay-by. Harry hoped his hunch was right, and hoped even more fervently that they would have the good luck to see the reported vehicle again. Razor pushed his snout past the passenger seat and Harry gently pushed him back; then, with a tremendous shock, he suddenly confronted the fawn ute, standing a little way off the other side of the road, quite plainly in view, not far from a bridge that he'd noticed on the constable's map.

'That's him! That's the ute.'

Jim immediately slowed and indicated to make the necessary turn, craning his neck to see. Harry leaned over and picked up the radio.

'We've got a suspect utility off the highway, facing east, just past the Gimpy Creek bridge and turn-off. We're going after him.'

But Jim was finding that he had to pull over to the left and let a string of cars go by before he could make the U-turn. 'Come on, *come on*,' he muttered, then, 'Oh shit,' because the ute's lights had come on over the other side of the road and it had started to pull away fast, vanishing behind them.

'He's seen us,' said Harry. 'The bastard's seen us.' He grabbed the radio again and Razor grunted in the back. 'Suspect utility now driving east along the highway. We're on him.'

Jim finally made the turn, but by the time they'd settled down and cleared a rise, the ute had taken its anonymous place somewhere ahead of them in a string of moving vehicles. Only the tail lights were visible.

'Where are you, you bastard?' Harry asked. Then one of the vehicles in the group about a hundred metres ahead suddenly made a left-hand turn off the road. 'That'll be him,' Harry yelled.

'How do you know? What if it's not?' Jim said.

'It will be. We've interfered with his plan so he'll be running on unconscious flight pattern and he's right on track with that lefthand turn.'

Jim accelerated and took off, passing two vehicles and tucking in behind another. 'That's the turn,' said Harry, indicating a narrow bitumen road turning off the highway, signposted 'Ellersley 6 kms' together with a graphic depicting 'Caution Kangaroos'.

Jim nearly overshot the turn-off and had to break and swing the car, skidding on the gravel as he did. Ahead of them, speeding down the Ellersley road, they could see the red tail lights of the ute. 'Be ready for a right turn now,' said Harry. 'If there's one available he'll take it.' Almost as Harry spoke, the utility made a sudden right-hand turn which Jim repeated moments later.

'Be ready for another,' said Harry. 'Two or three. Then he'll go back to a left.'

Jim glanced at him. 'How do you know this?' he asked.

'Because even though he's Angus Wetherill, he's a human being,' said Harry. 'And we're all hard-wired the same.'

Now Jim was flat to the boards but failing to make any ground because the ute had raced away ahead of them, recklessly speeding.

'I'll never catch up with him,' Jim shouted. Harry could see the sweat on his friend's face gleaming in the dashboard light. The night roared past them outside at speed; Jim's hands whiteknuckled on the wheel. The needle on the speedo was wavering in the red, at 160 kilometres per hour, when suddenly the utility ahead seemed to shudder in the middle of the road, partly explode in a spray of brilliant diamonds, veer wildly, then skid right onto the shoulder, bouncing and rocking off the road, collecting a wire fence on its way.

'What's he doing?' yelled Jim, wrenching the wheel to avoid overshooting the place the ute had left the road, wrestling to follow it. 'What's the bastard doing?' The utility continued to bounce along in a nearby clearing, over granite outcrops and piles, until it collided with a young sapling sprouting from a rock, spun round and stopped with its front wheels halfway up an embankment. One headlight still shone crazily up into the trees.

Harry jumped out of the car and let Razor out, hooked the line onto the harness and the old dog drew away fast, pulling Harry along with him, racing towards the crashed utility. 'This is the one,' his body language signalled. Harry took a firm hold of the line in his left hand, steadied the dog, unfastened the holster and drew his weapon. Angus Wetherill would not get any chances this time. This was high country they were in, rugged terrain and well-known to both Harry and Angus. Boolabimbie was tucked dozens of metres beneath them in the valley to the left. Harry ducked out of the headlights of their vehicle, crouched down and waited with Razor. He was aware of Jim doing the same beside him. Ahead of them, lit up by their headlights, the cabin of the ute was rocking wildly.

'What's he doing? What the fuck's going on?' Jim's voice was a harsh whisper.

They moved in closer, keeping low, almost right up to the ute where they took cover behind a rocky outcrop. Harry heard the sound of a distant watercourse. 'There's someone else in there with him,' said Jim. In the heavily shadowed interior of the utility, it seemed two figures struggled.

'Come out of there!' yelled Harry. 'Put your hand out the window. Open the door using the outside handle. Do it now. Slow.'

Thumps and bangs came from the cabin and more sprays of broken windscreen glass caught the light. 'Angus Wetherill! Out of there now!' Harry shouted. But the struggle in the ute continued. Then came a terrible, choked-off scream. As Harry and Jim watched, the passenger door opened a little and a glistening red hand flopped out.

The scent picture here was of hot metal and engine fluids leaking into the night, but there was something else that reminded him of a war zone after a battle.

'What's going on?' Jim repeated. Harry squinted, trying to see. He could smell the steamy odour of stomach wounds and the stench of alcohol. When the door suddenly banged wide open, Harry jumped with fear. He slipped Razor, who stood beside him awaiting further orders and shivering with readiness, and raised his weapon into firing position. Then he realised what was happening.

'Jesus,' he whispered, lowering the weapon. A huge, twisted kangaroo, with one paw dangling useless, sprawled out of the ute's now wide-open door into the circle of light, struggled to its feet, hobbled sideways, then jumped crookedly and vanished in darkness. From inside the cabin, the man's red hand fell further out, slowly followed by the arm and shoulder, until finally, with an extraordinary and chilling grace, gliding in the mess of his own bloody disembowelment, the rest of Angus Wetherill slid out upside down onto the earth.

Jim, Harry and Razor went back to the beginning of the skid marks on the road. Harry shone the powerful torch on the ground. He studied the kangaroo tracks and tyre marks until the pictures started coming to his mind. It was the same big animal whose tracks he'd noticed at the spot beside the river where he'd camped for the night. By the time Harry straightened up, he had it all. He turned to Jim as the story unfolded in his mind.

'This big fellow is standing in the middle of the road . . .' he said, showing Jim the place of collision, the beginning of the skid, the blood spray pattern from the impact '. . . frozen by the headlights of the ute. But Angus Wetherill just drives straight at him. See there? No attempt to swerve. He knows the bullbar will deal with this fellow. But instead of the bullbar throwing him off sideways onto the roadside, the roo somehow gets tangled up with it and comes flying over the top of the bonnet, crashes through the windscreen into the cabin, starts kicking and flailing around, trying to escape. Back legs like threshing machines; claws like razors. Angus Wetherill's trying to regain control of the vehicle. Trying to stop it, to get out away from this monster with the big claws slashing everywhere.'

The two men followed the careering track of the ute back to the rocky embankment against which it now rested. Water dripped from the radiator.

'But the more Angus struggles to get away,' Harry said, 'the more terrified and aggressive that big fellow gets. One final kick and the kangaroo lays him open from arsehole to breakfast.'

They had come round to the driver's side of the vehicle and now stood by the body of the dead man where it lay on its stomach. Harry saw the molten gleam of viscera under the collapsed body. He felt nothing but relief in that moment, that it was over after all these years. The end of the hatred. For both of them.

Jim went to the car to radio for assistance while Harry and Razor headed off into the scrub to deal with the injured beast, following the blood trail.

The sound of the watercourse became louder with every

step they took, and from the lie of the land and his own local knowledge, together with the familiar scent picture, Harry suddenly understood where they were. This was the high country directly above the Wetherills' property, Maldon Downs. The watercourse he could hear ended in the very fall that cascaded over the precipice in summer and down into the swimming hole of the Boolabimbie River. It was where he and Angus used to swim together in the shade of the giant river gum, with the overgrown scars of ancient shot pellets puckering its smooth white surfaces.

Harry found the kangaroo a few minutes later. It stood panting in the beam of the flashlight, with its broken paw and twisted pelvis, proud and stunned, blowing a red bubble from its snout with every breath, no longer able to move. The beautiful eyes in the kangaroo's stern, long face seemed to stare straight into Harry's. He stood a moment, panting with it. 'I'm sorry, brother,' he said, raising the weapon to dispatch it. But the creature's eyes were filled with luminosity and Harry found himself staring back into them, through to another place. It was as if his eyes, ears and nose – so much keener now than they'd ever been – had found yet another dimension. Around him, the whole night seemed to swing, pulsing in slow waves, and within his own body he sensed an inner undulation that moved in time, touching every organ, every cell. He lowered his weapon, unable to fire, and the eyes of the kangaroo dilated, the luminosity growing as the pupils relaxed. This was the third time in his life he had gazed into dying eyes. Now the data that his senses offered him increased in ever-widening circles, like the ripples on an inland sea, and moved outwards to encompass every tree, every mountain, the stars and beyond, into unknowable darkness.

Harry's mind widened and opened out so that for a second

he thought he might tip over backwards into infinity. And in that moment, Harry knew that nothing was the way he'd thought it to be. He knew now that a huge mystery surrounded and included him, everyone and everything, including Angus Wetherill and himself, including the kangaroo and the earth and the universe. Nothing was left out. Nothing was lost.

Then the kangaroo coughed, and gently toppled dead at his feet in a graceful tangle. The holographic vision faded and Harry was just a man standing with a dog in a dark place. He shone his flashlight on the dead kangaroo. I will take your skin, Harry thought, and make something precious out of it to remember this by. And then I will find out where she's living and take it to her as a gift. I'll ask her what my real name is. I'll bring my children to meet her and together we'll go back to the swimming hole and see if we can still see the marks of the shotgun pellets on the big river gum and I'll tell her about this night and how the big kangaroo finished that old business. She can teach me how to pray again.

Harry looked up at the stars, and the seven sisters blurred as the tears filled his eyes.